Abide With Me

Also by E. Lynn Harris

INVISIBLE LIFE

JUST AS I AM

AND THIS TOO SHALL PASS

IF THIS WORLD WERE MINE

Abide With Me

a novel by

E. LYNN HARRIS

DOUBLEDAY

NEW YORK LONDON TORONTO

SYDNEY AUCKLAND

PUBLISHED BY DOUBLEDAY
a division of Random House, Inc.
1540 Broadway, New York, New York 10036

DOUBLEDAY and the portrayal of an anchor with a dolphin are
trademarks of Doubleday, a division of Random House, Inc.

This novel is a work of fiction. Names, characters, places, and
incidents either are the product of the author's imagination or
are used fictitiously. Any resemblance to actual persons, living
or dead, events, or locales is entirely coincidental.

Book design by Brian Mulligan

ISBN 0-385-48657-X

Printed in the United States of America

This novel is dedicated to three magnificent people

Martha K. Levin for changing the course of my life, and then becoming a treasured friend

Blanche Richardson, the best friend a writer (or anyone) could ever be blessed with

Rodrick L. Smith (a.k.a. Everick) for friendship, and an abiding love I can depend on

❖   ❖   ❖

In Loving Memory
Maye F. Raymond (Aunt Maye)
Colton Delano Sledge
Rosa Hilda Brown

Acknowledgments

I am grateful for God's grace and blessings amid life's quiet storms. I am thankful for my family, for their support of my life and writing career, and most especially my mother, Etta Harris, and my aunt, Jessie L. Phillips.

I am thankful to all my friends, both old and new, who always understand when I lock myself away from the world to write my novels. Special thanks to the ladies who've been my support system for over two decades: Lencola Sullivan, Vanessa Gilmore, Regina Daniels, Cindy Barnes, Robin Walters, and to the new ladies in my life: Debra Martin Chase, Deanna Williams, Yolanda Starks, and Sybil Wilkes. To the men in my life: Rodrick L. Smith, Carlton Brown, Troy Danato, Kevin Edwards, Tim Douglas, Anthony Bell, and my new friend and brother, Brent Zachery.

I am also thankful for the friends whose vast information helped tremendously with this novel: the beautiful and talented Broadway diva Brenda Braxton, Adrian Bailey (Mister triple threat), and Brian Evert Chandler (the best Curtis Taylor Jr. I've seen on the stage). To the casts of *Smokey Joe's Café* and the most recent national touring company of *Dreamgirls,* special thanks for showing me so much love. Thanks also to

Tracey Davis of Wichita, Kansas, for the Jackson information and support.

Special shout-outs to my brothers and sisters who write wonderful books (especially my sisterfriend Julia Boyd for your information about Seattle). A special shout to a woman who has become near and dear to my heart, Iyanla Vanzant. I thank you, Iyanla, for your friendship and wonderful writing, but more importantly your powerful prayers during my stormy days and those filled with sun. You are amazing!

A standing ovation for my support team: my agents, John Hawkins, Moses Cardona, and Irv Schwartz (three of the best in the business); Laura Gilmore (the best assistant in the world); my attorneys, Amy Goldson and my uncle, Councilman Charles E. Phillips; and my accountant, Bob Braunschweig. I also would like to thank my hair-cutting brothers, who are also great friends, Shannon Jones (Chicago) and Anderson Phillips (Scissors New York).

In the publishing world I am also blessed with outstanding people; Stephen Rubin, the president of Doubleday, is the type of leader writers like me would follow anywhere. Welcome back, Steve. Thanks to my publicists, Sherri Steinfield and Patricia Blythe; and to Mario Pulice, the best art director in publishing and a man who always makes me smile (thanks for another great cover!).

I couldn't do what I do without great editors. Again, I've been blessed with the best: Blanche Richardson and Charles Flowers have helped me craft three bestsellers. Blanche and Charles are not only great editors but great people, and friends I know I can depend on. A special thanks to my line editor, Austin Foxxe of L.A., a talented writer whose work I hope to see soon on bookstore shelves. And to Rosalind Oliphant, for being my friend and test reader.

The last person I want to thank has been a godsend through one of my storms. Janet Hill at Doubleday had always been a great supporter and friend. So I was excited and nervous when she agreed to be my in-house editor. Not only did she become the valuable leader of my team, but an even closer friend. How many people can say that about people they work with on a day-to-day basis? So thanks, Janet, for being, as the young kids say, *all that.*

Finally, to my fans, the *invisible* friends I don't know who read my books and give me the best word-of-mouth support in the industry. I couldn't do it without *you.* (I love the cards and letters.) Thank you so much. This one is for you! God bless you all.

BOOK ONE

What You Can't See When Your Eyes Are Closed

1

Summer came, tucked behind a flawless spring. Raymond loved perfection, but he did not know that with perfection, sorrow would soon follow. It started with a late evening phone call. Raymond Winston Tyler and Trent Michael Walters had retired to their large, loft-style bedroom after an uneventful Friday. The two were trying to decide if they should watch the local news or one of the three videos they had rented for the weekend.

Raymond answered the phone on the nightstand after a couple of rings. He started to let the answering machine pick up, but the ring sounded unusually urgent and important. Maybe it was his younger brother, Kirby, or his best buddy, Jared.

After about ten minutes of "Yes . . . Yes . . . I can't believe this," Raymond walked over toward the large bay window. As he held the portable phone to his ear Raymond gazed at a burst of orange and blue lightning slice through the clouds as the sky opened up and sheets of rain began to fall. It was both beautiful and frightening.

Trent realized this call was important and went downstairs to the kitchen. A few minutes later he returned with a bowl of microwave popcorn, a box of peanut M&M's, and two bottles of water, just as Raymond was hanging up the phone with a stunned look on his face.

"Is everything all right?" Trent asked with concern in his voice.

"You're not going to believe this," Raymond said as he rubbed his forehead.

"What?"

"That was the chief of staff for Senator Patricia Murray's office," Raymond said.

"The U.S. senator? And?" Trent quizzed.

"I've been nominated for a federal judgeship," Raymond blushed.

"Get the fuck out! That's great," Trent said as he hugged his broad-shouldered partner.

"I still don't believe this," Raymond said as his lips parted into a huge smile.

"Why not? I've always known you're the best lawyer in the world," Trent said proudly.

"Do you realize the next step would be the Supreme Court? What is this . . . I'm getting ahead of myself. Supreme Court, my ass! My pops isn't going to believe this," Raymond rattled off.

"Call him," Trent urged.

Raymond looked at the digital clock on the phone and realized it was past midnight in Birmingham, Alabama. But Raymond wanted to share the news with his parents.

"Do you think it's too late?"

"Raymond, how often does someone get nominated for the federal bench?" Trent asked.

"You're right," Raymond said as he grabbed the phone and dialed his parents' number. After three rings Raymond started to hang up when he suddenly heard his mother's sleepy voice. A voice more familiar to him than any sound he'd ever heard.

"Ma," Raymond said.

"Ray? Is everything all right?" she asked.

"Everything is fine. I'm sorry to call so late. Where's Pops?"

"He's right here. You want to talk with him?"

"Yeah, but I want you to hear this too. Put me on the speakerphone." Raymond knew his father hated the speakerphone, but he heard a click and then his mother's voice suddenly sounding far-off.

"Ray Jr.? Are you all right?" Raymond heard his father ask.

"I'm fine," Raymond assured him.

"Then this better be good. Do you know how late it is?"

"Yeah, but I thought you'd like to talk with the future federal judge from the Western District Court of Washington," Raymond said. He liked the sound of his possible new title.

"What!" Raymond heard his father exclaim. Raymond could hear his mother in the background singing, "My baby . . . my baby going to be a judge." She sounded like the mother in the movie *The Nutty Professor* singing "Hercules, Hercules."

Raymond heard some clicking in the phone and then he could hear his father's voice more clearly. Raymond Sr. had turned off the speakerphone.

"Is Ma all right?"

"She's fine. When did all this happen? Why is this the first I've heard of this?"

"I didn't know I was even being considered. I knew there were some openings, but everybody in my office thought they were going to pick an Asian-American or this lawyer Charles Pope. I'm still in shock," Raymond said. "I guess we can thank the Simpson trial and my taking your advice about helping out Norm Rice in his race for governor."

"Did Norm have something to do with this?" Raymond Sr. asked.

"I have no idea," Raymond answered. "I got the call from Senator Murray's office. Her chief of staff said they had been trying to reach me all evening. But I guess we should all calm down because I haven't been put on the bench yet. There is the confirmation process," he warned.

"Don't worry about that. You'll get it. I know they need some local color on that bench."

"I hope you're right, Pops. I hope you're right."

After hanging up the phone, Raymond sat on the edge of the bed silently, listening to the rain and thinking about how his life was getting ready to change. Again.

During the Simpson trial Raymond had served as a talking head for the local NBC affiliate and had become something of a local celebrity, partly because he never seemed to take sides and also because Raymond was a very good-looking man. The station had been swamped with calls, faxes, and letters from women wanting to know Raymond's marital status. Raymond and Trent would spend some evenings reading some of the offers from viewers. Ray had his secretary send each viewer a thank-you note stating, *Mr. Tyler is very happy in his personal life.* When the station offered Raymond a permanent position, he politely declined.

His father was a retired family court judge and state senator who had always dreamed his son would follow in his political footsteps, and had suggested Raymond parlay his newfound celebrity into political prominence. It had been years since his father had encouraged him to pursue politics. His mother just wanted him to be happy.

❖   ❖   ❖

Raymond Winston Tyler, Jr., is one of the good guys. At least most of the time. Raymond is not perfect, but he wants the world to be perfect. The kinda guy who loves Oprah and Rosie, but might not admit he likes Jerry Springer as well. You know the type: he wants to please everybody.

The firstborn of Raymond and Marlee Tyler, big brother to budding Northwestern Wildcats football star Kirby Wayne Tyler, and a great friend to many. He's thirty-seven years old and already worried about turning forty. Ray's a Southern boy, born and raised in Birmingham, Alabama. A graduate of the University of Alabama and Columbia Law School, Raymond has spent part of his adult life living and practicing law in New York and Atlanta.

The last three years, he and his life partner, Trent, an architect, have been living in Seattle, Washington. They have been in a committed relationship for a little over five years. A successful partner in a small law firm, Raymond has finally discovered his paradise, in Trent, his fraternity brother, after years of going back and forth between male and female lovers. He once described himself as a sexual mulatto, but now he knows the true color of love. Now, this doesn't mean he didn't love the women in question or the men before Trent. He did. Nor does it mean he's totally accepted his sexuality, but he has come a long way. He still doesn't introduce himself with "Hello, I'm Raymond and I'm gay"; he doesn't think it is everybody's business.

Being in a stable relationship with Trent has helped Raymond a great deal and it's given him a sense of peace and security. With Trent, Raymond finally started to believe that true love with a man was possible. This was something Raymond thought was the impossible dream.

But this judge thing might bring back some of those doubts he had when he was moving between the gay and not-so-gay worlds. Times have changed, but is the world ready for a black, gay federal judge?

Trent is a lot different than Raymond, but like that old saying goes, *he loves Raymond's dirty drawers.* Loved him since the first day he laid eyes on him when they were both pledging Kappa Alpha Omega at the University of Alabama. So what if it took almost fifteen years to admit it to himself or Raymond? He always considered Raymond the unattainable pretty boy. Trent figured it wouldn't have mattered if Raymond was gay or straight; there was no way Raymond would want to be with him.

Trent can best be described as a basic boy who turned into a basic kind of man. He works hard and enjoys the simple things in life like cheeseburgers on white bread. Trent doesn't mind being in the background, or being a team player. Maybe that's because he comes from a large family where there was little room for a star. A family of eight boys—Trent was the baby boy—and three girls, all whose first names start with *T.* Like Terry, Tracey, Terrell, Timothy, Tamela, Thomas, Theresa. Well, you get the picture. Trent is also a father to a preteen son, Trent Jr., who lives in

Atlanta with his mother, Beverly, Trent's college sweetheart. Like Raymond, Trent ignored his own sexual desires and went along with the norm, until he met a Raymond look-alike while he served in the U.S. Marines and finally realized who he really wanted.

Trent is a Southern boy, born and raised in Mobile, Alabama, the son of working-class parents. Like Raymond's parents, Trent's folks were also involved in the civil rights movement, but in a more quiet and personal way.

In 1963, Trent's older cousin, Donald Walters, integrated Mobile's Murphy High without the fanfare of Little Rock or New Orleans. Donald was the son of Trent's father's brother who lived in Pensacola, Florida. He came to Mobile to attend Murphy High when his own colored high school didn't offer chemistry. Trent remembers how his father spent many a sleepless night standing guard in their living room with a shotgun, expecting Klansmen or other citizens of Mobile who weren't happy that an outsider had integrated their lily-white high school.

But there was no reason for shots to be fired. Mobile, unlike many other cities in Alabama in the sixties, took the high road when it came to race relations. Blacks and whites were distant, but respectful of each other's space. Sure, Donald was pushed around and kicked downstairs, but he stood firm. He had a dream and purpose. Today, Dr. Donald Jackson Walters teaches at the medical school at the University of Florida. Trent still adores his focused and determined cousin.

It was Donald who one Christmas gave Trent a set of Lego's and showed him how to build things. Trent loved the colorful toys and took them everywhere he went, including his first dorm room at the University of Alabama, where he received a degree in architecture. The Lego's even found a place in the Queen Anne Hill area of Seattle, an enclave of dignified, spacious, high-ceiling homes. The three-story, cedar-sided home is one of his most treasured designs. Trent, who as a child managed to find his own space in a three-bedroom clapboard house with twelve other people, is now designing houses and buildings where everyone who enters finds his or her own space.

2

The midtown apartment was quiet. There was no furniture, except for a couple of barstools, a television, and a queen-sized bed. It looked like the apartment of a struggling actor or a newly wed couple.

It was a little past noon as Nicole Marie Springer studied the face of her husband of four years, Jared Stovall, who sat at the bar with his left hand cupping his chin.

Nicole started to remove the deli sandwiches they had picked at for the last half hour, but instead she remained still. She gazed at her ruggedly handsome husband, a confident, biscuit-brown man, who at six foot three and 220 pounds looked exactly like the man she had fallen in love with some six years ago.

After a moment of pensive silence, she asked, "So you think I should take the job?"

Jared looked at his wife and said, "It sounds like they really want you. But what do you want?"

"Yeah, I mean I didn't even have to audition. And it's not like people have been beating down my door. I told you once you leave New York, people forget about you," Nicole said.

Jared removed himself from the barstool, took a few steps, and gently placed his arms around his wife's waist. He kissed her softly on the lips and then said, "Nicole, you know I support you. It's just the thought of not having you here with me . . . well, it makes me sad. But we moved here for your career and we'll just deal with it," Jared said firmly.

Nicole gave Jared a quick kiss and smiled. "Remember, Jared, it's only six weeks on the road and I'll be home before you know it."

"It doesn't mean I'm going to miss you less," Jared said with a sweet boyish smile. Jared Taylor Stovall would do anything for his wife. He had given up his hopes that being a wife and hopefully one day a mother would keep Nicole totally satisfied. When the aggressive real estate agent sold their house in Atlanta, with a nice profit after one showing, Jared knew he was headed to New York City. He couldn't resist his wife. He actually felt he loved her more each day. He knew he sounded corny and whipped, but he loved her more than the first time he saw her. He was in New York City, visiting his best friend, Raymond, when Raymond and Nicole's friend Kyle was dying of AIDS. The first time she walked into Kyle's bedroom and smiled, Jared knew it was all over. He loved her more than when he proposed to her in a Little Rock hotel, and more than the day he married her in an opulent wedding that people in Little Rock were still talking about.

The job in question was the starring role in a revival of *Dreamgirls,* a Broadway musical Nicole had been in almost a decade before. A role she had once turned down for the first national tour because she was in love with Raymond Tyler.

When she was first approached to take the role of Dena Jones, a role she had once understudied, Nicole was hesitant. The show was heading across the country for a bus and truck tour, but the producers were confident they would be back on Broadway the moment a suitable theater opened up. The producers were so interested in having Nicole in the role that they had promised she'd only have to be on the road the last six weeks, and only when they were certain a Broadway theater had been secured. When Nicole told them she didn't really want to do a role made famous by another woman, the talented Sheryl Lee Ralph, the producers told Nicole about the new, young, and soon-to-be-hot director they had hired. He was going to make additions to the show and make it all fresh: new costumes, a new choreographer, and even some minor changes that would make the role of Dena Jones even bigger.

And as she said, it wasn't like there were other acting opportunities for Nicole. She had been back in New York for almost three months and had only auditioned for three shows and a few workshops. Only one had called her back for a second audition, the workshop for *Dottie,* a musical planned on the life of African-American actress Dorothy Dandridge. Nicole had rushed out and purchased a copy of Donald Bogle's biography of the first black female superstar and had read it in two days. When she turned the final page, Nicole was in tears and knew she had to be a part of this production. A few days after her callback, Nicole got the word from her agent that the workshop had been canceled indefinitely, due to lack of funds. She realized not much had changed since she'd married and decided to follow her husband south to Atlanta, where he had a promising career as an investment banker. Money and race still ruled Broadway, the Great White Way.

Opportunities for acting were few and far between in Atlanta, and especially for a dark-skinned, African-American actress, so Nicole had concentrated on being a good wife. For a while she was happy with her new role, even though she resisted invitations from some of her Spelman sisters to become active in organizations like the Links and Junior League. The only organization she made time for was her Alpha Kappa Alpha sorority, and even that was on a limited basis.

To keep in touch with her craft, she had taken a part-time job as an instructor in the drama department at her alma mater, Spelman College. She enjoyed teaching, but really missed being in front of the camera or on a stage. With the exception of Atlanta's Alliance Theater, there were few opportunities. Whenever an opening for work on a film or a shoot for a commercial appeared, she would audition, but only if the schedule allowed Nicole to sleep in her own bed at night. Sometimes she ventured from Atlanta, like the time she went to North Carolina to audition for the Oprah Winfrey production of *The Wedding*. The producers and director loved Nicole, but since she was too young to play the role of Rachel, they could only offer her the role of a maid, or as they put it, "the dark-skinned nurse." Nicole had vowed to never play a maid, and she wasn't about to play a nurse who had just five lines.

It was only after a call from a New York agent telling her about the *Dottie* workshop that Nicole felt she was missing a big part of her life, the Broadway stage. Nicole Springer realized she wanted to live her dream life twice.

Nicole walked slowly to the window, gazing at the sun that poured like champagne over West Forty-ninth Street, and then walked back near Jared. She put her hand delicately on his, but with a slight hesitation. "Are you sure you're okay with this?" she asked.

"Baby, you know I'm cool with this. But it was you who said people forget about you when you leave. Right?" He removed his hand from under Nicole's and placed his strong one on top of the softness of hers and rubbed it affectionately.

"Yeah, I know, but this is different. I mean, when the show comes back to Broadway, even if it's for a short run, it might bring work."

"Look, this might be for the best. I'm going to be spending a lot of time at the office, finding out who's who and what's what. I've got to hire an executive assistant I can trust. You might as well do something you love."

Nicole smiled at Jared. What he said made a lot of sense. And what would she do while Jared kept long hours getting adjusted to his new position as a senior vice-president at Morgan Stanley? Both Nicole and Jared knew it was a good sign when Jared requested a transfer to New York and received a promotion and raise with the deal. They both still wanted children desperately, even though after two miscarriages, adoption seemed more likely. Nicole's mother was against her daughter moving back to New York, had told her she should be concentrating on having children. Nicole did not want to give her mother an opportunity to tell her once again that it was time to grow up and be a full-time wife and mother and leave acting behind.

"So when are you going to call the producers and tell them you're going to do it?" Jared asked.

Nicole looked first at her husband and then at the phone and said, "I guess there's no time like the present."

3

John Basil Henderson, ex-college and pro football star, had been seeing the therapist on the Upper West Side for almost three months. Yet it still took him several minutes before he broke the awkward silence of each meeting. The first three sessions, Basil, as he preferred to be called, hadn't spoken a word until his time was up, and then only to confirm the date of his next appointment.

Toward the end of the third session Basil finally broke the silence by asking the doctor, "So is this all we do, sit here and look at each other like fools?"

"Why are you here, Mr. Henderson?"

" 'Cause a whole lot of people been fuckin' with me. And if I don't deal with it, then the whole world gonna know when I lose it!"

"What people?"

"Well, we could start with my sick-ass uncle who took my manhood before I was even a man. I had to block the shit out of my head, but it showed up and caused me to lose a woman I loved and made me obsessed over a man I might have loved."

"Well, you've taken the first step by admitting to yourself that you were abused."

"So why don't I feel better?"

"One day you will. This is where the healing begins."

At the beginning of his fourth session, Basil shocked the doctor when he announced, "I guess we might as well get this over with." He stood up, seductively and slowly unbuttoned his tight-fitting royal-blue knit shirt, kicked off his loafers, unbuckled his leather belt, and dropped his beige linen pants. "I thought you needed to see what all the hoopla was about," he said as he stood before the doctor wearing only a black nylon jock-strap that looked more like a male dancer's belt.

The doctor studied the way Basil stood there practically nude, with his double-barrel chest and an epic ass, a body part all by itself. The features of his perfect body, including a semierect penis, betrayed the marks of a man who knew from an early age the power of being breathtakingly handsome. The doctor's face was composed and unreadable as he mur-mured, "I see." Basil gave him a cocky I-thought-so smile and put his clothes back on. The private strip show forever broke the ice between doctor and patient.

"You know that woman I told you about? The real pretty one that reminded me of Yolanda?" Basil asked as he leaned forward in the brown leather chair.

"Which one?" the doctor asked, peering over his tortoiseshell glasses.

"Beautiful brown-skinned sister. Looks like a model. Damn! I forgot what she did for a living. Anyway, she's the one I met in front of the locker room at the Knicks game. Said she was there with her sister who dated one of the Knicks. Probably a groupie," Basil said. "You know what a groupie is, huh, Doc?"

"Yes," the doctor said, and nodded for Basil to continue.

"Well, I had a date with her a couple of days ago."

"And how did it go?"

"It didn't," Basil said with a sinister smile.

"What happened?"

"I had given her my digits so she could call me. I don't call them first, you know." Basil settled back into the chair, feeling a little more sure of himself. He stretched his long legs in front of him and continued.

"She called once, twice, three times. I said to myself, 'This might be interesting.' I let the bitch call one more time and then I called her back. Well, I knew she lived way up in Harlem or some-fucking-where, so I invited her to dinner and made reservations at Cafe Luxembourg here on the Upper West Side. I told her to meet me there. 'Cause I figured, if she wanted to get with me, she'd find her way there. The woman said yes before I even got the address out of my mouth." Basil laughed, but the doctor just maintained a professional and distant look.

"Please continue."

"Anyway"—Basil sat back up stiffly—"I show up late on purpose.

She's standing near the maître d' dressed fly and lookin' lost. She gives me this big smile and I give her a little peck on the cheek and tell her I'm sorry I'm late—which I'm not. But she says it's okay, she really didn't mind the wait, whatever. We got seated immediately 'cause they know me there, you know?"

"Go on." The doctor's face remained expressionless.

"So I ordered a Beck's. She ordered a Kir—you know, one of those drinks women and sissies like. And then . . . I don't know . . . maybe it was just the stuck-up way she ordered her drink . . . I don't know, but something hit me. The whole thing was wrong."

Basil thought he saw a faint glimmer of interest seep through the doctor's facade.

"What do you mean, Mr. Henderson?" the doctor asked flatly.

"I really don't know what it was. At first she reminded me of Yolanda; then I thought about Raymond . . ."

"Raymond? You haven't mentioned him in a while. Did you finally call him?"

"Naw, I ain't called that mofo. He didn't answer my letter, so why in the hell would I want to call him?"

"Correct me if I'm wrong, but didn't he call you after the letter and suggest you see a doctor?"

"Yeah, but it was a phone call that lasted less than a minute long. It was like he was saying, 'I'm concerned about you but I ain't got the time to deal with you and your life. I got my own,' " Basil said as he stared blankly.

"You were saying you thought of Yolanda and then Raymond?"

"Oh, yeah. Then—don't ask me why, Doc, 'cause I don't have a fuckin' clue."

"Why did you think about him at the restaurant?"

"Who?"

"Raymond."

"Because I've been thinking how I'm gonna get that mofo back! I'm gonna make him pay for ignoring my ass," Basil said firmly. "Anyway, I just felt like that being in this restaurant with a dumb-ass sistah was the last place on earth I wanted to be. I had bigger fish to fry."

"And what did you do then?"

"I excused myself. Told her I had to go to the men's room. She just smiled and said something like 'I'll be waiting.' I went up to the waitress who was at the bar picking up our drinks and told her to cancel the Beck's, gave her a twenty, and walked my ass right on outta there."

"So you just left the young lady sitting in a restaurant. Then what?"

Basil put his arms behind his head, as if he was stretching out on the beach, somewhat satisfied that he'd gotten even the slightest rise out of the doctor.

"What'd I do then? Stopped my ass at a Mickey D's, a block away, got me a fish sandwich, and took my ass home!" Basil burst out laughing, but the doctor didn't even crack a smile.

4

It was Monday evening, a week and a couple of days after Raymond had received one of the most important phone calls of his life. He and Trent were enjoying the afterglow of a spectacular sunset lingering over the wooden deck in their backyard.

Relaxing on matching chaise lawn chairs, Trent was drinking a beer and Raymond was nursing a glass of white wine. Raymond still had on his work drag and Trent was comfortable in gray warm-ups and a black muscle T-shirt. They talked about the weekend just past, when Raymond's parents had surprised them with a trip to Seattle to celebrate his nomination for federal judgeship. His parents had called Thursday and casually asked what Raymond and Trent were doing. When Raymond said, "Nothing special," his father responded, "Great, me and your mom will be there tomorrow evening, so pick us up at the airport." It was the first time Raymond's father had visited them since they had told him they were a couple. Raymond's mother had visited a couple of times and always stayed at their house, but this time she stayed at the Four Seasons Hotel downtown with her husband. When Raymond suggested he get the guest bedroom ready, his mother responded, "You know your daddy don't like sleeping in strange beds." Raymond teased that hotel beds must not count.

Despite the sleeping arrangements, it was a wonderful weekend. Trent had taken the Tylers on a tour of the city, while Raymond made sure his caseload was in order. He had been advised to make sure there weren't any controversial cases outstanding that might derail his nomination. Since he mostly handled corporate clients and a few sexual harassment cases, he wasn't that worried, but he made sure.

Saturday evening, the four of them had gone to see the movie *Soul Food* and then enjoyed a delicious Italian dinner at Marco's, an elegant supper club, posh with pretense. Sunday found them enjoying service at Mount Zion Baptist Church and then brunch at Mecca. Trent was happy about this since Raymond didn't go to Mount Zion as often as he did. Trent went every Sunday, sometimes on Wednesday, and anytime there was a gospel musical. Trent loved gospel music. Raymond couldn't count the number of times he had come home and caught his lover swaying from side to side like he was directing a large mass choir. He loved everyone from Tramaine Hawkins to Sandi Patti. Just as long as the song had a little Jesus in the lyrics.

Sunday evening, Raymond had tears in his eyes as he bid good-bye to his parents. In a tender embrace, his father told him how proud he was of him. His mother shared the same sentiment and whispered how much she loved him.

"I think your folks had a great time, don't you?" Trent asked.

"Yeah, I think so. Thanks again for helping out," Raymond said.

"I love your folks. They're like family and it was my pleasure."

"Even my pops, with his sometimes evil self," Raymond laughed. He didn't think his father was evil, just a little difficult at times, or as his mother put it, stubborn as a country mule. It was a part of his charm.

"Your pops is cool. He's coming around. Besides, he's so excited by the fact his son is going to be a judge, one day soon he might even accept us as a couple."

"My pops accepts us," Raymond said defensively. Raymond Sr. had never really voiced opposition toward Trent, at least not to Raymond. He couldn't understand why Raymond Jr. wanted to move to Seattle when things were going so great for him in Atlanta, or so he thought. The truth was, Raymond had become bored with Atlanta, bored with his job, bored with his social life. When he fell in love with Trent, they both wanted a new beginning.

"Really?" Trent quizzed. Raymond smiled at his partner as he gazed into Trent's cinnamon-brown eyes with their rims of dark charcoal. After a few quiet moments, Raymond spoke of his father's pride.

"Yeah, I think Pops is cool with us. I know he's pretty excited about this judge thing, but I don't know what he's going to do if I don't get confirmed."

"Of course you'll be confirmed. Are you worried about that?"

"Naw. If it's to be, then everything will be cool," Raymond said confidently.

"Are you excited about it?" Trent asked. His face took on a serious expression.

"What do you mean?"

"Aw, you know. This confirmation process sounds like a bitch."

"Yeah, it could be. But this is an opportunity I can't pass up. You should see how the people in my office are acting. It's like I've been appointed to a court in heaven," Raymond said.

"You know I support you two hundred percent if this is what you want," Trent said. His full lips curved into a tender, loving smile.

"So you think I should do this?" Raymond asked.

"You're kidding, right? Didn't you hear me? I'm behind you all the way. We need people like you on the bench."

"I know that, but the FBI is going to be getting into my business."

"Have you done anything you're ashamed of?"

"Yeah, but I was acquitted of those charges," Raymond responded with a marvelous, deep-throated laugh.

"What are you going to do when they ask about your marital status?" Trent asked as he took a slow sip of his beer.

"I'll tell them I'm in a strong, stable, and loving relationship," Raymond said. "Besides, they must know I'm gay."

"Have they said so?"

"Not really, but you gotta know they've already done some investigating before they nominated me."

"Yeah, you're right. Did your father give you advice on how to handle this?"

"Not really. Just to make sure I tell the truth, but don't tell them anything they don't ask," Raymond said as he loosened the gold metallic tie that lay against his snow-white shirt.

"What's your mother sending you?" Trent asked.

"Huh?"

"She said something at dinner about sending you something that would help with the nomination process. Don't you remember?"

"Oh, yeah. It's probably some good-luck charm or some of her cookies and brownies. I hope so, 'cause it's been years since she sent me some. Kirby gets them all now."

"Maybe she thinks you're too old for her cookies," Trent joked.

"You're never too old for your mother's cookies. Never too old," Raymond said as he savored the last of his wine.

5

Nicole felt a gentle tap on her shoulder. She turned around to face a pretty young lady in the lobby of a downtown rehearsal hall. Nicole immediately noticed her beautiful wheat-colored eyes, full of innocent intensity. She looked vaguely familiar, maybe because she looked a lot like Nicole, only a few years younger and a few shades lighter, almost golden, like the color of apple cider.

"Miss Springer, I'm Yancey Braxton. I think I'm going to be your understudy and I'm just so excited to meet you again. I met you once and you gave me your autograph," Yancey said nervously.

"Yes, I've heard some great things about you. Nice meeting you," Nicole said as she extended her hand to Yancey. As they exchanged warm smiles, Nicole suddenly remembered seeing her photo in the office of the producer of the revival of *Dreamgirls*.

"Miss Springer, I know we just met, but I have a big favor to ask you," Yancey said.

"Sure, but please don't call me Miss Springer. I'm just plain Nicole. What did you want to ask me?"

"Can we go and get a cup of coffee or some tea?"

"I wish I could, but I'm waiting for my husband to pick me up. We're still unpacking. I don't know if you know, but I just moved back to New York."

"I didn't know that. I heard you were teaching down at Spelman."

"Yes, my husband, Jared, and I lived down in Atlanta for about three years, but to tell you the truth I'm so glad to be back in New York," Nicole said gleefully.

"And I'm sure New York is glad you're back. Well, it was nice meeting you and I look forward to working with you."

"Me too. And we'll get the chance to get together real soon."

As Yancey turned and walked away, Nicole looked at her watch and realized it would be about thirty minutes before Jared would pick her up.

"Yancey," Nicole called out.

"Yes, Nicole," Yancey responded as she turned around quickly.

"I didn't realize how early it was. I've got a little time. Why don't we just sit in the theater and talk a little."

"I would love that," Yancey smiled.

"Are you from New York?" Nicole asked as they walked into the semidark theater.

"No, actually I'm from Memphis," Yancey said.

"Wow, that's not that far from my hometown. I'm from Arkansas."

"Yeah, I knew that. I remember when you won Miss Arkansas."

"You remember that? Child, that seems so long ago," Nicole said. "Here, why don't we just sit here in center row," she suggested. The two ladies dropped their bags in a seat directly in front of them and sat down for a visit.

Yancey told Nicole how seeing her win the Miss Arkansas title had inspired Yancey to start participating in pageants at a young age. Yancey Elizabeth Braxton had been first runner-up for Miss Tennessee for two consecutive years, but had never made it to Atlantic City as a contestant for Miss America. She told Nicole that she was devastated when she didn't win on her second try. Yancey felt despite the success of Vanessa Williams and Debbye Turner, her race had worked against her in Tennessee. She became so disgusted that she gave up a full academic scholarship at Vanderbilt University and transferred to Howard University to study theater when she discovered Vanderbilt's program was geared toward music performance. After performing in every student production available, Yancey felt she was ready for Broadway and had left D.C. right before her senior year at Howard.

"You know you need to get that degree," Nicole advised.

"Yeah, I know. I might do it later on. But there can't be any better training than understudying someone like Nicole Springer," Yancey said.

"You're too kind. But after two years of teaching I don't know what you could learn from me. I think I'm still in training myself."

"Oh, Miss Springer . . . I mean Nicole. You don't need any training. I've seen you perform. You're the best," Yancey said.

"Yancey, you're just too sweet. When did you see me perform?"

"Actually, I've seen you in *Dreamgirls, Jelly's Last Jam,* and, of course, Miss America. My parents used to bring me to New York every summer and my mother and I would just go to shows. When it came to your shows, we would often see them twice. We were so proud of you . . . with you being from Arkansas and all," Yancey gushed.

"So you always wanted to be an actress?"

"It's been my dream since I knew I could have dreams. It's all I've ever wanted to do."

"How did you hear about this revival?"

"My agent sent the producers a tape and they flew me up from Washington, D.C.," Yancey explained.

"They did? Who is your agent?"

"Some local guy down in D.C., P. J. Stencil and Associates. They were good for D.C. and regional theater, but I've made up my mind that I'm getting myself a major agent. Somebody like William Morris," Yancey said.

"You want to be with a big agency like that?" Nicole quizzed.

"Honey, I heard they are one of the best and that's what I want," Yancey said confidently. Nicole admired her self-assurance and started to tell her she was going to need it. They continued to chat with ease, more like old friends than newly introduced castmates. Nicole told Yancey how, after two years in Atlanta teaching theater, and being the perfect wife, she had convinced her husband to move to New York, because she missed the Broadway stage. She shared how Jared, a real Southern man, supported her desire even though he was perfectly happy living in Atlanta.

"Where are you living?" Nicole asked.

"I'm subletting a friend's loft in SoHo, but I'll be looking for my own place once I find out how long we're going to be on the road," Yancey said.

"Well, I've heard we're not going to be out on the road that long. Plus we're in D.C. and Detroit for more than a week. My contract is for three months and then we're supposed to come back to Broadway. I have a husband who doesn't like me gone for long periods of time."

"I hope you're right. I want to be in New York, and not in Podunk, U.S.A.," Yancey laughed.

"I know that's right," Nicole giggled.

"Do you plan on having children?"

"I hope so. Jared would have a houseful if it was up to him," Nicole said as she looked at her watch. She decided not to mention her miscarriages and problems with conceiving.

"I can't wait to meet your husband. I mean, if that's all right," Yancey said.

"Sure, I'd love for you to meet the man in my life. Maybe once we get settled we can have you over for dinner."

"That would be just wonderful. I'll even cook for you guys if you want. I make this wonderful shrimp pasta dish. It's not that fattening like most of the Southern food I grew up on."

"You won't have to do that. And from the looks of you, fat wouldn't know where to find you," Nicole said as she noticed Yancey's shape, one that would look splendid either in a beauty pageant swimsuit or the jeans and sheer sweater she was wearing.

"How sweet of you, but trust me when I say I've had my moments," Yancey said.

"Haven't we all! Look, I've got to go. It's been so wonderful talking with you. I guess I'll see you tomorrow," Nicole said.

"Thank you so much for giving me this time," Yancey said as she grabbed Nicole's hands and shook them over and over. When Nicole stood up, Yancey stood also and suddenly gave Nicole a big hug as she whispered, "Thank you, thank you."

6

It was Thursday afternoon, 2:00 P.M. sharp.

"How was your week?" the doctor asked.

"It's been all good," Basil said.

"Tell me about it."

"I went on a date," Basil said.

"With a man or a woman?" the doctor asked.

Basil became visibly upset and looked sternly at the doctor. After a moment of silence, he asked, "What do you mean a man or a woman? I told you I don't date men. I just sleep with them." Basil felt his body become sweaty thinking about where the doctor was headed with a question like that. Once again, he thought the sessions were not helping.

"Did you have a good time?"

"It was all right. You know, dinner, a movie, and then back to my place for sex."

"On the first date?"

"Of course."

"Did you enjoy it?"

"Damn straight. I met this woman walking down Fifth Avenue near Tiffany's. She was beautiful. I caught her eye and she smiled and stopped. You know when they stop they want some play. So that was my cue. I went over, introduced myself, and got the digits. I waited the mandatory three days, called her, and invited her out," Basil said confidently. "But she was slick in a way . . . I mean making me call because she wouldn't take my number."

"So how did you end up in bed?"

Basil gave the doctor a faint smile of amusement and said, "It was easy. We went to this nice seafood joint and both ordered lobster, and after a couple glasses of wine she leaned over and whispered, 'I bet you eat pussy real well,' and I looked at her and said, 'And you know it!' "

"Did you tell her you sleep with men?"

"Fuck no! She didn't ask. That's why I think women are so stupid and why I hate them sometimes."

"Hate is a strong word."

"I know, but that's how I feel sometimes," Basil said somberly. For a second he thought about Yolanda, the last woman he had loved.

"Why do you hate them?"

Basil balled his left fist and pressed it into his cupped right hand. As he turned it firmly, he wanted to hit something or somebody, but he controlled his anger.

"I hate them and I love them. I usually try not to make eye contact with women because when I see them and I see that smile and that ass, then I immediately want to fuck them. And after I fuck them, I hate them. You know, when I get my nut."

"Do you think that's hate?"

"I don't know what you call it, but for me it's a strong reaction. I suddenly become sick at the sight and smell of them. And you know what I really hate is when they ask, 'Do you love me?' I want to tell them that pussy is the best truth serum."

"What do you mean?"

"I mean women ought to ask a man if he loves them right after they've fucked. 'Cause if he says he loves you before you fuck and he stutters after sex, then he don't love the woman, he loves the pussy."

"Why do you think that's true?"

" 'Cause I used to date this honey once and I couldn't stand her. But I couldn't break up with her 'cause the pussy was so good. She had this beautiful ass and I couldn't stand the thought of somebody else hittin' it."

"What didn't you like about her?"

"She was a dumb bitch but she thought she was so smart. I mean she had gone to City College or some school like that and she thought she knew everything. But the truth of the matter was the bitch didn't know shit. She would misuse big words all the time and that just drove me crazy."

"Why didn't you tell her or correct her?"

"The bitch was so stupid she wouldn't have figured it out."

"And how do you feel about men?"

"What do you mean?"

"What do you think of men?"

Basil suddenly had a picture of Raymond in his head, but quickly replaced it with Monty, a man who had threatened to announce Basil's bisexuality to the world. Basil couldn't stand Monty. Basil really hated his uncle.

"Aw, they're just as bad. If they're gay, then they fall in love with the dick. Mofos love a big dick. And the mofos who ain't gay fall in love with the pussy and the pussy controls them."

"And where does that put you?" the doctor asked.

"On top of any situation 'cause I know what the real deal is when it comes to sex. I understand the power of sex. And once you understand something completely, you can control it."

"Do you feel the need to have sex with anyone right now?"

"Why not? I'm not depressed or anything like that, and when my jimmie gets up, I've got to feed him."

"Do you feel like you're addicted to sex?"

"Didn't you hear what I said just a minute ago? I ain't addicted to jack."

"Do you plan to call this woman again?"

"Fuck no!"

"Why not?"

" 'Cause I got what I wanted. If she's lucky she might get a booty call in a couple of months."

"A booty call?"

"Yeah, you know . . . well, maybe you don't. It's when you call some-body late at night, at least after midnight, and you ask them to come over and they know what the deal is."

"I see." The doctor nodded.

"I do know that right now I can't have no honey riding my jock. Calling me every five minutes asking me what I'm doing. That's how they try to get control."

"So you're okay being alone?"

"I ain't alone." Basil knew he had a thick phone book with plenty of numbers to call whenever he became lonely.

"Are you interested in sleeping with men?"

"Not really."

"What does that mean?"

"Like it sounds."

"What about Raymond?"

Basil didn't answer. Again Raymond's face came into his mind. He was silent for about five minutes and then he looked at the doctor and asked, "Isn't my time up?"

"Yes. I'll see you next week."

"Yeah, right."

7

Raymond removed his suit coat and began reviewing the mail when he suddenly noticed a large brown package with a note from Trent. *Hey babe! Hope you had a great day. This package just came for you. I'm at the gym, then off to do some work. See ya. Love, Trent.* As Raymond picked up the package he thought he should be at the gym with Trent.

The package was heavy and Raymond could tell from the handwriting that it was from his mother. But it didn't feel like cookies, brownies, or any type of food he had been expecting. Raymond tore open the package and out spilled a black leather photo binder. Taped to the front of it was a note on frilly paper from his mother. *My Dearest Son, I hope this helps with the confirmation. I've been looking forward to the day when you might need this. I love you and I'm so proud of you. Your mother.*

The house was quiet and the evening sun bathed the den in a golden glow. The room was large, with hardwood floors, a beautiful Persian rug, black leather furniture, forty-six-inch television, and an antique rolltop mahogany desk. This was the room where Raymond and Trent spent many quiet evenings enjoying each other, watching sporting events or reading while snuggled on the couch. Raymond leaned against the desk and opened the binder.

On the first page was a copy of his birth certificate and his footprints. He looked at the date, June 20, the time, 4:56 A.M., and his weight, 8 pounds 6 ounces. He read his father's name and "student" listed as his occupation and his mother's maiden name of Gaines and her occupation of "teacher." Raymond couldn't recall the last time he'd seen his birth certificate and the black-and-white photograph of him as a newborn. Curly hair, eyes closed tight. Only three days old.

As Raymond slowly turned page after page, he realized the treasure he was holding: a memoir of his life from his mother's eyes. A magical binder that included photographs, report cards, teachers' names, school names and addresses from kindergarten to high school.

There were pictures and awards from football, basketball, and tennis camps that Raymond had attended during his youth. Photos taken with Santa and other special activities like the Cubs and Boy Scouts. His first NAACP membership card, certificates from Sunday school, vacation Bible school, and articles that appeared in school and local newspapers. A tattered picture of Raymond in his high school football uniform, holding his younger brother, Kirby. Memories that had slipped from Raymond's mind.

There were letters and cards Raymond had sent his parents and even letters his mother had discovered from his first love, Sela, the young lady he had fallen in love with on sight at a high school basketball game. Numerous pictures of Raymond and Sela at their high school prom, parties, and sporting events, and fraternity and sorority mementos from their days at the University of Alabama. Every important person and event that occurred up until his graduation from law school was lovingly placed in this special book.

During his parents' weekend visit Raymond had mentioned how much he was dreading tracking down all the information required for his confirmation. The financial stuff would be easy. All Raymond had to do was call his accountant and the reports would be ready. But the FBI wanted more. Organizations in which he held memberships, papers he had written, and a random sampling of cases he'd handled as a lawyer, not just in Seattle, but throughout his career.

They also requested information on the schools he attended, including the names of teachers and friends who might vouch for his good character, and evidence that he had always been a good citizen. His mother appeared pleased when she said she might have something that would help him out. When Raymond and his father asked what, she had said, "That's my little secret and I don't know if I'm ready to let go. What did I always tell you? Save some secrets for yourself."

Some of the secrets Raymond had saved for himself didn't make the book. There were no pictures of Kelvin, the handsome University of Alabama football player who had seduced Raymond on a beautiful fall

Friday during his senior year. But how would Raymond's mother know about that life-changing experience? He wondered where Kelvin might be at this exact moment, whether he was dead or alive, if he had remarried or was spending his life with a man. There was one picture of Kyle, Raymond's first openly gay friend, in a group photo his mother had taken on a visit to New York, but no pictures of Kyle during his last months on earth, before he succumbed to AIDS. Raymond's smile disappeared as he thought about Kelvin and Kyle, but it returned quickly when he thought of the great times he had shared with each of them. The romantic snowy night when Raymond and Kelvin came oh so close to making love with only a winter sky covering them. Raymond could hear Whitney Houston singing "You Give Good Love," even though no music was playing. He thought of a warm spring night in New York's Greenwich Village, standing outside of Keller's, where he and Kyle would comment on the good-looking men going in and out of the bar, waging bets on who would take home the best-looking guy. Moments like these were missing from the book. Moments in his life he'd never shared with his mother or any member of his immediate family, simply because he thought they just wouldn't understand.

But there were other memories of his New York tenure in the binder. A newspaper article about Nicole Springer, the Broadway actress Raymond had fallen in love with harder than ever before, harder even than with Kelvin. He'd always known in his heart of hearts that Kelvin and he wouldn't last. Nicole was now an official part of his family after she married his best friend and play brother, Jared. There were no photographs of the hospital hallway where Raymond confessed to a stunned Nicole his sexual desires for men. Yet, like hearing the silent music, Raymond could still see Nicole's horrified face.

There was a picture of his mother, himself, and Sela on her wedding day—to someone else. For a moment, it looked like the picture everybody in Birmingham thought possible. Raymond and Sela married. There they were, Raymond's mother looking like the mother of the groom, Sela in a beautiful wedding gown, and Raymond smiling in a handsome black suit. He was not the groom but only a guest, at a wedding that occurred a few weeks after his confession to Nicole. The day he realized there would be no wedding day for him.

Raymond smiled to himself, and his eyes became moist as he reviewed the melancholy milestones of his life. And then a tear escaped from his left eye and rolled down his cheek. He felt overcome with emotion from the gift his mother had given him. He wanted to call her and thank her and share some of the moments she'd left out simply because he hadn't shared them with her before. But Raymond didn't pick up the phone, only inches away. He wanted to share this moment with Trent, and yet a part of him relished being able to review his life in solitude. It was a special feeling, a special moment. And even though the house was still silent, he could hear Trent's voice after the first time they made love in their new home, quiet like now. Trent had whispered in his lover's ear, *"Some of the best moments in life are when we don't have a clue of what to say or do."*

Later that evening, Raymond got a call from Trent saying he was working late and asked if he wanted him to stop and pick up something to eat.

"Naw, that's okay. I'm not that hungry," Raymond said softly.

"Are you all right?"

"I'm fine. Just enjoying the evening and life," Raymond said.

"What was in the package?" Trent asked.

"A really special gift from my mother. It's hard to describe it, but I'll show it to you after I've enjoyed it," Raymond said.

"Okay. I'll see you later on."

"Trent?"

"Yes, Raymond?"

"Thanks for being such a gift to me," Raymond said.

"What a nice thing to say. Are you sure everything is okay?"

"Never been more certain," Raymond said.

After hanging up, Raymond picked up the phone and called Jared. Nicole answered the phone. He still loved the sound of her voice.

"Nicole, how you doing?"

"Raymond? Of course it's Raymond. I'm doing fine, sweetheart. Is everything okay?" Raymond was thinking people close to him didn't understand the sweet sadness he was enjoying. But how could they?

"I'm doing just great. I know you're happy to be back in the Big Apple," Raymond said.

"I sure am. Matter of fact, I'm on my way out the door. Going to a party one of the members of the cast is giving. Want to speak to your boy?"

"Is he there?"

"Sure, let me get him. It's nice talking to you, Raymond. I hope we'll see you and Trent real soon," Nicole said.

"Same here. It's always nice hearing your voice," Raymond said.

After a few seconds Jared came on the phone.

"Whassup, whassup, my niggah?"

"You, my brother. How is everything?"

"Everything's cool, couldn't be cooler if I was sitting in a tub of ice," Jared joked.

"You sound happy."

"Why wouldn't I be? Life is sweet."

"I'm not keeping you from nuthing, am I?"

"You know I always got time for you. Besides, Nicole's gone to her party and I'm getting ready to look over some work and hit the sack," Jared said.

Raymond and Jared spent the next hour talking like they hadn't talked for months. In reality they spoke briefly at least once a week, sometimes two or three times.

Raymond, knowing Jared was really a small-city type of guy, asked him how he was dealing with New York. When Jared said he was loving it, Raymond teased him about how he used to say he could never see himself living in New York.

Jared asked how things were going with Trent and the confirmation and if he had any dates for the hearings.

"You know, I know people in D.C., so when you go down there for the hearing, I want to be in the front row. In case any of them congressmen wanna act stupid. I got yo' back," Jared said.

"And you know it," Raymond said.

"Are you sure you're all right?" Jared asked as the conversation neared an end. Before answering the question, Raymond told Jared about the gift his mother had sent and how it had got him to thinking about his life and everything.

"Your moms and pops are some special people," Jared said. "What a wonderful gift."

"So you see, my brother, I'm fine. I just wanted you to know what a gift you are to me. And I love ya, man," Raymond said.

"And I love you back," Jared said.

8

"I did something strange the other day," Basil said.

"You want to tell me about it?" the doctor asked.

"There was this honey at the gym. I noticed her checking me out for a couple of weeks, but, of course, there was nothing strange about that. I mean honeys and knuckleheads check me out all the time. Sometimes I speak . . . sometimes I don't. It all depends on how I'm feelin' at the particular time."

"What was strange about this lady?"

"It wasn't anything strange about her physically. I mean, she was beautiful. I couldn't even tell if she was black, probably mixed with something. She kinda reminded me of this honey in Spike Lee's movie *Mo' Better Blues,* the one with Denzel Washington. Did you see that?"

"No."

"Cynda Williams, that's her name."

"The young lady?"

"No, the actress, but back to the honey I was talking about. She was beautiful. I said that, didn't I? So anyway, the other day she finally walked up to me and asked if I was John Basil Henderson, which was weird 'cause everybody calls me Basil. When I said yeah, she looked at me and said she'd been wanting to meet me for a long time. I'm thinking she must be a reporter or something, but I suddenly find myself looking at her eyes. They're hard to ignore, brownish-gray baby-doll eyes. There was something sincere and sad in her eyes."

"How so?"

"It's kinda hard to explain. I mean, it was like she knew me."

"Was she a reporter?"

"I asked her and she said no," Basil said.

"Did you ask her if she knew you?"

"No. But, of course, she did know me. She knew my full name at least. When I was playing ball, I was in the newspaper and magazines all the time. And honeys, just like little boys and some men, collect photos of their favorite players. And now with my gig at ESPN, I have a whole new group of fans," Basil said confidently.

"So she knew you from your football playing days or your current position?"

"I think both. We didn't talk about it that much. We went to lunch and she didn't want to talk about sports at all. And she wasn't really coming on to me, but I know she wants me."

"How can you be certain?"

"Think about it. A good-looking honey comes over and says she's been wanting to meet you for a long time. I mean, come on. Her approach may be a little different, but in the end I'm certain she wants what they all want . . . a piece of the beef. The honeys nowadays are getting slicker all the time. They're starting to think and act like men. I kinda feel sorry for the dumb mofos making all that money playing sports. Honeys be reading the sports section like it's a romance novel or something. They do their research and then they go in for the kill. The next thing some of those mofos know, they're in court trying to work out child support payments."

"What did you and the young lady talk about during lunch?"

"First just some general things. And then she asked me about my childhood, and even though I didn't tell her much, she seemed really interested in me. She asked me about my father. Said she had read an article on me where I talked about how tight I was with my father, since he was a single parent. I started to tell her don't be trying to analyze me, I've already got somebody doing that," Basil laughed.

"Are you interested in pursuing a relationship with her?"

"I don't know. I ain't really hanging with anybody seriously. I might 'cause she is fine, and I like it when honeys want to talk about something besides sports and who I fucked that was famous. You know?"

"You want somebody who's not interested in what you do for a living?"

"Yeah, that's right."

"That's understandable. So you had a nice time talking with her?"

"Yeah, I did."

"Are you going to see her again?"

"I don't know. Maybe. Maybe not."

"Does she have a name?"

Basil looked up and smiled at the doctor like a mischievous little boy and said, "Yeah, her name is Campbell. Like the soup!"

9

On Friday, Trent prepared a special celebration dinner for Raymond, who was looking forward to a quiet evening with his partner. But Trent had invited Dexter, who invited his own guest. Trent didn't actually invite Dexter. He invited himself, by leaving a message saying he was going to drop by, even though he knew that Friday was Trent and Raymond's regular date night. By the time Trent called to tell Dexter and remind him of that, Dexter and his friend were already ringing the doorbell.

Dexter Paul Johnson was more Trent's friend than he was Raymond's. If there was a major flaw in the relationship between Raymond and Trent, this was it. Raymond didn't always like Trent's choice of friends, but he never made it a big issue. He placed entertaining some of Trent's friends in the what-I-do-for-love category.

Trent was the kind of guy who would bring home a stray dog. Raymond would take the animal to a nearby shelter. He'd make sure it was the best shelter, but a shelter nonetheless.

Trent and Dexter had met while working out at the downtown Seattle Athletic Club. Trent had told Raymond how Dexter had come on to him during their initial meeting, but when Trent told him about his better half, Dexter pursued Trent's friendship instead. Dexter had a lover, a white one, but he was anything but a snow queen. With his perfect gym-toned body, Dexter loved men of all types. He had told Trent that his lover, David, was HIV-positive and very wealthy.

When the two of them met, Dexter figured David had two years if he was lucky, but now with the new drugs, David was suddenly robust. After hiring someone to run his gallery while he was on disability, David had returned to his occupation as an art dealer and business was booming, like his T-cell count. Dexter hadn't counted on that.

While waiting for David to kick the bucket, he had made sure his name was on the insurance policies. It was a rare event when Dexter escorted David to social events or clubs. It was a very strange relationship, and Raymond didn't think it was good for Trent to be so close with someone who had no respect for relationships. It didn't help when Dexter would encourage Trent to go club hopping without Raymond. Trent and Dexter both knew Trent would decline the invitation.

His betrayal of David was just one of the reasons Raymond didn't care for Dexter. He considered him a big-time user. Although he had a degree in economics from Washington State, Dexter wasn't working in his field. Instead he would secure clerical jobs, and count the days until he would become eligible for unemployment benefits. He'd get himself fired, then live off $300-a-week checks until they ran out, spending his free time in the gym and bars around Seattle. He didn't have to pay rent in the three-bedroom condo he shared with David, and was still driving the BMW David had bought him as a congratulations gift the time Dexter got a management job with CoreStates Bank. The job lasted all of thirty days before he quit or was fired. Several times during his brief tenure at CoreStates, Dexter had asked Raymond questions about suing his employer for sexual harassment, since everybody he worked for wanted to *have* him.

On this special evening, Dexter had brought his latest not-so-special piece of trade, Billy Ray, who could best be described as a wanna-be Puff Daddy, but really looked more like Huggy Bear, of the seventies television drama *Starsky and Hutch.* He had a face that was almost square, a Caesar-style haircut, and jumpy and intense brown eyes. Billy Ray had a lanky and gangling basketball player frame with unusually large arms. He was wearing tight jeans, which made him look like he was concealing a couple of plums, and a short-sleeved, pale blue work shirt that smelled of stale sweat. Raymond realized it was going to be a long evening.

"Are you mixed with sumthin'?" Billy Ray asked as he studied Raymond like a book.

"Excuse me?" Raymond asked. He looked at Billy Ray, then Dexter, and finally Trent.

"You know what I'm sayin'. Look at yourself. Mellow yellow, green eyes, and good hair. If one of yo' folks ain't white, then I know they came from the big house," he said in a full-throated, masculine voice.

"Both my parents are African-American," Raymond said sternly. He eyed Trent for a reaction, but Trent made sure there was none.

"What did you cook for dinner, Trent? Something smells good," Dexter said, obviously trying to change the subject.

"Wait till we sit down, Dexter. I know your mother gave you a little home training," Trent teased.

"What do you guys do for a living?" Billy Ray asked.

"Why is that important?" Raymond asked. He was praying Dexter hadn't told Billy Ray of his occupation.

"It must be sumthin' else. 'Cause you brothers are sho livin' large," Billy Ray said as he surveyed the L-shaped living room. Raymond was wondering if he should start bolting down anything of value.

"Why don't we go into the den and get something to drink?" Trent suggested.

The four of them walked from the living area into the den. Trent immediately went to the bar and pulled out a beer. "What are you guys drinking?"

"I'll just have some wine," Raymond said.

"Sounds good to me," Dexter chimed.

"You got any Courvoisier?" Billy Ray asked. Raymond started to say, *Only if you can spell it,* but resisted.

"Yeah, we do. What do you want with it?" Trent asked.

"Straight up! Ya'll ain't got nuthing against something straight, do ya?" he laughed.

Raymond rubbed his temple and wondered where on earth Dexter met these men. Not that he didn't know a thing or two about trade from his days in New York. He knew guys like Billy Ray from personal experience and from Kyle, who preferred guys like Billy Ray more than someone like Dexter. Guys called them trade because they would barter their sexual prowess for money, cocktails, and drugs.

Billy Ray checked out the furnishing in the den almost as if he was casing the joint.

"Damn, that's a big-ass TV," he commented as his eyes came to rest on the entertainment center.

"Yeah it is," Dexter said. "And when the fights break out on *Jerry Springer,* you feel like you've got a ringside seat," he added. Raymond was getting ready to ask Dexter when was the last time he'd watched anything at his home during the day, when Trent gave him a half-pained look that said, "baby, please be nice."

Raymond was happy when Trent announced dinner was ready. He

cringed every time Trent would leave the room and Billy Ray would once again begin the questioning. The second time Trent left for the kitchen, Raymond followed. Trent was checking something in the oven and Raymond, shaking his head and laughing, asked where Dexter had met Billy Ray.

"Dexter said he's one of the maintenance guys at the building where he's working," Trent said.

"Why am I not surprised?" Raymond asked sarcastically.

"Now, baby, why you always dogging my friend?" Trent said.

"And I guess he's supposed to be straight?" Raymond questioned.

"Well, I think he's married, but we know what that means," Trent said.

"Yeah, absolutely nothing," Raymond said as he pulled Trent close and kissed him gently on the lips.

"Thanks for being so understanding. I really wanted this to be a special evening for you and me," Trent said.

"I know. We will have plenty of time later," Raymond hinted.

Raymond left Trent in the kitchen and returned to their guests. As soon as he entered the den, Billy Ray had a question.

"So you ever been with a woman, Raymond?"

Raymond rolled his eyes and answered in his lawyerly, almost snobbish tone, "Excuse me?"

"Why don't we put on some music?" Dexter said as he leaped from the sofa. It was like he was running for cover.

"Women. Honeys. You know. Do you like hit some pussy every now and then?" Billy Ray asked as he pulled out a package of cigarettes from his shirt pocket. Raymond didn't answer the question but told Billy Ray if he wanted to smoke he'd have to do it outside. Billy Ray raised his eyebrow and gazed at Raymond for a quick second and then said he could wait since dinner was being served. As they were walking toward the dining area Billy Ray spoke again, "What about the tunes?"

"I'm still looking," Dexter said as he surveyed their CD collection.

"See if they got some Lil' Kim or Foxy Brown," Billy Ray suggested.

"I don't think so," Dexter said, almost singing his reply in a mock opera tone. Trent came to the door and announced dinner was ready.

He had prepared a meal of beef brisket, string beans with onions, and a sweet potato casserole. Billy Ray packed his plate so full of food that even Dexter looked embarrassed. Billy Ray took a piece of brisket from the platter and slurped it down before it touched the plate. Then he retrieved a couple more pieces of the thinly sliced meat without looking up. Making matters worse, when Billy Ray ate he made a loud smacking and sucking sound. When he took a brief break from his plate, he needed something else.

"Can you hook up a brother's drank?" he asked as he lifted his glass toward Trent. "Ya know red meat makes a bro thirsty," Billy Ray said as he stuck his fork into the beef.

"I'll get it," Raymond offered. He wasn't being sociable, but had suddenly lost his appetite. It was a good thing, because by the time Billy Ray finally pulled himself away from the table, there was very little food left.

10

In a few short weeks, Yancey Braxton had become not only Nicole Springer's devoted understudy but her shadow as well. One of the male dancers in the show commented that Yancey stuck to Nicole like lint on a cheap suit.

Whenever they took a break from rehearsals or Nicole indicated she might have a few minutes to spare while waiting for Jared to pick her up, Yancey would leap at the chance to spend time with her mentor and new friend.

Over a three-week period, Nicole had learned a lot about Yancey and often smiled to herself at their similarities. Besides the beauty pageants, they both knew that one day they would star on Broadway and move on to the big screen. They both grew up in small Southern towns, near big cities. Nicole was from Sweet Home, Arkansas, right outside of Little Rock, and it turned out that Yancey wasn't actually from Memphis, but had grown up in Jackson, Tennessee, a town just east of Memphis. Both women had strained relationships with their mothers, because they didn't understand what performing meant to their daughters. And both had lost their fathers, whom they had adored from birth. Yancey told Nicole her mother had further complicated things by marrying her father's best friend a year after her beloved father's death.

One day, while they were sharing a large plate of shrimp fried rice in a small Chinese restaurant, Nicole asked Yancey if she had anyone special in her life. A gentle look of amusement crept over Yancey's face as she answered very softly, "I think I've met the man I'm going to marry. He's a doctor right here in Manhattan. A pediatrician."

"You're not going to get married right now, are you?" Nicole asked. She assumed Yancey's career was very important to her, or so she thought.

"Oh, no, I'm not even trying to get married no time soon. But he's the one, and I know I can string him along until I'm ready," Yancey said confidently.

"Sounds like you got everything under control," Nicole said.

"I think so," Yancey replied. She paused for a moment to sip some of the tea from the tiny white cup in front of her, and then her voice turned semiserious.

"Nicole, could I tell you something and you not get upset with me?"

"Sure, why would I be upset with you?"

"Well, this doctor, my future husband, well, you know. Well, he's white," Yancey said with a touch of embarrassment in her voice.

"You think I would get mad at you for that?" Nicole asked.

"I didn't know how you felt about that kind of thing."

"Listen, love is love and I know it doesn't have a color. In fact, I was engaged to a white man once upon a time."

"You were? I had no idea! And here I was thinking I knew everything there was to know about you. What happened to him? Did you meet Jared and then fall madly in love with him?"

"Actually, I did fall in love with Jared rather quickly, but I was long over Pierce. We just grew apart. I had some happy times with him, but in the end it just didn't feel right."

"What did Pierce do for a living?"

"Funny you should ask. He was a doctor also. Made a lot of money and became a Broadway producer almost like a hobby, because he kept his practice open. I guess he's still doing both, although I haven't heard his name associated with any shows."

"See how much we have in common? But how could you leave a Broadway producer? Girl, that's a ticket I would like to get punched."

"It just wasn't right," Nicole said.

"Didn't you tell me you met Jared through a former boyfriend?"

"Yes, that's right."

"Was it Pierce?"

"No, I met Jared through Raymond, who I dated before Pierce. Raymond and Jared are best friends. Once I got over my anger with Raymond and we became friends, then I met Jared," Nicole explained.

"Was Raymond black?"

"Yes."

"Then I bet I can guess why you were angry," Yancey said.

"You think so?"

"Yes, honey, I bet he was a stone-cold dog. I bet you caught him with another woman. Am I right?"

Nicole sipped some of her tea and began to laugh.

"What's so funny?" Yancey asked.

"Well, it wasn't another woman. Let's just say I lost Raymond to nature," Nicole said.

"Nature. What do you mean?"

"Raymond was gay," Nicole said in a matter-of-fact tone. She was surprised how easy that rolled off her tongue, but was proud also. Nicole knew that time heals all wounds and tears are temporary.

"What!!" Yancey squealed. "Girl, naw, see that's why I don't date men in the theater and why black men are only good for one thing," she added.

"But Raymond wasn't in the theater. He's a lawyer, who just got nominated for a judgeship. And what do you mean black men are only good for one thing?"

"Wait, before I answer that . . . are Raymond and Jared still good friends?"

"Yep. Even though Raymond lives with his lover in Seattle, they still talk at least once a week," Nicole said.

"And you don't have a problem with that?"

"No, not at all. They were never that type of friends, and besides, I trust them both without reservation," Nicole said while Yancey eyed her with a don't-be-no-fool look. She heard a little voice inside her head say, "Damn, this is one real naïve sister. What I'm planning will be a cakewalk."

"I've got a little secret. Now, I'll be the first to admit that there are some fine, fine brothers out there. I mean just look at the men in our cast. I ain't gonna get my heart broken, though a woman has her needs," Yancey smiled.

"Right, but what does that have to do with black men being good for only one thing?"

Yancey explained to Nicole how her first boyfriend, Albert, had broken her heart in high school. Right after she gave her virginity to him, he left her for a white girl. But he continued to have sex with Yancey. Told her she was the best ever. Yancey thought she loved Albert and could win him back with great sex, but her plan didn't work.

Yancey was crushed, because on their prom night, even though Yancey had a great-looking date, she ended up dumping him and sleeping with Albert. On that night Albert had promised to dump his girlfriend and marry Yancey. Truth be told, Albert married the white girl right after their graduation.

"So every brother I meet is paying for what Albert did. I'll give them a little action, because, and I know this is a stereotype, because most of them are great in bed. This way I can hold out on Peter—that's my doctor friend—which makes him want me all the more. But I've told him, he ain't even getting close to sniffing distance until I have a ring on my finger."

"He doesn't think you're a virgin, does he?"

"No, I didn't go that far. But I told him I'm not that experienced. And he doesn't know about the brothers on the side."

"Do you think that's wise? I mean, what about these so-called brothers on the side? What happens if one of them wants to get serious with you?"

"Then it's their fault, because I tell them right up front what my deal is. I tell them I'm into my career and I don't have time for love. Now, if they just want a little sumthing-sumthing and I do too, then we can deal. Otherwise, it's no play," Yancey said.

"I hope you're careful," Nicole said.

"Trust me, Nicole. I'm always careful," Yancey said with a smile and quick wink.

11

"I'm a little down today," Basil said as he crossed his legs at the ankles. He was carrying a rolled-up copy of *USA Today*'s sports section, dressed casually in starched jeans and a loose-fitting long-sleeved cotton shirt, and wearing a scarlet and gray Ohio State baseball cap. The doctor noticed the black animal-skin loafers he was wearing sans socks. His face was clean-shaven and he was wearing slender gold loop earrings in both ears. He looked like a model for an all-American campaign.

"What's bothering you?"

"I finally spoke to Yolanda," Basil said.

"Yolanda, the young lady you were dating right before you started seeing me, right?"

"Yeah, that's the one," Basil smiled. The thought of Yolanda still touched a part of his heart.

"Tell me about the conversation."

"Yolanda was always a class act, and I think she's really trying to be my friend."

"You have a problem with that?"

"Damn skippy," Basil replied indignantly.

"Why?"

"She treats me like I'm not a threat to her and her so-called relationship."

"A threat? What relationship?"

"I think she's hanging with this guy she went to school with named Dwight. You know that there's no way, nohow I can get next to her. Therefore, we can be friends. But it's really not a friendship at all. It's very businesslike. I know she cares for me, but she always says, 'I want to be your friend and help you deal with your issues.' "

"Did she say what issues?"

"Didn't have to. What else would she mean when talking about *my* issues? I know where she's coming from."

"You mind sharing that with me?"

"Might as well, that's what I'm here for. It's like, ever since she caught me in the act with that mofo Monty, Yolanda treats me like I'm some sorta gay buddy, like that doctor friend of hers. I hate it when bitches try and discount you because you hit it both ways, or they catch you in some incorrect shit." Basil paused and pressed his lips together and then used his tongue to moisten them and continued. "To tell the truth, I don't even know why I called her. Maybe I was just curious, 'cause she made me wait a year before we talked. I guess she had to get me out of her system. I tried to call her a couple months after we broke up, but sistah wasn't having it. Never answered her phone, never returned my calls. One of the first things she asked me after we had gone through our 'how you doin' . . . good hearing your voice' kinda thing was if I had met a nice man. That shit made my skin burn. I mean, I ain't *never* talked to women about my sexuality and I'm not about to start some crazy shit like that right now. I like to *show* a woman what I can do rather than sitting on the phone, like a couple of bitches, chitchatting about what you like to do in bed, and telling me how big a dick the niggah you hittin' it with has."

"Why won't you refer to what you did with Monty as lovemaking or a sexual relationship?"

" 'Cause it wasn't. I was just trying to get myself out of a situation. You know with him threatening to drop my name in an interview he was doing. I didn't want that homo talking about my bizness to anyone. All he wanted was the beef, and anytime you don't kiss, then you sure as hell don't call it making love. It's just hittin' skins."

"So you used sex to get yourself out of the situation?"

"Always works, Doc," Basil said confidently. "It always has."

"Let's get back to why you called Yolanda."

"I wanted to see if she'd come to her senses and decided to give me another chance."

"Why do you want another chance with Yolanda?"

"I don't know," Basil said quietly.

"You don't?"

Basil was silent for a few moments, then he turned to the doctor and asked, "Could it be that I am, or was, actually in love with her?"

"Is that so hard to believe?"

"She touched places no one had ever come close to," Basil said almost wistfully.

"And how do you think she did that?"

"She just . . . listened when I talked."

"And no one has ever done that with you?"

"They always seemed to be looking someplace else. At me, through me, around me . . ." Basil's voice trailed off as he stared blankly at the floor in front of him, as if to illustrate his point.

"No man has ever touched you emotionally the way Yolanda did?"

"Naw."

"Not even Raymond?"

"He came close, but he blew it. When he just ignored my letter, it showed me the niggah wasn't shit. Just like the rest of the mofos, interested in the beef."

"It sounds like you have a difficult time loving, or accepting the fact that someone can love you for you."

"Love is for punks, suckers, and females."

"So you're saying you don't have any hope for love?"

"Love has never offered me any fuckin' hope. I'm outta here, Doc!"

12

A fine mist covered downtown Seattle. There was nothing unusual about that, but Raymond was glad Trent had reminded him to wear his black trench coat for his important meeting. He removed the coat during the bumpy elevator ride and happily noticed there were no signs of the dampness outside on his navy-blue suit with thin gold stripes. His red and yellow silk tie looked brand-new. Raymond felt good as he arrived on the nineteenth floor of the Federal Building.

"I'm here to see Ms. Lisa Lanier," Raymond said to the receptionist.

"You must be Raymond Tyler. Ms. Lanier is expecting you," she said.

"Thank you," Raymond smiled.

"Can I get you some coffee and maybe a muffin, after I take you into Ms. Lanier's office?"

"Some coffee, light with cream, would be nice," Raymond said.

Moments later Raymond was sitting in Lisa Lanier's office. Her office rang with clues that she wanted to be a politician herself one day. It was cluttered with photos of her smiling alongside the president, the governor, and Senator Murray. There were campaign buttons and stickers everywhere. Raymond thought Lisa aspired one day to be more than just the chief of staff to a United States senator. This was a woman with high political aspirations.

After a few pleasantries, *so nice to meet you, what part of town do you live in,* and so on, Lisa got down to business.

"I'm sure you know this confirmation process is a tough nut to crack, but don't worry, I'll be with you every step of the way," she said confidently.

"Thanks, I'm ready," Raymond said.

While sipping her herbal tea, Lisa looked over some of the information Raymond had submitted. "Give me just a minute," she said as she spread butter on a blueberry muffin. "Are you sure coffee is all you need?"

"The coffee is just fine," Raymond said. While Lisa was reviewing the FBI information and his financial records, Raymond studied Lisa Lanier. She had a slender face and sandy-colored hair with blond natural streaks. It was softly styled and fell right below her shoulders. When she looked up from the file, Raymond noticed her grayish-blue eyes were gentle and peaceful. After a few moments, she said in a kind voice, "Everything looks fine. This should be a piece of cake."

"I hope you're right. I've never been through anything like this," Raymond said.

Lisa dabbed her lower lip with a Kleenex and asked, "You're single, right?"

Raymond took a deep breath. He always hated this question. Could he consider himself single? Didn't the people who nominated him know of his living arrangements? He could hear his mother's voice saying, "Tell the truth, baby."

"I'm in a committed relationship," he said forcefully.

Lisa's eyebrows raised ever so slightly, but before she could ask for further clarification, Raymond added, "With a man."

Lisa took a bite of her muffin and said, "Oh."

"That's not going to be a problem, is it?"

"Oh no. I'm just glad you told me. We have judges on the federal bench who are gay. In fact, there is an African-American woman who's gay, I think, somewhere in the South. But you can be sure the FBI will ask you this in the interview, so shoot straight. I mean, tell them the truth," Lisa said as she grinned at her pun.

"No problem, I will," Raymond said.

"But I will be honest with you. Your lifestyle will open you up for all kinds of questions. They will check your partner and close friends," Lisa advised.

Raymond hated it when people referred to his life with Trent as a lifestyle, but he had become used to it, so he asked Lisa what type of questions.

"You know, like what do you think of the 'don't ask, don't tell' policy, and more than likely the gay marriage thing."

"Would you like to know how I might respond?" Raymond asked.

"Not right now, just think about it. We have more than enough time to cover the specifics."

Lisa spent the next fifteen minutes explaining her duties, while Raymond was thinking how he would answer the gay marriage question. He knew very well that people felt passionately about the issue on both sides. Lisa told Raymond she would set up and videotape mock confirmation hearings. Raymond could watch his performance and make changes where needed, especially with questions about gay issues. Lisa also pointed out that he would be questioned about his feelings on affirmative action.

"I don't see that being a problem, you're so articulate," Lisa said.

"Thank you," Raymond grimaced. Another thing he hated was when white folks used the term *articulate* when describing his speech. He couldn't stand the a-word. A code for black people who spoke the King's English like it was a second language. It was like whites and some lower-class blacks were so surprised. Surely someone had seen him in the courtroom, or heard some of the lectures he'd given while teaching constitutional law at the University of Washington law school. Anyone who knew Raymond Tyler knew he was an articulate and skilled conversationalist. Whenever he worked on a case with other partners in the office, they always wanted Raymond to do the closing argument for that reason alone. There had been many times when he won cases because of his persuasive and powerful manner that others had assumed were certain defeats.

"The good news is, we've passed the first big hurdle. The local bar association has approved your nomination," Lisa said.

"I'm glad to hear that," Raymond said. He hadn't anticipated any problem, though, because the current president had worked with Raymond at the University of Washington and was one of the first people to call with congratulations.

"Once we get a date for your confirmation hearing, our office will make your travel arrangements. Will your partner be going with you?"

"I hope so. His name is Trent Walters. And I'm certain my parents and younger brother will be attending as well," Raymond said.

"They must be so proud of you," Lisa beamed.

"Yes, they are pretty excited, especially my father," Raymond said.

"That's it for now. You'll be contacted when the FBI has completed its research. Of course, they will want to talk to you about any questions that might arise during the investigation."

"Okay," Raymond nodded.

"We'll work on getting an endorsement of some kind from the NAACP and the Association of Black Lawyers," Lisa said.

Raymond smiled, thinking how happy he was about being a member in good standing with both organizations.

He had been a member of the NAACP since he was nine years old when his parents gave him a membership for his birthday. Raymond didn't realize then what an important gift he had received.

"Do you have any questions?" Lisa asked.

"How long is the confirmation process?"

Lisa laughed to herself and said, "That's a good question. It could be a few months or a few years. But let's remain hopeful. There is a lot of pressure on Congress to give either a timely yea or nay on the president's appointments. No matter what, I'll keep you posted."

"Thank you. I will appreciate that," Raymond said.

Lisa stood and extended her long and narrow hand with a simple gold band on her middle finger and smiled. "It's been a pleasure meeting you, Raymond. I look forward to the day when I can greet you as Judge Tyler."

"So do I," Raymond said as he shook her hand.

❖   ❖   ❖

It had been a long day for both Raymond and Trent. Raymond told Trent about his meeting with Lisa, then Trent told Raymond about a big project in South Africa he wanted to be assigned to. But since Brenda Taylor, the other African-American in his office, was project leader, Trent thought it might prevent him from a spot on the team for this dream assignment.

"I didn't know your office had the 'one is enough' rule," Raymond teased.

"I didn't either, but then I've always been the only one," Trent said.

"Doesn't the project leader have a say?"

"Yeah, and Brenda's cool, but you know how *we* can sometimes be our worst critics."

"If this Brenda is as cool and smart as you say, then you're on the team," Raymond assured him.

Dog-tired, Raymond and Trent decided to retire earlier than their usual 11:30 bedtime.

Wearing a white, hooded, terry-cloth robe, Trent was pulling back the comforter on their bed when Raymond, wearing only a lime-green striped towel, walked behind him and kissed him gently on the neck.

"I've got something to ask you," he whispered.

"Now, you know you don't have to ask," Trent joked as he turned to face Raymond.

"Would you marry me?" Raymond asked.

"What?" Trent could not believe the question. His soft laugh sounded like a cough.

"I'm not asking you right now, but this is a question that might come up in my confirmation hearing. Would you marry me? I mean, if it was legal."

"I . . . I . . ." Trent stammered. His face was coolly composed and unreadable. Just as he was getting ready to explain his hesitation, Raymond's private line rang. His hesitation wasn't because he didn't love Raymond, but all he could think of at the moment was his mother. He could hear her sigh with a loud sound and tell Trent how his father would roll over in his grave at such an event. Trent couldn't think of getting married without his mother's blessing. And he was sure Raymond felt the same about his own parents' response.

"Hello," Raymond said as he answered the phone somewhat distractedly. Trent took a deep sigh of relief and was getting ready to go into the bathroom when Raymond put his hand on the receiver and whispered, "It's Kirby, I won't be long."

A few minutes later Trent returned to the bedroom wearing only a white muscle T-shirt and a smile. Raymond was already in bed with his back toward Trent. With only a wedge of light coming from the hallway, the room glowed like a dusk-covered evening.

"So how's your little brother?" Trent asked.

Raymond turned and faced Trent. When he noticed his bedroom attire, he smiled and said, "He's cool. Can you believe he's already in Evanston?"

"For what?"

"Football practice."

"Well, it is getting close to that time," Trent said.

Raymond sat up in the bed, moving the pillows to support his back, and said, "So you didn't answer my question." For Raymond it was a semiserious question. He had never really thought about marrying Trent, or any other man for that matter. He simply assumed when he accepted his sexuality that marriage was not an option. Now that he might be faced with taking a position on gay marriage, he wanted to know how Trent felt.

Trent smiled and started moving from side to side in a little electric slide type of groove and started singing.

"I'm so in love with you. Whatever you want to do . . . is all right with mee . . . mme," Trent sang in his rich tenor voice as he swiftly removed

his T-shirt. Raymond admired Trent's splendidly muscle-packed body and had a sudden urge to embrace him. As Trent was dancing in front of him still singing the Al Green tune, Raymond felt a tremendous charge of energy, then he felt Trent move closer to him, grinding to the sound of his own voice. Whenever Trent's body touched his, Raymond felt a rush of joy spread through his body. Trent suddenly dove into the bed and nestled his head in the curve of Raymond's chest, breathing in his familiar scent. He hadn't answered Raymond's question.

13

"Well I'll be. Look what the cat done drug in," Peaches said as Nicole walked into Cuts 'n' Cobblers, located in Harlem on 127th between Lenox Avenue and Adam Clayton Powell Boulevard.

"Peaches, it's so good to see you," Nicole said as she gave the small, red-bone, and wiry middle-aged woman a big hug. "Where is everybody?"

"Miss Thang, didn't I tell you brunch, not dinner? It's almost four o'clock. You do know what brunch is and that I do have a personal life, don't cha? And who is this light-skinned look-alike you brung with you?" Peaches asked as she noticed Yancey standing slightly behind Nicole. Peaches thought Yancey looked like her cousin Mabel Lee. Her cousin who lied so much Peaches said you could only believe every fifth thing she said.

"This is my new best friend and my understudy, Yancey Braxton," Nicole said as she moved so Peaches could get a look at her new friend.

"Braxton," Peaches said as she took Yancey's arm, looked her up and down and then up again. "You any kin to that singer? What's her name?"

"You mean Toni?" Yancey asked.

"That's her," Peaches said.

"Yes, she's my cousin," Yancey lied. Nicole looked a bit surprised. She was learning something new about her friend every day.

"So I guess sanging runs in your family," Peaches said.

"Yes, Miss Peaches, I guess so," Yancey replied.

"Ain't no need of calling me Miss. Peaches will do." Peaches thought Yancey's kiss-up demeanor also reminded her of Mabel Lee.

"So did we miss dinner? I mean brunch?" Nicole asked.

"Yeah, but there's some food back there. I'll fix you ladies some plates to take home. But I thought you came here to help," Peaches said.

"We did," Nicole said.

"Dressed like that?" Peaches said, noticing both women were dressed in their Sunday best. Yancey and Nicole were wearing similar silk dresses with pearls.

"And you missed all my kids. You know I've been tellin' them about you, Nicole, my Broadway diva friend. I know they git tired of me talking about people they ain't never met. A couple of them even heard of you. I got this child—you know, she a *translation,* you know a man wanna be a woman. But she's some kinda beautiful. I told her all about you and she knows who you are. Her stage name is Miss Kitty Cotillion and she's a mess." Peaches laughed to herself, then pulled out a pack of cigarettes from her off-white waitress uniform.

"I look forward to meeting her," Nicole smiled. Suddenly Nicole remembered Peaches in Kyle's apartment with a cigarette in one hand, a drink in the other, encouraging Nicole to read Bible passages to Kyle while he rested. When Kyle fell asleep, Peaches would tell Nicole to read them to her. She loved Nicole's theatrical reading of the Scriptures.

It was Nicole and Yancey's plan to come to Harlem to help out with the weekly Sunday brunch Peaches cooked for HIV-positive patients in Harlem. It was just one of the things an organization called More Than Friends did for patients in the Harlem area. The small organization also made sure patients on their client list got some kind of cheerful card every two weeks and they didn't let a birthday or holiday go unnoticed. Peaches was also working with GMHC (Gay Men's Health Crisis) to ensure people in Harlem had access to the new AIDS drugs and rides to their doctor appointments.

More Than Friends had been set up in the memory of Peaches's son, Kyle Alexander Benton, who had died of AIDS almost six years earlier. Nicole had been a close friend of Kyle's and had met Peaches during the last months of his life. She fell in love with the quick-witted Kyle moments after Raymond introduced the two. Nicole also fell in love with Peaches instantly, since mother and son shared a wonderful sense of humor. Not even AIDS could get them down.

Though it was a small organization, More Than Friends had a big heart. Its board consisted mostly of Kyle's family and old friends, like

Raymond, Jared, and Nicole, and some new friends Peaches had met once she decided to move from South Jersey to Harlem. Peaches had said she needed to be in New York to be closer to her son's spirit during his happy times. Kyle loved New York City. Besides, without Kyle's monthly visits, Peaches felt she had nothing to look forward to in Jersey.

Raymond, who was instrumental in getting the organization off the ground, had offered to hire a full-time administrator once he and Trent moved to Seattle, but Peaches wasn't having it. She was determined to keep her promise to Kyle, a son she liked, adored, and loved with her whole heart.

Raymond had done all the paperwork in creating the nonprofit organization, and Jared had taken some of the funds from Kyle's insurance policy and invested some and put the remainder in a trust. Jared had also written proposals for funds for which he thought the organization might qualify. But it was Peaches who made it work. She didn't depend on funds from the trust, but used her lottery winnings for an operating budget. She only called on her son's friends when she needed business advice. Nicole had put on a couple of small benefits before she left New York, but had lost contact once she moved to Atlanta.

Not only was Peaches the driving force behind More Than Friends, but she also had her own small business: she was part owner of Cuts 'n' Cobblers. She was the cobbler part, being the head cook in charge of baking some of the best peach, apple, and blueberry cobblers to ever come out of Harlem. Add to that the special nutmeg-spiced coffee Peaches prepared and suddenly Harlem had a new institution. Mornings were a madhouse with the lines out the door for the coffee and thick-crusted cobblers Peaches prepared. She sold them in the front part of the establishment. Peaches was proud of her double-shelved, refrigerated showcase. A couple of carpet pieces and a black leather mat covered portions of the steel-gray concrete floor. There were a few tables that were made for sitting, but customers used them for packages and brief-cases while they chowed down on the sweets, because the shop was always so crowded during the morning and evening rushes. There was an old-fashioned cash register that constantly displayed in the same black and white characters the total of $5.00, the cost of a large slice of cobbler and cup of coffee. A whole cobbler was nine dollars. The register didn't always work, so Peaches had a small calculator right under the shelf. Whenever there was a rush, which there usually was, she would survey a customer's purchase and say, "Just give me twenty dollars and we even."

The "Cuts" part belonged to Enoch Kitchens, master barber, and owner of the two-chair barbershop that was in the rear of the store. Enoch had been in the haircutting business in the same location for more than twenty-five years. His shop was one of the few in Harlem that refused to go unisex. Enoch wouldn't even hire female barbers.

Enoch, a widower for almost ten years, was from Church Point, Louisiana, but considered Harlem home for over thirty years. Enoch had moved there after leaving the army with his new bride. He wasn't looking for a storemate when Peaches walked in some four years ago, but with a lot of men now getting their hair styled instead of cut, business was slacking off. Besides, he was instantly smitten by the fast-talking, take-no-mess Peaches Gant. While he was still thinking, *I don't know about this,* Peaches slipped some peach cobbler in his mouth, and the deal was done. "Listen, ole man, you got all this space and it's just wastin'. Who knows, I might bring you some new customers," Peaches told Enoch.

"Neither one of you ladies don't happen to have a Sunday *Post,* do ya?" Peaches asked as she looked around to see if anybody had left one.

"I don't," Yancey said. "You want me to run and get you one?"

"Naw, that's all right. I can find out if I'm a millionairess later on," Peaches said.

"Peaches, I feel so bad. I could have sworn you said you were serving dinner," Nicole said as she looked at her watch.

"We were really looking forward to helping," Yancey interjected.

"I might have said dinner. You know this ole girl is getting old. But not to worry. The group will be back next week, just like today," Peaches said as she took a seat at one of the card tables that were set up for the brunch.

"Can we wash dishes or do something?" Nicole asked.

"Not in them pretty dresses. Washing dishes is Enoch's job," Peaches said. "I tell him all the time everybody got to do their part."

"Is that the man who answered the phone when I called? Where is he? He sounded so nice on the phone," Nicole said.

"He's upstairs, probably watchin' baseball or sumthin' like that. Let him stay up there for now. Why don't you ladies just sit down? I'll get some punch or sumthin' and we'll just have girl talk," Peaches said.

"That would be nice," Nicole said. There were only two chairs at the table, but Yancey noticed others leaning against the wall. She quickly grabbed one, unfolded it, and took a seat. Peaches noticed this and said, "I like this girl. She got some git-up-and-go. Don't have to tell her nuthin'. Where you from, darling?"

"I'm from Tennessee," Yancey replied.

"Oh, you a Southern gal, just like our Miss Nicole. Nicole, where is that fine husband of yours?"

"He's at the office."

"On a Sunday?"

"Yes. As soon as church services were over he headed for the subway and his office. But he told me to give you a big hug and a kiss and tell you he promises to be here next Sunday."

"Aw, ain't that sweet. Tell him I'll wait and git that hug and kiss from him. Just make sure he does it in front of Enoch. Let 'em know he got some comp," Peaches said.

"So this Enoch is more than a business partner . . . huh? Now, don't tell me Miz Peaches got a man," Nicole teased.

"Mind your own business, Miss Nicole. I swear. You ain't changed a bit," Peaches smiled. "Not one damn bit."

14

"Campbell is getting kinda weird," Basil said.

"What do you mean?"

"The other day we went out to lunch and she brought up my mother again. All she wanted to talk about was a mother I didn't know."

"And that makes her weird?"

"Don't you think it's weird? I mean, asking me if I ever saw a picture of her and did I know what she looked like."

"Have you ever seen a picture of your mother?"

"Naw. My pops said he had one, but he lost it during a move. Said he had one taped to a truck he was driving and someone stole it. From what I can tell, I mean from the way he talks about her, she must have been really good looking. I know I got my eyes from her, 'cause ain't nobody on my pops's side got gray eyes."

"Does it make you miss your mother?"

"That's a dumb-ass question," Basil said angrily.

"What's that response about?"

"How in the fuck can you miss something you never had?" Basil said. "I asked you that the last time. Explain that to me!"

"Has Campbell said anything about her own mother?"

"She said her mother was dead."

"Maybe that's why she keeps asking you about your mother."

"I don't see why."

"You don't? Did she say how long her mother has been dead?"

"I didn't ask. Look, I don't want to talk about Campbell. I ain't gonna hit the guts, so why should I be wasting my time?"

"So you're not interested in relationships with women unless they are sexual in nature?"

"You got it, Doc!"

"What about with men?"

"You know, I got my dogs . . . my boys. The ones who ain't interested in riding my jock. I certainly don't consider those gay mofos who want the beef friends and no way I'm going to be hanging out in public with them. When I say my dogs, I'm talking about some of the guys I used to play ball with and some I've met since I've been working at ESPN. But I don't want to talk about them either."

"Then what would you like to talk about?"

"I don't know."

"What about your father?"

"Don't want to talk about my pops."

"Your uncle?"

"Hell the fuck no!"

"How's work?"

"Work is cool. They love me over at the network, but I got bigger fish to fry. ESPN was cool for a starting job, but CBS just signed an exclusive deal with the Southeastern Conference and the Big Ten, which means they will be doing more games and they'll need some new talent," Basil said.

"So you like what you're doing?"

"Yeah, it's a cool gig. I study a little the Friday night before the game. Talk to the coaches and some players. Get up the next morning, put on a sports jacket they provide, and make a few intelligent comments and I pick up a nice paycheck. What's not to like?"

"Then what part of your life makes you unhappy?"

There was a long silence and then Basil said, "The dumb shit I let my jimmie get me into."

"Your jimmie?"

"You know, my dick," Basil said with a smirk. His hands were folded over his lap and he hunched it upward for emphasis. "Now, Doc, I've told you once before what a jimmie is. Now, if you gonna hang with me you've got to keep up."

"And how does your jimmie cause you problems?"

"Takes me places I don't wanna go."

"I don't understand."

"Makes me deal with mofos I have no bizness having in my life."

"Are you talking about men?"

"I'm talking about one man," Basil said sternly.

"Raymond?"

"Naw, that mofo Monty," Basil said with a grimace.

"Refresh my memory. Who is Monty?"

"Monty is the wanna-be pop singer who I was hittin' when Yolanda walked in on us. The mofo who ruined my one chance at happiness. Remember I told you he threatened to go public about being gay and was going to tell some reporter that he and I were kicking it."

"So you've been seeing him again?"

"Yeah, somewhat. I mean not like dating or any shit like that."

"Why?"

"I don't know why. I mean I don't go out looking for guys and I still have these urges to kick it with a dude and I can get Monty anytime I want. And since his career didn't take off like he thought, he's not much of a threat to my privacy. Ain't nobody interested in what some mofo who's singing in the subway station got to say about shit."

"So it's only about sex?"

"Damn straight. If I was going to settle down with a dude, it wouldn't be with a crazy, punk-ass mofo like Monty," Basil said.

"Then why do you see him?"

" 'Cause he's convenient." Basil stopped for a moment as if he wasn't sure what he wanted to go on between Monty and him. He cupped his chin for a few seconds and then continued. "But sometimes I just want to bust him upside his head, and sometimes I just try to drill him like I'm drilling for gold. I love making that mofo scream like a bitch," Basil said.

"But how does that make you feel?"

"Real good. Like I'm making his ass pay for being so damn tempting."

"But you said it made you feel bad."

"I'm just talking shit. I like putting that mofo in pain and then telling his ass to get up and get the fuck out of my sight," Basil said.

"And he does that?"

"You got that right. Just like the bitch he is."

"Well, I think we should stop here."

"Whatever."

15

Not accustomed to being home in the middle of the day, Raymond treated himself to a salami and cheese sandwich for lunch, with a few potato chips on the side. Absorbed in his own thoughts, he had come straight home after an interview with FBI agents.

The interview had gone well, Raymond thought. The red-faced man with the short hair of a military officer had spent the first few minutes talking about the upcoming football season. Asking Raymond what kind of team his brother's Northwestern Wildcats were going to have and what would happen if Northwestern ever played Raymond's alma mater, Alabama. He told him his father would sit on the Northwestern side while his mother would split her time equally.

"Sounds like you have a very supportive family," the agent said.

"I do," Raymond said quietly.

The only tension occurred when the agent said, "I understand you live an alternative lifestyle." There was that word again, he thought. "Lifestyle."

"If you mean I'm gay, then I guess the answer is yes."

The agent came back quickly with a question. "You guess?"

"I'm gay," Raymond said. Never in a million years did he envision a day when he would be telling an FBI agent that he *did* men. The agent asked for the correct spelling of Trent's name and date of birth and that was that.

Sitting at the table in the airy skylit kitchen, Raymond assumed the interview was going to be like a police interrogation. Two men in tight gray suits of impressive girth, spouting off question after question about his life. "Where were you, Mr. Tyler, when Waco went up in flames?" "Did you ever cheat on a college exam or your taxes?" "Have you ever cheated on your lifetime partner." But it turned out to be nothing like that. Just two guys talking about football.

Raymond had taken the last bite of his sandwich when the phone rang. He swallowed his fruit punch and grabbed the wall phone. He thought it might be his father or Trent. Both men had been more nervous than Raymond about the interview. His father had called him the night before and even called him on the car phone this morning advising Raymond to just look them in the eyes and tell the truth or "your version of the truth." Raymond thought his father's advice came from spending many years defending people whose version of events was their only defense.

"Hello."

"I got a call 'bout you," the voice said. Raymond knew the voice. Couldn't forget it if he wanted to.

"Basil Henderson," he said.

"Raymond Tyler. Whassup?"

"You, Mr. Henderson. Who called you about me?"

"Said they were from the FBI. Asked me what kind of lawyer you were," Basil said.

"And what did you tell them?"

"Told them you kept me out of jail. Told 'em it cost me a lot of money."

"Anything else?"

"Naw, then they wanted to talk about football. Asked me if I was the former pro player. I told them, you the FBI—don't cha know who you talking to?"

Basil Henderson wasn't exactly what Raymond would call a friend. He was more like an associate. Raymond met the unforgivingly handsome Basil while living in New York under some strange circumstances. Basil was paying Raymond's best friend, Kyle, for sex. Basil's closet door was tighter than the doors at Fort Knox; one of those people who depend on their own version of the truth regarding everything. Raymond and Basil would reunite some years later in Atlanta when Raymond represented Basil after he beat up a gay guy making a pass at him. It didn't matter that Basil was in the wrong and was gay or bi himself. Basil would never refer to himself by either of those terms.

After he settled the case, Raymond had done the unthinkable. He began an affair with his client. It was a passionate and powerful relationship. Just the sound of Basil's voice took Raymond back to a humid summer night when they made love in a swimming pool. Raymond hated to admit to himself how many times he thought of that night. Even though it had been over five years ago, Raymond could still remember their first kiss, and the way the kiss made him feel. Like he had a fever covering his entire body. The heat would break when Raymond thought about the night he spent amid Basil's clothes, trapped in his closet while he made love to a female friend.

When Ray and Basil's relationship ended, the two maintained a strange connection. Both knowing how to push the other's buttons, and doing it whenever there was an opening. But today, Raymond decided to handle Basil with kid gloves. He knew it wouldn't be beyond Basil to call the agents back and say, "I forgot to tell you we fucked. Often!"

"When you asked the FBI agent if he knew who he was talking to, what did he say?" Raymond asked.

"Aw, he just laughed. So why is the FBI calling me about you?"

Raymond shared his big news and how the FBI was checking into past cases and former clients. Raymond was not surprised Basil's case had attracted the FBI's attention. Raymond's "alternative lifestyle" would undoubtedly cause the bureau to dig up quite a few people from his past.

"Man, that's deep. My buddy is going to be a judge. Ain't that some shit," Basil said.

"We'll see. So how are you? The last time we talked you were having some problems," Raymond said.

"Everything's on the down low. Still doing the football commentating gig. How's your little brother?"

"He's doing great! I think he might start this year," Raymond said proudly.

"Cool. Maybe the next time I'm in Chicago I'll look him up. Maybe I can give him a few pointers," Basil laughed. Raymond ignored the last comment. He didn't want to even think about what kind of pointers Basil might be talking about.

"So are you still dating the young lady in Chicago? I think her name was Yolanda," Raymond said. From their last conversation, Raymond felt he already knew the answer.

"Naw," Basil said quickly. Exactly what Raymond was thinking.

"So who you dating?"

"Nobody. How's yo' boy?"

"You mean my partner, Trent?"

"Whatever."

"He's cool."

"So when you heading to New York, so we can hang?" Basil quizzed.

"No time soon. I'm busy trying to wrap up all my cases and get ready for the confirmation process," Raymond said.

"Maybe I'll see you at a Northwestern game. I know we're covering a few of 'em."

"Maybe. So, Basil, it's been nice talking to you."

"Same here," Basil said.

Both men hung up thinking about their passionate escapades. Basil thinking if he could just get Raymond alone for one more night. Raymond thinking if you touched the stove more than once, soon you'd get burned.

16

Taking a meal break from rehearsal, Nicole and Yancey were teasing each other over who should take the last cheese-drenched potato skin when an attractive, plump, neatly dressed woman approached their table.

"Nicole Springer, I don't believe it," the gingerbread-colored woman with reddish-chestnut hair said. Her thick brown eyebrows and eyelashes gave her face strong definition.

"Della Price? How are you doing?" Nicole asked.

"I'm doing just fine, darling, just fine. It's been a long time since I've seen you. I heard you'd gotten married and moved to Atlanta, or was it Arkansas," Della said.

"I did get married, but my husband and I recently moved back here," Nicole said.

Della opened her arms and said with a big smile, "Well, do I get a hug or something?"

Nicole stood up and gave Della a hug, then turned to face Yancey and said, "This is my friend Yancey."

"Yancey, what a wonderful name. Nice to meet you," Della said flatly as she extended her hand. Yancey noticed a sparkling diamond ring the size of a smoked almond.

"So what are you doing these days, Nicole?" Della asked.

"I'm getting ready for the national tour of *Dreamgirls.*"

"Dreamgirls? Honey, are they still doing that show? And aren't we a little too old to be playing teenagers?" Della asked with a feigned sympathetic smile.

"The director and producers don't seem to think so," Nicole snapped back as she took her seat.

Yancey started looking for the waitress. When the waitress saw Yancey waving her hand in the air, she came over and asked what she needed.

"Can you move these plates and bring us two cups of coffee? And please don't take all day. We're in a rush," Yancey said with a great deal of disdain. "She is so slow," Yancey said after the waitress scurried to get the coffee.

Nicole looked at Yancey, wondering why she was being so rude toward the waitress, and then turned back to Della. "So are you still in the business?"

"That fake shit? No way," Della said. For the next five minutes Della stood hovering over Nicole and Yancey's table telling Nicole about her wonderful life while completely ignoring Yancey. It was like a Shakespearean monologue with a little "drama mama" thrown in for good measure. "My husband, Mike, is an import-export dealer. He made a lot of money with the market and now he has his own company. We do a lot of business in London and South Africa. You know, there is a lot of business over there with all the changes. It's such a beautiful country. Have you ever been? We even had dinner with Nelson Mandela, it was just so grand. Mostly, though, we just spend a lot of time traveling all over the world. Right now we're redoing a place on Fifth Avenue, so I'm spending a lot of time with my designer when I'm not in Sag Harbor, where we also have a house," Della said triumphantly.

"Sounds like everything is going great for you," Nicole said as she looked at Yancey and rolled her eyes.

"Yes, it is. I'll have to invite you and your husband to one of our parties. Last summer when we gave our housewarming at our place in Sag Harbor, everybody who was anybody was there. Barbara Smith, you know she owns B. Smith, her husband, Dan, Russell Simmons, Puffy Combs, and Ed Bradley. People are still talking about it."

"Sounds like it was a fabulous party," Nicole said.

"What, no Veronica Webb?" Yancey asked, her voice full of sarcasm. Della ignored her question.

"So, Nicole, what does your husband do? You didn't marry one of those fine chorus boys, did you?"

"No, I didn't. My husband, Jared, is a vice-president at Morgan Stanley. He just got a promotion and we still have a home in Atlanta."

"Isn't that nice? So, Yancey, what do you do?" Della asked as she finally turned her head in Yancey's direction.

"Is knowing what I do important to the continuation of your happy life?" Yancey asked.

"Excuse me?" Della said, her voice expressing complete surprise at the tone of Yancey's question.

"You heard me, Miss, or should I say, Mrs. Ghetto Fabulous, or whatever your name is. You've been standing up here running your mouth, completely ignoring me, and now you want to know what I do? I don't think so," Yancey said as she took a sip of coffee. Nicole was looking at Yancey with a shocked expression, but she wanted to stand and applaud her and sing out, "Brava, diva."

Della looked at Nicole and then back at Yancey and then, in a huff, turned and left the restaurant without so much as a "good-bye."

"Yancey, girl, you are too tough," Nicole laughed.

"Who does that bitch think she is? She made me want to pull up on her."

Nicole drank some coffee and then told Yancey how she and Della used to compete for roles on Broadway and national commercials.

"She competed with you? That dumpy-looking bitch? Look like somebody broke the seal on the biscuit can. And what was that she was wearing? Did she walk into a hotel lobby, look at the rug, and say, 'Make me a dress out of that'?" Yancey laughed.

Nicole smiled and said, "She has gained a lot of weight. But life and those biscuits must be good. I just don't know how you could tell right off she was bad news. I mean, you picked up on that right away. It usually takes me a little more time," Nicole said.

"Honey, I can see trouble coming, even when it's disguised as a high-society wannabe," Yancey said. She thought it didn't make sense for Nicole to be as old as she was and still naïve when it came to bad seeds.

"Della was very talented. I mean sistah could sing and act her butt off, but she was always stirring up a mess. She's one of those girls who could best be described as an 'I'm tired of talking about me, why don't you talk about me' kinda girl," Nicole said. "A lot of people used to call her Evilene behind her back, 'cause she'd smile in your face one minute and stab you in the back the next. Rumor has it that she was understudying a role in *Ain't Misbehavin',* and one night she put the star's dress in the toilet right before curtain. Everywhere Della showed up, trouble followed," Nicole added.

"If she did that to me, I would *still* be beating her down. I guess most of us have some evil bitch in our past. Mine was this child named Nisey Mitchell. Her father and mother were both attorneys and thought they were hot shit. Nisey and I were in dance class and pageants together ever since we were about eight years old. Always the only two black girls. But she was so two-faced, and she had about as much talent as an ant. But in a small town that doesn't stop you. I got her ass good in the end, though," Yancey said proudly.

"What happened?"

"She wanted to be a cheerleader so bad, but couldn't even do a cartwheel. But we had this rule at our school that since most of the football team was black, then there had to be at least one black cheerleader. Everybody wanted me to try out, but Nisey pleaded with me to try out for drill team. She even offered to pay for my uniform and drill team camp. So during her junior year it looked like Nisey was going to live her dream by default 'cause she was the only black girl trying out for the cheerleading squad. But then, even though I had promised her I had no interest in being a cheerleader, I showed up at tryouts," Yancey said.

"Did you make it?" Nicole asked.

"Of course I made it," Yancey said with a laugh. She and Nicole slapped palms in a midlevel high five.

"So she never got to be a cheerleader?" Nicole asked, suddenly wishing she hadn't given Yancey that high five. She felt like black women needed to stick together, but reasoned that Yancey was still young.

"Not really. She was selected as an alternate, but when I quit right before the season started, they wouldn't let her on the squad because she didn't know all that stupid stuff they do. Like I said, I had no interest in that shit. I was trying to concentrate on my dancing, not shaking some pom-poms."

"It's sad to see black women treat each other so badly, but I guess in this business we've all got a Della or a Nisey in our past," Nicole said mournfully. She was thinking of some of the evil young ladies she had met during her pageant days.

"Yeah, girl, but that's where they need to stay. In our past," Yancey said as she picked up the check.

17

Basil was feeling talkative and launched into a long narrative moments after taking a seat in the leather chair.

"I've been thinking a lot about whether or not this is helping. You know, I still haven't confronted my father or my uncle about what happened and to tell the truth I don't think about it until I come into this office. When I do think about it, I keep hoping you'll have some kinda magic pill that would make everything all right, but we both know that ain't gonna happen. It's not like I'm some crazy gonna-shoot-somebody-or-myself mofo. I should just maybe say the shit happened, it's over, move on."

"Is that what you want to do?"

"I mean, what's the point? I'm still attracted to dumb-ass women and knucklehead mofos. You ain't been holding back on me, Doc, have you? You don't have some kinda magic pill that's going to stop these desires I have, do you?"

"You know that's not possible, but let me play the devil's advocate here for a moment. If there was such a pill, would you take it?"

"Damn straight," Basil said firmly.

"Then that means your feelings for Raymond are only sexual?"

"I didn't say that, but I see what you gettin' at. My thing with Raymond is that if I'm going to have these desires about men, then I want it to be with him or somebody like him. I mean, I still have to keep my shit tight. Even though I'm not playing ball, I can't be out there just sleeping around with every mofo that looks my way. I mean dudes talk about who they sleep with much more than the honeys, and they lie."

"So you're not clear on what you expect from a relationship with Raymond?"

"I'm clear I want to make that mofo pay for ignoring my letter. When I found out he was up for that judgeship, I figure now would be the time to bust his ass. But knowing his honest-Abe ass—that mofo has already told them he was into dudes."

"You've never considered that Raymond didn't know how to help you?"

"Then he should have said that! Look, I don't want to talk about Raymond. Let's talk about something else."

"What do you want to talk about?" the doctor asked as he scribbled in his notebook that Basil kept changing the subject whenever something bothered him.

"I went out to breakfast with Campbell. We had a nice time, but the conversation was kinda strange."

"How so?"

"I don't think she's interested in me sexually. I think she's just looking for a friend."

"What makes you say that?"

"First of all, she showed me these pictures of this white dude she been going out with. I mean, they live together, got a kid, and have a couple of dogs and she seems pretty happy. And I was right about her being mixed, but she didn't say which one of her parents is white," Basil said. He didn't tell the doctor how he had thought about bedding Campbell when she showed up in tight jeans and a yellow sweater that highlighted her breasts and skin tone.

"Does that disappoint you?"

"Not really. Getting close with some honey right now is the last thing I need. I lost my heart not that long ago, and I'm not going down that road again."

"Not even with Raymond?"

"I was talking about Campbell," Basil said firmly.

"So are you going to see her again?"

"Yeah, 'cause I really like talking to her," Basil smiled.

The doctor asked Basil what he was smiling about. At first, Basil started not to answer because it reminded him of the times women and men had asked him what he was thinking about when he became silent. It drove him crazy. But Basil answered the doctor anyway.

"I was thinking if I continue to feel so comfortable talking with Campbell, then I won't need you. I mean I could just schedule a lunch or a dinner with her once a week and talk to her," Basil laughed.

"Why do you feel comfortable talking with her?"

"I don't know, maybe because she makes me think about things I've tried not to think about."

"Like what?"

"She asked me about what kinda ladies I dated."

"What did you say?"

"I told her I dated all kinds of women. Started to tell her my jimmie didn't discriminate," Basil laughed.

"Do you think she's interested in dating you?"

"Naw, 'cause she went back to that mother shit. Asked me if I'd known my mother, would it make a difference in the type of women I dated."

"What did you say?"

"I said maybe. I told her there were things I think I missed by not having a mother."

"Were there things you missed?"

"Yeah, sorta. When I was a little boy and I would see other children with their mothers at school or at a football or baseball game, I knew I was missing a big part of my life. All I had was my aunt and whoever my father was bonin' trying to take the place of my mother. I mean, maybe if I had a close day-to-day relationship with a mother, then maybe I would have more respect for women." For a moment, Basil's mind wandered back to the Little League playing fields in Jacksonville, Florida, where he had first excelled in sports. But now he only saw the faces of the mothers of all his friends and heard his father's voice shouting, "That's my boy."

"Didn't your father teach you to respect women?" the doctor asked.

Basil didn't answer immediately. He was thinking about when he was a little boy, and his father would sometimes use his lady friends as live-in baby-sitters for him, while he played cards and chased other women with his buddies. When he couldn't recall any of the ladies' names or their faces, he finally broke his silence.

"My father taught me to be a man and to try and do what's right."

"And don't you think treating women with respect is the right thing?"

"You have to earn respect," Basil said defiantly with a disapproving stare.

18

"So you think they think we punks," Trent teased.

"That was an educated crowd, they figured it out," Raymond said.

"Madam chairwoman sure did have a nice house," Trent said. "I really loved the way she had the buffet set up."

"It *was* nice, wasn't it?" Raymond agreed.

"And the food was off the hook."

"Yeah, sister laid it out," Raymond said, speaking of the elaborate buffet of cold tiger shrimp, pastas, chicken, salads, and roast beef.

"Didn't you think it was funny that most of the wait staff was white or Asian?" Trent asked.

"I guess like they say, we've come a long way, baby."

The two were sitting at the kitchen table late Saturday evening. They had just returned from a dinner given in Raymond's honor by the local NAACP chapter. Lisa had warned Raymond they would be checking him out, even though many of the members already knew him from his work in the community.

"What did you think of Charles Pope?" Raymond asked. He was another one of the lawyers being considered for the bench. He was a partner with one of the larger firms in Seattle making big bank. A native of Washington, Charles had graduated from the University of Washington and Yale Law School. He had also clerked for Supreme Court Justice

Marshall. Rumor was he was a big womanizer and had far too many skeletons in his closet, including a child out of wedlock with his law clerk. He seemed particularly interested in Raymond and Trent's relationship, but something prevented him from asking them point-blank if they were more than roommates.

"He seemed like a nice guy. But his wife didn't match," Trent said.

"What do you mean?"

"Well, she seemed so shy, almost matronly, but she was certainly gulping down those vodka gimlets. There is an awful lot of pain going on there," Trent said about the woman who had sat next to him at dinner.

"I didn't talk to her that long," Raymond said.

"Yeah, that's why I think they knew what the deal was. You know with the seating arrangements. They sat me next to Mrs. Pope and you next to the hostess's husband. Something right out of B. Smith's book on entertaining," Trent said.

"Yeah, I did notice that," Raymond said.

"Charles asked where we met," Trent said.

"Did you tell him?"

"Yeah, you know he's a frat."

"I didn't know that. I've never seen him at any meetings."

"He ain't true. He pledged in the grad chapter in one of those walk-right-up-and-sign-in things."

"I guess that explains why I didn't know he was a brother."

The last two weeks had been busy for Raymond. Not only was his calendar filled with sudden social obligations like dinners and drinks, but he was also spending a great deal of time with Lisa preparing for his hearing. When he wasn't in meetings with Lisa, Raymond was boning up on recent court rulings and scheduling appointments with members of Washington's congressional staff members. All of this time spent shoring up support for his nomination was causing a little concern around his office. Their small size made a billing lawyer a valuable commodity. Feeling the subtle concern, Raymond had decided to resign. The partners wouldn't hear of that, but felt maybe a leave of absence might be better. Besides, they knew it would be an honor for them to have a former partner on the bench, one who felt supported by his firm. They never knew when a lawyer from the firm might end up trying a case before Judge Raymond Tyler, Jr.

There wasn't a major concern about Raymond neglecting his clients or his workload. Most of his clients on retainer weren't experiencing any major legal problems. But now every time a new case was presented at staff meetings, Raymond had to decline it because of his impending hearing. Because the firm wasn't large enough to have a partner doing very limited billing, Raymond understood perfectly that a leave of absence was in order.

"So you sure you can take care of me in the lifestyle I've become accustomed to?" Raymond asked Trent. He really didn't need Trent to support him. He had a nice savings account, and his investments were paying off. It just felt nice knowing that if he needed help, Trent had his back.

"Of course, but you've got to turn over all your credit cards and develop a taste for fried baloney and egg sandwiches," he teased. "What do you want to drink?"

"I know I shouldn't, but let me have a little wine. I don't have to get up early in the morning," Raymond said.

"What did your father say about you taking the leave?"

"He thought it was a good plan. Said I need to use all my energy getting ready for those fools in D.C."

"You're not going to have a problem," Trent said as he handed Raymond a glass of white wine.

"Cheers," Raymond said as he tapped his wineglass against Trent's beer bottle and smiled.

"I had a nice time and I was real proud of you," Trent said.

"Thanks for going. It felt good having you near. I know how much you hate those type of things," Raymond said. Usually Trent only accompanied Raymond to the annual office Christmas party and sporting events. When Raymond needed an escort, he would invite his paralegal, Sara. Recently Sara had met her future husband while escorting Raymond to a client dinner party.

"I don't hate them. And you know I'll do anything you need," Trent smiled.

"I know and I appreciate you," Raymond said as he sipped some of the cold wine.

About an hour later Raymond was listening to Maxwell's mellow voice, blending with Trent's soulful snore, when the phone rang. It was late and Raymond figured it was his father asking about the dinner. He had talked with his father more in the last two months than in the entire previous year. And now when they spoke it wasn't about Kirby's football career.

"Hello," Raymond whispered. He didn't want to wake Trent. There was no response. Just silence. "Hello," he whispered again. Suddenly Raymond heard a deep, male voice. "Watch out, my brother. They're out to get you." The voice was both frightening and familiar.

And then Raymond heard a dial tone.

❖   ❖   ❖

Raymond didn't tell Trent about either of his phone calls. Not the call he received from Basil, who, Trent knew, had rocked Raymond's world at one point. And Raymond was feeling some guilt because the sound of Basil's voice made him sweat in places it shouldn't. Raymond didn't mention the strange late-night warning call because he didn't want to talk about it, he wanted it to go away. Besides, Raymond had convinced himself he was dreaming.

But it didn't take him long to discover which was the more ominous. A couple of days later Raymond got a call from Lisa Lanier.

"Looks like we've got a problem," she said.

"What type of problem?" Raymond asked.

"The NAACP is going to oppose your nomination," Lisa said calmly.

Raymond felt a sudden chill and then a cold sweat.

"Are you serious?" Raymond asked. He couldn't believe that the organization he had been a member of since he was nine was against him. His birthday gift. Not the organization where his father, mother, and brother were also lifetime members. This couldn't be, he thought.

"Yeah, but we're going to find out what's going on," Lisa assured him. "And besides it's just the local chapter. It's not like it's the national office opposing you. This happens all the time."

"Did they say why?"

"No, I think it's because they want Attorney Pope since he is a local boy."

"Are you sure?" Raymond asked. What he really wanted to know was could the NAACP be opposing him because he's gay?

"Yeah, I'm sure that's it. They wouldn't dare do it because of anything else. But nothing is final. They're holding a press conference in about an hour. I just didn't want you to turn on the television and find out about it that way," Lisa said.

"Thanks for warning me."

"And I don't want to be the bearer of bad news, but the FBI discovered something they want to talk with you about," Lisa said.

"Did they say what?"

"No, but I'm sure they will get in contact with you. Now, Raymond, don't worry, everything will be fine. If it was something major or something that would prevent the nomination, they would have informed the senator. Instead they want to speak with you directly. It's probably something about a date or some school you attended."

"Maybe it's my leave of absence," Raymond said.

"Don't worry, this is all part of the confirmation process. Before you know it, I will be calling you Judge Tyler."

"I hope you're right, Lisa. I hope you're right."

❖   ❖   ❖

About an hour later Raymond watched as his hostess from the NAACP dinner read from a sheet of paper. Several black men were surrounding her like bodyguards. A television graphic identified them as CCS, Concerned Clergy of Seattle. He noticed the Reverend Willie Mack, Trent's minister from Mount Zion.

"It's not that we don't feel Mr. Tyler is qualified. He's a fine lawyer and has been a wonderful addition to the Seattle area. We simply feel Attorney Charles Pope is a better candidate and understands the needs of our community, especially on issues regarding the survival of the African-American family."

With his arms folded across his chest, Raymond watched as Mrs. Ethel Mae Ware refused to answer the reporters' questions. He suddenly wished he had taped the press conference so he could replay her statement and try to understand the organization's opposition. Even though he felt he already knew. Because he was gay, they didn't feel he was a part of the African-American family.

19

"I'm so sorry about this," Yancey said as she looked at her sterling-silver watch. She nervously twisted her opal ring.

"Oh, girl, don't worry. He's probably just running late. You know doctors. I can't tell you how many times *this* man has been late for a dinner engagement," Nicole said as she patted Jared on the arm.

"Yeah, but I had a good excuse," Jared said as he smiled at his wife and then at Yancey.

"I am so looking forward to my day off tomorrow," Yancey said.

"Me too. But this is Broadway. It's only a week before we open in D.C.," Nicole said.

"I can't believe it's that soon. Can you believe they have us going to Grand Rapids?" Yancey said.

"So it's Broadway bus and truck, but I tell you what, we'll be sold out every night. In cities like that, the black folks are very supportive. Many come more than once," Nicole said.

"I hope you're right. I guess after this week there won't be many nights off," Yancey said.

"So you lovely ladies deserve a day and an evening off. Let's not talk about the bizness and just enjoy ourselves," Jared said.

"Okay, babe." Nicole smiled.

The three of them were gathered at Nicole and Jared's West Forty-ninth Street apartment for dinner on a late Sunday summer evening. The salad was tossed, steaks grilled, the potatoes baked, and the cheesecake delivered. The only thing missing was Yancey's date, Dr. Martin Beck. Nicole and Yancey had spent the first half hour talking about members of the cast, and how exciting it was going to be traveling around the country with the show. "But only for six weeks," Jared reminded Nicole. She smiled in agreement.

"Let's give him about fifteen minutes and then let's eat," Yancey said in an annoyed tone. She gazed with envy at the dining room table set with beautiful gold and white china and crystal water goblets.

"Why don't you call his office?" Nicole suggested, looking at her husband and so happy to be spending an evening at home entertaining. Nicole wanted to give Jared a long, deep kiss, but didn't want to embarrass her husband or Yancey.

"You think I should?" Yancey asked.

"Why don't you?" Jared agreed. He, too, wanted to kiss his wife, looking beautiful in a black silk pantsuit. Yancey could tell from the loving look in both their eyes that Jared and Nicole needed a few private moments. She looked at the phone on the kitchen wall and then asked Nicole, "Is there another phone?"

"Yes, yes there is. Use the one in our bedroom," Nicole said as she pointed toward the bedroom, now finally completely furnished. She was proud of the maple canopy bed and hunter-green velvet chaise.

"I'll be back in a heartbeat. Don't ya'll do nothing I wouldn't do," Yancey said with a mischievous smile.

"Don't worry. Ain't nothing I do with my wife wrong," Jared said.

"I ain't mad at cha," Yancey said as she grabbed her bag and headed toward the master bedroom.

Once inside, Yancey admired the tastefully decorated bedroom. She pulled open the nightstand drawer and saw several ballpoint pens and several fast-food menus. No secrets there, Yancey thought as she shut the drawer and debated whether or not she should look in the chest. Yancey decided against that and pulled out her electronic date book. She pulled up Martin's service number. If Martin showed up, it would be the first date for Yancey and the man she had met a couple of days before while walking out of her apartment. She couldn't decide whether or not to call Martin's office, his service, or his home number, which he had written on the back of his card. Yancey decided on the office, but after several rings the answering machine picked up. Instead of leaving a message, Yancey hung up. As she walked back into the living room, she caught a surprised Jared and Nicole in a loving kiss and embrace. The two of them didn't hear Yancey, so she cleared her throat in a very theatrical manner. Looking a bit flushed, Nicole patted her hair softly and pressed her lips together.

"Yancey, is there something wrong?"

"Naw, I just wanted to know if it's okay if I paged someone." Yancey was blushing like she had just caught her parents in an intimate situation.

"Aw, sure. Go 'head. You can even answer the phone. Tell them you're our executive assistant," Jared teased.

"Okay, sorry about the interruption," Yancey said.

Yancey returned to the bedroom, picked up the phone, and punched in Martin's number. When she heard the quick beeps, Yancey punched in Nicole's phone number and hung up. She got up from the bed, walked over to the dresser, and looked in the mirror to make sure her makeup and hair were in place. She picked up Jared and Nicole's wedding pictures. Not bad, Yancey thought. While deep in thought about the wedding she hoped to have one day, the phone rang. Yancey put the picture back in its place and rushed over to answer it.

"Martin, where are you?" Yancey asked, assuming this was the return of her page.

"I'm sorry, I'm looking for Nicole Springer. This is Sean Steward of *The Rosie O'Donnell Show.* Is this Nicole?"

"No, this is her assistant. Can I help you?"

"Well, we had a cancellation and we want Nicole and the Dreams to do our show in the morning. Is that possible?"

"I'm sure she'd love to do it," Yancey said. She wanted to tell him he didn't have to call her next, since she was a member of the Dreams as well as Nicole's understudy. But she was too busy thinking this would be her national television debut. *The Rosie O'Donnell Show.* The people in Jackson would be too impressed.

"Great. Do we need to send a car? We go on live at ten A.M., but we need Ms. Springer here no later than nine A.M."

"No, Ms. Springer likes to walk. She's not that far from the studio. I'll make sure she's there before nine," Yancey said. She suddenly heard a call-waiting beep. "I'll make sure Ms. Springer is there."

"Thank you. Tell her we heard great things and we want them to do 'One Night Only,' but we want to use the Dena, Lorrell, and Effie characters instead of the Michelle Morris character. Rosie loves the Effie character and loves B. J. Hudson, who's playing Effie."

"I will," Yancey said as her heart suddenly sank and she sat down on Nicole's bed. Yancey played Michelle Morris, which meant she wasn't going to make her national television debut. Nicole would be on Rosie, not her. Performing before a national audience as she had in the Miss

America pageant. Like when she was nominated for a Tony Award. For all the world to see. Again.

Yancey felt tears close, but blinked them back. She once again checked her makeup and hair, and rose from the bed in one effortless movement. She walked very slowly into the living room, smiled her best Miss Johnson County beauty queen smile, and announced to Jared and Nicole, "Martin can't make it. He has to deliver a baby."

❧   ❧   ❧

It was a rare Monday morning when Nicole thought she could sleep in. She was awakened by soft kisses from Jared, around 7:30. And was drifting into a dreamy state of sleep when the phone rang. It was Yancey.

"Nicole, I need to talk to you," Yancey said.

"Is everything all right?"

"I think Martin's trying to run a game on me. Can we meet at the gym, or go somewhere and take a quick dance class?" Yancey asked.

"Sure, but it doesn't sound like you're in the mood for a class. And I enjoyed another glass of champagne when you left, so I'm not either. Why don't we just get together and have breakfast?" Nicole said in a sisterly manner.

"Yeah, maybe you're right. And this Martin thing may be nothing. But I do want to talk this out before I make any rash decisions."

"Where do you want to meet?" Nicole asked.

"Why don't we go uptown? Let's go to Wilson's and get a real Southern breakfast."

"Sounds like a plan," Nicole said.

"How does nine o'clock sound?"

"I'll see you there," Nicole said as she looked at the clock. This would give her plenty of time for her prayer and daily meditation and a long, soothing bath.

"Nicole, I really appreciate this. I feel like you're the big sister I never had," Yancey said softly.

"That's a very kind thing to say, Yancey. And don't worry. Everything will be fine," Nicole assured.

She got up from bed and went into her small kitchen. She debated having a cup of the coffee Jared had made, but decided on a glass of cranberry juice instead. Nicole thought the coffee at Wilson's might taste better.

Nicole was heading back to her bedroom when the phone rang again. She thought it might be Yancey. Nicole remembered how she was when she was young and in love. Every single thing became major drama.

"Hello."

"I'm surprised you answering the phone so early. I figured I'd get that answering machine," Nicole's mother said.

"Hi, Mom, how are you? Is everything all right?" Nicole asked.

"Oh, everything's fine. I'm just checking up on you. I had a dream about you last night and I just had to call. Are you okay?"

"I'm fine," Nicole said. She knew this was going to be one of those calls.

"I still can't figure out why you had to move back to New York. I mean, you and Jared had such a beautiful home down there in Atlanta. Trust me when I tell you, Nicole, you need to have some babies. It might not bother Jared right now, but that boy likes kids and he wants some of his own," Nicole's mother said.

Nicole was used to this type of conversation from her mother. Over the years, their relationship changed like the weather. At times, they were a loving mother and daughter and then, with the speed of a tornado, a change, and they couldn't stand each other.

After thirty minutes of a rapid tumble of breathless words, her mother asked Nicole if she was still trying to get pregnant.

"Mother, I told you I just signed this contract to do *Dreamgirls*," Nicole said.

"Dreamgirls, Dreamwomen, or whatever. Is that damn play worth losing your marriage?"

"I don't know what you're talking about. Jared and I are even happier now than the day we married," Nicole said.

"Trust me when I tell you that ain't always going to be the case."

Just as Nicole was preparing to respond, she heard the call-waiting beep. "Hold on, Mother."

"Hello," Nicole said.

"Nicole. This is Peaches. I need your help," Peaches said hurriedly.

This was the reprieve Nicole was praying for. "Hold on, Peaches."

"Mother, I'll call you back later. I've got an important call."

"What's more important than what I'm saying? Is it some show business mess?"

"Mother, I'll call you later. Good-bye."

Nicole clicked the phone back. "Peaches, I'm sorry. What's the matter?"

"They trying to take my place," Peaches said.

"What place?"

"My shop. This jackass who owns the place is trying to sell it. Ever since his father died, he just been snooping around here askin' if the health department know I'm serving more than pies when I have my meals for my kids. When his daddy was alive, he'd come by and have dinner with us sometimes. But he dropped dead about six months ago and now his son's basically saying he don't care what his daddy promised us. What am I going to do?" Peaches asked.

"Calm down, Peaches. Everything will be just fine. Do you have a lawyer?"

"A lawyer. Not here in New York City. Raymond usually handles my legal problems," Peaches said.

"Have you called him?"

"Naw, I hate bothering him, but, Nicole, they can't stop me from cooking dinners for my kids," Peaches said.

"Don't worry, they won't. Listen, I think Jared said something about Raymond taking some time off. If you'd like, I could give him a call and see what he says," Nicole offered.

"Would you do that for me?"

Before Nicole could answer she again heard the call-waiting beep. She assumed it was her mother, who had probably thought of some other things Nicole was doing wrong, so she ignored the beeps. She was thankful Peaches had a real crisis.

"Peaches, don't you worry one bit. I'll call Raymond and I know he'll help out. And if he can't, Jared and I will find you somebody who can."

"Are you sure? 'Cause if Enoch lost this place because of me, well I just couldn't forgive myself. And my kids depend on me. I don't want to go back to Jersey. And we can't even think about finding another place in Harlem. I mean with the Gap and Disney moving up here, regular colored folks can't find a place to do their own bizness," Peaches said.

Nicole heard the call-waiting beep again. She ignored it.

"Don't worry, I have the day off. When I get back from my breakfast date, I'll call Raymond. Now you get back to making those wonderful cobblers and don't worry," Nicole said.

"Thank you, Miss Nicole. I already feel better," Peaches said.

"Everything will be just fine," Nicole assured.

"Thank you, sweetheart. If I ever, ever hear anybody saying you got the big head, I'll stop them dead in their tracks," Peaches said.

"Thanks, Peaches. I'm glad I've got a mother-friend like you."

When Nicole hung up the phone, she picked it up immediately and heard the rapid beeps which told her she had messages. Nicole had figured as much, and knew her mother's messages could be as hurtful as live conversations. So she ignored the beeps and got ready for her breakfast with Yancey.

❖   ❖   ❖

Yancey didn't meet Nicole for breakfast. Yancey received the phone call she had been praying for. At 9:30 A.M., the producer for *The Rosie O'Donnell Show* called to explain to Yancey how they were a half hour before show time with one Dreamgirl missing. Nicole Springer. The producer asked was there any way Yancey could make it to Rockefeller Center to go on for the missing Dream?

"Of course I can," Yancey said. "I've just done my makeup."

"You're a lifesaver, Miss Braxton," the producer exclaimed.

"I'm just happy to help out. A true Dreamgirl is always prepared."

Before grabbing her already packed bag, Yancey reached for the phone and hit speed dial number one. After a few rings, she listened to Nicole's cheerful greeting. When she heard the beep, Yancey said, "Nicole, I hope everything is all right and I'll see you at Wilson's. I hope." Yancey paused for a few seconds and then said, "Don't worry if I'm running a little late."

❧   ❧   ❧

When Yancey entered her apartment late that evening, after her national television debut, the phone was ringing urgently. She dropped her bag and almost tripped over the coffee table as she raced to the phone.

"Hello."

"Girl, you were fierce! Just fierce," Ava said.

"Did you see me?"

"Of course I saw you," Ava said.

"What time does *Rosie* come on down there? It's live in New York."

"It comes on at three P.M., and I just happened to be flipping the channels and I heard them say something about the Dreams. And I was so proud of you that I was in tears," Ava said.

"I'm so glad you saw it. I didn't call you because I didn't know if my plan was going to work," Yancey said as she kicked off one of her boots.

"How did you pull it off?"

"I was invited to Nicole and Jared's with a guy I just met who Nicole thinks I'm getting ready to marry. Nicole will believe anything. And I guess I was at the right place at the right time. I mean how else can you explain that I got that call instead of Nicole or Jared? I guess I just got some angels working overtime for me. They know it should be me playing Dena Jones and not Nicole Springer. Her time has come and gone and she's the only one who doesn't know it."

"It was probably Mama," Ava said.

"What about Mama?"

"Your angel," Ava said softly.

"You're probably right, but I don't care if it's coming from above or below. I mean today was just wonderful. Rosie and all the people on her staff were so wonderful."

"So what are you going to do to celebrate?"

"I'm going to take a bath. Drink me a glass of wine or something. And then I'm just going to wait for the phone to ring."

"The phone to ring? What do you mean?"

"From agents, from producers. From anybody who saw me today and can help my road to superstardom move just a little bit faster."

"And it will, darling. It will."

20

In the days that followed the NAACP press conference, Raymond's spirits changed like a summer thunderstorm. One moment he was feeling sorry for himself and the next minute he wanted to kick some butt and take names. Initially he wanted to withdraw his name from nomination, telling himself he didn't need this grief. If *his* people didn't want him on the bench, then he didn't want to represent them. Raymond convinced himself he would be happy practicing law and teaching. He wanted to call his father and ask him for advice. But then he thought about how proud his father was about the nomination. Raymond hated to disappoint him, so he didn't tell him or his mother about the group's stance. Trent and Jared were supportive and had encouraged him not to back down. So he had to fight. For his family, his friends, and his dreams.

It was Wednesday, and Raymond was meeting with Lisa, who had been very supportive in the aftermath of the NAACP's decision. They were mapping out a game plan at an Italian restaurant located in the Monaco Hotel. After the waitress poured some olive oil in a blue and white saucer, Lisa gave her a "please don't hover over us . . . we've got serious business" look. The waitress smiled and said, "Just let me know when you're ready to order."

Lisa returned her businesslike smile and went right to work. "So you know one of these guys who's opposing you?"

"I don't really know him. He was involved in a case I handled," Raymond said.

"What's the information?"

"I don't know if it's important or if it will help," Raymond said.

"Let me decide," Lisa said as she dipped a piece of sourdough bread into the olive oil. Raymond nodded and began to tell Lisa about Barry Menton. After reviewing the videotape of the press conference, Raymond had recognized the middle-aged black man with the salt-and-pepper Afro. Raymond had met Barry while defending a young man who had filed a lawsuit against his employer for sexual harassment.

Raymond's client, Steven Heggs, had worked first for Menton as a personal trainer and then was offered a job as his executive assistant at a large software firm. Steven was a recent graduate of Howard University and had moved to the Seattle area hoping to land a sales engineer position with a software design company. Once he started working for Menton, Steven was told his job would require him to travel with Menton.

On one of these trips, Steven discovered there was no hotel reservation for him. It had been mysteriously canceled, so he had to share a room with his boss. The story goes that during the night Menton's feet became entangled with Steven's and the next thing Steven knew, his married boss had his lips on a part of Steven's body where they shouldn't have been. Raymond, forever the gentleman, wouldn't say *dick* or *penis*, just saying "you know" when trying to explain to Lisa where Barry's lips were.

The advances didn't stop when Steven pushed Menton away and told him he was totally heterosexual. It got worse, and with each of Steven's refusals, Menton seemed more determined.

"So are you saying this man is a closet homosexual or, since he's married, bisexual?" Lisa asked.

"He denied that and the charges as well, but he settled out of court for a midrange six-figure sum. Menton convinced the higher-ups at his company that this wouldn't be good for business. We were going to haul a lot of them in for depositions. And my feeling is that my client was truthful on all accounts."

"But how important is this guy, and do you think he's trying to get back at you?"

"I don't know. I'm not even certain we should use this or bring it up. I just told you in case we determine they are opposing me because of my sexuality," Raymond said.

"It's good to have that information. We'll see if he shows up at the meeting when we talk with the leaders," Lisa said.

"So they agreed to a meeting?"

"Yes, with me and possibly the senator. I don't think it's necessary for you to be there," Lisa said. The waitress returned and Lisa ordered for her and Raymond.

After they finished their meal of lasagna and Caesar salad, Lisa suddenly appeared nervous. She searched the restaurant as if looking for someone and then started twisting the ends of her hair. When Raymond asked if everything was okay, Lisa pulled out a black leather binder from her briefcase and studied a white piece of paper that was sticking out.

"What's that?" Raymond asked.

"I don't really know how to bring this up," she said.

"Bring up what?"

"I got this from the FBI. I told you they had some more questions. Maybe you know about it, but it could cause us a few problems," Lisa said.

"Are you going to let me read it?" Raymond asked.

"I'm not sure. Let me just tell you the facts. The FBI discovered that your partner, Trent, was arrested on March 15, 1996," Lisa said. Her words emerged painfully slowly.

Raymond's heart was beating wildly with a strange mixture of rage and sorrow. His body became warm with moisture.

"That couldn't be," Raymond said. "That can't be possible."

"I had them double-check it," Lisa said sadly.

"Arrested for what?"

"He was picked up for approaching an undercover cop in an adult bookstore," Lisa said. "The report states Trent was seen in the parking lot several times during the week of March fifteenth," she added.

Raymond shook his head in disbelief and gazed at the walls of the restaurant. The color of the walls made him dizzy as they progressed from pastel blue to shrimp pink and then into a large window he hadn't noticed before.

"Are you all right? I really hate telling you this. I wanted you to know because if the NAACP or the ministers get this information, well, it wouldn't be good for our battle," Lisa said.

"This just . . . can't be. Not Trent," Raymond said. His voice trailed off weakly as the feeling of fury and disappointment raged in his throat.

Lisa gently touched his hand in a show of concern and support and said, "This isn't the end of the road. It may never come up. We'll be just fine." Lisa was trying to reassure Raymond, even though she knew the information might create a major roadblock for Raymond's nomination.

But Raymond didn't hear Lisa's words or see the concern on her face, nor did he notice the waitress pick up the check. He wasn't thinking about the NAACP, the ministers, or the position on the federal bench.

All Raymond could think about was the man he loved who promised him to always be faithful and true had lied.

❖   ❖   ❖

Raymond drove slowly and automatically, his mind numb, trying to forget Lisa's words. When Raymond arrived home, still in a semidaze, he was happy the house was silent. He immediately went to his office and located his executive planner for March '96. Where was he the day Trent was arrested? Had he been working on an important case which kept him at the office late or had he been out of town?

It took him only a few seconds to see New York and a squiggly line through the entire week. Raymond suddenly remembered being in New York, taking depositions for a case. He remembered his evening phone calls to Trent, who would always end the conversation by asking Raymond if he loved him and missed him. Raymond always replied, I do and of course I miss you. He also recalled when he couldn't reach Trent during a twenty-four-hour period. When the two finally spoke Trent told Raymond he'd suddenly decided to go to Wednesday night prayer meeting. As Raymond remembered that conversation, his face became warm with anger as he wondered how many lies Trent had told him.

The phone rang and Raymond hoped it was Trent. Maybe he knew what Lisa had told him and was calling with an explanation. Raymond knew this was only wishful thinking on his part. "Hello," he said.

"Raymond?" Raymond recognized Lisa's voice.

"Yes, Lisa."

"Are you okay?"

"I'm fine," Raymond lied.

"Are you sure? Is there anything I can do for you?"

"No, Lisa. This is something I've got to handle," Raymond said.

"If you need me, call. Do you have my home number?"

"I think so. Yes, I have it," Raymond replied. He didn't know where it was, but he knew he wouldn't call Lisa at home anyway.

"Hang in there. This is a small setback. Everything will be just fine," Lisa assured.

"I know," Raymond lied as he hung up the phone. He knew things might never be the same.

Raymond went to the kitchen and poured a glass of wine and forced himself to drink it slowly. He didn't need to be intoxicated when Trent arrived home. Raymond picked up the phone and started to call Trent at his office and demand that he come home immediately. No, he couldn't do that. He thought about calling Jared, but didn't know how he would tell his best friend how his partner had been unfaithful. Raymond didn't want Jared to think critically of Trent. He thought of his mother, but decided against her for the same reasons. Maybe this information wasn't true. But what if it was?

What would he do? Play the lawyer and try to uncover the facts, or just shout out to his partner, "How could you do this to us?"

After two glasses of wine Raymond felt a little relaxed, and decided to take a shower. As the warm water and soap slid over his body, he imagined Trent coming in and not knowing what Raymond knew. Often when Trent came home and heard Raymond in the shower, he would undress and join him. They both enjoyed making love in their oversized cascading shower. But now the way Raymond was feeling, he didn't even want to think about Trent in an intimate way.

After his shower Raymond had another glass of wine and checked his messages. There was a call from his father, who wanted to know if Raymond had a date for his confirmation hearing because he and his wife wanted to stay in D.C. for a couple days of sight-seeing. One of his law school classmates had called to congratulate him on the nomination, and the last message was from Trent saying he was working "real late so don't wait up." For the first time since he'd fallen in love with Trent, he wondered if he was really working late.

BOOK TWO

Imitation of Life

21

On a cloudy summer day that felt more like fall, the music of Erykah Badu enveloped the Springer-Stovall apartment as Yancey and Nicole were enjoying their last afternoon in New York City for a while. The two women would be traveling to Washington, D.C., the following morning for the first stop of the planned six-week tour.

Nicole and Yancey spent the day shopping for makeup, music, and books for the trip and were waiting on Jared for an early dinner at one of Nicole's favorite restaurants, JUdson Grill. She had just offered Yancey a glass of apple juice when the phone rang.

"Let me get this, it's probably my husband," Nicole said as she turned down the CD player.

"Go ahead. I'll get the juice," Yancey said.

"Hello."

"Is this Nicole Springer-Stovall?" Raymond asked.

"Raymond? How you doing, Mister Judge-to-be?" Nicole asked.

"I'm doing fine. I got a message you called me," Raymond said.

"Yeah. Seems like we got a little problem," Nicole said.

"What?"

"I got a call from Peaches, and she's having some problems with her landlord not wanting to renew the lease she and Enoch have. Seems like he wants to sell. This guy just inherited the place from his father, who had told Peaches and Enoch they could live there forever. But Peaches thinks the son wants them out because of the Sunday afternoon dinners she gives for AIDS patients," Nicole said.

"Well, if it is, that's totally illegal. And you could possibly make the argument of an oral agreement. The last time I talked with Peaches, she seemed so excited about the work she was doing. It would be a shame if she lost the place," Raymond said.

"Yes, it would. I told her I would give you a call. When Jared told me you had taken a leave of absence, I thought you might be looking for something to keep you busy," Nicole said.

"I can't tell you how true that is," Raymond said. Nicole detected a sudden sadness in his voice.

"Is everything okay, Raymond?"

"Huh . . . Yeah, everything is fine. But it would be good to get to New York and help Peaches out. It would be good seeing you too," Raymond said as his voice returned to a rich and clear tone.

"I'd love to see you also, but unless you get here tonight—then I'll miss you. I leave tomorrow for D.C. Didn't Jared tell you I was doing *Dreamgirls* again?"

"That's right, he did. I was surprised I didn't see you the other day when I was watching *Rosie O'Donnell*. What happened?" Raymond asked.

"It was a simple mix-up," Nicole said. She looked over at Yancey, who grinned at her as she placed the bottle of juice on the counter. "I was kinda sad about it, but I'll have my chance to be on *Rosie*. Besides, I have a great understudy," Nicole added as Yancey blushed.

"I know you will. Well, tell my niggah I called and hopefully I'll see him next week. I'm going to stop in Chicago and see my little brother and parents, then maybe I can head to New York. I'll give Peaches a call," Raymond said.

"I'll tell Jared. I'm sorry I'm going to miss you. But soon we'll all have to get together. How is Trent?"

"Trent is all right," Raymond said softly. "Look, I need to run, Nicole. Take care, I love you."

"And I love you. Good-bye."

Nicole hung up the phone, smiled to herself, and returned to the counter where Yancey was sitting.

"What is that smile about?" Yancey asked as she placed her sweating glass of juice on a plastic coaster.

"No reason. It's just always good talking to Raymond. Remember the man I told you about?"

"Yeah, the man that's your husband's best friend, who is also gay, who you used to date. Honey, this is a modern world we're living in!" Yancey laughed.

"Yes, isn't it?" Nicole asked as she refilled her juice glass.

"So you really loved this Raymond guy, huh?"

"Yeah, I did. But Raymond came into my life for another reason," Nicole said softly.

"What do you mean?"

"I think the Lord put Raymond in my life so that I could meet Jared. Some people come in our life to move us toward what we should be doing, and who we should be doing it with. I still love Raymond, but now like a dear friend," Nicole said.

"That's wonderful! I knew the moment I met you I wanted to have a woman like you for a friend," Yancey said with a honeyed voice.

"You can count on me, Yancey, and I'm glad to have a friend like you."

The two women smiled, drank apple juice, and enjoyed the music. After a few minutes of Erykah's silky voice, Yancey asked, "Nicole, will you tell me about the women in *Dreamgirls?*"

"What do you mean?"

"Tell me about the Dreams. Dena, Lorrell, Effie, and my character, Michelle. I mean, you know these characters better than anyone in the cast."

"I guess you're right. Let me see. I'll start with Dena Jones, my character. Dena has stars in her eyes. She knows what she wants and that's a successful career in show business, kinda like a Diana Ross or Diahann Carroll. But she also knows she's working with a limited amount of talent. I mean she can't sing like Effie, doesn't really have Lorrell's rhythm of life. But I think she'll do whatever it takes to make it," Nicole said.

Yancey listened attentively, not wanting to interrupt Nicole's flow, but after she paused to take a sip of her juice, Yancey asked, "Is that why she falls in love with Curtis?"

"I don't think Dena is in love with Curtis. I think she admires his strength and how he, like her, goes for what he wants," Nicole said.

"What about Effie?"

"Effie most definitely is the one with the voice. She is a major talent. And like most people with talent, it is no big deal to her. And Effie is truly in love with Curtis, but I think she treasures her friendship with Dena and Lorrell more."

"So you think the friendship isn't important to Dena?"

"Oh yeah, I think it is. But it isn't the most important thing and she's like a lot of ladies in our business, career first, friends and family later."

"What about my character, Michelle? You've played her, haven't you?"

"Yes, I did. I don't think Michelle is really into show business. I think that's why she falls for C.C. so easily. In some ways she's like Dena: beautiful, but working with a limited amount of talent."

"I'm so excited to be in this show and headed to Broadway. It has been my lifelong dream," Yancey gushed. "I know people who had the same dream and didn't even get close," she added softly.

"Well, you're in a great position," Nicole said.

"What do you mean?"

"You're young, beautiful, and talented. There are no young *black* divas on Broadway, with the exception of someone like Vanessa L. Williams or Audra McDonald. Most of the young ladies your age, well, they're all doing videos and going straight to Hollywood, doing pilots that never sell and an independent film every now and then," Nicole said.

"Don't you have any interest in Hollywood?"

Nicole pondered Yancey's question for a moment and said, "I'm happy right where I am. If Hollywood is for me, it will come," she said confidently.

22

Seattle's golden days of August became sobering, and Raymond was looking forward to autumn. Fall had always been Raymond's favorite season, but there had been some magical winters as well. Was it because of the upcoming football season when his father's attention would turn full force toward Kirby? Or simply because fall always promised hope to him, and he needed something to hope for? This fall he took note of the fact that Trent loved the summer and spring. Up until now this difference had not been a big problem.

A small blessing occurred when Trent got his dream assignment in South Africa to help build schools. Raymond thought of Trent's excitement about his business trip to South Africa, where it would still seem like summer. "I can still wear my short shorts," he marveled while packing. Their good-bye had been simple and sweet. A modest kiss before dawn when the car arrived to carry Trent to the airport. Trent still had no idea of what Raymond had discovered, and he attributed Raymond's aloof behavior to the confirmation process. Trent dreamed of returning home to a lover whose eyes danced when he walked into a room.

Raymond, on the other hand, was happy to have time alone, to figure out what to do about Trent, to attend more of his brother's football games. In Kirby's first year, Raymond had attended only four games, whereas his retired parents attended every single game. It didn't matter that Kirby played sparingly. They wanted to celebrate their youngest's achievement even if it meant watching him roam the sidelines.

During the five-hour flight to Chicago, Raymond was not looking forward to the questions his father might have about his confirmation process. At times it seemed that it was his father who was going through the process rather than Raymond.

Raymond arrived in Chicago early Saturday morning, the last one of August. Unlike Seattle, Chicago was beautiful in the throes of summer. It wasn't exactly football weather, but Northwestern was playing the University of Oklahoma at the Chicago Bears' Soldier Field in the Kick-Off Classic, the annual first game of the college football season. Raymond's parents had arrived on Thursday, only to find a big surprise.

Kirby was not only starting in his first collegiate game but was also in love. That wasn't a big surprise. During his first semester at Northwestern Kirby had broken up with Traci Davis, his high school sweetheart. Traci had received a full scholarship to Stanford, and neither one of them had wanted a long-distance romance. Kirby told Raymond this was his opportunity to become a bona fide *playa*. From their conversations, Raymond knew something was up because Kirby had said he had someone he wanted Raymond to meet when he came to Evanston. When Raymond had asked how his training was going, Kirby had joked he was doing more than lifting weights during the summer. Raymond assumed Kirby Tyler, playa-playa, was about to turn in his membership card for a new girlfriend.

Before the game, Raymond met his parents for brunch at the downtown Chicago Hilton. That's when he found out why Kirby had been so secretive about his new girlfriends. Right after his father had explained to the waitress twice that he wanted his eggs scrambled soft, with onions and cheese, the conversation turned to the Kirby absence.

"I can't believe he couldn't find a good-looking black girl like he dated in high school," Raymond Sr. said.

"Is she white?" Raymond asked.

"No, but she might as well be," his father said.

"Raymond Tyler, stop talking like that. Do you know how you sound?" Marlee, Raymond's mother, said.

"You need to mind your own business, woman, and I don't care how it sounds. You know how I feel about this interracial stuff. I want all-black grandkids," he said firmly.

"If they are Kirby's kids, then they will be black," Marlee said.

"Kids? Who said anything about kids?" Raymond asked as he took a small sip of apple juice. Neither one of his parents answered.

"And don't you think for one minute her parents ain't saying the same thing," Raymond Sr. said.

"So, if she's not white, then what is she?" Raymond asked again.

"She's Asian," Raymond Sr. said as the waitress placed his order in front of him.

"Aw," Raymond said as he stuck a fork in his cheese omelette to make sure the cook had included both Swiss and cheddar cheese.

"That's not totally true," Marlee said.

"What do you mean? Why are you guys talking in some type of code?"

"She's Asian and black. Her parents met in the service. I think she's very pretty and seems nice. We had dinner with them the other night."

"When do I get to meet her?" Raymond asked.

"You'll see her at the game," Raymond Sr. said.

"Is she sitting with us?"

"Naw, she's a cheerleader. So you'll get a glimpse of her before you have to meet her," Raymond Sr. said.

"I don't care what she's mixed with. Dawn, that's her name, seems to make Kirby happy and that's all I care about," Marlee said while pouring honey over her pecan pancakes.

"He's still a kid. What does he know about who can make him happy?"

"Did you know about this, Raymond?" his mother asked.

"Kinda. I didn't know she wasn't black, but I knew he had met somebody," Raymond said.

"Told me he was up here getting ready for the season and then we get up here and find out he's shacking up with some half-breed," his father said in a gruff voice. "I should take that car I bought him back home," he added.

"You ain't taking nothing back," his wife said firmly.

"Then his grades better not drop one point," Raymond Sr. countered.

Raymond was pleased that Kirby had once again taken the attention away from him. Not once did his father bring up the confirmation hearings. When he asked Raymond why he was going to New York, he explained Peaches's dilemma.

"Yeah, go up there and show them who's boss. I read something in the *New York Times* about how white folks are buying up all the property in Harlem and running us out," Raymond Sr. said.

"Did they say white folks?" Marlee asked.

"Didn't have to! Who else you think got the money to go up and buy a entire block and then tear it down?"

"I don't know, Pops. From what I remember about New York, brothers and sisters up there are pretty much in the mix," Raymond said.

"Yeah, but them brothers and sisters don't want no parts of Harlem. They would rather live downtown with white folks."

"I think it's time for us to leave for the game. I don't want to miss a single bit of my baby's big day," Marlee said.

"Neither do I, Mama. Let's rock and roll," Raymond said.

"I know ya'll just trying to shut me up. But you know that ain't gonna work. We need to have a family meeting about Kirby's girlfriend mess." In the Tyler household, a family meeting meant Raymond Sr. would tell the family how to react in a given situation. Like the time he went out and bought four burial plots without consulting anyone, including his wife.

"Sure, Pops. We'll do it in the locker room after the game," Raymond teased.

❧   ❧   ❧

Northwestern beat the highly touted Oklahoma 27–0. Kirby Tyler caught seven passes for sixty-three yards, including a fourth-down twenty-one-yard pass in the first quarter that led to the first Northwestern touchdown. The Tylers were jumping up so high and hugging so much that people sitting next to them teased them every time Kirby ran onto the field.

Raymond spent a great deal of the game eyeing Kirby's new girlfriend, who was cheering him on from the sideline. Since there were two cheerleaders who looked Asian, Raymond picked the one with the deep olive complexion. While surveying the Northwestern cheerleaders, Raymond noticed an attractive coffee-colored one, and was once again reminded that he was indeed his father's son. He, too, wondered why Kirby had not chosen the pretty black girl instead of the Asian combo. But unlike his father's, Raymond's main concern was his little brother, and if Dawn made Kirby happy, then that's what mattered most.

Right after the game, the Tylers rushed to the locker room door. Raymond realized his hunch had been right when Dawn Liu came over and gave him a big hug and a kiss on the cheek. She looked more Asian than African-American, with thin lips and a small nose, but her voice had an urban flair. Her eyes were brown and almond-shaped, and her pageboy hair was straight and eggplant-black. Raymond Sr. rudely turned away and acted as though he was studying the football program book from the game. Raymond had seen this show before, especially when his father first met Trent. Raymond Sr. had a way of letting a person know he wasn't interested in anything they had to say. Long ago,

Raymond and his mother had both agreed there was no way of changing Raymond Sr. The older he got, his ways set in like cement, but they still loved him.

"I knew you were Kirby's brother from the picture of you he keeps in his room," Dawn said with her cheerleader's enthusiasm.

"It's nice meeting you, Dawn," Raymond said.

"Same here. Wasn't the game great? I got a feeling we're going back to the Rose Bowl."

"Were you going to school here then?" Raymond asked. Northwestern's trip to the Rose Bowl two years earlier had been one of the reasons Kirby had selected the Wildcats during his senior year in high school.

"Yeah, it was my first year as a cheerleader. I'm a senior," Dawn said.

"Oh, you are?" Raymond asked. So Kirby was dating an older woman, Raymond thought.

"Yes, I graduate this year with my engineering degree but I'm thinking about going for my M.B.A. at Kellogg," Dawn said.

"So you're going to stay at Northwestern?" Raymond asked.

"If they will have me. You know how some schools don't like to take their own into their professional schools."

"Yeah, but I'm sure you won't have any problems."

"I hope you're right. Excuse me, I'm going over there to talk with your parents. Nice meeting you," Dawn said as she clasped his hand warmly. No matter what Raymond said, Dawn appeared genuinely interested in it. Raymond had known plenty of these girls in college, sweet as candied apples, but most of them were African-American.

"Nice meeting you as well," Raymond said. He started to tell Dawn his father would change, but Dawn struck him as the type of girl who didn't worry about what other people thought. As she walked away, Raymond noticed Dawn's graceful, almost gliding way of walking, like a trained dancer.

Raymond was watching some of the players emerge from the locker room when he felt someone walking up behind him.

"We've got to stop meeting like this."

Raymond recognized the deep, sensual voice immediately, and he slowly turned to face John Basil Henderson. He was wearing a cranberry-red knit shirt that accented his nipples, which looked as hard as cherry pits, and some tight black pants that looked like jodhpurs, embracing every muscle in his lower body. It had been a year since Raymond had seen Basil in the flesh, but the effect was, as usual, heart-stopping.

"Basil, what are you doing here?" Raymond asked. *This is the last person I need to run into,* Raymond thought.

"I wanted to see you," Basil said in a lustful tone. There was something soft and welcoming in the incredible grayness of his eyes. Each stare felt like a sexual encounter. Basil had a way of doing that to both men and women. For Basil, seduction was an art and a pleasure. The way he carried himself, the way he walked, and the features of his handsome face were the signs of a man who had been told more times than the law should allow how fine he was.

Raymond blushed. "Yeah, right."

"So where is little bro? He had a great game," Basil said.

"Yeah, he did. We're all very proud of him."

"Should I be calling you Judge Tyler, or is it still just Raymond?" Basil was standing so close that Raymond could smell the spearmint Certs Basil had popped in his mouth before greeting him.

"Still just plain Raymond," he said as he nervously stepped back slightly.

"What's up with that?"

"The confirmation process just takes a little time," Raymond explained.

"Right . . . right. Let me know if I need to git my boys on them," Basil joked as he reached out and patted Raymond on the shoulder.

Raymond gave him a half-smile and then looked at Dawn talking with his parents, or at least, with his mother. Raymond Sr. was still not looking in her direction. His father looked pitiful, like a puppy waiting for his master to return. Raymond knew he needed to rescue his father and save him from himself.

"Let me introduce you to my pops," Raymond said to Basil.

"Cool," Basil smiled. The two of them walked slowly through the throng of well-wishers waiting for the victorious Wildcats.

"Pops."

Raymond's father turned to face his son with a relieved look on his face.

"Yeah, Raymond," he said.

"I got somebody I want you to meet. This is Basil Henderson, who used to play for the New Jersey Warriors," Raymond said.

"Of course! You signed a football for me. It's a pleasure meeting you," Raymond Sr. said as he grabbed Basil's hand and shook it in a double clasp.

"It's nice meeting you, sir. Looks like you got a future NFL star of your own," Basil said.

"You think so?" Raymond Sr. asked. His dour face was suddenly full of excitement like he was meeting the president or Justice Thurgood Marshall.

"If he keeps playing like he did today," Basil said.

"You aren't still playing, are you?"

"No, sir. I'm working for ESPN," Basil said.

"So you here covering the game?"

"You could say that," Basil said as he looked at Raymond from the corner of his eye. Raymond Jr. started walking closer to the locker room door.

Basil and Raymond Sr. continued to talk about football for a few minutes while Raymond went over to check on his mother and Dawn. Raymond suddenly heard a loud burst of cheers and applause and looked up to see a smiling Kirby surfacing from the locker room door. Kirby was wearing a tight gray T-shirt and jeans, with a purple and white gym bag hanging over his shoulders. His close-shaven head was covered by a purple N.U. baseball cap, and a single diamond stud gleamed from his left ear. Raymond rushed over to hug his younger brother and whispered, "Great game, little bro, great game."

"Word . . . word. We kicked some Sooner butt today," Kirby said proudly.

"I mean," Raymond said as he smiled at his brother. Kirby Tyler was an imposing young man, brawny and tall with big whiskey-colored eyes.

"Did you meet Dawn?"

"Yeah, I did."

"So what do you think?"

"She seems real nice," Raymond said.

"Yeah, man, she's da bomb. Where are Mom and Pops?"

"Over there," Raymond said as he pointed toward his mother.

"Where's Pops?" Kirby asked Raymond as he looked at his mother and girlfriend chatting like old friends.

"Aw, he's over there with Basil Henderson."

"Basil Henderson is here? Was he covering the game?" Kirby asked quickly. Kirby took off his hat and ran his large hands over his head. He put the hat back on and tucked his T-shirt into his jeans like he was about to be interviewed for a television sports show.

"Naw, I don't think so. But I think he still works for ESPN," Raymond said.

"Let me go over there and pay a playa his respects," Kirby said.

"Go on, we will talk later."

"Are you going to stay here a couple days extra so we can hang out?" Kirby asked.

"Don't you have school?"

"Naw, I've got a couple of weeks before registration."

"You want me to?"

"Right . . . right. You could come to practice and we can hang out. And you could get a chance to know Dawn," Kirby said.

"Then it's a deal," Raymond said. He suddenly felt a dizzying rush of tenderness and love for his little brother. It was a love Raymond knew he could always count on.

23

"I saw Raymond," Basil said with a big smile. The doctor tried to recall the last time Basil had smiled so warmly and broadly.

"How did it go?"

"It went fine. Raymond didn't believe I had come to the game to see him, you know, he thought it was work related. I just had this feeling, knowing Raymond, he'd be at the first game his little brother was starting. He looked great and I even had dinner with him and his folks. His parents were real cool. We didn't talk that much. I still think he gets nervous around me."

"Why is that?"

"I think it's because he doesn't want me to know how he feels," Basil said confidently.

"Has he said that to you?"

"No, he doesn't have to. We're both men and men play games."

"Was his partner there?"

"No, and when I asked about him, Raymond gave me this stern look and said he's fine. And I noticed he didn't mention him during dinner and gave his little brother the same answer when he asked about him. Something's up with those two and I'm going to figure it out."

"And how do you plan to do that?"

"Raymond is coming to New York to work on some legal deal. And from what I can gather he might be here for a while. He said he was going to call, but if he doesn't, I'll call him. I heard him tell his brother's girlfriend where he was staying. I'll give him a couple of days and then I'll call."

Basil was silent for about five minutes. After his initial burst of excitement, his face had grown sad.

"Is there something about your meeting with Raymond that's bothering you?"

"Not really. I was just thinking about how nice it was having dinner with him and his family. I mean, they really seem tight. I know from past dealings with Raymond that he and his father have had their moments, but they seemed so close. And I could tell his mother spoils Raymond and all the men in that family. It made me wonder what I missed by not having a mother."

"Are you still planning on finding out information about your mother?"

"Someday. But I don't know where to start. I guess I could go to my aunt. But in the past she hasn't seemed willing to give me any information. And besides, what good would it do? I mean, she's dead."

"I thought the point was to find out about that side of your history."

"What if it's not a good history? I mean, what if I got uncles and mofos on her side of the family that are sicker than my father's people?"

"That's possible. But I know you can handle it."

"I don't think so, and I have second thoughts about that shit. I might just open up a can of shit I won't be able to deal with."

"So why did seeing Raymond with his family make you sad?"

"Who said it made me sad?"

"The look."

"I don't get sad about shit like that. I was just thinking how nice I felt. Even though Raymond was semishady, it was just good being around him. Seeing him smile and inhaling his scent."

"Have you told your father about our sessions?"

"Naw," Basil shrugged.

"I thought you were planning to."

"You're the one that suggested that. I've told you about my father and I'm sure he would think this was some weak ass sissy shit," Basil said firmly.

"Maybe if you told him what brought you here."

"What's that going to do?"

"It might make him understand."

"How can he understand this shit when I don't?" Basil asked. He noticed the doctor looking at the clock on the desk.

"I'm outta here. I know my time is up," Basil said as he leaped from the chair.

24

The tour of *Dreamgirls* was off to a slow rebirth. Lukewarm reviews and half-full houses had the producers concerned that the show might not ever get out of the nation's capital. The fourteen days of performances had passed very slowly. One critic had gone as far as to christen the production *Screamgirls* and predicted that Michael Bennett, the creator, was probably turning over in his grave. He was kinder to the men in the cast, praising the lead, David Brown, in the role of Curtis Taylor, Jr., a Berry Gordy, Jr., type character, and Vondell Thomas, who played James Thunder Early, a James Brown/Little Richard composite character. The only females mentioned were the lead character, Effie Melody White, and Yancey, whom he called "stunningly beautiful with an icy elegance" and "a star waiting to drop on the Broadway stage." It pained Nicole that neither her name nor her character's name had received a mention. But she knew that sometimes, when critics were brutal, you considered yourself lucky to go unnoticed.

Nicole was glad to be in Detroit, where she hoped things would be better, despite the fact she was missing her husband. Late night calls from Jared had kept her focused and upbeat, but she was always tired. After the Washington reviews, the director had started three-hour rehearsals in the morning, and then another two-hour session in the afternoon with the female principals. The only good thing was the overtime pay, but Nicole was willing to give up a few dollars for an afternoon nap.

On opening night in Detroit's Fisher Theater, Nicole and Yancey had a light supper before the bus that transported the company to the theater departed. In the two weeks since leaving New York, cast members were already beginning to pair off. Nicole was happy that she already had a good friend to shop, exercise, and have dinner with before the tour ever started. She knew with a cast this large, she could have ended up like the new kid on the first day of school, walking into the cafeteria and praying someone would invite her to join them. It didn't help that she felt like a mother to many members of the youthful cast.

Yancey and Nicole were waiting on their salads when Cedric Curry, one of the dancers in the show, walked into the hotel café. Cedric had on headphones and was moving his head and body from side to side, like he was in a dance club, when he noticed Yancey and Nicole. He removed his headphones to give them a wave and a bright smile.

"You think we should ask him to join us?" Yancey asked.

"Why not? I don't really know him that well," Nicole said. Cedric, a small man with a teenage boy's chest and dancer's butt and legs, had joined the cast during the last two days in D.C. Nicole assumed from his skintight jeans and the way he swung his bag over his shoulder that he was gay. The female members of the cast usually hit it off with their gay peers, as long as they told the truth about their sexuality. Broadway road companies were known for their whirlwind romances, both gay and straight, and nobody had the time to look for love on the wrong team. Nicole figured Cedric hadn't yet met a love or made a friend among the male cast members.

"Cedric," Yancey shouted as she motioned for him.

"Hey, ladies! Nicole and Yancey, right? Whassup?" he said as he dropped his large leather bag in the empty seat. "Are you ladies inviting me to join you?"

"Sure," Nicole said.

"Thanks, 'cause I hate eating alone," Cedric said as he plopped into the welcoming metal chair. "What did you ladies order, and how much time do we have?"

"We're just having salads," Nicole said.

"I've noticed that most of the men don't eat before the show," Yancey commented.

"Yeah, because we have to do all that dancing. But I need something in my stomach," Cedric said.

He ordered a bowl of soup and a dinner salad with low-fat ranch dressing, and while waiting for his food, he talked nonstop about how excited he was to be in the cast. *Dreamgirls* was his first national tour. The original *Dreamgirls* was the first Broadway show he had ever seen, when it came to Los Angeles in the late eighties. He told Nicole and Yancey how great it was to be receiving a regular paycheck and not have to work with a bunch of no-talent singers like he had while dancing in music videos. Cedric was beaming with confidence when he bet that before the show hit Broadway he would be understudying or playing C. C. White, one of the male principals.

"Who all have you worked with?" Yancey asked.

"You name 'em, I've worked with 'em. Janet, Jody, Paula, Vanessa, and Toni. You know, all the divas," Cedric said.

"Did you know Yancey was Toni Braxton's cousin?" Nicole asked. Yancey looked down as she took her fork and removed an olive from her salad.

"Get outta here! Miss girl is fierce!" Cedric said. "She should be doing Broadway also."

"Yeah, she's doing great. But enough about her. Give us the tea on those other divas. Who's nice, who's a bitch, and who can really sing?" Yancey asked eagerly.

"I don't know you well enough to tell you *all* my secrets. But, honey, don't give me no wine or a rum and Coke or these loose lips of mine will start waggin'. You call me a talking *Sister 2 Sister,*" Cedric said with a sneaky smile.

"I don't think I want to know who's faking," Nicole said.

"Well, I do," said Yancey. "So you can tell me."

"Nicole, we know someone in common," Cedric said.

"Really? Who?"

"Delaney Morris. I'm from San Diego and she choreographed and directed a couple of videos I did."

Nicole was visibly shaken. She stopped eating her salad. Her face became sad, as though someone had just told her that someone very close to her was dying.

"Yes, Delaney and I used to be great friends," she said sadly. She felt tears begin to run down her face, and she didn't know how she could keep Yancey and Cedric from noticing.

"Are you all right, Nicole?" Yancey asked.

"Oh, I'm fine. There's just something in my eye," Nicole said as she took the cloth napkin and dabbed her eyes.

"She had great things to say about you," Cedric continued, oblivious to Nicole's reaction.

"Ya'll not good friends anymore?" Yancey asked.

"Let's just say we don't talk as much as we used to," Nicole said.

"What happened?"

"I don't want to talk about it," Nicole said as she looked at her watch to see if the bus would save her from talking about Delaney.

"I'm sorry. I thought you guys were good friends," Cedric said when he finally noticed Nicole's agitation. "Lord knows I don't want to bring the star of the show bad vibes on opening night. Are you sure you're all right?"

"There is nothing to be sorry about. And I will be just fine," Nicole said confidently. For the next ten minutes, while Yancey and Cedric wrapped up their getting-to-know-you talk, Nicole kept her eyes focused on Yancey's soft, pink waffle-knit sweater. She was as still as a painting.

Nicole didn't want to talk about Delaney because it was just as painful as talking about her best friend, Candance, who had died of AIDS a few years before Kyle. But Delaney was very much alive and living a productive life in San Diego with her lover, Jody, and their son, Fletcher. Their once strong friendship had been weakened by distance and a disagreement, not Delaney's bisexuality. In fact, Nicole's friendship with Delaney had deepened and grown stronger when Delaney confessed she enjoyed both men and women.

A child had weakened their friendship; the child Nicole and Jared had wanted Delaney to bear for them. The two friends had not spoken since one morning when Delaney called to say she couldn't be a surrogate for Jared and Nicole. She and Jody wanted their own children and she didn't think it would be a good idea. Delaney's decision upset Nicole, not only because her hopes were high for motherhood, but especially since Delaney had suggested herself when they had been unable to find a suitable surrogate.

Nicole's mind wandered back to that day a few days before Christmas and how she had pleaded with her friend to reconsider. Delaney responded, "I'm sorry. I can't risk harming my relationship. You understand, don't you?"

Nicole replied, "No, I'm sorry, Delaney, I don't understand."

The waiter returned with the check and Nicole came out of her self-induced trance. She quickly placed a credit card in the chocolate-brown tray and looked at her watch and then at Yancey and Cedric. "It's show time, kids," she said. "We've got a show to do!"

25

When Raymond arrived in New York, he heaved a big sigh to be there. Pouring down from a cloudless sky, the warm sun felt like the welcoming arms of an old and dear friend.

Once Raymond reached his hotel, he dropped his luggage in his small, one-bedroom suite and decided he wanted to visit some of his old haunts. He walked up Central Park West and over to Columbus Avenue, enjoying the food smells of the city and listening to the sounds rising from the pulsating streets. To Raymond, the Upper West Side seemed trapped in a time warp. The busy neighborhood looked the same as it had a decade before. Abundant rows of colorful fresh produce outside the shops, street vendors hawking pretzels, hot dogs, and cold drinks, and vagrants asking for spare change all fought for sidewalk space with musicians, dancers, and throngs of fast-moving New Yorkers. The only thing different, Raymond thought, was that the horn-honking drivers of ten years ago drove different-model cars.

It was only when he reached Seventy-second Street that Raymond noticed a change. The Citibank where he frequently used his bank card had moved to the right side of the street in the former home of Popeye's Chicken. One of his favorite restaurants, Tuesday's, was now a fast-food Chinese place. He walked down Seventy-second and picked up his pace as he approached the location of the Nickel Bar, the infamous, mostly black gay bar where he had met Kyle and several sexual conquests. But the Nickel Bar was now history. The place where Raymond had met one of his best and most colorful friends was now an office supply store.

Raymond stood silently in front of the store. His thoughts drifted back to the late eighties when the Nickel Bar was one of the most popular spots on the Upper West Side. Instead of seeing rows of paper and office supplies through a glass door, Raymond saw a semidark watering hole, with a long oak bar and well-worn stools. He didn't hear the sounds of the busy Upper West Side, but the blasting music of Chaka Khan, Melba Moore, and Diana Ross. Raymond thought about Arnold, his favorite bartender, and Dennis, the burly bouncer who always flirted with him. Had they moved on to another bar, or had they met the same fate as Kyle and so many of the Nickel's other patrons and become people with AIDS?

After his walk down memory lane, Raymond was anxious to see Jared. He returned to his suite, brushed his teeth, and spread a warm towel across his face before going back down to the lobby, where he was to meet his friend. Jared was standing with his back toward Raymond, but when Raymond came within five feet of him, Jared could feel his presence and turned quickly to greet his friend.

Even total strangers could tell from the warm smile and the brotherly embrace they shared, not to mention the wet kisses they planted on each other's forehead, that these two were best friends.

"Man, am I glad to see you," Jared said as he placed his arms around Raymond's shoulders.

"Same here, my brotha," Raymond responded.

"You still lookin' good," Jared said as he gave his friend the once-over.

"I don't know about that," Raymond said as he rubbed his midsection. He had gained about thirteen pounds since he left his job, and about seven more since the last time Jared had seen him, last winter when they went skiing in Vail. Jared did notice the extra weight in Raymond's face, but knew his friend might be feeling a little bit sensitive about it. Raymond couldn't help but notice that Jared looked like he hadn't aged a day or gained an ounce since they first met in Alabama some ten years before.

"So what are we going to do? Do you want to get a drink and grab something to eat? How much time do we have?" Jared asked.

"Which question do you want me to answer first? Or should I just say I'm all yours?" Raymond asked.

"This place looks nice. I didn't even know this hotel was here," Jared said as he took another glance around the hotel lobby with its cool blue and gold marble floor and vaulted ceiling.

"Yeah, it is nice. I hadn't heard of this place, but the lady who handles my travel said she had heard a lot of great things about it. And so far, so good. Every room, I think, is a suite," Raymond said.

"Why don't we just stay here?" Jared suggested.

"Sounds like a plan to me," Raymond said as he placed one arm around his friend's shoulders and gently maneuvered him toward the automatic door that separated the sparkling lobby from the hotel restaurant.

The normally busy restaurant was quiet, the stillness broken only by the sounds of the bartender moving bottles of liquor. A hostess with two large menus in her hand escorted the two men into the dining room, smiled, and said, "Okay, gentlemen, take your pick."

"How 'bout that table over there?" Raymond said as he pointed to a brass-rimmed table with four chairs in the corner with a view of Central Park.

"Great!" The hostess smiled as she led them to the table and placed the menus in front of them as they took their seats. "Can I bring you something to drink?" she asked as she ran her hands through a tangle of brown curls.

"Two glasses of Pinot Noir," Jared said. "Naw, make that a bottle." Jared knew it would take more than one glass of wine for the two of them to catch up on the details of each other's life. After the hostess left, Jared rubbed his two large hands together and asked, "How was the trip to Chicago?"

"It was a lot of fun. Mama and Pops send their love. Kirby's doing great, and the little Negro is in love," Raymond said proudly.

"What? Who is the lucky lady?"

"A real nice young lady. Her name is Dawn, and guess what?"

"What?"

"She ain't black," Raymond laughed. He told Jared about Dawn's ancestry and how happy Kirby seemed.

"You kidding? How is your pops handling it?"

"That's still being decided," Raymond said. "I think the only reason he didn't have a heart attack is because at least she isn't white. How is your better half?"

"Nicole is doing great. She's in Detroit. To tell you the truth, I can't wait until this tour is over, and she's only been gone a couple of weeks."

"I can't believe she's doing *Dreamgirls* again."

"Neither can I," Jared said mournfully. Raymond noticed a change in the tone of his voice.

"So why did you let her do it?" Raymond asked.

Jared arched his eyebrows and looked Raymond dead in the eyes and said, "Let her do it? Raymond, come on, get real. You know Nicole. It wasn't about me letting her do it. She wanted to do it, and I want her to have whatever it is she wants and needs to be happy."

"You really love her something crazy, don't cha, boy?"

"And you know it!" Jared said.

"How long is the show going to be on the road?"

"I think a couple of months and then hopefully, fingers crossed, the show will come back to New York. So how is Trent?"

"Aw, Trent's cool. You know . . . working hard. He's over in South Africa working on some big project. So I guess you could say we both doin' without."

"So what are we doing with our lives, partner? Sounds like our spouses are blazing trails across the world," Jared said.

"You think so?"

"Yeah, but we're doing our share. Look at you. In another couple of months, my man will be a federal judge, and what can be more important than that?"

"Could be . . . could be not," Raymond said quietly.

"What do you mean 'could be'? Those people on Capitol Hill ain't giving you a hard time, are they? If so, let me know. I still got some connections down there."

"Naw, it's just a slowdown. I still haven't got a date concerning my confirmation."

"Well, don't worry. It's gonna happen," Jared said confidently. A waiter brought out a bottle of wine and showed it to Jared, who nodded his approval. While the waiter was opening the wine, Jared and Raymond remained silent, just enjoying the view of the park. Raymond was thinking that this might be the time to tell Jared what he had learned about Trent; he could ask Jared what he should do about it. Jared was thinking of sharing his concerns about his future in New York and if his marriage could survive the differences he had begun to notice.

After he had poured them each a glass of wine the waiter asked if they were going to have dinner.

"What do you think?" Jared said as he looked over the menu. Raymond did the same. After a few seconds they both looked at the waiter and said, "Let me have the salmon."

Raymond and Jared looked at each other and smiled. The waiter quizzed, "Are you two brothers?"

"Sorta," Raymond said as he lifted his wineglass toward Jared, who lifted his in response. When they toasted their friendship, all that could be heard was the sound of the glasses clicking. As the sound echoed slightly around them, both Jared and Raymond felt that in the company of the other, all was right with the world.

❖   ❖   ❖

On his second night in New York, Raymond couldn't sleep. As he lay on top of the crisp, cold white sheets of his king-sized bed, his mind raced faster than a horse at the Kentucky Derby. Raymond's body felt numb, tension knotted his stomach. He felt an extraordinary mix of anger, anxiety, and envy. He was angry that he had fallen in love with a man who cheated on him, that Trent was the best he could do when it came to lovers. Anxiety that he might not have any other choice but to leave Trent. He felt envy at his little brother and Jared, who didn't have to suffer such betrayal.

After almost a decade's absence, those "I wish I wasn't gay" feelings had returned. And his heart plummeted when he felt that because he was gay, love would always be a temporary thing.

Raymond's eyes moved from the television, where a muted episode of *Seinfeld* was playing, to the marble-topped nightstand where hotel personnel had set up bottles of spring water and chocolates. He couldn't decide if he should turn off or turn up the classical music playing on the tiny clock radio located on the left side of the bed.

It had been almost five days since he and Trent had spoken to each other. This lapse in communication had never happened since they had moved in together three years ago. Over the last few days they had left messages, but Raymond was avoiding Trent and had not called him back in South Africa. Raymond had left a few messages on Trent's personal telephone line telling him he was doing fine and had enjoyed the time with his family. Trent's messages were full of excitement as he described South Africa and ended each call with "I miss you and I love you." Raymond didn't really know if he missed Trent, and in many ways, he was relieved that business had separated them.

Raymond felt even more sadness because he was alone with grief. During times like these, he hated being alone and missed Kyle more than ever. Kyle would have understood and made him laugh about it. He could hear Kyle saying something like, "Chirl, men ain't good for nuthin' but slanging dick and some of them can't even do that right. Move on." But now there was no one Raymond felt he could tell. There was no one to understand his pain. He wanted to tell Jared or his mother but wondered how they would feel later if he decided to stay with Trent.

Then Raymond felt a twinge of guilt. Maybe he had done something to deserve an unfaithful lover. Maybe he had spent too much time at the office or with his students. But Trent maintained long hours as well. He tried to think of someone he had mistreated. For a few minutes Raymond couldn't think of anyone. The women he had lied to about his sexuality had forgiven him, or so he thought. Nicole said as much, whenever the subject came up.

Then Basil came into focus. His image was strong and vivid, like he was standing in the room, staring at Raymond with a lustful gaze. But Raymond hadn't mistreated Basil. Sure, he had treated him with a certain indifference, but he hadn't been mean. Raymond rationalized that his treatment of Basil was to protect himself. He was so proud of himself for not falling in love with Basil during their brief affair. Raymond knew that when Basil set his mind on someone, he was dangerous to *any* relationship.

Raymond's thoughts turned to Larry Pratt, an attractive law student from Fresno, California. They had shared a meal and a flirtatious relationship for a few months. The two of them would talk about the law and sports, and then trade stories about being in the life. Nothing ever happened sexually. Once, when Larry made an advance, Raymond rejected him sweetly by telling him he could never get involved with a student, even one he wasn't teaching. But Raymond did find himself attracted to Larry and he had thought of him a couple of times while making love to Trent. Larry's flirting made Raymond feel young and sexy in a bad-boy way. When Trent and Raymond moved to Seattle, they had agreed to a monogamous relationship, but that didn't include fantasies. As long as these fantasies weren't acted upon.

After an hour of such thoughts, Raymond glanced at the television where *All in the Family* was on. Finally the fatigue of his problems overtook him, and Raymond drifted into a restless sleep.

❖   ❖   ❖

Peaches didn't hear or notice Raymond when he walked into a quiet Cuts 'n' Cobblers. The morning crowd had disappeared, and Enoch took Mondays off. Peaches had her back to the front door and was watching a small television that sat on the counter. Before Raymond could say hello, Peaches said, "Don't be no fool, honey. Don't tell that man you got a credit card." Sometimes when she was alone, Peaches would talk to the television, especially when the commercials contained African-American actors. She also talked back to some of the people pushing products on the Home Shopping Network, sometimes yelling, "Bitch, ain't nobody a big enough fool to buy that shit!" Enoch would always ask her who she was talking to and she would tell him to mind his own bizness.

"Who you talking to, Peaches?" Raymond asked. Peaches knew this questioner wasn't Enoch and turned around quickly. She had a smile a mile long as she took a long pull off her half-finished cigarette.

"When did you walk in here?" Peaches asked as she raced into Raymond's open arms.

"I just walked in. So who you talking to?"

"This dumb bitch on the TV tellin' this man she got a new credit card. Don't she know he ain't gonna do nuthing but use it up like he's gonna do her?" Peaches said, shaking her head in disgust over the woman's foolishness. "I bet it was another man who ruined her credit in the first place."

Raymond knew he didn't have time to get the whole story, so instead he told Peaches how happy he was to see her. He felt a sense of relief in her presence, and a smile began to slowly brighten his face. There was nothing he could do to stop it.

"And I'm glad to see you, baby. You looking good . . . your face a little fatter but I guess that comes from livin' good," Peaches said.

"Yeah, I've picked up a little weight," Raymond said, blushing.

"Come on, sit down. You hungry? I can fix you something to eat. You want some coffee?" Peaches made her way over to the counter, where she poured herself a fresh cup of coffee.

"Naw, I had a little something before I left the hotel," Raymond said.

"Why don't you stay with Nicole and Jared? You don't need to be stayin' in no hotel. You could even stay here. I got a pull-out sofa."

"Thanks, but I'm fine. Jared offered me his place and I might stay there a couple of nights. It just depends on how long it takes me to take care of you," Raymond said as he looked around Peaches's place of business. "This is a nice place you have here."

"Do you mean that or are you being shady?" Peaches asked. Her eyebrows arched.

"Oh, I mean it. And what do you mean me being shady?"

"You know—high-hattin' me. Being all snoblike. Now, don't forget you talkin' to Peaches and I know you. This place ain't much but it's home and don't think for a moment I would call you if I didn't want to lose this place."

Raymond walked over to Peaches and put his arms around her. Squeezing her tightly, he said, "I'm going to do everything in my power to make sure you don't lose your place."

"Is that a promise?" Peaches said as she looked up at Raymond.

"That's a promise," Raymond said as he kissed the top of Peaches's head.

❧   ❧   ❧

Raymond made contact with the lawyers for Peaches's landlord, and was hopeful he could take care of things in less than a week. He learned from a former law school classmate that property in Harlem was hotter than ever, and most property owners were taking advantage of the trend, forcing several small businesses to close. But Raymond also thought not many of those small business owners had a well-trained, soon-to-be-on-the-bench lawyer working on their behalf, and doing it for free. He wondered how many Harlem small businesses would suffer without the benefit of expert legal advice.

Before calling it a day, Raymond checked his messages in Seattle. There was another message from Trent and one from his mother. Her voice sounded anxious, so Raymond decided to call her right away.

"Mama? Are you all right?" he asked when his mother picked up after a couple of rings.

"Raymond? How is my baby?"

"I'm doin'. Is this too late?" he asked while cradling the phone receiver on his shoulder. He loosened his tie and untucked his shirt.

"It's never too late for my baby," she said.

"I was just returning your call. Your voice sounded urgent. Is everything okay?"

"Oh, everything is fine. But are you all right? I mean, you've been on my mind and the last couple of times I've talked to you, well, your voice sounds heavy," his mother said with concern in her voice.

"I'm okay, Mama. Just getting used to being back in New York and trying to see what I can do to help Peaches out," Raymond said.

"How is Peaches? And how long you think you're gonna be up there?"

"I don't really know right now, and Peaches has got everything cooking. Just worried about losing her place. I can already tell this is not going to be easy. Real estate in Harlem is hotter than hot now, and landlords want to move in the people who are willing to pay top dollar."

"How's Trent?"

Raymond paused for a second and then said, "All right. I guess. I haven't talked to him in a couple of days. You know, with the time difference and all. How's Pops?"

"Still simmering over Kirby's new girlfriend. I told him he better get over it or he's gonna have a stroke or something. Worrying about something he can't change. I told him that was Kirby's business."

"What's his problem? She seemed like a really nice girl," Raymond said. He started to tell his mother how he expected his father to be ecstatic, given that Kirby was dating a woman and not a man. But he didn't.

"The same problem he has with everything. Being old and feeling like he's losing control over his family."

"You think he really feels that way?"

"Honey, pleeze. That man still feels like, when he says something, we should all jump," she laughed.

Raymond and his mother talked for another few minutes about their recent trip to Chicago. She wanted to know when they would see each other again, and Raymond agreed to look at his calendar as soon as he could. Just when he was getting ready to hang up, he asked, "Mama, what would you do if Pops ever cheated on you?"

"First of all, he's too old to cheat. Don't nobody want him but me. And why would you ask me something like that, baby? Are you sure everything is all right between you and Trent?"

"Mama, if I told you something, would you keep it to yourself?" Raymond knew he had to come clean now, but deep down, he really needed his mama's advice.

"Sure, I would, baby. What's the matter?"

Raymond didn't answer. He and his mother were silent on the phone for almost a minute, listening to each other breathe. His mother broke the silence.

"Raymond, please tell me what happened."

Raymond told his mother the information Lisa had uncovered. His voice ranged from sorrow to anger and he was concentrating on not crying, though his eyes ached with tears. When he said the words out loud, they became even more painful, like they were bruising his throat.

"My first response is an easy one. And that's to tell you, it's in the past and the past is over. But I got to ask you something."

"Yeah, Mama," Raymond said softly.

"Do you still love him?"

After a brief hesitation, Raymond said weakly, "I think so."

"Then if you're going to forgive him, you'd better know so," his mother said firmly.

"What do you mean?"

"I mean this ain't gonna be easy. How does Trent feel?"

"He doesn't know."

"What do you mean he doesn't know? You haven't told him about this?"

"No."

"Raymond Jr., is that fair? What if it's not true?"

"The information was double-checked, Mama. I know it's true."

"But you haven't heard his explanation."

"There is no excuse for this, Mama. He shouldn't have done it," Raymond said angrily.

"Baby, I don't mean to sound harsh, and I know this is hurting you. But you at least owe Trent a chance to explain his case. Boy, you're sounding and acting more like your father with each passing day."

"No, I'm not." This comparison made Raymond even more upset. He loved and respected his father, but he didn't want to be like him on any level. Not because he felt his father had always run their home with an iron-clad fist, but because they were from different times. Somehow, his mother, Kirby, and Raymond had allowed his father to live in the past, without challenge. Raymond did admire the way his father always spoke his mind, not backing down to anyone, and was always loving and respectful of his wife. Raymond had never seen his mother and father arguing, only minor disagreements.

"Whatever you say. But I'm telling you this sounds just like something he would say."

"I've got to go, Mama. Thanks for listening," Raymond said quickly. He felt he had just made a big mistake by telling her about his personal problem.

"Where you got to go?"

"I promised Jared I would meet him," Raymond lied.

"But we ain't finished talking about this."

"We are for now, Mama. And don't you worry about me. And please, please don't tell Pops about this," Raymond pleaded.

"I'll try not to. Good night, baby. I'll pray for you and Trent, but you got to get on your knees too."

"Night, Ma. I love you."

"And I love you too."

When Raymond hung up the phone, he felt uneasy. It was something his mother had said at the end of their conversation, when he had asked her not to worry or to mention his problem to his father. Raymond knew his mother wouldn't be able to do either.

26

After about ten minutes of silence and staring at the doctor's framed degree from Cornell University and a framed photograph of Times Square, Basil finally spoke.

"I did something stupid," he said quietly.

"How so?" the doctor asked.

"One of my honeys invited me to some model's party the other night. It was at the bar called Chaos down in the SoHo area. It was a typical Gee-ain't-I-fabulous party. You know, a lot of models, model groupies, and people who ain't never had their name on a guest list," Basil said.

"How did that cause trouble?"

"I'm gettin' to that. This honey, Valencia, was busy kissing ass to some of the so-called producers and video casting agents. So I went up into this level of the club where they had a cigar and champagne bar. It was real tight with antique chairs and real dark and everybody lookin' smooth, puffing on cigars, and sipping champagne. So I take a seat at the end of the bar and this plump but good-lookin' in the face brother comes over and sits next to me. He offers me a smoke, tells me it's Cuban, and I take it."

"I didn't know you smoked."

"I really don't, but cigars and a blunt every now and then is cool. Let me get back to my story. So me and this mofo . . . his name was Dan or something nondescript like that . . . start talking. I decided to engage him in conversation because he had given me this wonderful-tasting cigar and 'cause I noticed the gold wedding band he was wearing. Big mistake," Basil sighs.

"Why was that a mistake?"

"I start talking and he seems like a cool brother. Tells me he works on Wall Street as a vice-president for one of the brokerage firms. We talk about the market. I ask him for some stock tips and he grins and tells me he's not going to jail just because he meets a good-lookin' brother."

"How did that make you feel?"

"By then I knew what was up. And that bugle blowing in his pants was a true sign. I had a couple of drinks, and I'm thinking if this mofo is married, then I don't have to worry about him riding my jock, you know, after I bust the guts and move on."

"So you were attracted to him?"

"Not really. But he was smart and I like it when a brother got his shit together. We talked about the markets and investments and how long it was going to be before the bull market faltered. He mentioned his loft in SoHo and his beach home in the Virgin Islands. But no mention of a wife. While he was talking, I kept looking down at his finger with the gold band. Just to let him know I wasn't stupid."

"Did he notice?"

"Not really. He was one of these mofos who obviously liked the sound of his own voice, so he wasn't interested in nuthin' I was saying."

"So how was this a mistake? You met someone whose conversation you found interesting."

"I'm gettin' there, Doc. I'm gonna tell you. I guess I should get to why I'm so mad at myself. Long story, short. After a few more glasses of DP, I end up back at his loft. He tells me he has this awesome sound system, and a computer system that is linked to the foreign markets and some more cigars and vintage brandy. So I decide to check it out. Ole boy's place was the shit. I mean, you could tell he was doing all right for himself. The walls were covered with expensive artwork and the loft had a view that was all that. Anyway after one drink, I asked Dan to let me check out the markets and he says, 'Sure.' So he leads me down this long, dark hallway. About halfway down he suddenly turns and said, 'I've been dying to ask you this all night.' Then he whispers, 'Can I taste that love basket I've been staring at all night?' "

"What did you say to him?"

"I didn't say fuck. I just whipped it out. He started sucking on it like my dick was pumping life into his ass. He pulls me to this bedroom and the first thing I notice is this big-ass wedding picture, with him and some dumb-ass sister. He pulls off his clothes and the body is kinda plump, but my shit is up so I'm ready to get off. But then . . ." Basil paused.

"What happened?"

"He whispers to me again. This time he says, 'Fuck me like a woman.' " Basil turned away to the window with a look of disgust.

"How did that make you feel?" the doctor asked after a few minutes.

"Pissed me the fuck off. I pulled my pants up. Pulled my mutherfuckin' dick out of his face and got the fuck out of his apartment."

"Why did that upset you?"

"It just made me sick. Here is this married mofo begging for the dick, which I would have given freely, but then he started talking about treat him like a woman. I want to just bust him up side his head, but I didn't." Basil paused and looked at the doctor as if he were waiting for a sign. After a moment of meeting the doctor's stony stare, Basil said, "So I guess I'm making progress, huh, Doc?"

"Do you think so?"

"Yeah. The fact that I didn't hit him and that I went home and jerked my own dick off tells me I'm making a whole lot of progress," Basil said as he got up from the chair and headed for the door.

27

Raymond had just closed a book on New York real estate law when the phone rang.

"This is Raymond Tyler." He answered in his best business voice since he was expecting a call from the lawyer of Peaches's landlord.

"Is this my man? I can't believe I'm finally talking to you," Trent said quickly.

"Trent, how you doing?" Raymond asked in a voice that sounded more like he was talking to a distant friend.

"I'm doing a lot better now that I'm talking to you," he said.

"What time is it over there?"

Trent didn't answer Raymond's question. Instead, he started talking at a rapid pace. "Raymond, you have to come over here. This place is beautiful. Now I know why the white folks didn't want to give up power! But, man, do our brothers need help with some things. The architecture is not that modern. This junior high we're building will be one of the most modern pieces of architecture in the village. But the hotel I'm staying at, the Intercontinental, is tight. I mean it's better than any hotel we've stayed in anywhere in the States. And the place where we're building the school is called the Bopfa King Village. It's about an hour and a half from Johannesburg and get this, baby, the king of the village graduated from Howard. Make sure you tell your pops that! I know he'll be proud. And the king invited us to his compound for dinner and a wedding. Can you believe that! I'm going to a real African wedding."

"That sounds real good, Trent. I'm glad you're having a great time," Raymond said. The chill in his voice could have air-conditioned all of South Africa.

"Yeah, boy, it's just unreal, this place," Trent said, oblivious to Raymond's response. "We're going to Capetown this weekend and I hear it's even more beautiful than where I'm staying now. So how are you doing? How is Peaches? Jared? Nicole?"

"They're all doing fine," Raymond said.

"That's great. You know what's crazy? The people over here are the nicest people I've ever met and they are so interested in our culture. They seem to love African-Americans. Just the other day I was in this restaurant and they had Dru Hill blasting over the speakers. When I go to Capetown, I'm going to visit the jail at Robben Island where they held Nelson Mandela," Trent said as he stopped to finally take a breath.

"Have you talked with Trent Jr.?" Raymond wanted to remind Trent about his responsibilities back in the States.

"Yeah, a couple of times. He's doing fine. I want to bring him over here. And I want to bring you also. When can you come?"

"I don't know. This thing with Peaches is going to take a little bit longer than I expected. How long do you think you'll be there?"

"I don't know. But I can get a trip home whenever I want. And you know I have to come through New York. Maybe I'll make a trip to New York in the next week or two. I can't tell you how much I miss you. Do you miss me?"

A few seconds lapsed before Raymond said, "Yeah, I miss you."

"The only thing missing from this wonderful experience is not having you next to me when my head hits the pillow. What's going on with the confirmation? Have they set a date yet?"

"Naw, not yet."

"What's going on? There aren't any problems, are there?"

"No, not really. I'm trying not to worry about it."

"Are you sure you're all right? You don't really sound like yourself."

"What do you mean?" Raymond asked defensively.

"It's just your voice. If I was there looking in your eyes, I would be able to tell. You're sure everything is cool?"

"Not really," Raymond said. His reply surprised him. He was not ready to talk with Trent about the information Lisa had shared. But he had promised Trent to always be open and honest. Then Raymond thought, Trent had made the same promise. So much for love.

"What's up?" Trent's voice was calmer now, finally focused on what Raymond was saying or, rather, not saying.

"I don't want to go into it right now. But we need to talk real soon and this is a conversation we should have in person," Raymond said.

There was silence on the other end. After a moment Trent said, "Man, I can't believe this. What is going on? And does this have anything to do with me? With us?"

"Trent, like I said, we need to talk about this in person," Raymond said sternly.

"When? I'll catch a plane tonight. I don't like the way your voice sounds. You know you're the most important person in the world to me. This project can wait. If my baby is upset, then I'm upset."

"You don't have to do that," Raymond said. He needed to stall. He didn't want Trent showing up in New York or Seattle before he could figure out what he wanted to say to him. "Let's just look at our schedule and then plan it. What we need to talk about can wait. I'm busy and you're busy."

"Do you still love me?" Trent asked.

"Yes." His quick response surprised him. Raymond knew that if he really loved Trent, one huge mistake shouldn't destroy his love, but he also knew being analytical about it didn't stop his pain.

There was a relieved sigh in Trent's voice when he said, "I'm so glad to hear that."

"Everything will be fine," Raymond said. He had to appear strong, even though he felt tormented by the questions he had yet to ask Trent.

"Are you sure?"

"Yeah. Look, you go on out and have a nice dinner. I'll give you a call in the next couple of days," Raymond said.

"That's cool. As long as you still love me, then I'll be okay," Trent said.

"Okay, take care."

"I love you and I miss you," Trent said softly.

"Back at you," Raymond said as he placed the phone back in its cradle.

Raymond decided to have a glass of wine to mull over his conversation with Trent, but before he headed toward the small kitchen in his suite, the phone rang again. Hoping it was Jared, he picked up the phone on the second ring. "Hello," Raymond said.

"Raymond Jr.," the familiar voice taunted.

"Pops. How you doing?" Raymond asked.

"I'm not doing too good. What is this shit your mother tells me about this man you live with hurting your chances for the federal bench? You need to get rid of him right away. If this kinda shit gets out, it can not only ruin your chances for the bench but fuck up the rest of your life. What was he doing to get arrested by an undercover cop?" There was not a drop of calm or fatherly love in his voice.

"Pops, I don't want to talk about this," Raymond said.

"I don't give a damn if you don't want to talk about it. If you didn't want to talk about it, then why did you tell your mother? Now you got her worried about what kind of person you lie down with every night. If you'd listen to me, you'd kick his ass out and find some young lady who understands your problem, who'd be willing to work with you. I know a few men like yourself who have wives, kids, and successful careers. Them white folks don't want you on the bench anyhow and this will give them the ammunition they need to keep you off!" His father's words were rushed, making him sound out of breath and frantic.

Trying desperately to keep his voice soothing, Raymond said, "Pops, I didn't mean to upset you or Mama. I just needed to talk to someone, and Lisa, the lady helping me through the confirmation, doesn't think Trent's arrest is going to be a big stumbling block."

"Then both of you are the biggest fools I know living in Seattle," Raymond Sr. said as his deep voice boomed through the phone line. Raymond Jr. felt a bolt of nervousness blast through his stomach as he remained silent. He didn't understand why he was nervous instead of mad at his father's words, attacking both him and the man he loved. He knew he wasn't mad at his mother, but he was sorry he didn't think before telling her about Trent. She was still a mother and a wife. She was only trying to help her child, like any mother. It didn't help that her husband was the person she went to when she had a problem.

"Raymond Jr., are you still there? Did you hear me? Don't try that silent bullshit with me. You need to finally stand up and be a man and get that boy out of your life. You owe that to me, your mother, brother, and the millions of people who died so you could have an opportunity like this. Being on the federal bench wasn't even something my classmates and me could even dream of. And here you have it handed to you on a silver platter and you gonna let somebody who says they care for you fuck it up? As your mother says all the time, *I don't think so.*"

If Raymond didn't know his father was mad, he knew it when he used profanity. Raymond could count the times on one hand when he had heard his father use such words, but Raymond had heard enough. "Pops, I am a man and I will handle this. Trent and I will handle this. We don't need you or anyone to help us get through this. I'm only sorry this has you so upset," Raymond said calmly.

"Then prove it. And I don't want to hear about what you and Trent are going to do. Matter of fact, don't mention his name to me again. You need to do something about saving this nomination. Go to the senator's office and tell her you're getting rid of that criminal, that you've learned the error of your ways, and that you're getting ready to straighten your life out." Raymond could hear his mother in the background advising him to calm down or hang up the phone.

"Straighten my life out! Fuck that! And how do you propose I do that, Pops?" Raymond lost it. He had never used profanity toward his father or any member of his family, even when he was joking around.

"Don't get smart with me. And don't be cussing me, 'cause I'll get on a plane and dare you to do it to my face! You know damn well what I'm talking about. This is important, Raymond. Do something. Stop letting people *fuck* over you, especially black folks."

"Pops, I got to go," Raymond said.

"Go where? I'm not through talking about this," his father screamed.

Raymond didn't respond. What he did surprised him and shocked his father. He hung up the phone without another word. Raymond was able to blink back the tears of sorrow and fury that sprang into his eyes. And that made him proud.

❖   ❖   ❖

About thirty minutes after Raymond had hung up on his father, his phone rang again. Once again he hoped it was Jared, but he knew better. It was most likely his mother. By now she would have chewed his father out for his comments and would want to console her son. Raymond also knew that if he didn't answer the phone, she would call back until she reached him. Raymond figured since he wasn't going to sleep a wink, at least his mother should. But the phone stopped ringing, to Raymond's relief.

His comfort was short-lived. Two minutes later the phone started to ring again and this time Raymond answered quickly.

"Hello," he said with agitation in his voice.

"Whassup, yo?"

Raymond recognized the voice as the next-to-last person he wanted to speak with.

"Basil."

"Yeah, I told you I was going to call you. Whatcha doing?"

"Looking over some work."

"I hear tension in your voice. Are you all right?"

"I'm fine. What can I do for you?"

"Maybe the first thing is telling me what I can do for you. Let me do something to get that tension out of your voice," Basil said.

"I'm cool, but it's kinda late. Can I give you a call later on this week?" Raymond wasn't having any of Basil's seduction bullshit. Not tonight.

"Naw, you sound like you need something and I ain't trying to hear no. I know exactly what you need."

Now Raymond was getting annoyed. He knew Basil was the last thing he needed. Raymond would have welcomed the Jehovah's Witnesses before he would open his door to Basil.

"Basil, I don't think I'm interested in what you think I need. I've got to go."

"Now wait a minute. I ain't talking about that. I'm calling to invite you to the gym. Let's go work out."

"Work out? This time of night? And where are we going to do this? In your private gym?" Raymond asked sarcastically.

"I wish I had a home gym. Naw, I'm talking about a trip to World Gym. It's open twenty-four hours and it's only about six blocks from your hotel. A good workout will release some of that tension. And for the record—you're the one with the mind in the gutter, Mr. Tyler."

"But it's past midnight," Raymond protested.

"So?"

Raymond thought a minute. He knew after the phone calls with Trent and his father, sleep would be difficult, if not impossible. Maybe a tough workout would do the trick as well as a couple of drinks.

"Okay, give me the address," Raymond said.

"It's on Broadway between Sixty-fourth and Sixty-fifth and I think the address is 1926, right above the Saloon restaurant. Do you want me to swing by and pick you up?"

"Naw, the walk will do me good," Raymond said.

"Then let's say in a half hour."

"I'll see ya there."

28

Basil bounced into his doctor's office in a jovial mood.

"Wanna know why I'm in such good spirits?" Basil asked.

"Sure."

"I spent the night with Raymond," he smiled.

"And that made you happy?"

"Yeah."

"How did that happen?"

"I just called him, and to be truthful, I didn't exactly spend the night with him. The other night I was sitting at home thinking about how I could see him. I knew he'd put me off if I suggested we do dinner or anything resembling a date or an invitation for sex. Anyhow, you know how I go to the gym late at night?"

"Please remind me why you go to the gym late at night."

"Partly because it's a way to unwind after a long day, and partly to avoid all the faggots hanging around the locker room trying to get a whiff of my stuff. Some of them still show up late at night but not that many. I don't give a damn what gym you go to, they are always there." When the doctor didn't show any bewilderment at what he was saying, Basil continued. "So back to my story. I called Raymond and I must have caught him at the right time 'cause he agreed to meet me at the gym. We worked out for a couple of hours and then right before dawn we went and had coffee. We talked the whole time. Or at least I talked. He seemed to have a lot on his mind."

"What did you talk about?"

"I was telling him about some of our sessions and how I thought they were helping out. Now, before you start flipping cartwheels, I'm not sure if this shit is helping or not, but I knew that's what Raymond wanted to hear. That I might be making progress in accepting who I am. Whatever the fuck that is. I hinted that I might finally be accepting my situation, and when I worked everything out, I'd be looking for somebody permanent in my life."

"How did he react to that?"

"He didn't. He just had this blank look on that handsome mug of his."

"Did he say what was bothering him?"

"Naw, but I'm certain it has something to do with that boyfriend of his."

"How so?"

"Well, when I asked how the boyfriend was doing, he snapped at me, 'I don't talk about my partner to people he doesn't know.' It was one of those bitch moments of his I remember. But with Raymond I don't mind it like I do with the honeys and mofos like Monty. Raymond's bitch moments aren't like a woman's or Monty's. He seems more poised and in control, you know, like someone who knows they're a little bit smarter than you, but they don't want to be arrogant about it. Raymond has gained a little weight and I can tell it's bothering him, but he's still a great-looking man. I mentioned it to him and he seemed a little pissed, but I told him I could help him lose it and he really seemed interested. When gay men like Raymond gain weight, it's usually a sign that something ain't right."

"So meeting with him made you happy. Did you tell him that you're interested in him?"

"Fuck no. If he wants some of this and I know he does—Mr. Tyler will have to come for me," Basil said confidently.

"And what if he doesn't?"

"Oh, he will. But if he doesn't, then I'll have to give him a little help," Basil said slyly.

"And how do you propose that?"

"I'll just figure out a way of reminding him how sweet a piece of me can be. Maybe I'll plan a midnight swim. If the two of us get in the water together, I know he'll remember how it was when we kicked it in Atlanta. I just got to check my memory bank and figure out which one of my friends has a place in New York with a private pool. It's probably not that many."

"So you're interested only in seducing Raymond?"

"It's a good place to start," Basil smiled.

"But what about that *permanent* relationship you mentioned?"

"That was a part of the seduction. From what I know about Raymond, he's not going to sleep with me if he thinks I'm just looking for a good fuck."

"Do you think that's fair to Raymond?"

"Don't cha know, Doc?"

"Know what?"

"Life ain't fair. If it was, my mutherfuckin' uncle would be six feet under and my mother wouldn't be."

29

Yancey didn't have much time before Nicole would return to the room to prepare for the evening's performance. She rushed into their hotel room, put on the safety latch, and went into the bedroom. She dropped her gym bag on the queen-sized bed nearest the telephone and dialed Ava's number.

"Ava Parker speaking."

"Ava! This is Yancey." Yancey removed the light blue sweatband from her head, then released her ponytail.

"You sound out of breath, child! Is everything all right?"

"Fine. Everything is great. I just got in from the gym and wanted to talk to you before Miss Pretty gets back. You know, Ava, I don't know if rooming with her was such a good idea."

"Why not? How else are you going to get even with her?"

"It's just that she's always around. Like the bitch ain't got nothing to do but hang with me. Most of the cast members would die for the opportunity to spend this much time with Nicole alone, but she's always with *me*. I can't wait until next week when her husband comes to visit. I'm going to have a private room the last few days here in Detroit and then we'll have a chance to talk more." Yancey ran her fingers through her hair. She needed a shampoo and conditioning, and for once, she was thankful *Dreamgirls* had so many wig changes.

"Well, even though she's all up in your face all the time, you seem to be working it. I can't tell you how many times I've read the review you faxed me."

"I'm working them fierce and it's working everyone's last nerve."

"Including Miss Pretty?" Ava asked.

"That's the problem, everyone except Nicole! This is one seasoned diva. Whenever I get great reviews, she congratulates me with that beauty pageant voice of hers. Like she's trying to win Miss Congeniality or something. It's just so damn fake."

It was really beginning to wear Yancey out that Nicole was always so supportive and gracious. It didn't bother Yancey at all that her great reviews brought cold shoulders and looks of disdain from the other cast members. She knew where they were coming from. But Nicole, who should have been threatened by Yancey's success, was as nice as she could be. Bitch! Even when Yancey lied and told Nicole that the producers of *Chicago* were flying her back to New York to audition for the lead in the Broadway company, Nicole was deliriously happy for her. The truth was that Yancey had to pay her own way and the audition was only for the chorus. Nicole had even confided her disappointment when the same producers had turned her down because *Chicago* was a "Bob Fosse dancers' show." "But I can dance," Nicole had said. It was common knowledge among some Broadway casting agents that Nicole Springer was a singer who could act, but she had limited dancing skills.

"Where is she now?" Ava asked.

"Still working out at the gym. I know she's wondering how I can rehearse three to four hours a day, work out at the gym, and then turn it out when the curtain rises, but she's right there hanging in with me."

"So I guess she's got to work out to keep that shape," Ava said.

"I guess so, but not to worry, gravity will take care of her."

"I can't wait until she has a baby," Ava said, "then hopefully, she'll have those childbearing hips."

"That's why I'm calling," Yancey remembered. "I don't think Miss Girl was ever going to have any children. I don't think she can."

"What? Why not?"

"It's just a feeling I have. Do you know this friend of hers named Delaney?"

"Naw, never heard of her. Was she a pageant girl too?"

"I don't know, but I think they met in New York. Nicole has never mentioned her, but Cedric, one of the gay boys in the show, told me Nicole and Delaney used to be real tight. And when Cedric brought up Delaney's name in front of Nicole, well, you would have thought Miss Pretty had just seen a ghost."

"Now, I wonder what's up with that?" Ava said.

"It gets better . . ." Yancey paused dramatically, setting Ava up for the really juicy news. "It seems this Delaney person is funny. You know, a lesbo!"

"Girl, shut up! Naw! You've got to be kidding?"

"Now, tell me if I'm wrong, but I do believe there's a story there. And I intend to find out what it is."

"You don't think Miss Pretty has been bumping pussies, do you?"

"I don't know, but if she has, wouldn't it be special if you *and* Miss Delaney showed up at our dressing room one night just before a performance?"

"Darling, just tell me when," Ava said.

"First we have to find Miss Delaney. I'll see what information I can get from Cedric. He loves to run his mouth when he gets a little liquor in him."

"And I'll look through some of my old programs and see what I can find out," Ava said.

"You do that. I know we can find her. And Ava, guess what?"

"I don't think I can take any more news. What?"

"My new agent called and said some people in L.A. saw me on the *Rosie* show. They want me to come out there for pilot season!"

"That's great! Who are these people? And when are you going?"

Before Yancey could answer, she heard a knock at the door.

"Yancey?" Nicole called out. "The safety latch is on."

"She's back. I got to go," Yancey whispered into the phone. "Hold on, Nicole. Here I come, darling."

30

"I caught Raymond checking me out real serious last night," Basil said.

"How did that make you feel?"

"Damn good. It means I'm getting to him. It won't be long now," Basil said confidently. On their second outing at the gym, they had spent about a half hour going in and out of the steam room before slipping nude into the whirlpool, barely sharing a word. Every time Basil asked Raymond if everything was all right, he said yes. When Basil asked him if he was having a good time, Raymond said, "I am." The doctor listened intently to these details, nodding from time to time.

"When I took off my jock—the black nylon number I wear when I want attention, you remember that one, right—Raymond's eyes were glued to my every move, like he was in some type of trance. Yeah, all I have to do now is reel him in," Basil said.

"And what are you going to do when you *get* him?" the doctor asked.

"I'm going to sex him down so hard he'll forget about what's-his-name in Seattle."

"So you think that will help you solve some of your issues?"

"I don't have any issues, Doc. I just come here because I get to say what the fuck I want and don't have to worry about what you think. I can thank Raymond for that."

"What do you mean?"

"How many times do I have to tell you that Raymond was the one who suggested I go to therapy? And this is cool. I get to say whatever is on my mind."

"We haven't talked about your father and uncle recently."

"Don't need to," Basil said firmly.

"Are you ever going to tell your father what happened?"

"No."

"Why not?"

"Because he didn't do it. It wasn't his fault."

"I think you're avoiding something that has caused you great pain."

"But that's over. The past is the past. And my mofo uncle now knows I know. Just the thought of me bustin' him has him scared as shit."

"But you've never confronted your uncle. How does he know you remember what he did so clearly, and have you thought any more about writing him a letter?"

"I don't need to confront him or write him some stupid-ass letter. The last time I saw him, when his ass was almost dying in the hospital, I looked at him like I could just as soon kill him as look at him. Trust me, he knew what my eyes were saying. He didn't use a lot of words when he did what he did, and I don't need words either," Basil said passionately.

"When was the last time you talked to your father?"

"A couple of days ago. I call him at least once a week, at least I try to. But we never talk that long," Basil said. There was a quiet sadness in his voice. It was deep, but softer than usual.

"How does that make you feel?"

"What?"

"The length of your conversations. Would you like them to be longer?"

"No need. I find out whassup . . . tell him what's going on with me and bam, we're through. I tell him I love him and he tells me he loves me and we say, talk to you later."

"And do you love your father?"

"What kinda fool-ass question is that? Of course, I love my pops. He's all I got."

"And you're certain he has no idea what happened?"

"No, and I'm going to leave it that way. And you know what, Doc? Today you don't have to tell me time is up, 'cause I'm out of here. I got shit to do," Basil said as he leaped from the chair and headed for the door in a move reminiscent of his football playing days.

The doctor didn't even have a chance to nod before Basil was gone.

31

It was early Monday evening and Raymond and Jared had just finished a workout and swim at the hotel gym. Raymond had finished his brief routine first and was waiting for Jared in the empty steam room. The locker room was quiet with only an attendant trying to look busy folding towels.

"So I've got a little problem I need your advice on," Jared said as he walked into the ivory-tiled steam room wrapped in a towel.

"What kinda problems you got?" Raymond asked as Jared sat on the bench right above Raymond. He wanted to tell Jared he didn't *know* problems. The steam room had always been a place where Raymond and Jared talked over their problems. When the two of them had lived in Atlanta, they met at the gym four times a week before work, and even though they didn't talk a lot while hitting the weights, they always ended up sharing their joys and solving problems in the steam room. It was as though the heat loosened their defenses, as well as their muscles.

"You know, I still haven't hired an executive assistant and it's running me ragged. I mean if it wasn't for my workouts, a great friend, and a wonderful wife, I'd be running stark raving mad," Jared said.

"You haven't found anyone who fits the bill?"

"Actually I've found two, and I don't know which one to hire," Jared said as he pulled his left knee up almost to his chin.

"Tell me about them," Raymond said in his lawyerly voice.

"The first one is a sister named Connie Gamble. She's actually been with the company about five years. She completed her M.B.A. at Fordham while working full-time. Really seems to have herself on the ball. Confident without being pushy. Not married, not dating seriously, so the long hours won't bother her. Went to undergrad at FAMU and majored in engineering. And I really think we would work well together," Jared said.

"And the other candidate."

"A white guy who now works at Smith Barney. This kid is about twenty-six years old. Went to Brown undergrad and got his M.B.A. from Harvard. Sharp as a tack and great references and I got a good feel about him," Jared said. "I've interviewed him three times and he seems cool for a white guy."

"So what's the problem? Doesn't sound like you could go wrong either way," Raymond said.

"I don't know. Pick the wrong one and it could affect how my superiors look at me when it comes to my next promotion. Connie has her fans, but there were some problems with her last supervisor."

"What kind of problems?"

"When I asked her about them, she said racism and sexism. Her former boss refuses to discuss it with me, probably because I know the firm is worried about a lawsuit. If I don't offer the white guy the job, I might be accused of the same thing. Not sexism, but racism," Jared lamented.

"What's in her employment file?"

"It's vague. You know, I wonder, if she wasn't black would I even be considering her?" Jared said.

"How so?"

"Let's just say if the situation were reversed on a couple of levels. Say it was Jackson Gates, the white guy, who had the problems with a previous supervisor, then I would probably have already eliminated him," Jared said.

"Hey, boy, you know you're fair. What are you worried about?"

"I don't know. Maybe I'm worried one day I'll look around and I'll be working for Jackson Gates," Jared laughed.

"The way things are going these days, you could be working for Connie as well. That is, if you were just an average brotha, which we both know you're not. So I say go with your gut," Raymond suggested.

"I got another problem only you can help me with," Jared said with a serious look on his face.

"What's that?"

"How do I get the white folks and some of the snotty black folks to stop asking me what Chinese restaurant I work at when I'm dressed down and carrying food for my wife and me?" Jared laughed.

"Just start taking orders, but get their money first," Raymond teased.

"That's a great suggestion!"

"Hey, and you can make some extra money for Jared Jr."

"If that ever happens," Jared said quietly.

"Trust me my brother . . . it will."

"Have I told you how glad I am you're here?" Jared smiled as he stepped down from the top level of the steam room.

"That's the first time today. And I'm always happy to hear it," Raymond said.

"You ready to get outta here and grab something to eat?" Jared asked.

"I'm done, but don't you remember? I've got to meet Peaches in an hour," Raymond said, lifting his body from the slippery tile.

"Ain't this kinda late for business?" Jared said as he pushed open the glass door.

Raymond followed close behind and said, "You know Peaches ain't business."

"I know, but my mama would be in bed by this time," Jared joked. He walked over and took a clean towel from the attendant.

"Peaches ain't your average mama," Raymond laughed.

"And you know it."

"You want to go with me?"

"But you guys are discussing business, right?"

"Now, how much business you think I'm gonna be talking with Peaches after a couple of drinks?" Raymond laughed.

"In that case, I'd better pass. I've got some work to do and I don't want to miss Nicole's call after her show tonight," Jared said.

"You're really in love, aren't you, my friend?" Raymond asked as he placed his towel on a brass hanger and opened the shower door.

"You need to ask?"

Raymond glanced at the peaceful look on Jared's face and said, "That *was* a dumb question, my brother," as he walked into the shower.

❖   ❖   ❖

Raymond could hear the clatter of dishes and voices as he reached the top steps of Peaches and Enoch's apartment on the top floor of Cuts 'n' Cobblers.

The door was open, so Raymond walked in and saw Peaches talking on the phone and attending to several pots and skillets on the stove.

"Puddin', I got to go. I ain't got time for yo' mess. My baby just walked in the door. Oh yeah, don't forget to play my numbers," Peaches said as she hung up the phone.

"What's going on?" Raymond asked.

"So what did that crooked asshole say?" Peaches asked Raymond as he pulled out a chair at the small dining room table in the kitchen.

"Don't I get a hug or something first?" Raymond asked with his arms open.

"Yeah, baby, but you the one who pullin' out the chair. Don't worry, Peaches saved you some supper," Peaches said. She gave Raymond a hug around his waist. "Um, you smell good, baby. Got on some of that expensive cologne."

"Thanks, Peaches. Where is your man Enoch?"

"Who said he was my man? He's down there cuttin' heads. You know he got his regulars who always come late," Peaches said while pulling out a pan filled with pork chops covered with onion-filled brown gravy. On the top of the stove was a pot of spaghetti and another one with green beans and mushrooms.

"That food smells good," Raymond said. He pulled out a yellow legal pad from his leather bag.

"You know it's good. Look who cooked it," Peaches said as she set a chipped plate in front of Raymond. She placed a paper napkin and a set of mismatched silverware on the side.

Peaches's kitchen was a cheerful blend of function and down-home comfort. Sheer Swiss dot curtains covered the lower half of the windows that reached from one end of the wall facing the street to the other end. Enoch had attached a redwood planter to the outside of the middle window so Peaches could plant an herb garden. He had also built the floor-to-ceiling knotted-pine shelving on the adjoining wall according to Peaches's specifications. She kept the shelves stocked with every kind of can, bottle, box, and bag of food she needed on hand to create what Enoch called "her magic."

The only thing that seemed out of place was the huge white refrigerator that took up almost one whole wall by itself. A calendar for the Good Shepherd funeral home, a broom, sponge mop, and the folded-up ironing board shared the wall with what Peaches had called a "monstrosity" when it was first delivered. But she was beside herself with joy that Enoch had spent so much of his hard-earned money on her birthday present. While the fancy new refrigerator happened to have all the features that Peaches had pointed out in the mail-order catalog she kept alongside her bed, the real selling point for Enoch was the automatic ice dispenser on the outside of the door. It pleased him to no end to fill glass after glass with crescent-shaped ice cubes to demonstrate the feature to friends. In fact, Enoch had changed his favorite place at the table, from the chair facing the stove to the chair facing the big, shiny refrigerator, where Raymond now sat.

"I have some good news and bad news," Raymond said.

"I don't wanna hear no bad news. So give me the good news."

"I didn't talk to the alleged asshole, but I spoke with his lawyer. He is interested in selling the place. To the highest bidder. So that means we got a shot. But from what I get from his attorney, he knows what a prime piece of real estate this place is. A group of investors, fronted by an African-American law firm, is buying up every inch of Harlem. You were right on the money when you said Harlem is hot again."

"I sho hope that's the bad news 'cause you know I can't afford no whole bunch of money," Peaches said as she slid a pork chop onto Raymond's plate with a plastic spatula.

"I looked at the lease and had another lawyer friend look over it. All they have to do is give you ninety days' notice of their intent to sell the place. It doesn't matter what this guy's father told you or Enoch."

"Did you ask 'em why they want us out? Enoch's been here since the beginning of time. It's got to be my kids."

"No, I didn't bring that up," Raymond said as he stuck his finger in the gravy and then put the tasty sauce in his mouth.

"Then you ought to, 'cause I tell you that's why they tryin' to get us out of here," Peaches said, pulling a tin of homemade rolls out of the oven.

"I know you said that, but what makes you so sure?"

" 'Cause once, the mutherfucker who owns the place came over with his ugly ass to pick up the rent, and I was having a cup of coffee with Miss Kitty and he acted like she had leprosy or sumthin'. His father wasn't like that. And you know I know prejudice when I sees it. I was raised in the South and he acted like some of them crackers I used to run into when I was a little gal."

"Peaches, I got to ask you before we proceed. How much money do you think you can come up with, say, for a down payment?"

"How much I'm gonna need?"

"Depends on what kinda loan I can get."

"Are they gonna wanna check my credit?"

"Yes."

"Then we can forget that."

"So your credit's not good?"

"That's one way of puttin' it."

"What about Enoch?"

"You'll have to ask him. I do let him keep some of his bizness."

"Are you interested in buying this place?"

"Yeah. This is my home and what kinda fool question is that?" Peaches asked as she lifted her green and white apron over her head. She folded it neatly and sat down beside Raymond. Peaches's face was full of concern as she prepared her own plate.

Raymond took a bite of the moist pork chop and a sip of the lemonade Peaches had prepared.

"Let me see how much they want for this place and then we can pool our resources. I can talk with Jared and Nicole, and we'll do what we can to make a decent bid. I think Jared said you had a nice little nest egg with your investments. So all is not lost."

"It better not be, 'cause if I have to give up my shop and my kids . . . well, it ain't gonna be nuthin' nice," Peaches said. Then she finally sat down to enjoy her magic.

32

After spending most of the day dealing with Peaches and her pending housing problems, Raymond decided to spend the evening returning phone calls. First he called Lisa, who had left several messages for him in Seattle. He looked at the clock and realized that it was almost five in the Pacific Northwest and figured she was still at her office. Lisa picked up after a few rings.

"This is Lisa Lanier."

"Lisa, Raymond Tyler returning your call."

"Raymond! It's great hearing from you. How is everything in New York?" Her voice was full of a teenage girl's excitement.

"It's coming along. It's great hearing from you also. Have you got some news for me?"

Lisa was silent for a few seconds, then said, "Well, honestly, I don't know if you'll consider this good news or not."

"Don't tell me there are more problems." Raymond was fearful that Lisa had discovered more secrets about Trent.

"Not really. I just wanted to run this suggestion by you. And to be perfectly honest, I'm not so certain I would do this," Lisa said.

"Do what?"

"We were talking about your nomination in the staff meeting the other day, and I was letting the senator and some of her top advisors know where we stood. I told them the NAACP was backing down, but if we promised to consider what's-his-face for the next opening, maybe they would go away quietly."

"What did the senator think about that?" Raymond asked.

"She didn't say anything, but one of her advisors, and let me just preface this by saying he's a good ole boy, Seattle style. He asked if you'd be willing to disassociate yourself from Trent and make a public statement to that effect."

Raymond went into a shocked silence. He reached for the remote control on the nightstand, clicked on the power button, and instantly hit the mute button and flipped the channels. He finally settled on VH-1 when he saw a Janet Jackson video and restored the volume.

"Raymond, are you still there?"

"You've got to be kidding, right?"

"This wasn't my idea. Trust me. But I had to at least bring it to the table. Besides, there is still no guarantee that the Senate is going to even bring your nomination up this session."

"I understand, Lisa. But let me make one thing perfectly clear: I will not be making any public declarations about Trent and my relationship. What I decide to do will be a personal and private decision," Raymond said firmly.

"I understand. I'm just doing my job," Lisa said.

"I know."

"When are you coming back home?"

"In a couple of weeks." *If I still have a place I can call home,* Raymond thought bitterly.

"Then let me take you to lunch. And I promise not to talk about the confirmation or Trent," Lisa said.

"Sounds like a plan," Raymond responded.

"Take care, and I'll look forward to that lunch."

"You do the same," Raymond said. Just as he was moving the phone from his ear, he heard Lisa call his name once more.

"Raymond, you know I would never ask you to do such a thing, don't you?"

"I do, Lisa. Like you said, you're just doing your job. Now, you have a good evening and don't worry about me," Raymond assured.

"Thanks a lot. Good night."

"Good night."

Raymond was heading toward the small kitchen in his suite for a glass of wine to calm his temper, but before he reached the doorway, the phone rang.

"Hello," Raymond said.

"Whassup, my boy," Jared asked.

"Gotta be you. Are you at home?"

"Now, you know I'm still at the office bustin' my chops. I got to make sure I got everything in order before I go spend a couple of days with my baby," Jared said.

"I forgot. When are you leaving?"

"Day after tomorrow. Bright and early."

"I guess you miss Nicole," Raymond said softly.

"And you know that. I didn't realize her being on the road was going to be this hard on me. What about Trent? Are you going over to South Africa or is he coming here?"

"We haven't decided. But something gotta give soon," Raymond said.

"You sound like me. We men do have our needs," Jared teased.

Raymond started to tell Jared sex wasn't the reason he needed to see Trent, but decided against it. "So how long you gonna be at the office?"

"At least another couple of hours. I'm breaking in my new assistant, Connie."

"So you went with the sistah?" Raymond quizzed.

"Yeah, but ole Billy Bob made it easy for me," Jared said. Billy Bob was a term Jared used when referring to white men.

"You talking about the white guy you were considering?"

"That's the one."

"What did he do?"

"He took a job with a senior partner. Which means he'll probably be my boss one day," Jared laughed.

"That's life in the big city called corporate America," Raymond mused.

"And you know that. I was just checking with you since I know it's going to be late when I get in. I've got to see you before I leave."

"Just tell me when. I'll make time," Raymond said.

"Let me see how much I get done tonight and early in the morning. I'll give you a holler and let you know before noon tomorrow."

"That's cool with me. Now, don't work too hard. Remember you gonna need your energy when you get to Michigan."

"I always got energy for my baby," Jared said.

"Later, boy."

"I'll holla at ya."

This time Raymond made his way to the kitchen and was savoring his glass of wine when the phone rang. He expected to hear Peaches's voice when he picked up the phone, but instead it was Kirby.

"Whassup, playa-playa?" Kirby asked.

"Lil bro. I was going to call you."

"I had to call you 'cause you know I got this curfew thing and I have to study and get my playa points in. I'm almost as busy as my big bro," Kirby teased.

Kirby and Raymond talked about football, Kirby's new love, and their parents. When Kirby said it was time to call it a day, he asked Raymond if he would see him the upcoming weekend. Kirby mentioned he thought he was close to convincing his father that he deserved a Range Rover instead of the used Mustang he got when he graduated from high school.

"Are Mom and Pops coming?" Raymond asked.

"For sure. I think they are going to stay a week. I mean, since they've retired, Pops likes to come up and catch as many practices as he can. It's like I never left home," Kirby said.

"Then I don't think I'm going to make it," Raymond said. He enjoyed watching his little brother play or stand on the sideline, but he was not interested in a face-to-face meeting.

"Why not?"

"Me and Pops need to give each other some space. We had another falling-out," Raymond said.

"When did that happen? You guys seemed cool when you were up here for the Oklahoma game."

"It's no big deal. Pops probably needs a couple of games to cool down. Besides, I know he likes spending time with you and your football playa friends," Raymond said generously. He wanted to keep Kirby out of his disagreement with their father.

"Is it the *gay* thing?" Kirby asked with some caution in his voice. The two of them rarely talked about Raymond's sexuality. In fact, Raymond had never told his little brother he was gay, but assumed Kirby, being an honor student and all, had figured it out when Raymond stopped talking about women and had that look of love in his eyes whenever he mentioned his fraternity brother Trent.

"What do you mean the *gay* thing?"

"I don't mean anything about that. I just know Pops can sometimes be close-minded about stuff. He is from the old school of playas," Kirby explained. Raymond was amused that his little brother was trying to let him know he was cool with Trent and his living arrangement, but like his father, he wasn't necessarily interested in the details.

"Naw, it doesn't have anything to do with that. Tell Mom to give you Pops's version. Better yet, let's just leave it alone. I'll make the next game. And your message said you had something important to talk with me about. It must be important 'cause you didn't even give me a chance to return the call. What's that about?"

"It can wait," Kirby said quickly. "I'm still waiting on some information."

"What kind of information?" Raymond thought maybe Kirby was going to come to him as backup in his quest for new transportation.

"Like I said, big bro, it can wait. I've got curfew. Later, playa," Kirby said.

"You hang in there, little bro. Give the folks and the lady friend my best."

"Will do."

Raymond had another half glass of wine, then removed his pants. He was preparing for a shower when the phone rang again.

"Whassup, playa hater?"

"Basil, whassup with you?"

"Just calling to see if you're ready."

"Ready for what?"

"Our midnight workout, of course. Didn't I tell you I was going to get you back into shape before winter comes?"

"Man, I don't know. I'm kinda tired and I've had a couple of glasses of wine. Maybe we can do this tomorrow."

"Naw, man, come on. I know you might be a little bit sore, but that's the best time to work out. Besides, I put off my workout waiting on you. Now, I'm not going to take no for an answer. Do you want me to swing by and pick you up or are you going to walk?"

Raymond thought about Basil's offer for a few moments and recalled their first late night workout. It had been an eye-opening evening that turned to morning, lifting weights and talking, while enjoying the view of some of New York's finest, not to mention Basil. No matter how Raymond felt about Basil there was no denying his handsomeness. Besides, another glass of wine would cause a restless sleep and extra, empty calories.

"I'll meet you at the gym," Raymond said.

"Got my jockstrap on tight and on my way out the door," Basil said.

The thought of Basil and his ass and sex covered only by a jockstrap made Raymond smile to himself as he rushed for his warm-ups and tennis shoes.

❖   ❖   ❖

When Nicole opened her eyes early Wednesday morning, she had an uneasy feeling. Yancey wasn't in her bed and it was obvious that she hadn't slept there the previous night. During her big-sister moments like this, Nicole wished she had a prayer partner to start her day. She had thought of asking one of her female castmates, but thought they might think of it as just something older women did. She brushed off her anxiety about Yancey's absence. Besides, Nicole didn't want the cast thinking she was old-fashioned or some kind of religious fanatic. And she considered her faith a personal thing and could hear her late father saying, "Let your life preach more loudly than your lips."

The two of them had spent the previous evening with several cast members at a local cabaret located close to the theater. It was a small, dark place with a middle-aged black man named Gus playing the piano. After a few drinks, several of them took turns at the microphone belting out tunes, much to the delight of Gus and the local patrons.

It was like the *Star Search* finals. Cedric had started it with a silky version of "I Who Have Nothing." Nicole followed with a sultry version of "Someone to Watch Over Me." But it was Yancey who brought the crowd to its feet with a soulful version of the Carpenters' hit "Rainy Days and Mondays."

Just as Nicole was moving from her bed toward the bathroom, she heard the door lock turn. In walked Yancey with a neon-bright smile.

"Hey, darling. You weren't worried about me, were you? Wasn't last night wonderful?" Yancey sat down on the bed and pulled off one of her black pumps.

"Yeah, it was a lot of fun. But from that look on your face, your fun must have started when you left the club," Nicole teased.

"You got that right. I destroyed another myth last night," Yancey said proudly.

"What myth was that?" Nicole asked as she reached for the plastic pouch where she kept her toothbrush and paste.

"That all dancers and chorus boys are gay."

"Oh, honey, I knew that," Nicole said. Yancey walked to her side of the room and removed her ivory silk blouse, her two perky breasts plopping out. Nicole was shocked for a minute. She could have sworn she saw Yancey put on one of her fancy silk bras after the show the previous night.

"So are you going to tell me what happened?" Nicole asked.

"I will when I come back, but first I'm going to pull myself together and run downstairs and get us girls a couple of steaming cups of coffee. How does that sound?"

"Sounds great to me. I'll take my shower, but it seems like you're the one who needs cooling off," Nicole teased.

Yancey grabbed a *Dreamgirls* sweatshirt and pulled it over her head, still minus a bra. "We'll see who needs cooling off next week when that fine husband of yours shows up," Yancey said.

"Point well taken, Miss Yancey. One point for you," Nicole said as she headed for the shower.

About fifteen minutes later Yancey returned with two tall cups of black coffee and almond croissants. Nicole walked out of the bathroom in a hotel bathrobe with a towel wrapped around her head. "That was quick," she said to Yancey.

Yancey placed the bag of croissants on the dresser and paused before she passed Nicole a cup of coffee. "You don't like sugar in your coffee, do you?"

"Naw, if I'm going to drink it, I take it black."

"Then this is yours. I put about five packets of sugar in mine," Yancey said.

Nicole removed the lid from the coffee and inhaled the strong aroma of Colombian caffeine. She sat at the standard hotel desk and took a sip of coffee before saying, "Now, tell me what happened last night. I looked around after your fan club thinned out and you were gone."

Yancey sat on the edge of Nicole's bed and took a long sip of her sugar-filled coffee, then said, "You know Devin Richardson, right?"

"He's a dancer. And isn't he understudying one of the male roles?"

"I don't think so, but I know you've seen that body of his. Well, anyhow, after I finished talking to some of the patrons at the club, he was standing against the back wall in tight jeans, looking good enough to eat. You know, I had never really paid that much attention to him. He really has a handsome face," Yancey said.

"I agree. He's a nice-looking man," Nicole said.

"So we talked a few minutes at the club and then he suggested we go to the local IHOP for some breakfast food. He had rented a car and said he'd give me a ride after we finished. We left the club, but we couldn't find the IHOP," Yancey said. She paused and had a deep gulp of coffee. Nicole followed her lead and took two long gulps.

"Did ya'll call information?"

"I don't think he really *wanted* to find the restaurant, because Devin suggested we go to his place. He was staying in one of those residence hotels with the kitchens and said he had some breakfast food and he would cook. I looked at him and took one whiff of this sexy cologne when I felt my bra strap loosening and my panties getting moist," Yancey said as she stood up and waved her hand in the air, the other hand on her hip.

"Yancey, you didn't?" Nicole quizzed.

"I didn't what?"

"You didn't sleep with him, did you?" Nicole wasn't passing judgment, but she wanted to warn Yancey about tour relationships.

"Oh no, we didn't do no sleeping." Yancey paused and gave Nicole a comical look. "But, honey, Mr. Devin fucked your lil sister down. I ain't had service like that in a long, long time," Yancey said like it was a musical cue.

"Are you going to see him again?" Nicole felt that most of the heterosexual male cast members could spell trouble, simply because of the attention they got when most of the men were gay, and didn't want Yancey to get hurt.

"Nicole, child, please lighten up. I have somebody and Devin is still just a chorus boy. I think we were both supplying our needs."

"Just as long as you both are on the same page," Nicole advised.

"Trust me, Nicole, we're on the same page, singing the same song."

33

On the day Jared was to arrive, Yancey had a surprise for Nicole. After their morning coffee and bagels, Yancey announced she had a day of beauty planned for the two of them as a way of celebrating her getting a little something-something from Devin and the arrival of Jared.

"Yancey, how much are you spending for this?" Nicole asked when they were greeted by a uniformed driver in the circle of the hotel driveway.

"Now, Nicole, being a good Southern girl, you know better than to ask someone how much a gift is costing. I just want you to be relaxed and looking beautiful when your husband arrives," Yancey replied.

"You are too sweet, just like your coffee," Nicole gushed. She was surprised and deeply touched by Yancey's generosity.

After a short drive to Dearborn, a suburb of Detroit, Nicole and Yancey began their day of manicures, pedicures, seaweed facials, and a deep-tissue massage. They passed on the hairstyling when they didn't see any black faces at the posh day spa located at the equally posh Ritz Carlton Hotel.

"I haven't been able to trust a white lady with my hair since the Miss America pageant," Nicole said when both of them decided against getting their hair done.

"What happened?"

"Child, all my hair almost fell out after I got back from Atlantic City. This stylist permed my hair with some product I know hasn't ever seen the insides of a black beauty salon. My hair came out in large clumps," Nicole said.

"What did you do?"

"I bought me a wig and then I just cut it short. Thank God short hair ended up being popular that year!" Nicole laughed.

"So you were a trendsetter. Ahead of Halle Berry and Toni Braxton," Yancey said.

"I guess so," Nicole smiled. The mention of Toni Braxton reminded Nicole of two questions she had wanted to ask ever since meeting Yancey. Why didn't she talk about her famous cousin more often? And was she ever coming to see the show? Nicole jumped at the opening.

"Yancey, do you talk to Toni often?"

"Toni who?"

"Your cousin, Miss Girl. The one with all the Grammys and that fabulous body," Nicole added.

"Oh, you know how it is when people get famous . . . they suddenly don't have time for the little people," Yancey said as she hung her clothes in the maple locker provided by the spa. They put on thick white terry-cloth robes with cobalt-blue piping and walked to the nearby massage room for their first pampering treatment. Shortly after their massage started Nicole resumed the Braxton family conversation.

"I'm sorry to hear that," Nicole said.

"Sorry to hear what?" Yancey asked.

"You know, what you said about your cousin. Toni struck me as such a sweet person. She's always talking about her family and what have you in the interviews I've read."

"Now, don't get me wrong. I'm just saying *I* don't talk to her often. I'm sure she still talks with her immediate family on a daily basis," Yancey said.

"That's good to hear. Now, how are you girls related?" Nicole was still curious about the famous cousin, even if Yancey was out of the family loop. Yancey didn't answer because she started coughing, her throat feeling scratchy and painful, then leaped from the table to get a glass of water. She moved so swiftly it startled the massage attendant and Nicole. A few minutes later she returned, hoping Nicole had finished her little examination of Yancey's family tree.

"Are you all right?"

"Yes, I'm fine. I drank a little water and squeezed a little lemon into it and I feel wonderful. Let's go and get our lunch, then talk about what you and Jared are going to do," Yancey suggested.

"That sounds great. I can't tell you how excited I am to see him, but I must confess I'm a little nervous," Nicole said as the two of them walked toward the dining area. The hostess offered them a seat on the terrace, but not wanting to risk her voice to the early morning fall chill, Yancey pointed toward a small table in a secluded area. When they sat down, Yancey returned to their previous conversation.

"You said you were nervous about Jared's visit. Why?"

"Oh, don't get me wrong. I'm not nervous about seeing him. I can't wait. But when I talked to Jared this morning, he said he had some exciting news. Now, with Jared that means one of two things," Nicole sighed.

"What two things?"

"Either it has to do with his job, which means he's gotten some kind of promotion that might mean leaving New York, or he's unhappy with his new boss and wants to go back to Atlanta," Nicole said. "Or it could be the baby thing again. I don't know if I told you, but one of the first things Jared did when we got to New York was look up all the adoption and surrogate agencies. But I just can't get my hopes up again for a child."

Yancey looked confused at the mention of the agencies, so Nicole explained that she had lost two babies to miscarriage and had explored the possibility of hiring a surrogate.

"Have you given up the hope of having your own child? I mean your doctor didn't say it was impossible, did he?"

"No, he didn't, but after my last miscarriage I don't know if I could go through it again. And as much as Jared loves me and says he understands, I know how bad he wants a child."

"The miscarriages must have been really difficult, huh?" Yancey asked softly.

Nicole was silent for a few moments as she looked off into space and recalled her last pregnancy. Her eyes welled with tears, but she felt comfortable sharing her tragedy with Yancey.

"The last time was pretty bad. It happened only after a couple of months. I was on my way to an audition for a limited run of a Pearl Cleage play at the Alliance. About a half mile from the theater I felt an awful pain and then I noticed a pool of blood in my car, all over this yellow cashmere sweaterdress Jared had given me. The amount of blood scared me so much that I wasn't even thinking about my unborn child, but my own life. Later that evening in the hospital, with Jared holding my hands, I couldn't help but think of my reaction," Nicole said sadly.

"What reaction?"

"That I wasn't really worried about the child. I mean even though I was only a couple of months pregnant, it was still a human being. I began to think the reason I haven't been able to carry a child full-term was because subconsciously I'm not ready for a child."

"Did you tell Jared that?"

"I couldn't. But I often think about that day and how I felt. Especially when my mother and Jared and Jared's mother speak of the children and grandchildren they are looking forward to."

"What are you going to do?"

"About what?"

"I mean, are you on birth control?"

"Naw, I gave that stuff up. My mother has hinted that that might be the reason I'm having so many problems."

"I'm not trying to get personal, but does Jared use protection?"

"No. And I must tell you, Yancey, sometimes I worry more now about getting pregnant than when I was in college and trying so hard to win Miss Arkansas and get to Broadway. What about you? You are using protection, aren't you?"

"Honey, you betta believe it. Matter of fact, I made Devin put on two condoms the other night. I'm convinced he's one hundred percent hetero, but I don't need no little Devins or any STDs while I'm doing this show. Now, if it was some multimillionaire, then I might reconsider," Yancey said.

"You mean you'd give up the business for a rich man?"

"Who said I would give up the business? Honey, I'm still young. If it was the right man and the money was right, I'd take a little vacation, drop that load, and pick up right where I left off. With a rich husband in tow, show business would be a whole lot easier."

"What do you mean?"

"Well, with the kinda money I'm talking about for my future husband, I wouldn't have to audition for a show. I'd just have him produce it," Yancey said confidently.

"That would be wonderful," Nicole sighed.

"What? Having a rich husband?"

"No. Never having to audition for another show," Nicole said.

"You got that right! But you're pretty much at that level now. I mean, you didn't have to audition for this show," Yancey said as she signed the tab for lunch.

"This was different because the producers and director wanted me and had seen my work. I've still got to audition for shows, workshops, but in private, usually just before a few key people. I don't have to do any cattle calls, where every member of SAG and AFTRA are standing in line with sheet music in hand," Nicole said. She took the linen napkin and wiped her mouth.

"I look forward to that time in my career. You ready to get those nails done?"

"Let's do it," Nicole said, placing the napkin on her empty plate and gracefully raising herself from the chair.

❖   ❖   ❖

Nicole couldn't wait.

It was Saturday, and the company's last performance in Detroit. The cast would have a rare Sunday off, giving Nicole two nights to spend alone with Jared before traveling the hundred-plus miles for the Monday night opening in Grand Rapids.

Before leaving for the theater, Nicole packed her bags and had them transferred from the room she'd shared with Yancey to the suite where she hoped to be making mad, passionate love to her husband in a few short hours.

Jared arrived at the hotel a little after eight. The concierge had taken care of everything just as he'd requested. Two dozen peach-hued roses decorated the bedroom. Another dozen roses had been placed on the coffee table in the living area, along with fresh strawberries, smoked salmon, and thin triangles of toasted bread. A bottle of chilled champagne was nestled in a silver ice bucket on the wet bar.

Jared reached into a zippered compartment in his garment bag and pulled out a small bag that contained some of Nicole's favorite lilac-scented candles, which he placed on either side of the bed. Jared lit the candles and dimmed the lights to a soft, seductive glow. *Perfect,* he thought, anticipating Nicole's reaction to the romantic atmosphere he'd created. Jared had tried to think of everything. He wanted this precious time with his wife to be special, memorable. He knew that keeping their relationship tight meant never stopping the chase.

At intermission, Nicole was surprised to find a dozen of her favorite peach roses on her dressing table, along with a box from Victoria's Secret tied with a lavender silk ribbon. The card on the package read: "Call me at intermission. I've got a secret to tell you." It was signed, "The Man in Room 906." Nicole picked up the phone in the dressing room and called the hotel.

"Is this the man in 906?" Nicole responded to Jared's husky, whispered "hello." "I understand you have a secret to tell me?"

"I can only reveal the secret to the right woman," he teased. "You'll have to show me your credentials first."

"My credentials? You mean like a driver's license?"

"No," Jared said, his voice low and sexy, "a license can be easily forged. This is what you must do. Immediately after the final curtain, come to the hotel and knock just once on the door of room 906."

"And how will you know it's me? How will you know I'm 'the right woman'?"

"You must wear only the contents of the package that was delivered to you. I believe you have a black coat you can wear en route. But that's it. Nothing more. Your credentials will be evident and then, and only then, will the secret be revealed to you."

Jared placed the receiver back in its cradle before Nicole could respond. He had heard the breathless excitement in her voice and knew that his intended effect had been achieved. But the chase worked both ways, and Jared's sex was as hard as marble when he stepped into the shower.

It was all Nicole could do not to rush her lines. Her performance was more seductive than usual, fueled by her secret passion. The closing night audience was enthusiastic and showed their appreciation with not one, but three, standing ovations.

After dressing in record time, Nicole and Yancey shared a cab from the theater back to the hotel.

"Don't forget this," Yancey said as the cab pulled up in front of the hotel. She handed Nicole a flat, silver-colored box.

"Yancey, you never cease to amaze me." Nicole peeked under the lid at the nut-filled chocolate brownies.

"You didn't make these, did you?" Nicole asked.

"No, honey, even I ain't that good. A good friend sent them, but I thought maybe you and Jared could share them after you get your groove on."

"That's so thoughtful of you, Yancey. Remind me to send your friend a thank-you note." Nicole put the box in her bag and took out her wallet.

"I'll take care of the taxi," Yancey said. "You were fantastic tonight. Now, you just go along and enjoy yourself. You deserve it."

By the time the elevator reached the ninth floor, Nicole had dabbed an expensive scent behind her ears and on her wrists. She tightened the sash on her coat and slipped her stockingless feet out of her three-inch-high heels.

She followed the plushly carpeted corridor to room 906. Arriving at the room, she set her bag down beside her and placed her shoes on top. As she raised her hand to the door, her heart was pounding and her body throbbed in all the right zones. She took a deep breath and knocked once on the door.

"Who is it?" Jared asked, opening the door a crack.

"It's me," Nicole whispered, "the right woman."

"Prove it," Jared said, opening the door full, but barring her entry into the room with his muscular arms.

The sight of Jared's glistening body, covered only at the waist by a soft blue towel, sent a shivering thrill through Nicole.

"Let me in and I'll give you all the proof you need."

A young couple holding hands passed behind Nicole and giggled as they caught a glimpse of Jared in the doorway.

"I'm sorry, but you'll have to show me your credentials first."

Nicole looked anxiously to her right and to her left. The couple had disappeared around the corner and no one else was in the corridor. She loosened the sash and pulled her coat open and back, letting it slide off her shoulders to the carpet.

Jared took in every inch of Nicole's firm, curvaceous body. Her erect nipples pressed invitingly against the lace of her champagne-colored bra, and her long, smooth showgirl legs extended from the daintiest matching panties.

"Oh, yes," Jared said, "you are most definitely the right woman." He took Nicole's hand and led her into the room. He brought her coat, shoes, and bag inside and dropped them near the door.

"My mystery man," Nicole said, looking around the living room of the suite. "Everything is so beautiful!"

"You're beautiful, Nicole." Jared pulled her to him in a long embrace. His familiar clean, masculine scent excited her. He tilted her chin down and kissed her lightly on the forehead. He brushed her cheeks softly, slowly, with the backs of his hands and let his fingers slide down her arched throat to the round fullness of her breasts. Continuing down Nicole's body, Jared cupped her perfect butt in his hands and gently kissed her top lip, then her bottom lip, before parting them and entering her mouth with his tongue. They deeply explored each other's mouth until Nicole thought she would reach total satisfaction from the kiss alone.

Jared led Nicole into the candlelit bedroom. He shut the door and positioned Nicole so she faced the full-length mirror affixed to the back of the door.

"Look at yourself, baby. I must be the luckiest man in the world." Jared stood directly behind Nicole, the hair on his broad chest tickling the smooth curve of her back. His arms encircled her waist as he ran his tongue along the nape of her neck. She watched as he moved his hands slowly up her body and unclasped the front of her bra, letting her breasts fall free. He ran his fingers up and over her nipples, then back down to her hips. Nicole watched his every move. She felt like an actress starring in an erotic movie. The effect was titillating. Jared saw the pleasure in her eyes reflected back at him.

"Are you watching, baby?" he asked as he slid one hand down inside her panties and caressed her left nipple with the other. She watched as he parted the soft, downy hair between her legs and found her deep, pink, throbbing core.

Nicole moaned as Jared massaged her ever so slowly until she was slippery wet, and her moaning grew more intense. Nicole's breath was coming now in quick, short pants. Jared's fingers rubbed gently, but faster and faster as he sensed Nicole approaching ecstasy.

Nicole closed her eyes and reached behind her to hold on to Jared's hips for support.

"Open your eyes, baby," he whispered. He slid her panties down over her ankles, then knelt down in front of Nicole, between her and the mirror.

"I want you to see me do it to you." He placed his hands on her ass and pulled her to his full, wet lips. Jared ran his tongue slowly over her mound of swollen hardness, lingering at the tip until Nicole grabbed his shoulders, arched backward, and screamed his name. He thrust his tongue inside her until he felt her shudder from the release.

Jared rose and scooped Nicole up and carried her to the bed. He stood over her trembling body and announced that he was now ready to reveal the secret. He then let the pale blue towel fall, exposing his enormous erection, then said, "I'm all yours, baby."

❖   ❖   ❖

Yancey spotted Cedric in the hotel lobby and joined him for a drink in the bar before retiring to the solitude of her hotel room.

Yancey enjoyed gossiping with Cedric. They seemed to have a lot in common, like their interest in old movies and men. Cedric said his all-time favorite movie was *The Women,* while Yancey favored *All About Eve* because she loved the Eve Harrington character. And on this evening, Yancey took the opportunity to pump Cedric for information about Devin.

"Why all the questions about boyfriend?" Cedric asked.

Yancey was annoyed at herself for being so obvious. She shrugged her shoulders and looked away.

"It's okay, Miss Girl," Cedric said. "I share a dressing room with him, and I've seen the goods, not totally full frontal, mind you. Ole boy should be required to carry a warning with that fat piece he's packing! And I know he loves the ladies!"

Yancey couldn't prevent the huge grin from spreading across her face as she suddenly picked up her drink and headed to her room. She couldn't wait for Devin to knock at her door.

As soon as Yancey shut the door to her room, she removed her watermelon-pink sweater and thought how nice it was going to be to walk around the room nude without worrying about what Miss Pretty would think. She thought of possibly meeting her new fling in her birthday suit. She set her glass of wine on the nightstand and was removing her gold necklace and earrings when the phone rang.

"Hello," she said in a deep, trick-me-fuck-me voice, thinking it was Devin.

"Hey, darling, it's Ava. Did you give her the treats?"

"I sure did. I even made it look all pretty in a silver box with a big ribbon around it. Are you sure this stuff is going to work?"

"It should. There's enough Ex-Lax in those brownies to keep her running for days even if she only eats a couple of them. But if you want to be certain she won't be in any condition to perform on Monday, then put a couple of drops of that other stuff in her coffee or whatever she drinks Monday."

"That might be hard, you know. Her husband is here, so I won't be bringing her coffee in the morning."

"How long is he going to be there?"

"I think until Monday."

"But you are going to be her roommate in Grand Rapids, aren't you?"

"Yeah."

"Then give it to her Monday afternoon. Go out and get her one of those cold, flavored coffee drinks."

"Ava, this shit isn't going to kill her, is it?"

"No, but for a few hours she'll wish she were dead. In the meantime, you'll be on stage dazzling those producers."

"Oh, guess what, Ava? I heard a great rumor tonight." Yancey's voice was laced with excitement.

"What did you hear, child?"

"Well, I had a drink with Cedric in the bar before I came to my room. We're becoming good friends, you know. He's just as devious as I am. Anyway, Cedric told me that he heard from a reliable source that our director might be leaving real soon to go to Paris or somewhere to direct a new play." Yancey took a long swallow of her wine.

"So why is that good news?" Ava asked.

"Because he's the one who picked Nicole. He hasn't been feeling me at all. I mean, he's cordial enough, but he thinks Miss Pretty not only hung the moon but makes it shine as well."

"What if the new director likes her too? She has been around a long time. And Broadway is like the rest of the world—it's all in who you know."

"Well, unless it's somebody she knows, we'll be on equal ground," Yancey said.

"I see what you're saying. But if our little plan works and you go on Monday night, it won't matter who's directing *Dreamgirls.* You'll be on your way to stardom!"

"From your mouth to God's ears," Yancey said as she swallowed the last of her wine. She was confident she could not be denied if she got the opportunity to play Dena Jones just once.

"Now remember: all you need to do is to put a few drops in her drink. It's tasteless and she'll never know what hit her."

There was a knock at Yancey's door.

"Somebody's at my door, sweetheart. I'll call you tomorrow, or you can call me, since Miss Pretty won't be here."

"Good night, darling. I'll speak with you tomorrow."

"Night, Ava," Yancey said as she rose from the bed and hung up the phone. She greeted Devin at her door and took the bottle of wine and the street-vendor flowers he offered. At the sight of Yancey without her sweater, Devin's boyish grin broke into a lustful, hungry smile.

34

Early Sunday morning, before Raymond got to enjoy his first cup of coffee, or even skim the *New York Times,* his phone rang. When he looked at the clock and saw it was only 6:42, he assumed it was either Trent or his mother.

"Hello," he said, trying to sound like he had been lifted from a deep sleep. The truth was he had been awake for about half an hour, thinking about the previous evening with Basil.

"Hey, baby. I didn't wake you, did I?"

"Naw, Ma. What's going on?"

"Have you read the newspaper yet?"

"I'm still in the bed. What happened?" Raymond asked as he sat up in the pillow-packed king-sized bed.

"Kirby made a touchdown," she said proudly.

"He did? That's great. I can't wait to read the paper. I wish I'd been there," Raymond said. He was thinking this was the type of call his pops would normally make. He did it when Kirby was in middle and high school, giving Raymond the details of his brother's gridiron heroics. His mother's call was a clear sign his father was still upset with him.

"You could have been here. What did you do this weekend? And when are you going back home? And when is Trent coming home?"

"I just hung out with a friend. I'll be going home sometime this week, and I don't know Trent's schedule."

"Well, I hope you ain't going to stay away from your brother's games because of your father. You and he are so much alike. Kirby misses you. He won't make you feel guilty about it, but I will, because I'm your mother," she said.

"So what was the score?"

"They lost, but my baby was so good!"

"Tell Kirbro I'm proud of him, and I'll try to make the next game," Raymond said.

"You tell him yourself. You and your father must think I'm some kinda human Western Union," she joked.

"Is he there?"

"Who?"

"Kirby."

"No, he's not here, and I bet his little butt ain't in his dorm room either." Raymond smiled at the way his mother still called Kirby little, despite the fact he was now the largest member of their family.

"Is he at Dawn's?"

"I'd bet my retirement fund on it."

"So your little boy is now a man," Raymond said.

"What are you going to do today?" his mother asked, quickly switching the subject. Raymond smiled to himself at the way his mother didn't want to discuss Kirby's love life.

"Maybe watch a little football and take in a movie with a friend," Raymond said.

"With Jared?"

"Naw, he's in Michigan with Nicole."

"You going to church?"

"I doubt it," Raymond said.

"Now, you know you need to have yourself in church—and who is this friend you're going to the movies with? I hope it's somebody like Peaches."

"Mind your own bizness, lady. I said might, and we not gonna get into this church thing. It's much too early." For a moment Raymond thought of Sundays back in Seattle where he would be in the bed, reading the newspaper and watching Trent get ready for church. The two of them would talk about how they would spend the afternoon and make plans for dinner.

"You ain't too old for me to tap that rusty butt of yours," his mother teased.

"I got to go, Mama. I love you. Tell your husband I said whassup," Raymond said.

"You know I ain't tellin' him that, but I do love you. Save the newspaper with Kirby's name in it and send it to me. You know I keep stuff like that."

"I will and yes, I do," Raymond said as he remembered the memory book his mother sent him. "Tell Kirby I'm proud of him and I'll call him later."

"I will. Good-bye."

"Bye, Mama."

Raymond jumped up from the bed and had his early morning pee, and then, still nude, quickly opened his hotel door and picked up the thick Sunday *New York Times*. He walked back into the bedroom and located the sports section. No big headlines with "Kirby Tyler Scores Touchdown" on the front page of the section. On page eight under a column headed "Big Ten Results," Raymond read in small print, *Wisconsin 24 Northwestern 22.* He saw his brother's name and read *Kirby Tyler's 56-yard touchdown was followed by a failed two-point conversion which would have sent the game into overtime.* Raymond was turning the pages of the paper to the box score section to see how many yards Kirby had gained when the phone rang again.

"Hello."

"You thinking about me?" It was Basil. *Does this guy ever sleep?* Raymond wondered.

"Why would I want to do that?" Raymond joked.

"I was thinking about you."

"Why would you want to do something like that?" Raymond asked coyly.

"Well, not exactly about you," Basil retorted. "I was just looking at ESPN 2, and I see where your little bro scored a touchdown. They still lost, but the boy looks good. What speed!"

"Yeah, the boy is fast. I was just reading about it. So they showed him on television as well? I'll have to tell my folks," Raymond said.

"So how you feeling?" Basil asked.

"I'm cool. I'll be better after I shit, shower, and shave," Raymond laughed.

"I'll shave you and shower you."

"I think I can handle it alone." Raymond wasn't sure he could handle Basil being so flirtatious first thing in the morning. The previous night the two of them had spent the evening at the gym, then went by Basil's for pizza, where he had pulled out all the stops. First, after ordering the pizza, he made sure Raymond's wineglass was never empty. And then, although they had both showered at the gym, Basil felt the need to shower again once he reached his apartment, while Raymond drank wine and listened to Maxwell's *Unplugged* CD. After his shower, Basil walked into the living room nude, carrying some lotion and a pair of black silk low-cut briefs. He asked Raymond to rub some of the lotion on his back, and as he bent over and put on the sexy underwear, Raymond stared and stared, thinking nobody could fill out a pair of underwear like Basil.

After he finished with the lotion, Raymond came out of his mini-trance and returned the flirt by asking Basil, "Was that all you wanted?"

"That will do for now," Basil said. Then he asked, "What about your boyfriend? How long has it been since you've rubbed him with lotion like that?"

"Things aren't always what they seem," Raymond replied, something he immediately regretted saying when he saw Basil's sinister I-thought-so smirk.

"Just thought I'd ask," Basil said.

"And I appreciate that," Raymond said as he leaped from the leather sofa and announced his departure. Basil did manage a full-body brotherman hug in his underwear, but that was as far as he got. Now here was Basil, again with his sex still rock hard, no doubt working him again.

"So are we still on for this afternoon?" Basil asked, bringing Raymond back to the moment at hand.

"Maybe. Let me give you a call after I've gotten myself together," Raymond said.

"All right. If I'm not here, then page me. I gave you my beeper number, didn't I?"

"Yeah, and your cell phone and e-mail address," Raymond said.

"I get yo' point, you smug mofo," Basil joked.

"Later."

"I'll be waiting."

Raymond called room service and ordered a half pot of coffee with low-fat milk, orange juice, and a cranberry muffin. When he hung up, Raymond thought again about Saturday night with Basil Henderson. Was he playing with fire by going to Basil's apartment and seeing him almost every day? He did enjoy working out with Basil and was beginning to feel like he was losing some of the additional pounds he had gained. Raymond appreciated the time and care that Basil took to explain certain exercises and to give him a list of foods he should avoid until he had lost weight. On more than one occasion he had thought that maybe one night —or two—with Basil might be just what he needed to move on. Sleeping with Basil wouldn't help him forgive Trent, but it sure would make him forget about him, for a few passion-filled hours at least. Raymond was shocked and touched when Basil told him that he was the only man he'd ever kissed. Raymond didn't believe him, of course, but he was touched by the sentiment, nonetheless.

He had often thought, more than he wanted to admit, of the nights he had spent with Basil so many years before. The summer night they had made love in a pool under the moonlight was a memory that always moved some additional weight to his sex. Raymond recalled the dinner Basil had prepared that night and served on his wooden deck in Jersey City. When he indulged revisiting that night, he wanted to make it perfectly clear to Basil that he was in a relationship, and if they did do anything it would be mutual masturbation or something safe. No touching. No sucking. No fucking. It didn't matter how badly each of them wanted more. And even though he cringed at the thought, Raymond bet his father might accept someone like Basil as his son's partner, rather than someone who had jeopardized not only his dream job but his father's dream for his son as well.

❖   ❖   ❖

The night slipped away swiftly, and by midmorning Yancey was awakened by a flurry of soft kisses from Devin.

"Good morning, beautiful lady," he said. His voice was deep and gentle.

"Good morning. What time is it?" Yancey said as she rubbed her eyes and searched for the clock.

"It's almost noon."

Yancey leaped from the bed. "I've got to get rolling. The day is half gone."

"Relax. Did you forget we don't have a show today?"

"I know that, but I need to get in touch with Nicole so I can get a ride to Grand Rapids," Yancey said.

"Don't worry 'bout that . . . you can ride with me," Devin suggested.

"Naw, I can't do that. I promised Nicole and Jared I'd ride with them," Yancey said as she looked for a robe. She was wearing a taupe-colored silk T-shirt which was clinging to her body like a second skin. Yancey located her robe and sat at the dresser mirror to work on her hair, while Devin sat up in the bed staring at her.

"So you think we got time for one mo', before we check out of here?" Devin asked with an easy sexual assurance.

"I don't think so." Yancey smiled like an annoyed cosmetics consultant. For a moment she studied Devin's angular, unshaven face, with his well-defined mouth and round, mahogany eyes. He was not handsome, she thought, but interesting-looking in a strong, sensual way. He had a muscular, not massive, dancer's body. Yancey thought about the night before when her body had arched to accommodate his manhood, as she enjoyed the throbbing warmth between her legs.

"We might not get that many chances in Grand Rapids," Devin said.

"Why not?" Yancey asked as she started to brush her hair.

" 'Cause you're going to be back with Nicole and I'm going to have a roommate. You know how long this show is going to last, and I've got to save the Benjamins for rainy days," Devin said.

"You have a point there, but don't worry, mister-mister . . . I can get rid of Miss Pret—I mean Nicole, when I want to," Yancey said.

"So you ladies got a system?" Devin asked as he watched how Yancey's arms rose gracefully as she pinned her hair back.

"Yeah, we got a system. I just tell her I've got to take care of some personal needs. She might be square but she ain't dumb."

"You two get along pretty well?" Devin asked.

"I guess so. It's not like I'm going to move in with her once we get off the road, but I know I can learn a lot from her."

"Yeah, she's been around awhile, and she's very, very talented. I saw her in *Jelly's Last Jam* and in a show that never made it out of workshop called *To Tell the Truth.*"

"And was she good?"

"From what I can tell. I mean, I think she was nominated for a Tony one year, but she didn't win. She has the reputation of being a real trouper. The kinda girl who comes in and takes over when the divas move on."

"How many shows have you been in?" Yancey asked. She thought she might as well learn a little bit more about the man who brought her such sexual pleasure.

"Three Broadway shows—*Five Guys Named Moe, Smokey Joe's Café,* and *Tap Dance Kid*—and the national company of *Miss Saigon.* Seems like just when the unemployment checks are 'bout to run out, something comes along. What about yourself?" Devin asked.

"I was born to do this. You could say it's in my blood, and it's all I've ever wanted to do," Yancey said.

"I guess you've got big plans for yourself. What . . . winning a Tony and an Oscar?"

"You forgot the Emmy and Grammy, sweetheart. Trust me, I plan to have my name on each one of them before I leave this earth. I'm also going to be on the cover of *Essence, Ebony, Vogue,* and, of course, on the cover of *People* magazine's Fifty Most Beautiful People issue," Yancey said confidently.

"So Miss Yancey got it all planned, just like the great Miss Dena

Jones," Devin said, referring to the character in *Dreamgirls* Yancey felt she was destined to play.

"I sure do. But unlike Dena, I'm not going to let a man get in my way. I ain't looking for a Curtis Taylor, Jr. How did you get into acting and dancing?"

"Literally by accident," Devin said. He decided he wasn't going to get Yancey back into bed, so he stood up and searched for his underwear.

"Accident?"

"Yeah, I ran track in high school and played baseball. Got hurt training. Took a dance class as part of my rehabilitation and found out it was a great way to meet ladies," Devin said. He reached down and pulled his boxers out from under a blue-flecked bedspread.

"So all the gay guys don't bother you?"

"Not at all. I let them know right up front what's what, and they leave me alone. I love being one of the few roosters in the henhouse," Devin said slyly. Yancey noticed the trace of a smile touch his eyes as he pulled his jeans up and moved toward the dresser, where she was still sitting, preparing to put on a rose-colored lipstick. No matter how great Devin was under the sheets, she thought, after his last comment, she would make him wait a long time before he got back into *her* henhouse.

"I guess you want a kiss before you leave?" she asked.

"Would that be asking for too much?"

"Could be . . . could be not," Yancey said with a slight chill in her voice.

Devin rubbed his hands together and asked if that was a yes or a no. Yancey stood up dramatically and said, "I'd love to kiss you, Devin, but I've just combed my hair."

❧　　❧　　❧

Nicole was scraping seeds off a sesame bagel when she realized that after a weekend of lovemaking and just enjoying her husband's company, they hadn't spent much time talking. "Baby, what was the exciting news you had?"

"Damn . . . I forgot to tell you," Jared said.

"Tell me what?" Nicole asked, spreading grape jam over the toasted bagel.

Jared took a sip of his orange juice and said, "I got a call from a surrogate agency, and they think they've found a match." His voice was suddenly excited and anxious.

Nicole took a sip of her coffee and asked with a strained smile, "They found somebody black who's willing to carry our baby?"

"Not exactly. But she's not white either," Jared joked. He noticed the stress in his wife's face.

"She's not black . . . not white. What then?" Nicole asked.

"She's Hispanic, but I think she might have some African-American roots," Jared said.

Nicole didn't respond. She took another bite of her bagel as an awkward silence filled the room. Nicole was thinking of some of the beautiful Hispanic women she saw in New York, with their thick, curly black hair, olive-colored skin, and big eyes. Women who were beautiful, but who didn't look like her. If there was going to be a surrogate, Nicole wanted her black!

"Are you all right?" Jared asked.

"I'm fine. I'm just thinking about how our baby would look," Nicole said softly.

"It will look like us and it will be beautiful," Jared said with assurance in his voice.

"But is now the right time? I mean, my career is just taking off again."

"I know, and I've thought about that. But you won't always be on the road. I mean, if this show doesn't come back to New York, then there will be other work for you. And if push comes to shove, we could always hire somebody to help out."

"So you've got it all figured out," Nicole said.

"Now, Nicole, you know for something like this, we have to both agree. I mean, I don't even know if this young lady is going to work out. It's just an option. I asked the agency to send me some more information, and when you get back home, we'll meet her and take it from there," Jared said. He reached for Nicole's untouched glass of orange juice and finished it with one long swallow. Nicole was thinking about what to say next when the phone rang. "Hello," she answered.

"Hey, darling, you been having a good time?" Yancey asked.

"Yancey, are you all right?" Nicole asked. She thought she detected a sadness in Yancey's normally perky voice.

"I'm fine, but I've missed having you as my roommate," Yancey lied.

"That is so sweet. How was your time alone?"

"I wasn't exactly alone," Yancey said.

"Devin?"

"You got it, honey."

"Is that getting serious?"

"Pleeze . . . not on your life. I've got work to do. Have you guys had your morning coffee?" Yancey asked.

"Yes, darling, we ordered room service. It's not as good as the coffee you've been bringing me every morning."

"Do you want me to bring you guys some?"

"No, that's all right, we've both had enough. How are you getting to Grand Rapids?"

"That's why I was calling. Is Jared still planning on driving you?"

"I think so," Nicole said.

"Can I get a ride? I mean, if it's not asking too much. If you two want to be alone, I'd understand."

"Don't be silly. Jared and I would love for you to ride up with us," Nicole said as she looked at Jared, who was making a funny face and moving his head from side to side like he was dancing.

"You're sure now? 'Cause I could ride with Devin or Cedric or I could be really country and ride the bus," Yancey said. Jared was now putting his underwear on his head and doing his Stevie Wonder imitation, which always made Nicole laugh.

"You're riding with us. I'll call you when we decide what time we're leaving." Nicole laughed.

"What are you laughing at?" Yancey asked.

"You'd have to be here. I've got to go," Nicole said. She hung up the phone and rushed toward Jared, pulled the underwear off his head, and gave him a big kiss that led to another session of passionate lovemaking.

35

When the cast of *Dreamgirls* arrived in Grand Rapids, the city was damp and drizzly. That afternoon a fierce rain came and moved through the downtown area as though it had been prearranged. Rainy days and Mondays . . .

Nicole was missing Jared and adjusting to yet another convention center hotel attached to the theater where they would be performing. Jared had rented a car and drove her and Yancey to Grand Rapids and then drove to Chicago and caught a late flight to New York on Sunday night. Nicole was putting some clothes in the dresser drawers when Yancey walked in with two cold specialty coffee drinks in a cardboard carrying case.

"Honey, you'll never guess what I just saw," Yancey said as she carefully positioned the drinks on the desk. She had already sipped half of one of the drinks and gave Nicole the one filled to the brim.

"Thanks a lot. I can never get enough caffeine," Nicole said. "What did you see?"

"Before I went to get our afternoon pick-me-up, I stopped at the gym, and there was this overweight lady walking on the treadmill in heels and a skirt! Now, if that don't tell you how country this city is, then nothing else will," Yancey laughed.

"I kinda enjoy playing a town this size. You can rest assured that we will have full houses every night and standing ovations will be the norm. These people are so happy to see a Broadway show, and they're not as jaded as New York crowds," Nicole said. She sipped the cold coffee drink.

"You don't have any more of those brownies I gave you, do you? I'm kinda famished," Yancey said.

"No, honey, those things were good. And so is this. I ate two of them Sunday, and Jared had a couple also. But I need some real food. The restaurant looked interesting. Maybe we can go down and have some fruit or a salad before we have our walk-through," Nicole suggested.

"Yeah, that sounds good. What time are we supposed to be over there?"

"Four o'clock. I don't think we'll be there that long," Nicole said.

Yancey looked at her watch and said, "Then I think I'll take a quick shower. How are the towels? Are we talking Holiday Inn or Four Seasons?"

"I think something in the middle," Nicole said. Then she finished the last of her drink.

Shortly after Yancey went into the shower, the phone rang. Nicole was hoping it was Jared, saying he had arrived safely back in New York, but it was Dennis, her agent.

"Hello."

"Nicole, how you doing?"

"Dennis, I'm okay. Ready to get back to New York, but I'm good," Nicole said as she sat on the bed.

"Are you nervous?"

"Nervous about what?" She thought this was a strange question, since Dennis knew she could now play Dena Jones in her sleep.

"Didn't you get my message?"

"What message?"

"That some of the producers of *Dottie* are going to be at the show tonight, checking you and some other people out. I think they finally got the backing they need and they plan to bring the show to Broadway before the Tonys next year."

"Did you leave the message with Jared?"

"No, I think I spoke to your roommate in Detroit. She didn't tell you?"

"No, I don't think so. This is great news. But why on earth would they come to Grand Rapids?"

"It's funny. I think one of the moneymen is a big Amway guy. And I think Grand Rapids is the headquarters for Amway and he has a lot of family there. You know moneymen—cutting corners any way they can."

"Well, that's great news. I was telling Yancey how the crowds will probably be great. They're even doing an opening night party," Nicole said.

"Knock 'em dead, which I know you will. I'll let you know what I hear," Dennis said.

"I'll be waiting. Are they going straight to Broadway, or are they going to do a tryout in Boston or somewhere?"

"From what I hear, they're going to do a short workshop and then they're heading to the Great White Way."

"That could be both good and bad," Nicole mused aloud.

"I heard another rumor. Is there any truth that you guys are going to get a new director?"

"There have been some rumblings, but we haven't heard anything definite."

"Well, I heard it's going to happen—and real soon. I'm told the producers are bringing in an African-American director," Dennis said.

"I guess we'll see soon enough," Nicole said.

"Any way it goes, you'll be fine."

Nicole looked at her watch as Yancey walked out of the bathroom, wearing an eggshell-white hotel robe and a towel wrapped around her head. "Dennis, thanks so much for calling, but I've got to run. I want to get something to eat before I'm due at the theater."

As Nicole hung up the phone, Yancey removed the towel from her head and started massaging her hair. "Was that the hubby?" she asked Nicole.

"No, that was my agent, Dennis. Did he call me when we were in Detroit?" Nicole asked.

Yancey paused for a moment and a quizzical look crossed her face like she was thinking really hard. "What's his name?"

"Dennis Hopkins," Nicole said.

"Yeah, he did call. I forgot. I don't know where you were since we're together so much, but he did call. I'm sorry," Yancey said.

"Oh, that's all right, but he gave me some good news," Nicole shared.

"What? Are we on our way to Broadway?" Yancey asked, fully aware of why Dennis had called.

"It looks like they got the money to do the show *Dottie,* and some of the producers are going to be here tonight to check me out," Nicole said proudly.

"That's great. But for which role?"

"Dorothy, I hope," Nicole said.

Yancey was quiet for a moment and then asked, "Wasn't Dorothy Dandridge mixed?"

"No!" Nicole snapped. "Both of her parents were black. As a matter of fact, her mother was real dark. Even darker than me. She was also an actress who played a lot of roles as a domestic."

"Oh, I'm sorry. I didn't mean anything by that. I just remember looking at the cover of the book about her you were reading. And she kinda favors Halle Berry."

"She favors Janet Jackson as well, and we both know both her parents are black," Nicole said.

"Well then, they have to be considering you for Dorothy. Why else would they come to Grand funkin' Rapids to see you? And what other female leads are there?"

"There is the role of her sister," Nicole said.

"What about her mother?" Yancey asked.

"They better not try to offer me that role. I ain't ready to play nobody's mama."

"I know that's right," Yancey laughed, and gave Nicole an airborne high-five slap.

"Let me check my face and then let's go and get something to eat," Nicole said.

"Okay. What are you going to wear?" Yancey asked as she walked over to her side of the closet and touched a light blue cashmere sweater, wondering if it was cool enough to wear it.

"What I have on," Nicole said. "It's just a check-out-the-theater thing."

"That's not what I heard," Yancey said, pulling the sweater off the wooden hanger.

"What did you hear?"

"I ran into Cedric when I was at the coffee shop and he said we're in for a big surprise this evening."

"What did he say?"

"I think Dan is out as director. I heard they're bringing in somebody black. And ain't nobody seen hide nor hair of Dan since the last show in Detroit. For all we know he might already be out of the country."

"I hope that's not true. I love Dan," Nicole said as she brushed some loose hairs back into place.

"I like him too, but maybe we need some new blood in this show," Yancey said.

"Like my daddy used to say, if it ain't broke, don't fix it," Nicole said. She pressed her lips together and decided she needed a new layer of lipstick.

Yancey started to tell Nicole that there were a lot of things wrong with the show, like the fact that she wasn't playing Dena. But Yancey decided Nicole would learn soon enough.

❖ ❖ ❖

Yancey and Nicole were running late for the cast walk-through of their first performance at the Devoss Theater. They'd had a light but filling dinner at the hotel restaurant, but skipped the coffee to get back on time.

It was 5:30 P.M. by the time the cast toured the theater and made minor adjustments to key scenes to fit the new stage.

Nicole, Yancey, and two other female cast members shared a dressing room that included a brightly lit, mirrored row of dressing tables along one wall and a water cooler, wet bar, and chaise lounge against the opposite wall. Their costumes hung on a circular rack at the far end of the room near the two-stall rest room.

A fresh carafe of coffee brewed on the wet bar's counter, next to an open chest of colas and fruit drinks.

Nicole placed her makeup bag on the dressing table in front of the middle chair.

"Mmmm," she said, "that coffee smells wonderful. Anyone else want a cup?" She walked over to the wet bar and took a Styrofoam cup from the stack on the counter.

"Wait!" Yancey yelled. She jumped up from her chair and rushed over to Nicole. "Let me get that for you. I brought some mugs from Detroit. You don't know where those cups have been."

"Thanks, Yancey. You're so sweet, and these cups do look a little dusty," Nicole said as she returned to her seat and began removing makeup from her bag.

With her back to the dressing tables, Yancey pulled out the mugs and a tiny eyedropper from her large black satchel. She took a quick glance over her shoulder, then added three drops of a clear liquid to the empty mug and poured hot coffee into it. Yancey then poured herself a cup and made sure she filled it with cream, and placed it in her left hand. "Here you go, darling," Yancey said, and placed the mug from her right hand in front of Nicole.

"Thank you, darling." She took a small sip. "Mmmm, this is good and hot," she said.

While applying their makeup, Nicole and Yancey talked about the previous weekend, and whispered to each other when discussing the producers who were going to be in the audience. Yancey had suggested that the other cast divas didn't need to know that important producers were casting a new musical.

About thirty minutes later, with their makeup and coffee completed,

Yancey and Nicole started to put on their costumes for the opening act. While Yancey was zipping up Nicole's dress, Nicole felt a wave of nausea roll from her stomach to her throat. She fought back the urge to vomit and the nausea seemed to diminish after a few moments.

"Nicole," Yancey asked, "are you all right? I didn't zip you too tight, did I?"

"I'm okay, thanks. And no, you didn't zip me," she smiled. Nicole returned to the mirrors to make sure her makeup was in place, and while touching right under her eyes, her hands felt shaky.

Yancey watched her in the mirror and looked truly concerned. "Are you sure you're okay, darling?"

Another wave of nausea hit at the same time a violent abdominal spasm doubled Nicole over. She grabbed her stomach and rushed to the rest room.

Yancey waited a few moments, then went in to check on her. She could hear Nicole groaning behind one of the stall doors.

"Nicole? What is it? Are you sick?" she said with a touch of alarm in her voice.

Nicole opened the stall door and stood bent over, bracing herself against the door frame. "I think it must be something I ate," she said weakly. "Maybe it was the smoked salmon Jared and I had."

"Oh, Nicole, you look terrible. Poor baby. Come lay down. I'm going to get Vincent." Yancey helped Nicole to the chaise lounge and the other women crowded around, trying to make Nicole comfortable. During the commotion, Yancey took the eyedropper from her bag and went to find the stage manager. She didn't want to leave any evidence of her bad deed around.

When they returned to the dressing room, Nicole was feverish and tiny beads of sweat formed on her forehead and across her upper lip. Vincent felt her blushing cheeks.

"My God, Nicole, you're burning up!" he said. "Do you think you can go on? It's almost a half hour before curtain."

Nicole sat up and struggled to her feet. "I've got to get to the rest room quick," she said. The other two cast members took her arms and walked her to the rest room just in time.

"I'm calling a doctor," Vincent said. "Yancey, do you know the number to the hotel?"

"No, but I can get it," Yancey offered.

"No, don't worry, I'll get it. You need to change costumes. You're going to play Dena Jones tonight!"

Vincent hurried out of the dressing room, leaving Yancey alone in front of the bank of mirrors.

"I *am* Dena Jones," Yancey said to herself, smiling broadly at her own reflection.

❧   ❧   ❧

Yancey located a bank of phones outside the ladies' room at the Amway Hotel. She had finally managed to escape a group of local well-wishers at a festive party being given in honor of the *Dreamgirls* company. Yancey looked around to see if any of her castmates were in the area before dialing Ava's number.

"Hello," Ava answered.

"It's me, and I can't talk long," Yancey whispered.

"Where are you?"

"I'm at the hotel, at a party a group of sororities is giving the cast, but I had to tell you what happened," Yancey said excitedly.

"Tell me. Did my little care package work?"

"Like a charm! Right before the show Miss Pretty got sick as a dog. She was sweating, and from what I heard she was hugging the toilet in more ways than one, but I think she's okay. The stage manager called a doctor and he said it was probably food poisoning or something. She's up in the room now, sleeping."

"So you got to go on as Dena?"

"You got that right. And guess what? We did get a new director, and he was in the cast of *Dreamgirls* when Nicole was." Yancey smiled at one of the ladies going into the rest room.

"Is that going to be good or bad for you?" Ava asked, sounding a bit concerned.

"I think it's going to be good, because Nicole was not happy when she found out who the new director was. When I asked her why, she told me that Chris, that's the director's name, was upset with her when she didn't accept a role on the first national tour. It seems she kept him waiting and then decided not to do the show," Yancey said. She had stopped whispering because the area near the phones was empty.

"So how did it go? Did you sing them up out of there?"

"It was glorious! When I came out and took my bow, the audience started standing up. They went wild! I mean, it almost brought me to tears. I got almost as much applause as that dreadful child who plays Effie."

"Oh, I wish I had been there," Ava said.

"I wish you'd been there too. It was just magical. The gowns looked marvelous on me. I hit all my marks, didn't miss one line, and I sang and acted my ass off," Yancey boasted.

"How long you think Miss Pretty is going to be out?"

"I think only a day or so. But you can bet your last dollar that after hearing me tonight, Nicole will not miss a single performance. You might need to send me some more of that magic potion," Yancey laughed.

"Does she know how well you did?"

"I think so, because she was in the rest room close to the dressing room during the first act and half of the second act before they carted her ass back to the hotel," Yancey said. She noticed Monica Evans, one of the members of the chorus, walking toward the phones. Yancey smiled and gave her best fake wave, then turned her back toward Monica.

"I've got to go," she whispered into the phone. Suddenly she felt someone touch the back of her shoulder. Yancey turned to find Monica standing right behind her.

"You were fierce, girl! Just awesome. You blew them out of there," Monica said.

Yancey told Ava to hang on for a minute as she turned to hug Monica and say, "Thank you so much."

"And I heard the reviews are going to be good," Monica said.

Yancey raised her eyebrows and smiled. She had forgotten that in cities where they stayed less than a week the reviewers came out the first night. "I hope you're right," she said.

"Let me get in here before I burst," Monica said, pointing toward the ladies' room.

"Okay, thanks again," Yancey said, and returned the phone to her ear. "Ava, I gotta go. Thanks so much. I never could have done this without you."

"Yes, you could, but we ain't finished yet. We've got to make sure you're Dena when the show hits New York," Ava said.

"Good night, darling. I'll talk to you when I can."

"Good night, baby, and congratulations."

Yancey hung up the phone, took a deep breath, and let out a satisfied sigh.

36

The Harlem fall morning was clear, with a crisp chill in the air. Just as Raymond reached for the door of Cuts 'n' Cobblers a fast-moving Peaches came out carrying a large brown paper bag with both hands. She moved past him purposefully, as if she were the drum majorette for the FAMU Marching 100.

"I thought I was goin' to miss you. Come on, you going with me. We can talk about my bizness in the cab," Peaches said.

"Where are we going?" Raymond asked as he followed Peaches to the curb and waved his hands in the air, signaling a taxi. There were very few yellow cabs still in Harlem, but after a few moments, a steel-gray Buick pulled over. Raymond looked a bit apprehensive, but Peaches didn't blink as she turned toward Raymond and said, "What you waitin' on? Open the door for me."

The cab smelled of aromatic tobacco. The driver was a robust black man with a gray and black conductor's cap on his head, a smoking pipe dangling from his mouth.

"How much you charge to take us to 143rd and Lenox?" Peaches asked the driver.

"Seven dollars," he said in a mild Haitian accent.

"Seven dollars, man, you crazy! You know it can't be no more than four dollars. Five tops! Now, do me and my friend have to git out at the corner or are you gonna act right? You ought to be ashamed of yourself, trying to take money from honest, hardworking folks."

The driver took the pipe from his lips and pointed the stem at Peaches.

"What you say? I *am* honest, hardworking folks! Who you been paying five dollars, lady? I'll make it six, but you know you ain't right."

"Five dollars or me and my friend get out right now."

"Mon dieu," the driver muttered under his breath.

"Peaches, don't worry about it, I got it. But where are we going?"

"You can pay it, but you ain't gonna pay no more than five dollars," Peaches said as she met the Haitian's glare in the rearview mirror. "And we're headed for Miss Kitty's house."

"Sir, you heard the lady. Put out your pipe, please, and get us there safely, and I promise you a nice big tip," Raymond said.

"You ain't said nuthing but a word," the driver said as he tapped the contents of the pipe out in the ashtray.

Raymond gave him a wink and then turned to Peaches to ask her again where they were going.

"Up to Kitty's house. You know, one of my chil'ren. She ain't feeling too good and I promised to bring her some food," Peaches said.

"Is this how you've been delivering food?"

"Not usually. I have some helpers. I cook it and they drops it off to some of the peoples who can't come by and pick up their meals. But Kitty is special, and I think some of my cabbage and ham hocks is just what she needs," Peaches said.

"Is that what you've got in that bag?"

"Yep, and some sweet potatoes and a baked chicken," Peaches said proudly.

"Now, who is Kitty? I haven't heard you mention her."

"Yes, I have. You'll love Miss Kitty. I thought I had told you about her, but I guess that was Nicole. She and her little show bizness friend met Miss Kitty. She's a translation," Peaches said.

Raymond took in every detail as the cab moved up Lenox Avenue. He had spent many a Sunday attending church in Harlem and remembered the delicious meals he had eaten at Harlem institutions like Sylvia's and Copeland's.

"Now, Peaches, what on earth is a translation?" Raymond asked as he studied the people and buildings like it was his first visit to Harlem.

"You know, she's a woman now, but she wasn't born that way. And I guess she's a woman, 'cause I ain't seen her stuff," Peaches laughed. "I guess what we see now is the remix version of Miss Kitty."

"You mean Kitty is transgender?" Raymond's voice was careful, his tone measured.

"Trans . . . what? What kinda word is that? We both might find out what she is if we have to bathe her," Peaches said.

Raymond began to feel moisture on the back of his neck. He was nervous about meeting Miss Kitty. It was one of those things he still had a problem with, mainly because he didn't know what to do or say when it came to the transgendered people he met, which weren't that many. When he went to gay bars, he managed to avoid conversations with them, unless they were the bartender. Now he faced the possibility of assisting Peaches in bathing one.

"Five dollars, sir," the driver said.

"What?" Raymond asked, coming out of his minitrance. He looked to his right and saw a red-brick, three-story walk-up next to a small grocery mart and a junk-filled vacant lot, followed by a continuous row of brick buildings, none higher than five stories.

"Pay the man, Raymond. Miss Kitty lives right there," Peaches said, moving her head slightly to the right.

Raymond pulled a ten-dollar bill from his wallet and handed it to the driver.

"Keep the change," he said.

"Merci beaucoup." The driver nodded toward Peaches, who was already halfway up the steps. "She tough, that one, no? She remind me of my own dear mother. Tough, but big heart, no?"

"Yes, sir, she has a really big heart," Raymond said as he exited the car and ran to catch up with Peaches.

She turned around and said, "If you got so much money to throw away, then maybe *you* should buy the place."

"Speaking of, when are we going to talk about your business? How long are we going to be here?"

"As long as Miss Kitty needs us. And let me warn you if you thought Kyle was a mess, well, you ain't seen nuthin' yet," Peaches said as she passed the bag of soul food to Raymond and searched her purse for keys.

"What are you looking for?"

"Kitty's keys."

"You have apartment keys to the clients you serve?" Raymond asked incredulously.

"They ain't clients. They my kids. They trust me, and I trust them," Peaches said. She located a ring with several keys.

Raymond thought how committed Peaches was to the work she had started; the work he had promised Kyle he would support. But what kind of support had he given? A check now and again, versus the hands-on approach Peaches managed daily. He was brought up knowing that he owed his community much more than an occasional check. He could hear his father's voice saying, "You've been lucky, Raymond. And you know that to whom much is given, much is expected."

"I'm so glad this chirl lives on the first floor," Peaches said as they entered a tiny tiled foyer. To the right was a stairway with badly worn carpet, leading to the upper floors. To the left was a maple door with tarnished brass numbers nailed to it that read "101." Raymond noticed a stack of newspapers next to the stairs and a rust-colored wastebasket that held two umbrellas. Peaches placed a key in the door, turned it, then stopped. She looked at Raymond and said, "Brace yourself, child, you'll live through this."

"I'll be fine," Raymond said.

"You'd better be." Peaches smiled, then opened the door and called out, "Miss Kitty. It's me, your fairy godmama, Peaches."

Raymond took a deep breath, exhaled loudly, and followed Peaches Gant, fairy godmama, into another world.

Peaches moved quickly once inside. She took the bag of food from Raymond and went straight to the tiny kitchen separated from the rest of the apartment by a wood-beaded curtain. She placed the food on the counter and turned the oven on. She turned on the spigots over the enamel sink and searched the cabinet under the sink for dishwashing liquid. Peaches hummed a gospel tune as she moved briskly about, heating the food and washing the dishes. She emerged back through the curtain of beads some minutes later to find Raymond still standing just inside the front door, looking about nervously.

"Raymond, baby. What are you doing—waiting on an engraved invite? C'mon in and sit down." The room was dark and stale. Peaches walked over to the heavy drapes behind the sofa and pulled them open, letting a stream of bright sunshine into the room. Although the room appeared well kept, the light exposed a thin veneer of fine dust on the glass-topped coffee table and the hanging plants in front of the window.

"Give me a hand with these windows, Raymond. They always stuck!"

Raymond crossed the polished hardwood floor to the sofa and forced both windows up. He gulped fresh air into his lungs as though he'd been holding his breath, then sat down on the sofa.

Peaches knew that the stuffy, sickly air reminded Raymond of Kyle's last days. She had felt the same way the first time she visited Miss Kitty. She sat next to Raymond on the sofa and patted his knee.

"It's okay, baby. Peaches knows. You collect yourself and I'll go see if Miss Kitty is awake and presentable so you can meet her."

Raymond loosened his tie and tried to relax. He leaned his head against one of the starched lace doilies that hid the worn spots on the rose-colored sofa's cushions and armrests.

The room was Goodwill chic. The sofa and matching overstuffed chair, the ashwood end tables, the glass lamps, were all in good condition, but clearly recycled. But here and there, Miss Kitty had added cheery splashes of color. There were bright orange throw pillows on the sofa, and red, pink, and teal-blue scarves hung from a wooden coatrack near the front door.

A large steamer trunk that sat against the far wall boasted plump fuchsia cushions on top. The wall behind the trunk was covered with framed photographs. Some appeared recent, while others, Raymond surmised, were "pre-Kitty" photos. The most striking was of a somber-looking boy holding the hand of a tall, thin, brown-skinned man with a stingy-brimmed hat tilted rakishly to one side.

Raymond was listening to the soft sounds of gospel music coming from the bedroom when the door suddenly opened.

"Come on in and meet the lady of the house," Peaches said.

Raymond searched Peaches's face for some clue as to what awaited him on the other side of the door.

"Come on," Peaches said, "she don't bite!"

A large four-poster bed dominated the tiny bedroom. The only other furniture in the room was a nightstand covered with all shapes and sizes of prescription medicine bottles and a long chest of drawers with four Styrofoam heads on top. Three of the heads flaunted differently styled and colored wigs. Someone had drawn faces on each head. One smiling, one frowning, one laughing, and one coquettish-looking face with lips puckered up for a kiss. The frowning head was bare.

"Miss Kitty, I would like for you to meet my dear friend Raymond Tyler."

Miss Kitty was propped up on peach-colored satin sheets under a mauve comforter. A box of tissues lay alongside something Raymond hadn't seen in years: a pink Princess phone with a rotary dial!

Miss Kitty did not look well. She seemed sunken into the red kimono robe, and the frowning-face auburn wig now atop her own head was off center. Her eyes were dark brown and solemn.

Her voice and mannerisms, however, were strong and brash.

"Raymond, is it? It's absolutely divine to make your acquaintance. Peaches has told me so much about you. She said you was good-looking, but she didn't say you were phine, baby," Miss Kitty said as she tapped the bed with her ruby-red polished nails. "Please. Do have a seat."

Raymond looked nervously around the room, to no avail, for another place to sit. "Here, sit here," Miss Kitty said, patting her bed.

"I can stand," Raymond said as he tried to manage a friendly smile.

"Well, suit yourself. I hear you're going to help Miss Peaches save her place," Miss Kitty said.

"I'm doing my best," Raymond said.

"I just think they want her out so they can git rid of people like me. But they don't know who they fuckin' with, do they, Miss Peaches?" Miss Kitty said as she looked at Peaches.

"You got that right," Peaches said. "You feel like eatin' sumthing, baby? I made some ham hocks."

"Yeah, make me a little plate while I sit here and talk to this man. I can't tell you the last time I had a man in my boudoir, but that's what got me in this mess anyhow." Miss Kitty laughed.

"Are you taking the new drugs?" Raymond asked.

"Yeah, baby, I am when I can git 'em. They so expensive, though, and some of 'em make me sicker than I was before I started takin' 'em."

"Why are the drugs hard to get?" Raymond wondered aloud.

"They cost money, baby. And since Mommy can't shake her groove thang and work, then I have to depend on my little disability check and Miss Peaches."

"What kind of work did you do?"

"I'd do a little hair every now and then. And I did some of my good-good girlfriends' taxes, 'cause Mommy was good at math, but mostly I was a performer. You know, impersonations. My favorites were Patti LaBelle and Tina Turner. Honey, I would work the kids' last nerve when I was in my prime. I gave them fever," Miss Kitty said in a high and pinched voice. She clapped her hands and clearly was enjoying the memory.

"I bet you were something else," Raymond said as he sat on the edge of Miss Kitty's bed. Her laughter had made him feel more comfortable.

While Peaches prepared Kitty's plate, Raymond learned her history. Miss Kitty had been born in Columbia, South Carolina, and christened Kendall David Summerhill. Kendall had moved to New York when he was sixteen, after he was nearly beaten to death by a local football player who had unknowingly fallen for Miss Kitty's beauty and charm, without knowing the young Miss Kitty was actually Kendall.

Miss Kitty told a story of young love gone bad.

"I used to dress up in my sister's clothes and go downtown, away from my neighborhood, where nobody knew me. I would put on some of her best outfits and underthings and one of my mama's many church wigs. I would put the things in my book bag, catch the bus, and go to the Grey-hound bus station and change. That's where I met Steven, and for almost a year, we would meet. He had no clue what I was packin' between my legs."

Raymond couldn't resist a question. "So I guess you guys weren't intimate?"

"Child, yeah, we were intimate. That's why he tried to kill Mommy. I would tuck my stuff real tight between my legs and when Steve would feel down there it felt just like pussy. And since we would always be in the car, and it would be at night, he never knew. That is, until I got silly and let him go too far."

"So he was pretty mad, huh?"

"You ain't said nuthin'. But I packed up my beat-up face and I went back to that Greyhound bus station and caught a bus to New York City, to become a star, darling! And I was."

"What did your parents say?"

"Those country-ass, low-life mutherfuckers didn't have a chance to say nuthin'. After I was nearly beaten half to death, my daddy, who always smelled like he had fallen into a liquor well, tried to kill me too. Tellin' me what a disgrace I was. I wasn't having it. So one night when they were all asleep, I booked. And it was good riddance to small towns and small minds," Miss Kitty said as her voice broke and her eyes welled with tears.

Silence filled the room for a few seconds. Raymond didn't know what to say or do. He realized how brave and strong she was. Miss Kitty/ Kendall was thrust by fate in the front ranks of the gay rights movement, one of those gay people who were abused just because of their physical appearance and mannerisms. Raymond and Trent were never mistreated or disrespected by strangers because they were black gay men, because most hatemongers couldn't tell they were gay by just looking at them. They had never been physically threatened because of their sexuality. Raymond knew Miss Kitty and others like her made him nervous be-cause he had always been afraid that when he acknowledged that he was gay, people would assume he wanted to look and be treated like a woman.

Now he wanted to comfort Miss Kitty, but instead he shut his eyes tightly and felt the emotions knotting up his stomach. Suddenly he heard Peaches's voice.

"Kitty, you ain't scaring Raymond, are you?" she asked as she came into the bedroom carrying a plate on a TV tray.

"Well, he still here, ain't he?" Miss Kitty said as she took a tissue from the bedside supply and dabbed the corners of her eyes. After regaining her composure, she firmly placed her back against the pillows lined against the headboard.

"Yes, he is. And ain't that a blessing," Peaches said, placing the tray over Miss Kitty's lap.

37

For Raymond, Wednesday, hump day, had been a good day. He was making progress with a loan officer and the landlord's attorney. He figured he could wrap up everything within the week and return home. Raymond discovered the workouts with Basil, or maybe just nervous energy, had helped him lose some pounds. The suit pants he had brought from Seattle were not fitting the same way. Now he needed a belt. The weight loss was further confirmed when he went out and bought several pairs of black, size 32 jockey underwear, which fit snug and sexy. He was almost back to his prerelationship weight.

Raymond was even looking forward to an evening with his trainer/nemesis, Basil Henderson. He had decided to give himself his full five-step date-prep grooming treatment. Before he started, Raymond smiled and thought of Kyle and how the two of them had created their grooming prep when they were both single and heading out for a night on the prowl. First he splashed cold water on his face and then warm water. He took a buff pad and poured on a liquid cleanser and scrubbed his face. Next he took an ivory gel shaving foam and massaged it into his face, then took a blue disposable razor and shaved slowly. Raymond splashed more cold water on his face to close the pores and then put on a layer of Noxzema. He located an orange tube of a facial mask he once used at least twice a week and laid it next to a dry white facecloth.

While he allowed the cold cream to sink into his pores, he went into the kitchen and poured himself a glass of wine. As he took his first sip of wine, he thought back to his subway ride from Cuts 'n' Cobblers to the hotel, when he had been thinking not of the progress he was making for Peaches, but of his evening planned with Basil. He knew Basil was setting him up for the big seduction, and for the first time since he had committed himself to Trent, Raymond was open to being seduced. He was remembering how great Basil looked in the gym and at his apartment when Raymond caught a glimpse of him in his sexy underwear. He thought of Basil's clean and masculine scent, how he smelled great even after a two-hour workout, the sweat and his body chemistry mixing beautifully. He thought of his dazzling, sneaky smile and that amazing body, which Raymond thought had gotten better with age. At this moment, the only question in Raymond's mind was where the seduction would occur. Would they reunite at his hotel, or Basil's spacious apartment?

As he walked back toward the bathroom to remove the cold cream, the phone rang. It was Jared, and there was panic in his voice.

"Raymond."

"Whassup, dude? You sound kinda breathless."

"I just got back from Grand Rapids," Jared said.

"Aw, that's sweet, you miss your wife so much you went back," Raymond teased.

"I do miss her, but that's not why I went back. Nicole was sick. She even missed a couple of performances," Jared said.

"What's wrong?"

Jared told Raymond about a phone call from Yancey telling him how Nicole had almost passed out before the opening night performance in Grand Rapids. When Jared finally saw Nicole, she had convinced him everything would be fine, it was just a mild case of food poisoning.

"Maybe she's pregnant," Raymond suggested, knowing how badly Jared wanted a child.

"I don't think so. I think she's back on birth control. We talked about it before we moved back to New York. You know the trouble she's had with the pregnancies, and we both agreed to give her career a couple of years before we started trying again," Jared said.

"Is there anything you need me to do?" Raymond asked as he touched the now dry cream on his face.

"Naw, just keep us in your thoughts and prayers."

"I'll do that," Raymond said.

"Want to grab some dinner?" Jared asked.

"Aw boy, I've made some plans."

"Anybody I know?"

"You dipping . . . What about tomorrow?"

"That's cool," Jared said.

"Then tomorrow it is."

"Just give me a call either later on tonight or first thing in the morning."

"Deal," Raymond said as he hung up the phone.

Raymond went into the bathroom and rinsed the dry layer of cream from his face with lukewarm water. Looking at his reflection in the mirror, he thought about Jared and Nicole and how lucky they were to have each other. The "damn I wish I were straight" thing streamed through his mind for a moment, but the phone interrupted his thoughts.

"Hello."

"You ready?" It was Basil, always anxious to see him.

"Ready for what?" Raymond asked, trying to be coy.

"Whatever happens, happens."

"Just about. Still got to shower, but I'll be on time," Raymond said.

"You want me to come over and scrub your back or whatever?" Basil teased.

"I think I can manage," Raymond replied quickly.

"You need me to pick you up?" Basil asked. "I've ordered a car."

Raymond thought for a few seconds before asking, "The restaurant's on Eighty-sixth and Broadway, right?"

"Yeah."

"Naw, it feels good outside. I think I'll walk," Raymond said.

"Whatever suits you, but be on time."

"Then I need to get off the phone."

"I'm looking forward to this," Basil said softly.

"Me too," Raymond said, and hung up the phone. He looked at the clock and realized he had less than an hour to give himself a mini-facial and shower. He went to the closet and pulled out a pair of black pleated slacks and a sky-blue cotton shirt and laid them on the bed right next to each other. When the phone rang again, he decided to let the hotel answering machine handle it. Raymond assumed it was probably Basil calling again, with something smart and sexy to say, or maybe it was Jared, who he knew would hang up and call right back if it was important. After he applied the smooth green algae to his face, Raymond checked for the red message light, which was dim. Whoever called hadn't felt the need to leave a message.

Raymond stepped into the shower and continued his pampering by applying a body polish touted as a skin-purifying exfoliant he had purchased at the hotel gift shop. He rubbed the grainy, oatmeal-like substance over his body and moved under the needles of hot water. He poured some of the hotel-issued combination shampoo and conditioner over his head. His thoughts drifted to visions of a nude Basil in the gym shower, his butterscotch-colored body glistening against the white tile. By the time he ended his shower, his sex had expanded and was demanding attention. As he dried himself off, Raymond thought that giving it the satisfaction it craved might make him less vulnerable to Basil's seduction, but when he looked at the clock he realized there wasn't time. Basil would have the upper hand.

❧   ❧   ❧

When Raymond walked out into the cool autumn night, he was greeted by two surprises. First, even though it was close to theater time, there wasn't a long line waiting for taxis outside the hotel. There were only two couples in front of him. As he watched the first couple, two sixtyish-looking people, enter a taxi, Raymond noticed the comfortable look they had with each other. He couldn't help but think about his own parents when the tall, bespectacled bald gentleman gave his wife a little peck on the cheek before sliding into the cab. The next couple in line were closer to Raymond's own age, and couldn't keep their hands off of each other. Raymond wondered if they were a happily married couple or two people engaged in a torrid affair. Either way they looked happy and in love. *Looks like everybody's getting some but me,* Raymond thought. Suddenly Raymond's train of thought was broken by the doorman saying, "Sir, it's your turn." He opened the taxi door, and Raymond moved down the steps and stood directly behind the doorman, allowing the current passenger to exit. As the passenger leaned over to pay the driver, the trunk popped open and a bellman suddenly appeared to remove several pieces of luggage and set them on the curb. The instant Raymond recognized the black leather duffel and matching garment bag with the gold initials *TMW,* Trent stepped out of the taxi. Trent handed the bellman a tip and turned to see a startled Raymond looking at him.

"Raymond!"

"Trent, what are you doing here?" Raymond asked.

"I came to see you, boy," Trent said as he hugged Raymond enthusiastically and kissed him on the ear. Raymond, in his semishocked state, hugged Trent back lightly and tried to force a smile of excitement.

"Why didn't you tell me you were coming?" Raymond asked.

"Aren't you glad to see me? Man, you're looking great. What have you been doing? Looks like you've lost some weight. Where are you on your way to?" Trent rattled off a string of questions. The doorman looked at Raymond and asked if he still wanted the taxi, since another couple was waiting.

"No, that's okay," Raymond said. He then turned and headed up the steps back into the hotel.

"So you didn't answer me," Trent said as he followed behind Raymond.

"Answer what?" Raymond asked while walking through the automatic sliding glass door. He was looking at the bellman in front of him instead of at Trent. He told him to take Trent's luggage to his suite.

"Aren't you glad to see me?" Trent repeated.

"Of course, I'm glad to see you . . . it's just that I wasn't expecting this," Raymond stuttered as he retrieved Trent's bags and led him toward the elevators.

"That's why it's called a surprise! This is a nice hotel," Trent said as he stepped into the walnut-paneled elevator. As the two of them stood side by side, Raymond's stomach was suddenly filled with nervous energy. Trent asked about Jared and how things were going with Peaches and her problems. Raymond told him about the progress he'd made and how Jared seemed to always be working. As the elevator reached the twelfth floor, Raymond was thinking about what he would say to Trent and wondering if this was the time to confront him about the bookstore incident.

When the two of them entered the suite, Raymond walked quickly into the bedroom and placed Trent's duffel in the closet. Trent was standing in the parlor section as he called out, "Where you running off to?"

"Hold up," Raymond called back. He took a deep breath and walked into the area where Trent was standing with a big smile. Trent walked toward Raymond and put his arms around him, then kissed him warmly on the lips. Trent's arms slowly started to slide down Raymond's body, as his sex pressed into Raymond, whose sex, which had been so full before, now felt nonexistent.

"Are you all right?" Trent asked as Raymond pulled away.

"I'm fine. Are you hungry? Do you want to get something to eat?"

"I'm okay. They served us about three meals on the flight over. Were you on your way to dinner?"

"Yeah."

"With Jared?"

"Yeah, with Jared," Raymond lied. He suddenly thought about Basil and realized he needed to call him at the restaurant. Raymond walked over to the blond-wood desk, picked up the room service menu, and started thumbing through it. Trent was talking nonstop about South Africa and its beauty and how he was going back to Seattle for a couple of days before stopping in Mobile to pick up Trent Jr., and how he had gotten special permission for him to miss a week of school so he could travel to South Africa. Raymond put down the menu and pretended to listen and sound interested when Trent came toward him and said, "I love you, and I've missed you so much." Something suddenly went through Raymond when Trent professed his love, and from nowhere the words shot out explosively, "Is that why you've been unfaithful to me? Is that why you've been having sex in bookstores?"

Trent looked at him with the disbelieving expression of a child and then stuttered, "Ray, what are you talking about?" His voice expressed complete surprise.

"You know damn well what I'm talking about. Were you or were you not arrested for having sex in a downtown bookstore?" Raymond asked as though he was cross-examining an alleged rapist.

Trent slowly shook his head and said, "I wasn't having sex."

"Oh, you were just looking for sex. Tell me this, Trent . . . have you always been faithful to me? Answer that!" Raymond shouted.

Trent dropped his head slightly, then lifted it and asked, "Have you always been faithful to me?"

Raymond looked into Trent's eyes and with a rush of anger shouted, "Hell the fuck yeah! So this is what you're going to do? Turn your fucked-up shit on me? I can look you dead in your eyes and without question say that I have always honored my commitment with you." Raymond's emotions suddenly became an uncontrollable force, like a tornado sweeping through a trailer park, furious and quick. "I can't believe this shit! You get caught in some mess and you're going to try and turn the tables on me. How many times were you unfaithful, Trent? And with who? Were they black or white? Is he somebody I know? Here I am going around thinking I've got the perfect relationship and we ain't got shit. We're no different from all those motherfuckers we've turned our noses up at. You remember them, don't you, Trent? The friends we've given up when they've flirted with one of us or tried to engage us in group sex. Are we like *those* people, Trent?" Raymond's voice trailed off weakly as feelings of sadness and anger burned in his throat. He could tell by the frightened look in Trent's eyes that there had been others in his sexual life.

"Let me explain," Trent said. Raymond didn't answer, and the room seemed engulfed in an unnatural stillness. Then Trent began to speak without pause. "You were working all the time. And when you came home you were in front of the television, watching those political shows and sports. And sometimes, Raymond, you can be uptight. There are a lot of things I used to do sexually that I don't do anymore because I don't think you'd want to. But I don't mind because I love you. Do you hear me? I love you with all my heart, but I'm human and I've made mistakes.

It was just one of those moments," Trent said as silent tears fell down his face.

Raymond was unmoved by the tears, and with cold anger in his voice he said, "You're supposed to spend those moments with me!" Trent didn't answer and silence stretched between the two of them for almost an hour. Raymond felt a sadness in his heart because everything he had felt since his lunch with Lisa had been proven true. Trent felt a deep sadness as well. He could see from the wounded look in Raymond's eyes how badly he was hurting. Trent's own feeling from their conversation that something was wrong had also proven true.

The silence continued until the phone began ringing. Raymond knew it was Basil and he just let it ring. Trent finally asked him if he wanted him to answer the phone, and Raymond said firmly, "No." Raymond walked into the bedroom, picked up the phone, and listened for the dial tone. He then pushed 0.

"This is the hotel operator. How can I help you, Mr. Tyler?"

"Would you put a 'do not disturb' on my phone until further notice?"

"No problem, Mr. Tyler. Would you like a wake-up call in the morning?" Raymond looked at the clock and realized it was almost 10:30. "No, that won't be necessary."

When he hung up, the red light on the phone began flashing frantically. As Raymond walked back into the living area, Trent was standing with his arms folded across his chest and gazing out the window at the sea of yellow taxis moving slowly around Columbus Circle. When he heard Raymond walk back into the room, he turned and asked, "So what are we going to do? Are we over?"

Raymond wanted to say, "So you can go out and fuck whoever you want?" but he did not. Instead he just looked at Trent and said, "I don't know. I'm carrying my ass to bed."

Raymond felt like he had just returned from a funeral as he undressed and lay on the bed, not even bothering to remove the bedspread. He pulled out a couple of pillows and propped them against the headboard, and then stared at the ceiling as his emotions assailed him from every direction. He felt mad. He felt sad. And he felt totally alone. Who could he talk to? Who would understand the pain of infidelity? Raymond felt the answer was no one.

About a half hour later Trent walked quietly into the bedroom. He had tried to sleep on the sofa, but it was too small. When he walked into the bedroom, he noticed Raymond's eyes were closed, but sensed he wasn't asleep. Trent started to ask his partner if it was all right if he slept in the same bed with him, but he did not. He simply removed his yellow polo knit shirt and navy slacks and lay next to Raymond. Trent gazed at the ceiling and noticed the thin slice of light coming from the nearby bathroom. He wanted to hold Raymond and plead for forgiveness. Trent wanted to explain his weakness, and how it hadn't happened in years. He wanted Raymond to know how deeply he loved him and how he would do anything in the world to take back those moments.

Raymond's thoughts were more questions. What would he do? Should he leave Trent? He had always told himself that if he was going to be in a relationship with a man . . . then it had to be perfect. It was clear to him that this relationship wasn't perfect.

Raymond and Trent had both fallen into an uneasy sleep when the phone rang. They both leaped up, and again Trent asked, "Do you want me to get that?"

Raymond knew it was Basil, but he didn't want to talk with him. He figured it would suit Trent well to know that other men were interested in him, so he said in a smug tone, "Suit yourself," as he turned his back on his partner. Trent didn't answer the phone and turned his back too, away from Raymond. A few moments later the phone rang again, and this time Raymond jerked it from the cradle and shouted, "What!"

A shaky-voiced operator said, "I'm sorry, Mr. Tyler, but the party has called five times in the last thirty minutes. I told him you had a DND on your phone but he said it's an emergency. A family emergency," she said.

"Can you ask who it is?" If it was Basil, then Raymond would give the operator a firm no.

"Sure, I can do that. Hold on, Mr. Tyler." A few seconds later the operator came back on the line and said, "He says he's your brother. He said his name was Kirby Tyler."

Raymond still figured it was Basil and was going to instruct the operator to make him give a middle name. But instead he said, "Put him through."

"Right away, Mr. Tyler."

"Ray." It was Kirby, and for the second time that evening, Raymond heard panic across the phone line.

"Whassup, Kirby?"

"Ray . . . you need to come to Chicago. We think Pops had a heart attack. You've got to come quick, bro, 'cause they don't think he's going to make it and Mama's freakin'," Kirby said.

"What? When did this happen? Is he still alive?" Raymond sat up in bed as his heart began to race. A warm film of sweat began to dampen his neck.

"We were out eating. He was talking and then he just passed out. I don't know if he's still alive. I'm at the hospital now and they're not letting Mama or me know anything. We need you, Ray," Kirby said, as though he was near tears. He sounded not like a star football player, but like a little boy suddenly afraid of the dark.

"I'm on the first thing outta here, Kirby. Tell Mama to hold tight."

38

"I think this is the first time some shit like this has happened to me," Basil said. His voice was solemn and deeper than usual.

"How did that make you feel?" the doctor asked.

Basil had predicted this question, so he let off the anger he had felt since the night before.

"How does it make me feel? Is that the only thing you fuckin' doctors know how to ask? Is that the first thing they teach you in med school? Just ask the patients how it makes them feel? It made me mad as fuck. How dare that mutherfucker stand me up and not even call. And when I call him, his punk-ass boyfriend answers the phone. He never said anything to me about his boyfriend coming to town. That goddamn Raymond wasn't even man enough to talk to me and tell me he didn't want to go to dinner with me," Basil said.

The doctor wanted to ask Basil if it made him think about some of the women he had stood up, but after Basil's tirade he decided against it. Instead, he asked, "Why do you give Raymond so much power over your life?"

"That mofo ain't got no power over me. I'm the one with the mutherfuckin' power. I just don't understand why he tried to make a fool out of me. There I am sitting at the bar, drinking beer after beer, and eating stale-ass peanuts. Having to give my don't-fuck-with-me look to men and women who tried to strike up a conversation with me," Basil said as he stood up, placed both his large hands on his knees, and bent over, trying to relieve some of the tension in his lower back. After a moment, he straightened up and walked toward the bookcases, his aching back to the doctor.

"How long did you wait?"

"Almost two hours. I called his hotel and he didn't answer the phone and then I called and the bitch-ass operator tells me, 'Mr. Tyler has requested a do not disturb.' Ain't that some shit?" Basil asked but didn't wait for an answer. "I carried my ass home and pulled out my phone book and wasn't nobody home. Couldn't even get ahold of that faggot-ass Monty. I started to just call a ho."

"So you wanted to spend the evening with somebody?"

"I wanted to get my jimmie off. That's what I wanted," Basil said firmly.

When the doctor asked Basil how could he be certain it was Raymond's partner who answered the phone, he told the doctor how, when someone finally answered the phone early the next morning, he had said, "Raymond?" and the person on the other end said, "No. Raymond's not here. This is his partner, Trent."

"And you still haven't spoken with Raymond?"

Basil turned and stared menacingly at the doctor. "Do you think I'd be mad as fuck if I'd talked to Raymond?" Basil shouted. "Do you think I'd be talking about this if I'd had the chance to tell that mofo how don't nobody stand me up?" Basil saw a bit of fear in the doctor's eyes and tried to concentrate on keeping his voice under control. He gave a fake laugh that sounded more like a cough when he said, "I guess my father was right when he said love and sex makes strong men into fools."

Through the smoldering anger in his eyes, the doctor could detect a deep sadness and a crack in Basil's veneer of toughness. "And which one of those things applies to Raymond?"

"Which what?"

"Is it love? Or is it sex?"

"I don't know," Basil said softly.

"You don't?"

"Maybe I don't want to know."

"So what are you going to do?"

"Do about what?"

"About your relationship with Raymond. Are you going to try and contact him?"

"You know I've got to get him now. And all I gotta say is it ain't gonna be pretty."

39

Raymond arrived at Chicago's O'Hare Airport. He was traveling light, so he went immediately to the ground transportation area and caught a taxi to Northwestern Medical Center, located in downtown Chicago. He was tired, since he had been up since Kirby's call. Trent had offered to come with him, but Raymond declined his offer, telling Trent he would call as soon as he heard anything, one way or the other. When he left the hotel suite, just before dawn, Trent held him tightly and whispered, "I love you," and Raymond replied, "I know," and kissed his cheek. He was relieved that Trent realized that their problems would have to wait.

Raymond's response to his father's collapse surprised and confused him. Initially he was scared.

The fear he could understand; he didn't want his father to die. The love he felt for his father, though uncertain at times, was equally over-powering. This was the man who had nurtured him, sacrificed for him, meant the world to him. Raymond couldn't imagine not having his father in his life.

What shocked him were the feelings of anger and betrayal. He felt secretly ashamed and guilty that he was so angry at his father for this crisis. His father's death, he thought, would be the ultimate betrayal, robbing Raymond of the opportunity to vent his unwanted anger.

Although he struggled to conceal his true emotions, Raymond was overwhelmed when he arrived at the hospital to find his father semicomatose in the intensive care unit.

The front wall and door of the large room were glass, and Raymond could see his mother and Kirby seated on opposite sides of the bed.

Raymond Sr. looked peaceful, like he was enjoying a blissful dream, and didn't appear to be suffering. When Raymond's mother saw him standing at the door, she rushed to greet him.

"Oh, Raymond. Baby. Thank God you're here," his mother said as she embraced her firstborn son. She cried softly into his shoulder. Raymond held her tightly and felt her body shudder with each tearful sob.

Kirby stood and joined in the embrace. "Me too, bro. I'm glad you're here."

Dr. Hector Rodriguez was the cardiologist on call when Raymond Sr. had been admitted to the hospital. He hesitated outside the glass door and decided to allow the family a few minutes before entering. He rapped his knuckles on the door before coming inside. "I'm Dr. Rodriguez," he said to Raymond. "I'm sure your mother and brother are happy to have you here."

"How is he, Dr. Rodriguez?" Raymond asked. "Is my father going to be all right?"

"Right now, Mr. Tyler, we don't know much at this point. He's stable for the time being, but the next forty-eight hours are critical. Only then will we be able to tell if he'll survive this episode and what, if any, disabilities he might have. My experience tells me that it is of the utmost importance that you are all here with him now, loving him, supporting him, and pulling for him. I will be checking in on Mr. Tyler periodically, but feel free to have me paged if you have any questions or concern." With that, the doctor turned and left the room.

A deep sob rocked Mrs. Tyler's medium frame. Raymond's concern now turned to his mother. She was always so strong: the glue that held the family together through tough times. And now she seemed to be falling apart with no pretense even of a solid front.

"Come on, Mama. You know Pops. He'll pull through. He always comes through in a crunch. Besides, he's too stubborn to die." Raymond hugged his mother and tried to believe his own words. It was clear to him that he would have to be the one to put up the strong front. His mother was badly shaken, and Kirby looked like a scared little boy.

Raymond turned toward Kirby and asked what had happened.

"We were having dinner at a steak house not too far from here. And Pops and I got into sorta an argument," Kirby said, "right before it happened."

"Now, you know it wasn't your fault, son," Raymond's mother said, resuming her place at her husband's side. She placed Raymond Sr.'s hand between hers and began to rock quietly back and forth in her chair. "Your father's stroke had nothing to do with you. Nothing at all."

"So are they sure it was a stroke and not a heart attack?"

"The doctor said it was a stroke," Kirby said.

Raymond motioned for Kirby to follow him to the hallway. When the two of them got outside the room, Raymond looked at Kirby and said, "Tell me what you and Pops were arguing about." Kirby hesitated before he answered Raymond. His eyes appeared bigger, filled with fear. Raymond had seen this look before, but then Kirby had been fourteen years old and caught having sex with a neighborhood girl in the back of Raymond's parked car. Finally he spoke. "Whenever your name came up during dinner, Pops would roll his eyes and make this grunting sound. I told him I thought he should lighten up on you, you know? He said you were holding up your own confirmation by not kicking Trent out. And I told him it was none of my business, his business, or the business of the federal government who you choose to live with. Pops went off on me something terrible. If I'd known he was gonna get so upset, I would have kept my mouth shut. But I didn't, and now we're all here in this sterile-ass hospital wondering whether he'll live or die."

"You're right about one thing, Kirby. Trent is my business," Raymond said firmly, "but Pops's health is between him and God. You, Kirby, are not in charge of that. You, little brother, are not responsible for Pops's condition."

"But I meant what I said," Kirby insisted. "It just pissed me off that Pops was mad at you. He was saying that I needed to change my major to prelaw. Said some shit about how somebody had to protect the Tyler legal legacy. I told him I had no interest in being a lawyer or a judge. He's the only one in the family who cares about that shit. I think I really hit a nerve when I said he was the one who wanted to be a federal judge, not you. I told Pops he can't live his dreams through us. It's not fair."

"What did he say?"

"Told me to stop disrespecting him and Mama. He was so mad it looked like smoke was coming out of his eyes and ears. He started sweating and a few minutes later his eyes rolled into the back of his head and he fell out of the chair."

"That must have been scary," Raymond said, reaching to grab Kirby by the shoulders. "Thanks for sticking up for me, little brother. It means a lot to me that you did that."

"I just hope the price isn't too high," Kirby said as he looked through the window at his father's fragile form. "I don't think I could handle it if he didn't make it."

Raymond put his arms around Kirby's shoulders and whispered, "Everything is going to be all right, little brother. No matter what happens, the Tylers will survive. Now let's go back in that room and make sure Mama knows that."

40

After a three-day absence, Nicole was ready to reclaim her role of Dena Jones. A local Grand Rapids doctor had given her a tentative clean bill of health. She returned to her hotel room to pick up her makeup bag after seeing Jared off in a taxi to the airport. Nicole had assured her husband that she had just suffered a little case of food poisoning and was fine. She was touched that he loved her so much that he flew to Grand Rapids to make sure. She felt like the luckiest woman alive.

Nicole picked up a note from Yancey telling her that the director had called her for a meeting, so she would meet her at the theater. Nicole was thinking about her loving husband and enjoying the silence when the phone rang.

"Hello," Nicole said.

"Nicole. I'm so glad I caught you." It was her agent, Dennis.

"I was just getting ready to leave. How are you doing?" Nicole asked.

"I'm doing fine. It's just that I have some bad news."

"Bad news? What kind of bad news?" Nicole asked.

"This is the part of my job I hate. You know I love having you as a client, don't you, Nicole?"

"Sure. You're not dropping me, are you?" Nicole asked as she sat on the bed.

"Of course not! We're going to make each other a lot of money. I think you're talented, beautiful, and will have a long, long career."

"Then what's the bad news? The *Dottie* producers haven't gotten their money situation straight?"

Dennis's voice changed to an apologetic tone. "I just hate this and I don't understand what has happened. I mean, in all my years of working with producers and directors, I can honestly say this just blows me away."

"Come on, Dennis. I'm a big girl. Tell me," Nicole demanded.

There was a brief silence, and then Dennis said, "You're not coming back to Broadway with the show. They want to buy out your contract for the rest of the tour."

Nicole was stunned and silent. Was she hearing Dennis correctly? She got up from the bed and walked toward the window; she rustled the curtains gently as she gazed out at the lights of the small metropolis sparkling seductively below. The night looked clear and peaceful. Nicole's mind traveled to other times of great disappointment in her life: the night in Hot Springs, Arkansas, when she was named a runner-up instead of the new Miss Arkansas, and again when she finally made it to the Miss America pageant in Atlantic City, where again her name followed the words "and the third runner-up is . . ." She thought of high school, where she wasn't even allowed to audition for a principal role in a production of *Brigadoon.* Back then Nicole still had the future to look toward, but now the clock on achieving her dreams was ticking loud and fast.

"Nicole? Are you still there? Are you all right?" Dennis asked frantically.

"I'm here, and I'm okay. When did this happen?" Nicole asked.

"The producers called me this afternoon. And I laid into them and told them we were going to take this to the union. They assured me they are willing to pay out the rest of your contract, and if you're so inclined you can stay with the show. They just didn't think it was fair to have you think you've got the role when it comes to Broadway. They even had the gall to suggest the standby role for you when the show comes back to New York. I told them 'hell no,' " Dennis said.

"Standby for who? Who are they replacing me with?" Nicole asked calmly.

"What have you heard?"

"Nothing, I'm not really in the gossip loop. I didn't even believe the director rumors and look what happened. They're probably going after a name. I mean, since they weren't able to convince Jennifer Holiday to come back, it makes sense they would want a big name for Dena. Someone like Audra McDonald or even Toni Braxton. I read somewhere she was interested in doing Broadway," Nicole said quietly.

"So what should I tell them? Have them write us a check now or later?" Dennis asked.

"I'm doing the show," Nicole said firmly. "At least tonight. I'll let you know about tomorrow," Nicole added, her voice cold with anger.

"Are you sure?"

"I'm sure," Nicole said as she looked at her watch. "I've got to go. It's almost seven-thirty."

"You're something else, Nicole, and I respect you more than any actress I know."

"Thank you. I'll call you in the morning. I've got a show to do," Nicole said as she hung up the phone.

Nicole grabbed her leather makeup bag and caught a glimpse of her hurt and pained look in the mirror. She fought back an oncoming panic, though she wanted to open her mouth and just scream. Nicole didn't scream, but she was unable to stop the tears that flowed silently and easily as she walked out of her hotel room.

❖   ❖   ❖

In the office of the general manager of the Devoss Theater, Yancey Elizabeth Braxton was getting some good news. And even though she reacted as if she were shocked and stunned, Yancey had expected nothing less.

"Are you serious? This isn't some kind of sick joke?" Yancey asked as she performed for the new director and two producers.

"No, we're not kidding. We want to offer you a contract to play Dena Jones once we hit Broadway," Jim Keith, one of the producers, said.

"Yancey, when I saw you perform the other night, I knew you were born for this role," Chris, the new director, said. "I mean, I've seen a lot of Denas, but I'm certain you're what Mr. Bennett had in mind when he conceived this show. You're talented, young, and beautiful. You are Dena Jones and the critics in New York are going to love you like they did here."

Yancey brought both her hands to her cheeks and said, "Oh my. This is wonderful. I don't know what to say."

"Just say you'll do it. We know you're close with Nicole, but we all know this is a business," Chris said.

"But what about Nicole? I mean we're friends and she'll be devastated," Yancey said with a sincere look of concern on her face.

"Nicole is a professional and there will be other shows. Besides, she's probably tired of this role."

"You think so?" Yancey asked.

"Of course."

"If you think Nicole will understand, then I'll do it," Yancey said. "When do you want me to start?"

"Maybe as soon as tonight," Chris answered. "Legally and, of course, worrying about the union, we've offered a buyout of Nicole's contract, but we've agreed to let her play out the tour. But usually in situations like this the actor or actress will take the money and run."

"So what do I do?" Yancey asked.

"About what?"

"Tonight. Should I prepare to play Michelle or Dena?"

"Just go to your dressing room and let's play it by ear. Don't say anything until we make an official announcement. If Nicole shows up, then put your Michelle face on. If we hear from her agent that she's not going to make it easy for us, then we'll take it from there."

"I can't thank you enough," Yancey said. "I promise I will not let you down. I will give you the performance of a lifetime every time I hit the stage."

"We know that, Yancey, and that's why we're making the change. We've contacted your agent and we'll begin working on a contract that you'll be satisfied with."

"I'm not worried about that. This is a role I'd do for free, but since I don't have to . . . well, I just don't know what to say." Yancey got up from the chair and started hugging each of the producers and the new director and kissing them on the cheek. When she left the office, her only regret was that she didn't have enough time to call and tell Ava, the woman she treated as a big sister, who was actually her mother, the great news.

BOOK THREE

Save Some Secrets for Yourself

41

Ava Rose Parker had lived her life large and hard, with few regrets and fewer attachments.

An accomplished entertainer, she had performed her jazzy renditions of classic ballads in the best clubs, drunk the best wines, and eaten the best foods that all of Europe had to offer. She had dined with Moroccan royalty, partied with rich Frenchmen, and been pursued by the wealthiest members of Spanish society.

Although Ava had been a celebrated cabaret performer for fifteen years, she had never forgotten her less than auspicious beginning in Jackson, Tennessee.

Ava was a traffic-stopping beauty, with big, round, doe-brown eyes and long thick lashes, dimples that punctuated her glowing butterscotch cheeks, and thick black hair permed to tameness that tumbled just past her shoulders. When she strolled down the streets, the boys in Jackson catcalled her Miss Brick House; her male suitors across the Atlantic referred to her as statuesque.

At age sixteen, she had been a contestant in the Miss Ebony Mid-South beauty pageant, a popular pageant for African-American young women from Tennessee, Arkansas, Mississippi, and Louisiana. Besides receiving wonderful prizes, the winner continued on to the Miss Black America pageant as a front-runner. Beginning with their first rehearsal for the pageant, Ava assumed Nicole Springer was her only real competition. During the two-week event, each of them had won swimsuit, talent, and evening gown competitions on their respective nights. Ava surmised that if she could get Nicole out of the way, she'd be certain to win the crown.

To get Nicole disqualified, Ava started a vicious rumor that she was pregnant by one of the pageant producers from her home state. The rumor spread like grease on a hot skillet and, in the interest of fairness and avoiding embarrassment, the pageant's board of directors had all of the contestants tested.

Only Ava's test came back positive.

After Ava was forced from the pageant and sent back to Jackson, Nicole went on to become Miss Ebony Mid-South, but then shocked officials by giving the crown to the first runner-up. Nicole had been so disgusted by the test and rumors, she vowed to never again enter a pageant for African-Americans only. Three years later Nicole Springer was competing for the title of Miss America. In Jackson, Ava was trying to track down Bobby Earl Braxton, local football star, for child support for her two-year-old daughter, Yancey.

Ava loved her pretty little baby, but motherhood was not on Ava's agenda. When Yancey was five, Ava left her with her mother, Essie Dean, and headed to New York and Broadway. On her final callback for a role in *Dreamgirls,* Ava recognized the young lady auditioning right before her as Nicole Springer. When Nicole walked right by Ava without even a glance, Ava became furious. Nicole got the part and Ava returned to Jackson, but not for long.

Five months later Ava headed to Europe, where she had heard that it was a lot easier to break into the business. Ever since Josephine Baker, Europeans had welcomed black women artists, and Ava saw a second chance for a stage career. So she left her baby again with her mother, who had loaned her the airfare to Paris, as well as money for a month's hotel stay.

Ava worked hard honing her singing and dancing skills while waiting tables. She was talented and ambitious, and knowing whom to sleep with was an asset as well. After Bobby, Ava knew instinctively who the little fish were, and she wanted to swim with the sharks. She controlled, contrived, and connived her way until her career took off, then soared. Virtually unknown in the States, Ava Rose became a household name throughout Europe and even had a hit song in Japan.

Ava and her mother stayed in close contact through letters, postcards, pictures, and the rare transatlantic phone call on Yancey's birthday. Each week, Ava sent a package to her mother and daughter. There were little inexpensive gifts at first, but later, when the money began to flow, she sent designer dresses and jewelry.

Yancey received a constant stream of letters and pictures from Ava as well. Her vanity mirror was bordered with pictures of Ava decked out in evening gowns at clubs, or in sundresses and wide-brimmed hats on the Riviera. Yancey idolized her glamorous mother and wanted more than anything to be just like her. Yancey never forgot her own frequent trips abroad to visit her mother beginning when she was nine years old, but could not forget the sadness she felt when she returned to Jackson to her devoted grandmother. Her father was never around, so as a teenager she fantasized that he was related to Toni Braxton, full well knowing it wasn't true.

Ava made sure there was plenty of money for Yancey's ballet, tap, and modern dance classes, and for her singing and elocution lessons too. Yancey sent her mother her report cards, her class pictures, and trophies from Little Miss pageants she won all around the mid-South. More than anything, Yancey took to heart Ava's advice to not let anything or anyone get in the way of her dreams. And though they were an ocean apart, Yancey grew to be just like her mother, in more ways than one.

Ava returned to the States at least once a year, spending a little time in Jackson, but weeks in New York City pursuing her Broadway dreams. She came close several times, but Ava's last shot at Broadway occurred when she was assured a major role in a Bob Fosse musical, *Big Deal.* Ava was certain this would be the part she had worked all her life for, but it was not to be. One of the producers and a casting agent had promised her the role after catching her act in Paris and two New York auditions. But the day before rehearsal started, the casting agent and producer were replaced and so was their leading lady. Ava's agents didn't get the bad news to her in time, and when Ava was told at the stage door of the theater the part had gone to *Dreamgirls* alum Loretta Devine, Ava vowed to never return to New York. It was a horrible day for Ava, and to make matters worse, she literally bumped into Nicole Springer, another member of the *Big Deal* cast. Again Nicole didn't even recognize Ava, and only smiled and said, "I'm sorry." Ava felt lower than low and cried all the way back to her hotel. Ava couldn't bear to tell her daughter that she wouldn't be performing closer to home as she had often promised.

When Ava returned to Europe, her yearly trips to the States stopped, and so did the visits from Yancey. Ava married a French millionaire; she divorced him some two years later, but was financially set for life thanks to a generous clause in their prenuptial agreement. Ava's interest in her cabaret career began to wane the more time she spent shopping all over Europe. Every now and then, she thought of staging and producing a stunning show-'em-what-they've-been-missing New York cabaret debut. But something always stopped her from following through with that dream, and instead her focus shifted to Yancey's dreams for Broadway.

It was only when she received a call from Yancey informing her that Mama Essie was ill that Ava returned to the States. When Essie died two months later, Yancey prayed that she would finally have her mother to herself. And for about a year, she did. The mother and daughter, who were more like sisters, grew closer. Ava attended Yancey's pageants and dance recitals. The two of them took trips to London and spent weeks attending shows on the West End. And during that time Yancey heard the stories of the evil Miss Pretty and how she had forced her mother to pursue her showbiz dreams on another continent, taking Ava away from her mother and the daughter she loved. All those years, all her life, all that time without her mother. *All because of one person,* Yancey thought. Someone had to pay.

42

It was Saturday; day three of the Tylers' vigil. Raymond and his mother had checked into the Marriott on Michigan Avenue and took turns sitting with Raymond Sr. so that at least one of them was always at his bedside, talking to him, even though he couldn't respond, touching him, praying that would come out of his coma. Kirby would take the evening shift after football practice, bringing his books and playbook as he sat by his father's bed. This would give Raymond and his mother time to sit down and eat a real meal and freshen up. Kirby was grateful for Northwestern's open football date, which allowed him to spend more time with his father.

One evening, Raymond and his mother sat quietly at a table in the hospital coffee shop, each lost in their own troubled thoughts.

It was Mrs. Tyler who broke the strained silence.

"I need to call your Aunt Mattie and see if she will go over to the house and send me your father's insurance papers and burial plot information," she said quietly.

"Why are you going to do that?" Raymond snapped. "I don't want to hear no mess about some damn burial plots!"

"What's wrong, Raymond?"

"What do you mean? You're talking about burial plots, Pops is laying in the hospital unconscious, that's what's wrong!" Raymond lied.

"Raymond Tyler, Jr., don't you dare lie to me. I can see something's bothering you in the way you look at your father. You don't touch him like Kirby and I do. Tell me what's going on."

"Mama, I feel like a dog saying this, but I'm so conflicted about Pops. I'm so mad at him and the way he's treated me lately. I'm mad at him for the things he said about me and Trent, I'm mad the way he's throwing Kirby's accomplishments up in my face, like I've let him down and he doesn't want anything to do with me anymore. Why can't he accept my decisions about my life? I mean, I love Pops, you know I do. But if I've got to live my life according to his rules or lose his love, then I might learn how to live without his love. I'm a grown man and Pops has got to respect that."

"Your father does love and respect you. He just wants the best for you and Kirby," his mother said.

"He should want for us what we want for ourselves. And I know this might sound ugly, but I hope he doesn't die on us and leave me with all this anger."

Raymond couldn't look at his mother after his last statement. He fully expected her to call him selfish and everything but a child of God. But she didn't. Instead she asked, "And what else, son? You might as well get it all off your chest. What about Trent? That's what started this episode between you and your father."

"What about Trent?"

"You really love him, don't you?" she asked with a soft smile.

The question surprised Raymond. He and his mother had never discussed such intimate details of his relationship. It had always been limited to "How's Trent? Tell him I said hello."

Raymond paused a second, took a deep breath, and said, "Yes, Mom. I do. Very much. But . . ."

"But what? I know we've never spoken about your relationship, but I knew you two loved each other. I could tell that when we visited you guys in Seattle. And if you love him, then that's all that really matters. Your love is the only thing you have control of."

"What do you mean?"

"Son, you can't control how someone else feels about you. Of course when you love someone, you hope that love is returned with equal measure."

"So I'm supposed to love him even when he cheats on me. Endangers my career and my relationship with my pops?"

"Trent is human. People make mistakes. You aren't perfect, and neither is your father, or me, for that matter."

"But I feel so stupid. Having some stranger tell me about the person I love. I thought everything was fine between us. I mean, when I was with the firm, I was always pretty busy and sometimes under a lot of stress, and maybe I didn't spend as much time with Trent as I should. But he should understand that and how much I love him. Now that he's confessed to what I heard, well, I don't know what to do."

"You pray about it and do what your heart tells you," Mrs. Tyler said.

"Listen, I know I sound so selfish. Here I am thinking about myself while Pops is fighting for his life. But somehow it all seems connected. Everything I thought was solid and secure in my life is suddenly washing away like dust in a rainstorm. I just think I'm mad at the world right now and I don't know what to do about it."

"Oh, Raymond, you're not mad at the whole world. You're just disappointed with two men in your life. Both of whom are good men. Both of whom you love. And both of whom have hurt you deeply."

Raymond looked at his mother with a perplexed expression on his face.

"Raymond, your father and I taught you to always be fair. You've always been kind and sensitive to others, always righting wrongs and defending those who need defense. But, son, you got to fight for yourself now. How are you going to be the head of the family if your father doesn't make it through this? You got to let Trent know how you feel, how angry and hurt you are. And if your father makes it through this, you've got to let him know how you feel. You can't keep it all bottled up inside."

Marlee took her son's hand and continued, "You know, Kirby was right. Your father wanted very badly to be appointed to the federal bench and even the Supreme Court. When we first met, he told me one day he'd reach his goal. But it didn't happen. But when you got nominated, well, I don't recall ever seeing him more proud. It was like his dream had come true. A Tyler man was on track for the highest court in the land."

"Why didn't I know Pops dreamed to be on the Supreme Court? I always thought when he was elected state senator, he'd achieved his dream."

"Because your father always shared his dreams with one person. Me," his mother said as tears sprang from her eyes. Raymond reached across the table and touched his mother's hand softly.

"I'm sorry, Mama. This helps me understand Pops's reaction better."

"Baby, you've got to make it clear to your father that this is your life. Life is too short to spend it pleasing other people. Even if those other people are your parents. And if this judge thing is not your dream, then you got to tell him that also. He may not want to hear it, but he'll respect you for telling him."

Several minutes passed in silence. Raymond stood and walked around to his mother's side of the table, then knelt next to her. He wrapped his arms around her and pressed his face to her bosom.

"Thank you, Mama. Thank you. I know you're right. I just need some time to let it all settle. To finally figure out what my dreams are." She stroked his head and patted his back like she had when he was a boy.

"Like I said, son, life is short. Tomorrow is not promised."

43

Nicole arrived at La Guardia feeling defeated and alone, even though Jared met her. When Nicole saw Jared looking tired and worried himself, she smiled, although tears were streaming down her makeup-free face.

"Hey, baby," he said as he kissed her passionately. "I haven't been able to sleep since I talked to you last night." He took his hand and wiped away her tears.

A few moments later Nicole's tears stopped, and she said softly, "I'm sorry I had you worried, but I'll be okay."

Jared picked up Nicole's luggage and retreated to the limo he had hired. During the ride home, Nicole gave him more details of the last forty-eight hours, and he responded by holding her tightly in the backseat while she ranted, cried, and ranted some more. "I couldn't believe the way that jerk Chris acted when I showed up to do my final show. When he asked me if I was sure I wanted to go on, I told him to get out of my way, before I had my lawyer and the union representative on his ass. And then I went out there and gave the performance of my life."

"That's my baby," Jared said, gently patting her hands.

Nicole told Jared how she had spent Friday debating whether or not to stay with the show until her contract expired or leave and return to New York. When her agent, Dennis, told her the producers had a settlement check ready to be messengered to his office whenever she gave the word, her mind was made up. Nicole told Jared she could hear her deceased father saying, "Don't stay nowhere people don't want you."

By the time they got home, they were both so spent they decided to fall into bed and talk in the morning. Jared held Nicole tightly all night, even after she'd fallen into a fretful sleep. Nicole's restless sleep continued throughout the weekend.

When Nicole awoke on Monday morning, it was a little after nine, and Jared had long been gone. He'd left a note on the pillow beside her that read: *Nicole, I love you with all my heart. You are and will always be the star of my show. Call you later. Love, Jared.*

Nicole felt like she'd been beaten with a stick. Her eyes were bloodshot and swollen, her body exhausted. She turned on the television, but put on the mute button while watching *Regis and Kathie Lee*. Nicole wanted to enjoy the perfection of the silence.

A few minutes later Nicole got out of bed and pulled her terry-cloth robe on over the Arkansas Razorbacks nightshirt she'd worn to bed. She stumbled into the kitchen, where Jared had made coffee, and she poured herself a cup. The sunny brightness of the kitchen seemed to emphasize her gloomy mood and disheveled appearance, so she retreated to the bedroom. She sat on the bed and considered taking a shower and getting dressed, but could not think of a good reason to do either. She just didn't have the energy, nor the inclination. She curled back under the covers and fell into a restless sleep.

Nicole woke up about an hour later and decided to watch *The View*. Nicole loved this show and hoped one of the hosts like Star Jones or Joy Behar would say something funny to make her smile. But today the four ladies were talking about the most recent kids-killing-kids incident. This time Nicole pulled the covers over her head and went into a deep sleep.

"Nicole! Wake up! Baby, wake up. I've been trying to call you all day." Jared shook her gently until she began to stir. "It's six o'clock. Have you been asleep all day?" he asked.

"I guess so," Nicole said. "I turned the phone off."

"Are you feeling all right, baby?" he asked with concern in his voice. "I was worried about you. Did you eat anything? Why don't I run you a nice hot bath and give you a massage? I can ease those blues right out of your body. Then I'll run out and get us some dinner."

"I'm not hungry. I just want to go back to sleep," Nicole said. She was thinking Jared didn't have a clue as to how depressed she felt. Did he think a bath and a massage could alleviate her troubles?

"What have you eaten today?"

"Nothing."

"Then I'm going to get us something to eat," Jared said as he pulled off his suit and changed quickly into some warm-ups. "What do you feel like eating?"

"I don't care," Nicole said. "Get whatever you want."

"How about barbecue? Or would you like something light?"

Nicole looked at Jared angrily and said, "I told you I don't care." And then she pulled the covers over her head and prayed for another deep, dreamless sleep.

❖   ❖   ❖

Morning dawned, and Yancey woke up ready to enjoy the beginning of her life as a star. She let out the sound of soft laughter and clapped her hands when the sun broke through the early morning clouds and the room suddenly looked golden. Yancey was getting ready to pick up the phone and order room service when it rang.

"Hello."

"Where have you been?" Ava asked.

"With Devin, who I got to figure out a way to get rid of now. How are you doing, sweetheart?"

"I'm doing good, but I've been going crazy. What did Miss Pretty say when she found out you got her part?"

"I don't know," Yancey said as she pulled back the covers.

"What do you mean? Didn't you see her?"

"I saw her right after her last performance. And Miss Pretty turned it out! I mean even I was in awe. But since we didn't know if she was going to stay with the show or leave immediately, I sorta stayed clear. I left her these sweet messages and said I was spending the night with Devin. But when I was certain she was gone and had left Grand Rapids, I came back to my room. I had to give up all that pussy to Devin, just so I could escape some fake teary good-bye with Miss Pretty. She left me this sappy note, and I'll send her some flowers with an *I miss you* note and that will be that. I'm on my way to Broadway!" Yancey said as she pumped her fist in the air.

"How is the show going?"

"Oh, it's fine. And last night I was fierce! The new director was all over me. I think I might have to give him a little taste."

"Now, be careful serving up favors. Make sure it's gonna earn you some brownie points," Ava advised.

"Oh, don't worry. If I give Chris some play, it will be for a good, good reason."

"So do you know when you're going to Broadway? And you better get your agent to get a contract now. Have them put it in writing," Ava advised.

"I already got them working on it. We go to Memphis after we leave here. And then we're going to close down and get ready for the Great White Way. During that off time, I will be getting some other things like a press agent and a manager," Yancey said.

"You need a press agent, but hold off on that manager stuff. You don't need to be giving somebody else ten percent of what you get. Trust me, girl, I know," Ava said.

"You're still coming to Memphis, aren't you? I mean I know you wanted to confront Miss Pretty there, but I'd love it if you came opening night."

"Don't worry, darling, I'll be there front and center," Ava said.

Yancey heard a knock on her door and told Ava to hold on. When she looked through the peephole, she saw a Mexican housekeeper with her cart and passkey. Yancey ripped open the door and yelled, "What do you want?" The frightened maid pointed to the Housekeeping Service Requested sign. "This is on the wrong side. Come back later," Yancey said as she slammed the door.

"Ava, let me call you back, honey. That was the dumb-ass maid and I need to go to the bathroom."

"Are you sure you're okay?"

"Mama, I'm on top of the world. And I can't wait to see you."

"And I can't wait to see my daughter play the great Miss Dena Jones!"

44

"They trying to send me over the top, Doc. Trying to send a brother over the top!" Basil announced as he took his balled left hand and smacked it into the palm of his right hand. Only moments before, he had walked into the office and started pacing around the tiny space like a horse waiting to be released from his stable.

"Who's 'they'?"

"You are not going to believe this shit, 'cause you know what? I don't believe it." He stopped pacing and leaned against the windowsill with his arms crossed in a defensive posture.

"Are you going to tell me what happened? Does this have to do with Raymond?"

"Fuck no! I still ain't heard from that mofo, but this ain't got shit to do with him," Basil said as he finally took a seat.

"Let's talk about what happened."

"First, let me tell you the story. Don't ask me how I feel, 'cause I don't know how I feel. Just let me tell the story, okay?"

"Fine. Tell me the story."

Basil was silent for a few moments and then released a long sigh, and his shoulders sank as he began to speak. "I was at home the other day, sad to say, waiting on a call from Raymond. Something is up with him 'cause neither him or his boy are at the hotel. He had checked out. Since he had stood me up that night I've been waiting to hear from him. Whenever the phone would ring, I'd answer it after the first ring. I'd take my cellular with me everywhere I went, even the gym and the golf course. So the other day, I'm at home and the phone rings, and it's Campbell. We talk about how we haven't talked in a while. I tell her I've been busy . . . she says she's been busy, and then she says she's gotta see me today. When I asked her what was up, she said, 'It's something I should have told you the first time we met.' So now she's got my attention and I agree to meet her at Dayo, this soul food restaurant in the Village," Basil said. He took a deep breath and continued. "I don't like going down to the Village because mofos are always hittin' on me. But it was the middle of the day and I figured no harm, no foul. So I meet Campbell down there and she's drinking a glass of wine and smoking a cigarette. But she's looking good! She had on this slammin' tangerine-orange sweater that looked like it was sewed on her body. I'm thinking sistah's ready to give a brother some skins, cool. I mention to her that I didn't know she smoked and how that's gonna mess with her workouts. She just smiles and says, 'I only smoke when I'm nervous.' I ask her why she's nervous and Campbell tells me to order something to eat or drink, she's paying. So now I'm really wondering what's up."

"Did she tell you?"

Basil gave the doctor a that-was-a-stupid-question look and nodded his head and said, "Oh yeah, she told me."

"What did she say?"

Basil stood up and started talking again, but his voice sounded disconnected, as if it wasn't attached to his body. "This bitch tells me that she's been keeping something from me. Tells me we're related. When I ask her how, she takes a couple of quick puffs from her cigarette and then says just real casual, 'I'm your sister.' I look at this bitch like she got two heads and both of 'em are fucked up."

"What did you say?"

"I looked at her and said, 'What kinda bullshit game are you playing? I ain't got no sister. And if I did it certainly wouldn't be no crazy-ass bitch like you. It's just me and my pops.' I thought that would shut her up, but she kept talking. Told me my mother only died recently. That she was living in New York on Long Island most of my life, but she had moved to Santa Fe, New Mexico, about five years ago. Told me some dumb-ass shit about how my father made her promise never to contact me. She said my pops had caught my mother with Campbell's father, some white mofo, and had banished her from Jacksonville, Florida. My pops ain't that kinda man, and so I'm thinking this bitch needs to be writing soap operas." Basil paused briefly. "Then she told me when her mother was sick, they spent a lot of time in her bedroom just watching television and how one day they saw me on the tube being interviewed after a game and her mother told her this fucked-up story. I wanted to say to her crazy ass, 'Don't you know they give sick people drugs?' Maybe her mom had some old-timers' disease or some shit like that."

"Did you ask her what kind of proof she had?"

"Naw, 'cause the bitch ain't got no proof. Campbell ain't my sister. She don't even look like me!"

"What did you do?"

"I told that bitch if she wanted to run a game on somebody, then I was not the mofo to be playing with. Told her I'd report her ass to the FBI for extortion."

"So she asked you for money?"

"Hell no. I didn't give the bitch a chance. I got up and walked my ass right out the restaurant."

"Did you ask your father about what she said?"

Basil released a wild, hysterical laugh as he fell back into the chair and said, "Fuck no. You think I'm gonna call my pops every time some crazy mofo shows up trying to tap me for some funds? I don't think so," Basil said.

"So you didn't believe her?"

"Hell the fuck no!"

"So why did it bother you so?"

"Who said it bothered me?"

"Your body language. Your voice."

"Hey, what am I supposed to do? Now I've got to watch the honeys just like the hardheads. Everybody got a game," Basil said as he got up from the chair.

"You want to talk about it some more? We've got a little more time."

"Naw, Doc. I've done all the talking I'm going to do about that crazy bitch. And you know, when I think about it, I'm sorry I wasted even this time speaking about it. I'm outta here," Basil said, and then dashed from the office.

45

Jared was worried, and his patience was shrinking. There had been no improvement in Nicole's disposition. She had not left the apartment since arriving from Grand Rapids and was still wearing the same night-shirt. She spent her days watching television and old movies like *Who's Afraid of Virginia Woolf?, A Patch of Blue,* and *Carmen Jones.* Depression was closing in on her like a winter storm.

Jared knew she had a lot to work out and that she was hurting. But after three days of no real conversation, he knew something had to be done. When he suggested she resume seeing Dr. Huntley, the therapist she had seen in the late eighties, Nicole was quick with a firm no.

One evening before leaving his office, he called her mother and expressed his concern. Her mother called immediately. When Nicole saw her mother's number on the caller ID Jared had recently purchased, she figured she might as well get the conversation over with.

Her mother was blunt and to the point, as usual. "Nicole Marie Springer-Stovall, you need to get over it! You're acting like a little spoiled brat who didn't get her way. I told you moving back to New York was a bad idea."

Nicole didn't respond as she listened to her mother on the speaker-phone. The familiar voice sent a chill through her, and Nicole pulled the ivory cashmere blanket she loved close to her chin.

"Now, I know you've suffered terribly," she said sarcastically, "and I'm sure you're not the only one in the world to ever experience a little setback, but it's time to get on with your life. It sounds to me like that acting thing has dried up and you're providing your own little drama. It's time to do what you should have done years ago. Start having babies."

"Mama, that is something Jared and—"

Nicole's mother interrupted her and continued. "You know Jared wants a child and you're not getting any younger. Wasting all those years trying to be an actress. See where it got you? You should have listened to me, but no, I don't know nothing. I think you need to count your blessings that you still have a husband, let alone a man like Jared. But you've always been so hardheaded. But a hard head still makes a soft behind. I hope them firing you will bring you to your senses."

Nicole's mother went on and on. Nicole just didn't have the energy to fight her anymore. She stared at the phone as though her mother's abrasive voice and hurtful words were poisonous snakes coming through the line. Finally she said, "Good-bye, Mother," and hit the disconnect button.

When Jared came home that evening, he announced he had a business trip to Chicago and was going to check in on Raymond's father and stop by Atlanta to check on his own mother.

"What happened with Raymond's father?" Nicole asked.

"Nicole, don't you remember? I told you his father had a stroke. He's in a coma."

"That's horrible. I'm sorry about that. I don't remember you telling me," Nicole said softly.

"Did your mother call you?" Jared asked, sitting on the edge of the bed.

"Yeah, and after she had her say, I hung up."

"Nicole, what is wrong with you? You're letting this thing eat you up. When are you going to snap out of it? It's not like you to sleep all day. And hanging up on your own mother. What's up with that?"

Nicole did not appreciate Jared's accusatory tone. Wasn't he supposed to be on her side? Didn't he see how hard this was for her? She just needed more time. She didn't know for what, but she knew she wasn't ready to face the world. Let alone her mother.

"Why are you two teaming up on me?" Nicole cried.

"What do you mean teaming up?" Jared asked, briefly closing his eyes and rubbing his temples. He felt a terrible headache coming on.

"All my mother wanted to talk about was that tired old it's-time-to-have-a-baby line again. She wants me to be a good little wife and mother now that my career is down the tubes, as she thinks. She's the last person on earth who should be advocating motherhood!"

"Maybe she's right," Jared said matter-of-factly.

"What did you say?" Nicole asked as her eyes narrowed to a cold stare. She couldn't believe he'd just said her mother was right.

"I mean, why not?" Jared persisted. "Why can't we start a family now? Would that be so bad? I mean, you're not exactly busy, are you? You haven't returned any of the calls to your agent, so you can't be that concerned about your career."

"I just can't take the rejection right now. Not from you or casting people," Nicole said.

"How have I rejected you, Nicole? I've been patient with you while you pursued your career. I moved to a city I'm not particularly fond of for your career. I've been patient. I don't think I deserve to see you dragging around here for days." He took a deep breath and continued. "You don't go out, and you haven't been taking care of yourself. You've had that damn nightshirt on since you arrived home. I wouldn't be a good husband if I stood by and watched you wallow in your self-pity," Jared said, dropping his voice to a deeper tone.

"Why are you putting all of this on me? You didn't say this when I asked you to move. Can't I take a few days for myself where I'm not worried about how I look?" Nicole asked as she tugged at the hem of her nightshirt.

"Sure, baby. You can take a few days to get over this. But it doesn't give you the right to be mean to your mother, and to act like I'm not even here. You haven't listened to anything I've said. The encouragement I've offered. How many times over the last week that I've told you I loved you."

"What if I can't get pregnant?" Nicole asked as she looked away to the window. She was a mess, she knew, and Jared's attention the past few days had barely registered. She knew what he was really after.

"Then we still have the surrogate route or adoption," Jared suggested.

"Oh no. I'm not going through that shit anymore," Nicole said firmly.

"What shit?"

"Adoption. Have you forgotten how those people wanted to pry into our life? Have you forgotten about how many times they had a baby for us, only to tell us later there was no baby? I can't go through that. And if you want a child that bad, then maybe you ought to find someone else. I can't take that pressure," Nicole said, her eyes filling with tears. She felt everything around her was collapsing.

"I can't believe you. Maybe I should leave tonight before I say something I'm going to be sorry for," Jared said as he looked at his wife. He couldn't believe what he was hearing. He knew he was looking at his wife, but the voice and words were those of a total stranger.

"Suit yourself. Go to Chicago. Maybe you can comfort Raymond and his family since you can't do it for me!" Nicole said, and raced past Jared and into the bathroom, where she locked the door and threw herself to the floor as the tears began again.

❖   ❖   ❖

It was late and Yancey was looking forward to a restful night of sleep alone when the phone rang. She unzipped her skirt and laid it on the dresser and grabbed the phone.

"Hello."

"Hey, darling. How was the show tonight?" Ava asked.

"It was great! I just love playing Dena, and Chris keeps telling me what a great job I'm doing. He wants me bad," Yancey laughed.

"Like I said, be careful. A cast member is one thing, but the director is another. If Miss Pretty hadn't been so shady with this guy before, she might still be doing the role on her way to Memphis with you. What are you going to do about this Devin guy?"

"I think he's getting the clue. Every time he suggests doing something I tell him I need to work on my new role, but he's still sniffing around. But if he calls or comes by tonight, I might give him some one more time. But you can be certain I will give him the heave-ho before we get to Memphis."

"That's good. I want to make sure we get to spend a lot of time together. But I sure hate it that I won't be able to see Nicole's face when she finds out I'm your mother."

"That would be fun, but I'm glad she's gone. I can't wait to get to Memphis. What day are you coming?"

"I'll be there the first day. I don't know if I'm going to drive or hire a car, and I plan to stay the entire week. It's going to be wonderful; we can go shopping at Goldsmith's and have some ribs at that place near the hotel. And we can visit the Civil Rights Museum."

"I'm looking forward to it. Did you take those announcements to St. Paul AME?" Yancey asked. She and Ava were going to blanket Jackson with the news that Yancey was starring in a show headed for Broadway.

"I sure did. I even put a couple of dollars in the church secretary's pocket to make sure she put it in the bulletin. I contacted this girl I went to school with, who is president of Links, and they're thinking about chartering a bus down to Memphis to see you turn it out. So it will be standing ovations every night."

"That's wonderful. Can you believe it? We got Nicole out before Memphis and New York. Ain't life grand?" Yancey asked as she fell back on her bed.

"Yes, it is darling. Life sho is grand!"

46

A son can never take too many walks with his mother. So on a crystalline Chicago Sunday, mother and son walked hand in hand along Lake Michigan, as a thin October wind blew. The sky was a layered patchwork of red and bronze broken by stripes of gray.

More than a week had passed, and thankfully Raymond Sr.'s prognosis had improved. He was moved to a private room which gave the family greater privacy and freedom to come and go. He was conscious much of the time, though he still couldn't speak. The left side of his body remained paralyzed, but in the last few days, some movement and feeling was detected. Kirby was able to turn his attention back to classes and football, while Raymond and his mother were able to leave the hospital each evening when visiting hours were over.

"It was good seeing Jared," Mrs. Tyler said after several minutes of silence. Jared had made a surprise visit to check on the Tylers while conducting business in Chicago.

"Yeah, it was. I think it made Pops feel better also," Raymond said as he watched a seagull scoop up something floating on the top of the water and then fly off.

"Is everything all right with Jared and Nicole?"

"Why do you ask?"

"Well, he just looked a little worried. Everything okay with him and Nicole?"

Raymond laughed and said, "Do you ever stop being a mother?"

"Can't do it."

"They've hit a bump in the road over when the babies start coming. But they will manage. I think I'll give him a call when I get back to the hotel to make sure he's cool. He was trying to be strong for us. But he's a bit troubled," Raymond said.

"And since you know I'm a mother twenty-four hours a day, I have a question. Is Trent going to come to Chicago before we take your father back home?"

"I don't know. I think it depends on how long I'm here," Raymond said softly.

Mrs. Tyler knew it was a difficult time for her son and that Raymond hadn't talked with Trent often since arriving in Chicago. When Trent called, Raymond would only speak for a few minutes, often telling Trent he needed to get back to the hospital. Raymond would leave brief messages for Trent when he knew Trent was away from their Seattle home. His mother would also watch Raymond sit for hours looking at his father, unable to say what was in his heart. She knew that Raymond needed to make peace with his demons.

"You know, Raymond, I'm going to tell you something I swore I'd never tell you," Marlee announced.

Raymond stopped walking and turned to face his mother before asking, "What, Mama?"

"Your father cheated on me once."

"Pops?" Raymond said. "Pops cheated on you? No! Pops would never do that! And when I asked you before, why didn't you tell me then?"

"It was our business," Marlee said firmly.

"I can't believe Pops would do something like that," Raymond said, shaking his head in disbelief.

"Well, he did," his mother said, "he most certainly did."

"I'm sorry, Mama," Raymond said as he hugged her tightly. "I know you wouldn't lie to me about something like that, but it's still hard for me to believe. I mean, the two of you always seemed so happy together. The one thing I always knew I could depend on was you guys being in love. What happened? How did you deal with it?"

"It was a very long time ago, Raymond. I haven't really thought about it in ages. And, of course, it's never happened again."

"How can you be sure?"

"I know. We were so young then. You were just a toddler and your father had just hung out his shingle. It was tough going. He was trying to build up his practice and I had a little rascal like you running me ragged and I was teaching and working a part-time job. I told your father he should apply at some of the large law firms. I mean, he had finished at the top of his class at Howard, and if he wanted to be a judge, he needed that experience. But large firms weren't interested in somebody your father's color. The money was short and so were our tempers. We seemed to be pulling apart instead of pulling together.

"Anyway, one night he didn't come home. I knew he was lying to me when he called with some silly excuse and it just about broke my heart. Not a day passed before he confessed that he'd been with another woman. Some out-of-law-school clerk who was helping him start his practice. It was like he couldn't wait to rub my face in it. I thought he must be the cruelest man in the world."

"Jesus, Mom. What did you do?"

"I did what you're doing. I ran. Wouldn't speak to him, wouldn't listen to nothing he had to say. I just grabbed you and went to my mother's. I was so angry, so hurt, I couldn't see straight. But the pain, the anger, the hurt that I thought I'd left behind, followed me around until I had to do something. As bad as your father had made me feel, I loved him something awful. Yes, I wanted to fix him, get even with him, but I couldn't imagine my life—or yours—without him. But my own mother pointed out that I had been partly responsible."

"No way, Mama. How could you have been responsible? What he did he chose to do. No matter what, Pops shouldn't have done that to you!"

The two of them walked toward some concrete steps and sat down, with the racing traffic of Lake Shore Drive behind them and the calm of Lake Michigan before them.

"Son, life is just not that cut-and-dry. People sometimes do hurtful things just to get the other person's attention. And what I discovered was that I hadn't been paying attention, or giving attention, either. The more I thought about it, the more I wondered why he hadn't cheated sooner. Now, maybe he could have just come to me, sat me down, and told me what was wrong, but I probably wouldn't have heard him. But it was my mother's advice that meant the most."

"What did she say?"

"She told me, 'If you love him,' she said, 'really love him, then forgive him, forgive yourself, and move on with your lives.' "

"So that's what you did?"

"That's what I did."

"Did it work?"

"Trust me, baby, it worked." She smiled and grabbed his knee playfully. "It worked."

"Forgiveness, huh?" Raymond said mostly to himself as he put his arms around his mother, buried his face in her neck, and gently kissed her.

❖   ❖   ❖

Raymond went to the lobby of the hotel and called Jared's cellular phone. Raymond didn't want to disturb his mother, so he went downstairs to the lobby and called Jared. He picked up after a couple of rings.

"Hello, Jared Stovall speaking."

"Hey, dawg. You miss me?" Raymond asked. He could hear the static of the portable phone in the background.

"Didn't I just see ya?" Jared joked.

"Yeah, but you've been on my mind," Raymond said.

"So you saw through me, huh?"

"And so did my mom."

"Don't worry, I'm cool. I'm down here in Atlanta enjoying Moms and my little sister and when I get home, Nicole and I will work everything out," Jared said.

"OK. I just want you to know, despite everything I'm dealing with, I'm here for you," Raymond said.

"I know that. And how are you doing? I'm still trippin' on what you told me about Trent. I mean, man, I don't know what I'd do if I ever found out Nicole was stepping out on me," Jared said. He was shocked when Raymond, out of the blue, had said, "I thought the knowledge that my lover is lookin' for dick elsewhere could be the worse thing that could happen and now this." Raymond dropped the bombshell and then stated emphatically that he didn't want to go into details. Jared had just deeply massaged his shoulders as Raymond stared out into space silently.

"Well, right now, my pops and you are my priority. I deal with Trent later," Raymond said as he looked at his watch. It was almost midnight and he had thought about calling Trent just to check in.

"Well, I'm here if you need me," Jared said.

"And you know that."

"And I might have a solution to my problem," Jared said.

"What's that?"

"I still want my own children, and I know one day that will happen. But while I was on the flight to Atlanta, I sat next to this sistah who worked with Big Brothers and Big Sisters. We got in a conversation and I thought about what an impact Nicole and I could make in some of these children's lives. And there is foster care as well. It will give us some training and help out some of the kids who need to know they matter," Jared said.

"That's a great plan. You'd be a great big brother or foster father. I know you're a perfect best friend."

"And so are you," Jared said.

"Let me hang up before we both get too mushy," Raymond said as he fought back the tears forming.

"I love you, Ray."

"And I love you back."

47

The last thing Nicole wanted was company. With Jared away on business, Nicole was enjoying her solitude by listening to the gospel song "Stand," over and over. When she became ready to face the world, Nicole would have a new theme song.

As she crossed the living room to answer the incessant buzzing of the intercom, Nicole was startled by her own reflection in the framed mirror near the door. She looked bad. The intercom buzzed annoyingly again and Nicole pushed the talk button.

"What is it!" she yelled at the speaker. She touched the arrangement of chrysanthemums sent by Yancey and Cedric, and breathed in the heavy fragrance of the apartment.

"It's me, Miss Springer. Clinton. The doorman. I'm terribly sorry to disturb you, 'cause your husband told me you weren't feeling well, but there's a Miss Morris here to see you, and she said she come from way across the country to see you." The doorman lowered his voice to a whisper. "And from what I can tell, I don't think she's going to leave without seeing that you're all right. What would you like for me to do?"

Miss Morris, Nicole thought. *Delaney!* "Please tell Miss Morris that I'm fine, but I really can't see her right now. Tell her . . ."

"Nicole?" Delaney's voice came over the intercom. "Girl, I'm on my way up there and you'd better open the door or I'm calling 911. And you can forget if you think Clinton here can keep me from coming up."

Nicole knew there was no stopping her old friend Delaney Morris. Not when she used that tone. By the time Nicole had put on a robe, turned down the gospel music she was playing, and unlocked the two dead bolts, Delaney was knocking on the front door.

Delaney was shocked at her friend's appearance. The first thing she noticed was Nicole's eyes, which were void of the sparkle Delaney remembered. Nicole's hair was tangled and wild, dark shadows encircled her eyes, and her lips were chapped.

Nicole felt shamefully self-conscious under her friend's close scrutiny. She felt the tears begin to well up in her eyes as she prepared to hear her friend tell her how messed up she was!

"Bad hair day?" Delaney said.

Nicole couldn't help herself. She laughed out loud and couldn't stop giggling. She laughed until her side hurt, and Delaney laughed right along with her. They grabbed each other and held each other so tightly and laughed so hard that Nicole began to choke. Delaney patted her on the back and told her to raise her arms. When Nicole put her hands up over her head, the coughing subsided, but when she took one look at Delaney, with her own tears falling from the corners of her eyes, Nicole began to cry again.

After a few moments, Nicole said, "Delaney, girl, what in the world are you doing here?"

"You got any tea in that kitchen?"

"Tea?"

"Yes, tea."

"I think so," Nicole said.

"Then c'mon in the kitchen and I'll make us some tea. Then I'll tell if you'll tell. Should I tell Clinton to take my garment bag out of the storage room?"

"I'll buzz him later."

The two friends walked arm in arm into the dark kitchen. Nicole sat at the counter while Delaney opened the blinds to allow the soft light of early evening to flood the room. She turned on the kettle, found the tea bags and two mugs, and set them on the counter. She pulled a barstool next to Nicole's and put an arm around her friend's shoulder, drawing her close.

"So you gonna let the bastards grind you down, huh?"

"What are you doing here?"

"I'll give you the short version: Cedric called and told me those bastards had you replaced in the show. He was worried about you 'cause nobody had the chance to say good-bye. I called you. You weren't answering the phone. I didn't leave a message. I called Jared's mother in Atlanta and she gave me his office number. After finally getting through that tough assistant of his, we talked. He told me you were taking it real hard and that he was worried about you. Said he thought maybe you should go see Dr. Huntley, but you weren't having it. I told him I'd pray for you 'cause I knew you weren't feeling me these days," Delaney said.

"You thought I was still upset with you?" Nicole asked with her head held down.

"I figured you'd get over it sooner or later, but Jared called me from Chicago and told me you guys had a big fight. And I know you don't like to fight. He said the fight was about him wanting you to stop your career and have a baby. I know how sensitive that is for you."

The high-pitched whistle of the teakettle put a temporary halt to Delaney's rapid-fire narrative. She poured the water over the tea bags and handed Nicole a mug. She set her own steaming mug on the table and picked up where she left off.

"Jared said you were sleeping too much, not eating enough, and depressed as hell. He said he didn't know what to do, that he'd never seen you act like this. But from his voice and our conversation I think Jared's in worse shape than you. Men hate it when they can't fix things," Delaney said. She took a sip of her tea.

A trace of a smile touched Nicole's eyes, and she said, "I know that's right."

"Anyway, Jared told me he was going to be in Chicago for a few days on business and then he was headed to Atlanta for business and to check on his mother. It sounded like he needed some space himself.

"So I said to myself, 'Miss Self, you need to get on a plane and get to New York and see what's up with my girlfriend.' Jody and Fletcher were on their way to Seattle to see my mama, so the timing was perfect. And, ta-da! Here I am. Come to save the day," Delaney said as a sweet smile softened her face. "Okay, your turn."

Nicole gazed for a moment at her friend, beautiful with a brownish-yellow skin tone like she had just returned from the Islands. She thought about how Delaney, who used to refer to herself as a "video ho," was now a leading director of music videos. She still had a dancer's body, and her thick, short curly hair gave Delaney the look of a woman who had to be taken seriously.

When Nicole began to speak, she told Delaney the events of Grand Rapids, with the new director, her sudden illness, and how she was dismissed. Just telling her old friend her side of the story made Nicole feel better than she'd felt in days.

"I will tell you this, though, girl. I walked out of there with my head held high. I gave them a performance of a lifetime. The only problem was when I got back to New York, where I thought my dreams were going to come true, well, I just crashed," Nicole said.

"And you're entitled to that every once in a while. But don't you for one minute let some lame-ass director define who you are. That sorry S.O.B. is just mad 'cause you wouldn't give him some back in the day. You know how these showbiz people are. And Chris is a diva hater if there ever was one."

"I know you're right. I probably wouldn't have taken it so hard, but I didn't have anyone to turn to. I mean, Jared tries, but I don't think he understands how important this is to me. And my mother, well forget that. And I didn't have a friend left. I didn't have a Candance. And I didn't have a Delaney," Nicole said as she touched her friend's hands gently.

"You'll always have Delaney, whether you want one or not. Now, you listen to me, Ms. Springer-Stovall. You are the most talented person I know. Anyone who knows you knows you're a wonderful actress, a great singer, and an okay dancer." Delaney laughed as she moved her hand side to side.

"I'll never be able to dance like you," Nicole smiled.

"And you don't need to. So what are we going to do about this baby thing?"

"What do you mean?"

"You still want a kid?"

"Now, Delaney, don't play me like that. I don't want you to change your mind 'cause you're feeling sorry for me," Nicole said.

"I ain't feeling sorry for you, and I didn't say that I've changed my mind. But you know it's important to Jared."

"I know. But, Delaney, I think I got to face why I'm so afraid of getting my hopes up. I also have to face that I got some real deep concerns about motherhood."

"Why?"

"I'm ashamed to say, but I'm afraid I'd turn out just like my own mother."

"Honey, from what you've told me and what I've seen . . . there is reason to be scared. But just like I can see your talent, I know you'd be a great mother. If that's what you want. Forget about Jared for a moment. He's a man, and even though he's a cut above the rest, he's still a man. And from what I remember about them, they think of themselves 24-7, 365!"

"But what if he leaves me?"

"Then he loses. But Jared ain't going nowhere. He is whipped! And he loves you."

"I'm so glad you're here. I'm sorry for being such a selfish bitch," Nicole said.

"Nicole, at some point in each of our lives, we all become selfish. It doesn't mean we're bad or bitches. It just means we're taking a moment for ourselves and we need to do that from time to time. Just don't make a habit of it, or I'll have to do a dyke pull-up on you," Delaney said, playfully putting her fists in a boxer's stance.

"So what do I do?" Nicole asked.

"About what?"

"About Jared and the baby business," Nicole said as she took the mugs and walked around the counter and placed them in the empty sink.

"Well, you kick the blues to the curb, girlfriend. Stiff upper lip. It's time to get on with life. Kick some butt, and take names."

"What should I do first?"

"We need to make a plan."

"A plan?"

"Yeah, and I know just what it needs to be," Delaney said forcefully.

"What?"

"We need to get a comb and a brush so I can fix your head before the Hair Police come in here and give you a citation for this do!"

"You're still crazy, Delaney," Nicole said with a smile. When she smiled, it was as though the sun had finally broken through the clouds.

48

Though Jackson, Tennessee, was seventy-nine miles east, the Memphis media treated Yancey like a long-lost favorite daughter. Partly because she had sent several eight-by-ten color photos and a press release touting herself as the greatest entertainer to hit Memphis since Elvis Presley performed his first concert in 1954.

WXTV sent a limo to whisk her directly from the airport to their downtown studio for a live entertainment segment of *Good Morning Memphis.* From there she went to a popular hip-hop radio show, where listeners called in and asked her questions about herself and the show. One caller asked if she was the same Yancey Braxton who had graduated from Jackson Central Mary High.

"Why, yes, I am," Yancey answered, pleased to be recognized.

"This is Nisey. We were in Delta Debs together and Ballards School of Dance. Do you remember me?"

"Nisey? I'm trying to remember. You know, most people might think Jackson is small, but we had about six hundred people in our class. I don't remember your name, but I'm sure if I saw you, I'd know you," Yancey said. She recognized the voice of her hated childhood rival, but wanted to make sure Nisey didn't enter Yancey's wonderful new world.

"Yeah, I'm sure you'll remember me when you see me. I've gained a little weight, but my face still looks the same."

"Oh, I'm sorry to hear that, but I hope you won't let that keep you from coming to the show."

"Don't worry. I'll be there with bells on. I have third row center seats."

"That's great! Come backstage and say hello," Yancey said.

But the caller didn't respond, because she had hung up. The radio show ended with Yancey singing a few bars of "One Night Only" a cappella.

After a busy morning, including an interview with the *Memphis Commercial Appeal,* Yancey was able to check into her hotel room. Most of the cast stayed at the Radisson Hotel in downtown Memphis. Except for Yancey. She was staying at the four-star Peabody Hotel, and Yancey Braxton walked in like she had a deed to the place.

Yancey moved into a modest suite on the concierge floor, unpacked her bags, and ordered a Caesar salad from room service. She called the concierge and arranged to have a light supper and chilled champagne in the room when she and Ava returned from the theater later that evening.

Yancey placed a flower-covered box of Ava Rose memorabilia on the sitting room's coffee table. She anticipated sharing the pictures, postcards, and letters with her mother that night. Though she carried the box of memories with her everywhere, it had been years since Yancey actually took the items out of the small box and looked at them. When she was a child, she would hold each letter in her hands, feeling the texture of the expensive stationery, staring at the picture postcards and photographs of her mother, and making up stories and fantasies about each one. By the time she was fifteen, Yancey had memorized every page, every line, every word of each and every letter in the box and could recite the whole bundle by heart. She had noticed that her mother's handwriting was somewhat erratic on the postcards, yet beautifully scripted on her letters. The box was Yancey's treasure, her heirloom, the closest she ever got to her real mother. That is, until now.

Yancey arranged a few keepsakes on the coffee table next to the box, ate her lunch, took a bath in lavender salts, and then decided to take a long nap before the evening performance. She dreamed of little girls in petticoats and ribbons dancing in meadows of wildflowers, while beautiful mothers in flowing dresses sat sipping mint iced tea and cautioning the girls to be careful of dancing so near the edge of a looming cliff. In her dream, Ava Rose reached unsuccessfully for Yancey's little hand, and Yancey fell backward off the cliff into the deep blue sea below. She awoke at the sound of the phone ringing. It was the front desk calling to tell her that flowers had been delivered to the hotel, but she had a Do Not Disturb sign on her door.

"Yeah, send them up," Yancey said, rubbing the sleep from her eyes.

Minutes later a young black man was knocking at Yancey's door with two dozen yellow roses. The card attached was addressed to "La Petite Diva," and Yancey removed the card which read: *Make me proud. I love you. Ava.*

The young bellman cleared his throat as he stood with his hands behind his back.

"Oh, I'm sorry. Let me get you something," Yancey said as she pulled a dollar from her purse and handed it to the bellman.

As the flowers filled her suite with their perfume, Yancey painted her nails with a dazzling ruby-red polish. Then she put on some of her best lingerie, a pair of baby-blue silk panties and matching bra, and a pair of seamless stockings held up by a satin garter belt.

When she looked at the clock, she noticed it was a little past six. She put on a tight black below-the-knee skirt and a tangerine-orange mohair sweater.

Before leaving the room, she called the hotel switchboard to see if Ava had checked in. "Not yet, but we are holding a key for her," the operator said.

"Can I leave a message for her?" Yancey asked.

"Yes, ma'am."

"Tell her to meet me backstage after the show. I'll leave her name on the guest list."

"I sure will, Ms. Braxton."

Yancey grabbed her bag, and a few minutes later she was striding through the streets of Memphis with pluck and ease. The newly renovated Orpheum Theater was only a few blocks away from the hotel, on the corner of Beale and Main. After a couple of minutes Yancey could see the throbbing lights from the neon sign atop the majestic theater. When Yancey saw *Dreamgirls* in big, bold letters, she thought the only thing missing was her name above the title. And even though it wasn't quite 6:30, a crowd of well-dressed white and black people were already gathering in front of the theater.

Yancey slipped through the stage door, and when she located her dressing room, she was greeted by more flowers, with the envelope again addressed to "La Petite Diva." Just as she was pulling the card out of the envelope, Yancey was startled by Monica Green entering the dressing room and giggling as she said, "I'll see you in a minute, sister friend."

Yancey's eyes widened slightly in surprise at Monica, then asked, "What are you doing here?"

"We're sharing a dressing room. Didn't you know?"

"No one told me. I was told I'd have a private dressing room because

I'm going to have some of my family and friends visiting me each night," Yancey said. Besides, Yancey knew Monica was one of the young ladies in the cast who was being considered for her understudy. Yancey had no intention of sharing a dressing room with someone who wanted to be where she was.

"Well, you need to check with the stage manager or somebody, 'cause this is where they told me to dress," Monica said, putting her bag on the dressing room table.

"Have you seen Chris?" Yancey asked.

"Look, Yancey, I don't know why you're tripping. But believe me when I say I'm not going to be in your way. When the show is over I will be out of here so fast, I could win a gold medal for quick change," Monica said. She was wondering why Yancey was acting so uptight.

"I don't care how fast you dress. This dressing room was supposed to be for me and my family. Don't you understand? You've got to *g-o*, go!" Yancey screamed. She felt tears beginning to form.

"I don't know what's wrong with you, but I'm not going to fight with you. I will find another dressing room even if I have to use the bathroom at the service station across the street," Monica said as she grabbed her bag and rushed from the dressing room, giving Yancey her best fuck-you wave and slamming the door.

"Dumb bitch," Yancey muttered to herself as she locked the door. She sat at the vanity and smelled her flowers. She looked into the mirrors, smiled, and said dramatically, "It's show time, diva. It's show time."

❧   ❧   ❧

Yancey would not disappoint her mother. From the opening curtain to intermission, her Dena Jones was inspired and flawless. She knew that Ava would be pleased, and hoped that perhaps her mother would even come backstage during intermission to tell her how wonderful she was doing.

When she burst through the door to her dressing room and found no one but her dresser, she realized that her mother was merely being professional in not distracting her at such a critical time. Ava knew the opening scene in Act Two was Yancey's time to shine. It was a Las Vegas–type showcase with Dena Jones arriving onstage from the ceiling in a tight red sequined gown, with a white mink wrap. Alone at center stage for a few precious moments.

Yancey was then joined by several hunky dancing boys, including the recently jilted Devin. There was a pivotal moment in the show when the lights would dim to a single spotlight, and Yancey would be at center stage holding an eager audience in the palm of her hand.

The audience seemed so still, Yancey could almost hear them breathe as one in anticipation. Given her natural flair for the dramatic, Yancey paused precisely five seconds before belting out the first bar of Dena's theme.

But something was wrong. There was some sort of disturbance in the audience. A woman's voice. Someone standing in the third row, making some kind of commotion. Members of the chorus continued to dance, but with questioning looks on their faces, while Yancey ignored the outburst and began to work her number.

Just as the two other Dreams were about to join her onstage, Yancey heard someone call out her name from the audience.

"Yancey Braxton, you stank ho!"

The voice sounded vaguely familiar, but Yancey couldn't quite place it. She continued to sing each note perfectly, but she felt a chill twisting through her body, like someone had placed a tray of ice cubes down her beautiful gown. She tried to will herself not to look into the audience, but with the stage lights out, she could clearly see a woman with a huge bust and with blond streaks mixed through auburn hair, wearing a short-skirted fire-engine-red suit. The woman was standing behind the mayor of Memphis and his wife, both of whom had turned around in shock to look at the bizarre scene.

In fact, much of the audience had turned in the woman's direction to watch four ushers pull her up the aisle and out of the theater. Halfway up the aisle, the woman forced herself free, and turning toward the stage, she yelled one more time:

"Yancey Braxton, bitch! Fucking stank ho!"

The audience gasped as the ushers pulled and pushed the woman out into the lobby, while Yancey sang the last soulful phrase of her song. After she held the last note an extra measure, the audience gave her a standing ovation.

❖   ❖   ❖

After the show, Yancey rushed to her dressing room for her reunion with her mother. Once there, Yancey quickly removed her makeup and was brushing her hair when she heard a knock at the door. Her heart was beating like a drum as she raced to open it.

It was Chris, the director. "Are you all right?" he asked as he entered the dressing room.

"I'm fine. Why do you ask?" a disappointed Yancey said, returning to her dressing table.

"That crazy woman in the audience. The theater called the police and they took her down to the station for questioning. She said her name was

Nisey and that she went to school with you. Would you like a police escort back to the hotel?"

"Nisey, oh, I'm not a bit surprised. That chile ain't never had any class. Probably was her first time at the theater. And no, I don't need an escort." *If I ran into that broke-down ho, I'd beat her ass down,* Yancey thought to herself. "Thanks anyway."

"Really? Okay, if you're certain. And by the way . . . you were absolutely wonderful tonight. I'm so glad I put you in the role of Dena," Chris said.

"And so am I. Well, if you'll excuse me, I have to get dressed. I'm waiting on my mother," Yancey said as she pulled her robe close.

"Was she supposed to be in your house seat?" Chris asked.

"Yes. Why?"

"Because I was looking out at the house, and that was the only empty seat in the place, that one and Nisey's after she was escorted out," Chris said.

Yancey felt she was close to tears as she asked, "How can you be certain it was my seat?"

"I know because I made sure you had the best seat available. It was second row center—right next to the mayor and his wife."

"Oh."

"Are you all right?" Chris asked as he touched Yancey softly on her left arm.

"I'm fine. My mother is probably at the hotel. I've got to hurry and get there," Yancey said. Her eyes lost their sparkle.

"If you need me, you can reach me at the Radisson," Chris offered.

"Thanks, Chris," Yancey said as she closed the door behind him. She released the fabric of the robe and got dressed. Maybe Ava's car had been delayed, or maybe there had been an accident, Yancey thought to herself. She had to get to her room.

Yancey bolted out of the theater and whisked past a group of teenage girls waiting for autographs. "Miss Braxton, you were so wonderful. Would you sign my program?" a young black lady asked.

"No, I can't, I'm in a hurry," Yancey said. "Try me tomorrow."

After practically running to the Peabody, Yancey rushed to her suite. The emptiness of the suite felt cold to her. But then she saw the message light flashing on the phone. *Of course,* Yancey thought. She has been delayed. Just as well with Nisey in the audience trying to upstage her. Yancey made a silent vow to herself to be even better tomorrow night when Ava would certainly be front row center.

Yancey pushed the button marked "messages." An automated voice informed her that she had two messages and to push the number 7 to play them. Yancey quickly pushed the button and heard Ava's voice. "Hey, sweetheart. I guess you know by now that I'm not there. I'm sorry but I won't be able to make it. I'm in Atlanta right now on my way to Spain. I got a call this morning from the producer of the show at Le Monte Carlo. He was in a bind. His star broke her leg and he was expecting the royal family of Luxembourg to attend his cabaret tomorrow night. I had to leave ASAP. I'm so sorry, and I wanted to be there so badly tonight, but you know the business, and trying to get out of Jackson . . . is so . . ." Yancey heard the dial tone, and she hit the 7 again. "Sorry, but that damn machine cut me off. Well, they're boarding my plane and I'll call you once I'm settled. I know you did great tonight, and don't worry, I promise . . ." Again Yancey heard the dial tone, only this time Ava didn't bother to call back.

Yancey slammed the phone down and poured herself a glass of champagne. She opened the French doors to her suite and walked out onto the small balcony. She looked at the dark sky with a handful of stars. After a glass of champagne, Yancey felt intoxicated by the stillness of the Memphis night.

She refreshed her glass, took a long sip of her drink and then couldn't decide what to do with the half-filled flute, twirling it in her hand from left to right. After a moment, she raced back into her suite, gathered up the photos, letters, and postcards in silence, and placed them back in the special box. And then she very slowly poured the sparkling, bubbling liquid into the box over her prized keepsakes. And then in a fit of rage and sorrow, Yancey tossed the glass across the room, where it crashed against the wall, breaking into several tiny pieces.

49

"Did you miss me last week, Doc?" Basil asked as he took a seat.

"I was a little worried."

"Don't worry, I know the rules. You'll get your check," Basil smirked.

"I'm not worried about that. What happened? Did you ever hear from Raymond?"

"Yeah, I did, and he had a good reason for standing me up. He left me a message. His father had a stroke. He sounded pretty sad, but I'm not here to talk about Raymond," Basil said.

"So what would you like to talk about?"

"I'm thinking my pops has been lying to me," Basil said without emotion.

"About what?"

"I think Campbell is telling the truth. Matter of fact, I'm willing to bet she's telling the truth."

"About her being your half sister?"

"Yeah, I think me and Campbell are related."

"Why do you believe her now?"

"About a week ago, I'm leaving the gym and Campbell is standing out front. The first thing I think is, now this bitch is going to start stalking me and I'm going to have to find another gym or contact the police. But when I saw her, I was just going to ignore her and walk past her."

"Why didn't you?"

"She had this little boy with her. He had a little football in his one hand and the other hand in his mouth. When I looked at him, I couldn't believe how much this boy looked like me. His eyes were exactly like mine. The color of his skin. His nose, even though it's small, looked like mine. It was like I was looking at myself as a child," Basil said.

"Who was this child?"

"It was Campbell's little boy. His name is Cade. I mean, Doc, when I looked at him, I couldn't believe it. I stared at Campbell and then I started wondering if I had slept with her. I mean the little boy was about six years old. I started thinking that if I hadn't slept with her, maybe she had pulled one of those stunts you hear that women do all the time. You know, giving their girlfriends the semen of somebody famous. But I'm hipped to that shit, and I always make sure I dispose of the condoms. At least with women, 'cause I know how sneaky they can be."

"What did you say to Campbell?"

"I looked at her and asked, 'Who is this?' "

"Did she answer you?"

"Yeah. She said this is Cade, your nephew."

"How did that make you feel?"

After a considerable silence, Basil stood up, trying to organize his feelings. He felt angry, he felt betrayed, and yet he was excited about his new family. Yet his emotions attacked him from every direction.

"At first I was mad, because, Doc, I could look at this little boy and tell that he was a part of my family. I even wished he wasn't just my nephew but my son," Basil said as he sat back down.

"Why?"

" 'Cause he's a great kid. After we talked for a few minutes, Campbell asked me if I'd like to spend some time with Cade. That let me know she wasn't fakin'."

"And what did you do?"

"At first, I was a bit hesitant. I mean, I haven't spent a lot of time with kids, but something made me say yes. And we had a great time. He can already play some video games and we went to this playground down in the Village and got on the swings. I mean, we had a ball. Last Saturday I took him to my place and rented the movie *The Lion King* and we went to that big toy store on Fifth Avenue and Cade ran me crazy. He's going to be some type of athlete. Says he wants to play hockey so I promised to teach him how to ice-skate. I didn't tell him I had to learn first. It was wonderful," Basil said, smiling.

"What's that smile about?"

"It's something Cade said to me when I took him home."

"What did he say?"

"He wouldn't let go of my hand, and when I tried to shake it loose, you know in a playful way, he said, 'Uncle Basil, stay with me.' I mean it almost brought tears to my eyes."

"Sounds like you got a new friend."

"Yeah, it does."

"So, Campbell wants you involved in your nephew's life?"

"Yeah, she does. Despite me actin' like an ass when she first brought this up to me."

"Did you call your father and tell him about what you've discovered?"

"Not really," Basil said with a slight waver in his voice as he continued. "I mean I called him and asked him if he knew anything about my mother's family. Where I might contact them and get a picture of her."

"What did he say?"

"He said he didn't. Asked me why I was asking about her."

"Did you tell him?"

"No."

"Why?"

"Because I could tell from his voice that he was lying. I needed to be looking at him dead in his face," Basil said.

"Are you going to do that?"

"At some point."

"Why are you waiting?"

Basil lowered his voice, as if he were speaking directly from his heart. After a deep breath he said, "Because when I do, I'll have to accept the fact that my father doesn't give a shit about me. How could he? How could he give a fuck about me by keeping me away from the woman who brought me into this world? All of his fucking manhood pride. Maybe he did know about what my uncle did to me. If he could keep something like this from me, then I don't know what kinda fucker I've got for a father."

"You know to bring closure to this, you've got to confront your father, don't you?"

"I don't have to do nothing. I don't have to deal with that crazy fuck, ever. I know I'll hear from him if I stop calling or sending him checks. But I don't give a fuck!"

"Basil, can I ask you something about your father?"

Basil narrowed his eyes and looked at the doctor with suspicion, then asked, "What?"

"Are you afraid of your father?"

Basil took another deep breath, and his gray eyes misted, but remained steady, and said, "I don't know."

"You don't know?"

"I don't think I'm afraid of him. Right now I'm just scared that my whole life has been a cruel hoax. Maybe I'm not fucked up because of what my uncle did to me, but because I'm my father's son."

"Say it," the doctor said firmly.

"Say what?"

"Say what your uncle did to you."

"I don't like thinking about it. I don't like saying it!"

"I know this is difficult for you. But I also know, as do you, that talking about it—saying what happened to you—gives you power. Every time you say it brings you one step closer to defeating it."

"But you know what he did. I've already told you."

"So, tell me again."

"Doc . . ."

"Basil. Say it."

Basil bit down on his lips. His eyes were watery with unshed tears as he sat in silence. When he finally spoke, it was not with the voice of a confident superstar football player and sexual conqueror, but that of a frightened little boy. "My uncle molested me," Basil said. "He fucked me."

50

Delaney's rescue mission had turned into a three-night slumber party for two old friends. Though Nicole had recovered from her mini-depression and seemed to be doing fine, Delaney was glad that Jared would be back before she left to go back to San Diego.

The first two days had been rocky. Nicole had poured out her hurt. It didn't help matters when Delaney informed her that Yancey had assumed the role of Dena Jones.

"Are you sure?" Nicole asked Delaney as they sat cross-legged on the bed in pajamas. Their sleepwear made them feel like teenagers rather than two grown ladies.

"You didn't know? Cedric told me. I know you were in bad shape when I got here, but I told you how tight Cedric and I became when I hired him to be in a couple of videos. What kinda girl is Yancey anyway? Cedric seems to like her."

"Oh, she's a sweetheart. But I'm a little bit surprised they gave her the role, since she's so young, but I guess nothing in this business should shock me," Nicole said. "I'm just kinda sad Yancey didn't share her big news with me herself. But I guess she was being a friend by not rubbing her good fortune in my face."

"Now, Nicole, you know friends are rare in this business. One of the things I always hated and loved about you is your wanting to believe in the best in people. I ain't built that way. I'm always covering my *b-a-c-k*,'' Delaney said.

There were times when Nicole appeared both pitiful and vulnerable. During those times she would rush to her bedroom or bathroom and pray, and then listen to the gospel song "Stand" once more. Delaney had alternated between comforting Nicole with hugs and chamomile tea and threatening to kick her butt if she didn't stop feeling sorry for herself. Delaney didn't know which tactic had done the job, but she was grateful for the guidance that led to her friend's recovery.

On day three, Nicole was beginning to look, act, and feel like her true self again. She suggested they do a little shopping along Fifth Avenue and then spend the evening at home cooking dinner together. Delaney had suggested that they go out to Justin's, Puffy Combs's Chelsea restaurant, then realized that Nicole didn't want to miss Jared's nightly call from Atlanta.

Jared called at least twice a day, and again in the evening to whisper "Good night, and I love you" in Nicole's ear. No talk about their argument, no mention of babies, surrogates, and adoption agencies. Jared was ecstatic about Nicole's improvement and was looking forward to coming home soon. They both were eager to be in each other's arms again.

"Do you two really think you can live without each other?" Delaney teased after Nicole ended a long conversation with Jared by planting a big, juicy kiss on the telephone receiver. "I mean ya'll are acting like you just started hitting it."

"I can't wait to see him and make up," Nicole said. "I love him so much and I could have lost him by being so selfish and silly."

"Honey, you two are a mess. Still acting like school kids after all these years. I ain't mad about it!"

"What about you? You look good. Are you still in love?"

"Oh, I'm in love double-double. I love Jody like mad, and Fletcher, your godson, is a joy. You know what I ought to do is send Fletcher here for a couple of weeks so Jody and I can take some time away. We'll see how truly interested Mr. Jared is in being a father," Delaney laughed as she placed a bag of popcorn in the microwave while Nicole opened a bottle of wine. Nicole had taken the goose-down pillows off her bed and the quilt off the guest room bed, and brought them into the living room, where the two women snuggled up to watch a tape of *The Preacher's Wife*.

"You could send Fletcher up here for a whole year and I don't think it's going to change Jared's mind about children. Everything is okay right now, but I know sooner or later something's gotta give."

"And you'll handle it when you have to. All you got to do is put on that damn gospel song 'Stand' and give me a call. With the combination of you praying and me giving kick-ass advice—well, obstacles don't stand a chance."

"I'm going to miss your silly behind," Nicole said, and reached over to hug her friend.

"I love you, Nicole, and I'm very proud of you. If you ever need me," Delaney said, hugging her friend, "I'll be there for you. Always."

Nicole didn't answer because her eyes were filled with tears as they embraced each other and rocked back and forth.

❖   ❖   ❖

On the last day of Delaney's visit to New York, she and Nicole started the day at Scissors New York, a popular salon a couple of blocks from Nicole's apartment. Scissors was *the* place in the theater district to have your nails 'cured, and your do done, and at the same time rub elbows with Broadway's hot and, sometimes, not-so-hot talent.

At first Nicole protested, telling Delaney there was no way on earth they could get an appointment at such a late date.

"Do you know how popular that place is?" Nicole asked.

"I know, darling. But Anderson the owner and I go way back. We're in like Flynn."

Just as Nicole and Delaney were leaving for their day of beauty and lunch, the phone rang. Nicole hoped it might be Jared, so she answered the phone.

"Hello."

"May I speak to Nicole Springer?" an unfamiliar male voice said.

"This is Nicole Springer."

"Ms. Springer. This is Dr. Rodrick Gordon. I examined you when you took ill in Grand Rapids."

"Oh yes, Dr. Gordon. What can I do for you?"

The doctor paused and then said, "Ms. Springer, I just got your test results back and I wanted to bring something to your attention."

Nicole raised her eyebrows and threw her left hand in the air as Delaney encouraged her to hurry up by tapping her left foot.

"Yes?" Nicole asked.

"Well, I know how young women, especially in your line of business, watch their weight, but trust me, taking laxatives is not the way."

"What are you talking about?" Nicole quizzed.

"Ms. Springer, we found a large amount of citrate of magnesia in your system," Dr. Gordon said firmly.

"What's that?"

"It's a clear laxative that has a slight lemon flavor, and I've known people to put it in tea and beverages."

"I've never heard of it and trust me, Doctor, I would never use a laxative unless I was instructed to do so by a physician."

"Good. Laxatives can be very dangerous if they're abused." He paused and then continued. "Everything else looks fine, Ms. Springer, but I just wanted to speak with you myself—just in case."

"Thanks for calling, Dr. Gordon, but I'm fine," Nicole assured.

When she hung up the phone, Nicole had a puzzled look on her face. She told Delaney what the doctor had said and wondered aloud if he had mixed up her results with someone else's.

"Delaney, Grand Rapids is a small town. Anything could have happened. A lot of time they have high school kids working in labs. But I'm going to talk with my doctor here about it," Nicole said.

"Do you think somebody put something in your drink on purpose?" Delaney asked.

"Who would do that?"

"Maybe some guy, trying to get in your pants."

"But a laxative? I haven't been anywhere where men would have had a chance to drop something in my drink," Nicole said.

"What about some of the women in the cast? What about this Yancey child?"

"Oh, Yancey would never do anything like that," Nicole said.

Delaney walked over to Nicole and took both her hands and said, "Nicole, honey, I know you want to see the good in everybody. It's one of the things I love about you. But everyone you meet who acts like they're your friend, ain't your friend. Everything that glitters sure ain't gold," Delaney warned.

"I know that, but I'm sure there's been a mistake. I'll get a checkup and I'll have my doctor re-evaluate the results, but Yancey would *never* do something like that," Nicole said confidently.

"Never say never."

"I know. Come on, honey. Let's go get our 'dos done," Nicole joked. But as she closed the door, the memory of Yancey bringing her coffee each morning came to her. Nicole especially remembered Yancey's always smiling face.

❖   ❖   ❖

When they arrived at Scissors New York a little after lunch, Nicole and Delaney sat beside one another on one of the padded benches in the waiting area, across from an attractive black man who had his face buried in the current issue of *Essence*. Nicole and Delaney were flipping through an old copy of *Vibe* when they spotted an ad for men's underwear featuring their waiting-room neighbor.

"That's him!" Delaney whispered, pointing to the model in the ad.

"Who?" Nicole asked.

"Girl, keep your voice down. It's him!" Delaney nudged Nicole's shoulder with her own and nodded toward the brother on the opposite bench. Nicole looked down at the page, then at the man sitting across the room, then back at the ad showing him clad only in briefs.

"You're right, that's him," Nicole whispered. "I can't wait for Jared to get home, 'cause even though that old boy is fine, my baby would give him a run for his money."

Delaney turned her attention to the walls of the posh salon nearly completely covered with framed photographs of Broadway stars, models, and a few nonindustry people like the first black female astronaut, Mae Jemison.

"Isn't that the child you understudied in *Jelly's*?" Delaney asked as she pointed to a photograph above the magazine stand.

"Yeah, that's her," Nicole said.

"What is she doing?"

"I heard she's pumping out babies," Nicole said as she picked up a *Body and Soul* magazine.

"Why isn't your picture on the wall?"

"It might be, but it's probably on the wall downstairs," Nicole chuckled.

"Well, when the owner, Anderson, gets here, I'm going to make sure we get a new picture of you right here, center wall," Delaney said as she stood and pointed to the space.

"Wait until I'm back on Broadway," Nicole advised.

"That will be sooner than you think. Trust me on this," Delaney said as a beautician's assistant came over and told the ladies it was time for their first step toward beautiful hair.

About three hours later, and feeling beautiful, Nicole and Delaney walked over to B. Smith's for a late lunch.

"You look great!" Delaney said, admiring Nicole's bouncing and behaving hair.

"And so do you!" Nicole said.

"Yeah, that guy who did your hair was something else. Did you see all those tattoos he had?"

"Honey, they were everywhere. If he wanted to, he could probably walk around nude and nobody would know," Nicole laughed.

"And he was just singing and singing. I started to tell him to let the people getting paid sing the songs. It didn't matter if he was singing a

Jody Watley or Gerald Levert song. I mean his voice wasn't that bad, but he needs to stick to doing hair."

"I know that's right," Nicole said.

The late lunch of sea bass with champagne sauce was predictably superb. The two women leisurely strolled the three blocks home enjoying the balmy autumn weather. When they walked into the apartment, they found Jared popping the cork on a bottle of champagne. His face lit up when he saw his wife. Their embrace and kiss was so long and tender that Delaney coughed to remind them she was still in the room.

Jared released his wife and walked over to Delaney and gave her a big bear hug that said more than words could ever convey.

"Back at you," Delaney said. "Let's have some champagne and make a toast to friendship and love."

After a few sips of champagne and more toasts, the buzzer sounded and the doorman announced that the driver had arrived to take Delaney to the airport.

"Well, guys," Delaney said, "I guess this is it for now. You two had better keep in touch."

"You want me to help you with your bags?" Jared asked.

"Naw, it looks like you're busy. I can make it," Delaney smiled.

Delaney came over and gave Nicole a hug and whispered, "I miss you already."

"Me too," Nicole said as she fought back tears. And with a wave and sad little smile, Delaney was gone.

There was an awkward moment as the door closed and Jared and Nicole stood in the foyer suddenly realizing they were alone for the first time in almost a week.

"I sure am glad to see you, Nicole." Jared's voice was husky with emotion. "I didn't know I could ever miss anyone like I've missed you." It was obvious to Nicole that Jared's anger had passed and given way to something more powerful: an abiding love.

After a moment she said in a whisper, "And I've missed you too, Jared." She took his hand and led him toward their bedroom. Jared followed and grabbed the champagne bottle as they passed through the living room.

Nicole dimmed the bedroom lights. Facing the mirror over their dresser, she had a clear view of Jared sitting on the bed behind her. She turned and smiled at him and asked, "So you got any more secrets for me?"

Jared began to unloosen his tie and whispered, "And you know it!"

51

It was such a beautiful fall day that it almost seemed cruel that Raymond was facing an emotional mountain. When he woke up, Raymond saw a note from his mother telling him she was at the hospital and he should take some time for himself. After eating breakfast alone, he decided to return some phone calls.

He had received bad news from the real estate lawyer in New York, and there had been two urgent messages on his answering machine at home from Lisa, saying she had to speak with him today. It was almost 11:00 A.M. in Chicago, so Raymond knew Lisa would be in her Seattle office. He located her name in his date book, dialed the number, and sipped the last of his lukewarm coffee.

"Lisa Lanier speaking."

"Lisa, this is Raymond Tyler. How are you doing?"

"I've done better. Thanks for calling. I'm afraid I have some more bad news, and we've got to act on this right away. Are you still in New York?"

"No, I'm in Chicago," Raymond said.

"When will you be back in Seattle?"

"That's up in the air. What's going on?"

Lisa told Raymond that a *Seattle Sun* reporter had contacted her office several times inquiring about an alleged arrest for solicitation by

Raymond. The reporter wanted to know if that was the reason Raymond's nomination had been delayed.

"Where did that come from?" Raymond asked.

"Apparently, it's getting confused with Trent's arrest. Obviously, this guy hasn't done all his homework, but now we're getting calls from the gay newspaper and the African-American paper requesting interviews with you to clear this thing up."

"And how do you clear up something that's not true?" Raymond wondered aloud.

"We can hold a press conference denying the charges," Lisa suggested.

"Isn't that something your office can do? Why do you need me?"

"Raymond, what are you thinking? Of course you have to be here. You have to look those reporters right in the eye and tell them that it's just not true."

Raymond let out a big sigh. "When do you want to do this?"

"We needed to do it yesterday. But no later than tomorrow. Can you be back in Seattle tomorrow afternoon?"

"No, I can't do that," Raymond said firmly.

"Raymond, this is important. Are you sure you still want the nomination?"

"Lisa, I really appreciate what you've done for me. But the reason I'm in Chicago is because my father had a stroke and he's still in the hospital. My family needs me right now, and I can't leave."

"Oh, I'm so sorry to hear that. My mother had a stroke a few years back, so I know it's tough." She thought for a moment and then suggested, "Maybe you can make a press release or we could set you up with one of the local Chicago stations and have them feed the press conference back to Seattle. But I want to warn you, this might not be good for Trent."

"What do you mean?"

"If the reporters keep searching, they may discover the truth. You might need to clarify Trent's record in any press release or public statement you make," Lisa said.

"Say what? Tell the city of Seattle that my partner was arrested? There's no way I can, or would, do that. Trent made a mistake, but he didn't seek the public eye. That would be unfair to him. So I won't be making any statement that implicates him in any way," Raymond said. His tone was clear, confident, and powerful. Raymond's anger toward Trent had dissipated, leaving a residue of hurt. His mother's words of advice to forgive echoed in his mind.

"This might be the biggest hurdle of your nomination. I don't think this is going to blow over," Lisa said.

"Would that be true if I withdrew my name from nomination?"

"You aren't going to do that, are you?"

"Look, Lisa, right now my family is the most important thing in the world. And Trent is a part of my family. I won't subject him to this, so I think I need to prepare a statement withdrawing my name." He didn't feel sad, but relieved, like a wall inside him had dissolved. "It looks like the NAACP and Charles Pope will get their wishes," Raymond said.

"Raymond, why don't you think this over? I mean, we've worked so hard, and I want to see you on the bench. Isn't this your dream?" Her voice sounded soothing and compassionate.

Raymond thought for a few minutes, then stared at the unmade bed and the breakfast tray on the desk. It was clear to him at that moment he didn't want to be a judge. Raymond wasn't even certain he wanted to continue practicing law. He thought of all the years he spent hearing the rain of his dreams, trying to please his father, a man he once dreamed of becoming himself.

"No, Lisa. It was my father's dream, not mine. I need to get to the hospital, but you'll get my letter of withdrawal later today by fax. I also want to thank you for all your help, but I know this is the best thing for everyone concerned," Raymond responded.

"You sound sure," Lisa said softly.

"I am," Raymond said. "Good-bye, Lisa."

Raymond hung up the phone, then picked it back up and dialed Peaches's number. Having made the decision to withdraw his name, Raymond felt he'd climbed halfway up the mountain. *Might as well keep climbing,* he thought. Talking to his father and Trent would take him over the top.

"Cuts 'n' Cobblers, this is Peaches."

"Peaches, this is Raymond. How are you doing?"

"I'm doin', baby. What about you? How's your daddy doing?"

"Well, he's out of intensive care, but he still can't speak or walk. The doctor said it's going to take some time."

"You tell him and your mother that Peaches is prayin' for him and I gots me an angel up in heaven who makes sure God gits the word," Peaches said.

"Thanks, Peaches. But I have some more bad news."

"What, baby?"

"The attorney for the real estate company left a message saying they rejected our offer. Property up in Harlem is going crazy. Someone has bid $575,000."

"What? That's getting close to a million dollars. Baby, I ain't got that kinda money. What am I going to do?"

"We can look at some other places. As soon as Pops gets better, I'll come and help you and Enoch find a place where you can have both your home and business," Raymond said.

"But this is our home. It ain't fair. Can we make another offer?"

"Sure, Peaches. But even with all your money and what Jared and I can kick in, we can't come close to that number. Our last offer was only $350,000."

"Then call them and offer them mo'," Peaches said firmly.

"What? Where are we going to get the money from?"

"I don't know right now, but I know this is where I'm 'posed to be, and God wants me here. We'll figure the rest out later," Peaches said. "Now I got to go and sell some pies. Thanks, baby."

"I'll talk with you soon, Peaches."

"Raymond?"

"Yes, Peaches?"

"Make the offer."

"Whatever you say," Raymond said as he hung up the phone.

❧   ❧   ❧

Raymond and Kirby walked side by side down the polished tile floor of the hospital corridor. Kirby was wearing tan jeans, his navy-blue shirt was untucked, and he was carrying a leather book bag over his shoulder. The brothers were talking about Kirby's upcoming game against Michigan when Raymond suddenly stopped walking, grabbed his brother by his broad shoulders, and said, "Have I told you I love you lately?"

Kirby blinked his eyes, smiled, and said, "You don't have to tell me, I know."

"How are things with you and Dawn? I know you haven't been able to spend a lot of time with her."

"Everything is tight."

"I think that means everything is going well. Right?"

"See, you can still hang with the young playas," Kirby teased.

Raymond smiled and then his tone turned serious. "Would you mind if I went in and talked to Pops first? I got some things I want to talk to him about."

"Sure, but you know he's still not able to speak. He can't talk back."

"That's the main reason I want to talk to him." Raymond grinned.

"I get your point," Kirby said as he shook his head. "I've been excused from practice, so I'll go down to the coffee shop."

"I'll come and get you when I'm finished."

"Don't be long. Mom and I have cooked up a little surprise for you," Kirby said with a sneaky smile.

"What kind of surprise?"

"I ain't talking," Kirby said as he walked toward the elevators.

Raymond wondered for a moment what surprise Kirby was talking about as he walked toward his father's room. When he got to the door, he took a deep breath and walked in. His mother, sitting by the bed, much like she had the first night, rose to rush over and hug Raymond.

"Any change?"

"He's able to drink some stuff out of a straw. But still no movement and no talking. I've been waiting on you and Kirby, so I can go and talk to the doctor. I want to take my husband home, even if I have to get a home care attendant to help me every day," Mrs. Tyler said as she picked up her purse from the windowsill.

"You go talk with Dr. Rodriguez, Mama. I'll stay here with Pops and then Kirby will come up later."

"Make sure you're back at the hotel around seven, okay?"

"Why?"

"Don't ask questions. Just do what your mother says," she said, playfully tapping him on his backside.

"Whatever," Raymond said as he kissed his mother on her cheek.

When his mother left the room, he walked slowly to his father's bed and sat in the metal folding chair next to the bed's guardrail. Raymond Sr.'s eyes were closed, but when Raymond Jr. sat down, they opened very slowly. Raymond smiled at his father and studied his tobacco-brown skin, his sad, brownish-green eyes, and the network of lines around the corners of his mouth. Raymond Sr.'s face had a flat expression, like a lake reflecting a winter sky. Raymond gently touched his fine hair, which was more gray than black, and he realized he'd never touched his father's body in any way with the exception of an occasional hug. He slowly touched his face and was surprised by how soft it was.

Raymond bit his tongue and then his words began to fill the empty silence. "Pops, I know you're going to get better. I know this might not be the best time, but your stroke has made me realize that I'm not promised another chance like this. I want to start by telling you how much I love you and how proud I am to be your son. And I've been really mad at you for the last couple of months, and I've been scared. I was afraid that if I told you how angry I was at you, I'd lose your love. And lately I've been frightened because I almost lost you.

"When we got into the argument over what I should do with Trent, I started to write you a letter and tell you how I felt. I knew with a letter I could get my point across without you disputing or discounting what I had to say or how I felt. I guess that's the lawyer in you," Raymond chuckled.

He took another deep breath and continued. "When you came to Seattle after I was nominated for the bench, I was so happy. Not because of the nomination, but because my father had come to the place I called home. You were proud of me again. You know the last time I remember you being proud of me?" Raymond asked, knowing full well his father couldn't answer.

"Besides when I graduated from law school, which I don't know if you were that happy about, since I didn't go to Howard. It was when I was in high school and was playing football, and when some cheerleader would decorate our yard with toilet paper streamers and signs, and you and I would try and figure out which cheerleader was my secret pal. Remember how we would clean up the yard after the game and then go into the house and watch college games? This was before Kirby was interested in football or hanging out with us. During that time I felt like I was a son you could be proud of. As long as I did what you wanted me to."

Raymond felt his words may have been harsh but these were his true feelings and he needed to say them. He began to trace his father's face slowly with his fingertips, wondering how many of the lines he had caused.

"Do you know how hurtful it was when you told me you and mom didn't raise me to be no sissy? I can still see the anger and disgust in your eyes. Did you ever stop and think about how I felt when you gave me the silent treatment when I brought Trent home the first time and introduced him as my life partner? How you denied who I am whenever I wanted to talk about my sexuality. Did you think that reflected on you? It didn't. My sexuality was decided long before I ever knew what sex was.

"Now, I don't want you to think that all I remember is the bad stuff. You and I have shared some wonderful times. Remember when we would stay up late drinking beer and eating cold pizza when you were running for state senator? How we talked over campaign strategies? Do you know how proud I was when I worked with you in your firm and you would introduce me to your lawyer friends and judges with such pride? How we would come home and review our caseload and discuss if we wanted the firm to become larger or remain a family business. Those were wonderful times, Pops. You were treating me as an equal, as a man."

Raymond moved his chair closer to his father. "Now, Pops, I know this is something you don't want to hear, but you've got to hear it from me. I wanted you to be the first one I told when I was nominated and I wanted you to be the person on my side when I went through my confirmation, but that's not going to happen. I withdrew my nomination today because I realized that the only reason I wanted to be a judge was so that I could see that pride in your eyes again." Raymond paused and reached to take his father's hand in his. Together their hands were an anchor in the world.

"I was trying to live your dream, Pops. I didn't know until a couple of weeks ago that you wanted to be a Supreme Court justice. Why didn't you tell me that? You would have been a great one. Tough but fair.

"But this little crisis of ours has made me realize that I want to do something more with my life. Right now I don't know what that is, but I promise you it will be something that makes you proud. But it will be my dream, Pops," Raymond said as he removed one of his hands from his father's grasp, then beat his fist against his chest and tears began to fill his eyes.

"So you got to get well, so we can talk about the wonderful things we're going to do with the rest of our lives. What we're going to do for our family and for the world. 'Cause I know you're not finished, Pops, and I feel like I'm just beginning."

Raymond wiped the tears from his eyes with the back of his free hand, never letting go of his father's hand.

❖   ❖   ❖

When Raymond arrived back at the hotel, he discovered his surprise. Trent was sitting in a chair looking over some notes at the small table in the suite Raymond was sharing with his mother.

"Trent, what are you doing here?" Raymond asked as he placed the card key on the dresser.

"This time I was invited," Trent said, getting up from the table and walking toward Raymond. "Your mother and Kirby called me. They told me you need me."

"Oh they did," Raymond said as he sat on the edge of the bed.

"Yeah, that's what they said," Trent said. He sat on the bed next to Raymond. Trent put his hand on Raymond's knee and looked in his eyes and said, "Raymond, I love you deeply, with my whole heart. Since we've been together, one of the things I've wanted most was for the rest of your life to be the rest of mine."

"Trent, you did something I thought you'd never do. You hurt me," Raymond said as he looked sadly into his partner's eyes.

"I know, and I'm sorry. All I can say is that it won't ever happen again."

"How can you be sure?"

"Because I can see the hurt in your eyes. I must admit that when I was doing what I did, I didn't think much of how you might feel. But ever since I've left New York, I've been thinking how I would feel if you were unfaithful to me, and it's not a good feeling."

Raymond stared at Trent and tried to figure out what to say. A voice in his head was telling him, "You're on a roll, let him have it," while another was saying, "Raymond, stop being an asshole. You love this man. Forgive him and get on with your life."

Raymond chose the latter and said, "Trent, I know if we're going to have a future together, I must forgive you in my heart and I have. It's just, at times, I think about it and I still feel anger and sadness. I begin to wonder if we can ever have what I thought we had."

"We can," Trent said. He moved closer to Raymond. He breathed in Raymond's strong, clean scent and began to kiss him on his neck, and then his ears, his face, and finally Raymond's lips. Raymond didn't resist as he had in New York. He began to savor the taste of Trent's tongue. When they stopped kissing, they both stood up, and Trent noticed Raymond's face had softened. A tenderness had come into his eyes.

Then, in an unspoken agreement, they moved to opposite sides of the bed and pulled back the bedspread. In a single fluid movement, Trent removed the yellow knit sweater his biceps were straining, unbuckled his belt, dropped his pants, and removed his underwear.

Raymond stood, still fully dressed and gazing at Trent's deep-muscled chest, his flat stomach, and his plump and firm sex. He heard that voice again telling him this wasn't the way to resolve their problems. But a wave of desire moved through him as Trent moved closer to him with his silky, warm nakedness and began to undress Raymond slowly. The voice became silent. But suddenly Raymond thought of his mother and whispered, "Trent, we can't do this. My mother might come in."

He smiled seductively. "She's got a new room. Everything will be fine." The heat of his smile made Raymond's body warm with moisture.

When Trent removed Raymond's underwear, he stood back and marveled, "Damn, baby, you look better than ever before. And I didn't think that was possible."

Raymond and Trent began to make love with a certain caution, as if it were their first time. And in many ways, it was.

The Power of Silence

A Letter . . .

In the solitude of her apartment, Nicole decided to write a friend a letter.

My Dearest Delaney,

I hope this letter finds you, Jody, and Fletcher well and looking forward to the holidays. Jared and I are wonderfully blessed. It's a beautiful winter day here in the city. The sun is out, but there is a definite chill in the air. The weatherman said we might even have a White Christmas.

I was getting ready to send you one of my annual Christmas letters (please pray that this doesn't mean I'm becoming more like my mother . . . smile). Anyway, since you're such a special friend, Delaney, and you played such an important role in my life this year, I thought you deserved your own letter. It's funny how the art of letter writing has gone out of style and has been replaced by e-mail and the occasional postcard. Remember when I told you I had over ten pen pals at one time when I was a little girl? Sometimes I miss the days when all it took to excite me was an Alaskan postmark.

I want to thank you once again for showing up when I really needed a friend. I'm so sorry I caused us to lose so much precious time, but I promise I will make it up to you. Thanks also for the Iyanla Vanzant books you sent. Sistah knows she can write and tell the truth. I read from one of her books each and every day no matter what. Even when I'm on top of the world.

Jared is out right now, doing some Christmas shopping. I have no idea what he's getting me, but I'm thinking about getting him a cashmere overcoat. You do remember how cold it gets here, don't you? We are thinking about going down to Fisher Island in Florida for a couple of days, but that might change if everything works out with the foster child.

I'm sure I told you Jared and I passed all the interviews and could get a child any day. I'm nervous and excited at the same time. But Jared is even more nervous than I am. Every day he comes home and asks me the same questions: Did the agency call? When is the child coming? Is it going to be a boy or a girl? Just between us I know he wants a boy.

My career is picking up. Please don't say I told you so. I've done some voiceover work and I've been approached to do a gig at The China Club. They have this cabaret series on Sunday nights featuring Broadway stars. Can you believe it? Like I'm a star! Speaking of Broadway . . . did Cedric tell you it looks like Dreamgirls *might not be coming to Broadway after all? At least not this summer, but maybe next. I'm dreading the thought of the show coming back before Jared and I move out of the theater district. I hear the producers are having trouble finding a suitable theater, and are thinking about going to London before coming to New York. I'm happy about that, 'cause despite how I was treated, those kids in the show gotta work.*

Yancey has called and invited me to lunch a couple of times, but I've been really busy with my voice and dance lessons. It's not like I'm avoiding her or anything, but I've thought a lot about what you said. I guess it is possible that she was trying to do me in. But if she really did try to harm me, she doesn't need enemies . . . she needs prayer and friends. I keep Yancey and other cast members in my daily prayers. If I'm ready to see her by the time she gets back from London, I might invite her over for tea. I wish her only the best, but sometimes you have to be a friend from a distance. I still find it hard to believe; Yancey seemed so sincere. But don't worry, from now on I'll keep both eyes open.

I recently got invited to audition for a new George Wolfe musical, and guess what? I'm one of the female leads! It was a close call, honey, because they had offered the role to La Chanze. You know sister not only can sing, but she's beautiful too. She turned them down to do Ragtime. *After I found out, I started screaming, "Thank you,*

Father!" as I skipped . . . yes, child, skipped home from my agent's office. I guess I got some angels pulling for me.

I'm pulling together a benefit for Peaches and More Than Friends. Jared and I are doing everything possible to make sure she has the money for her down payment. Raymond is coming back to help and I've already got the cast of Smokey Joe's, *plus Lillias White (with her singing butt), Brian Stokes Mitchell, and Vanessa L. Williams to perform. It should be just fabulous! I'll keep you posted about the details. I'd love it if you and Jody and that little manchild of yours can come.*

I've got a lot on my plate, but I'm looking forward to the new year. This year has been tough, but there have been joyful moments. Finally, I've realized how blessed I am to have a husband who loves me despite my faults, and to have someone like you to remind me of the true meaning of friendship. At last, I've learned one of the lessons my father always tried to teach me . . . tough times don't last long . . . but tough people do. So I guess you could say I'm getting tougher in my old age.

I'm going to close now. I think I might take a long walk after I drop this letter in the mailbox. I love you, Delaney. Thank you for being my sister and my friend.

Love Always,
Nicole

A Meeting . . .

It was the first Thursday of the new year. Basil carefully placed his black leather jacket on the coat rack, then rubbed his two hands together and blew his warm breath on them before taking his seat.

"It's cold out there, Doc," Basil said as he looked around the office. Today the small space didn't appear drab and depressing as it had on previous visits. Basil noticed the winter sun beaming through the windows, flooding the office with a natural light.

"How were your holidays?" the doctor asked.

"They were cool. I spent Christmas Day with Campbell and Cade. It was great. My little sister can cook. I mean, she cooked all this food, and I helped Cade play with a lot of the toys I bought him. It was a good day," Basil said, smiling a slow half-smile.

"So you decided not to go and see your father?"

A thoughtful frown crossed Basil's face as he said, "He kinda made the decision for me. He went to the Bahamas with one of his lady friends. But he's not off the hook."

"You still haven't told him what you think?"

"Not what I think! What I *know*. And I'll tell him when the time is right. Now I've got my entire future ahead of me and I'm only going to deal with the past when it's absolutely necessary. I can't let what my father and uncle did go without mention, but I'm finally getting a grip on my life. I'm not going to let them or the past ruin it," Basil said firmly. "Now I'm going to make choices that come from my own strength and not from what other mofos, including my family, might think or feel."

"Are you and your nephew still getting along great?" the doctor asked. He had decided to change the subject to something more pleasant.

"Yeah. Kids are so amazing. And he's already enriched my life more than all the mofos I've ever met put together. I guess children having a way of doing that," Basil said.

"You could say that," the doctor responded.

Basil plopped his left leg over the arm of the chair, then folded his arms over his chest and posed a question to the doctor. "So, Doc, are you gonna miss me while I'm gone?" He had a mischievous little boy's glint in his eyes.

"Where are you going?"

"Aw, I forgot to tell you. I'm going to take some time off," Basil said.

"Are you leaving town?"

"Yeah. I forgot to tell you . . . my little nephew is helping my love life. You should see the way honeys react to me when they see me with Cade. I mean, not that I needed any additional help, but this is a whole new pool of women," Basil smiled.

"So you've met someone?"

"Yeah, I did," Basil said.

The doctor looked at his watch, then said, "Do you want to tell me about the person? We still have a little time."

"Sure. This sister is slamming. I mean, she's beautiful and smart and even though we haven't hit the skins yet, I know it's going to be tight. She smells so good. And the way she carries herself. I mean, she's not like anybody I've ever met. This one might be my soul mate," Basil said confidently. "I was drawn to her like she was a candle and I was the flame," he added.

"Where and when did you meet her?"

"It hasn't been that long. We met Christmas morning. I was at Rockefeller Center with Cade, practicing our skating, while Campbell was cooking. You know, Cade and I are getting pretty good at this skating thing," Basil laughed. "Anyway, she was up by the Christmas tree, but I saw her checking me out. I smiled at her and she smiled back and waved like she knew me."

"She wasn't on the rink?"

"Not immediately. I guess she was visiting the Christmas tree. My first reaction was to pick Cade up from the skating rink and run up and find out her name. But I guess that's one of the changes in me. I mean, I wasn't only thinking about myself. Cade was having a great time and so was I."

"How did you meet her?"

"She came down to the rink. I kept looking up toward the tree, hoping she was going to come back. Every now and then I would look up when Cade had skated off by himself. Now one of my eyes was on him at all times, but maybe every other minute or so, I'd look up to see if this beautiful lady had returned."

"So did she?"

"Well, I got to speed this story up, 'cause I'm getting ready to meet her after I leave here. Cade and I kept skating. He would fall sometimes and so would I. Cade had fallen again, and I was bending over, holding his hands, kinda guiding him along, when this lady skated up next to us and asked if she can join us. Right as she skated up to us, she fell and I picked her up. When I touched her hand, I felt a wonderful energy. Her smile was so beautiful and she had on this beautiful but politically incorrect mink coat and a pair of diamond studs in her ears that just paled next to her smile. When I said sure, she slipped her arm in mine and we just skated for over an hour. She kept falling, but I just think she liked the touch of my hands. Neither one of us were wearing gloves. Cade liked her, especially when she suggested we get some hot chocolate."

"Well, Basil, I'm happy for you. Is that why you're leaving town?" The doctor noticed how Basil's face lit up when he mentioned his nephew.

"Yeah, she's an actress. A Broadway actress. And even though I said I wasn't going to date someone in show business, well, never say never. But she's in this musical that's going to London and she asked me to come over and see her. So I'm thinking maybe I need to get away for a little while, and then go deal with my father. I'm determined to make this year better. And why shouldn't it be? I got my sister and nephew and I got a new lady in my life," Basil said in a totally satisfied tone. "Who could ask for anything more?"

"So Campbell, Cade, Basil, and . . ." The doctor paused, allowing Basil to complete the sentence.

"Yancey," Basil smiled. "My new lady's name is Yancey Braxton."

A Reunion . . .

Under the canopy of a deep and endless blue sky, Raymond sat alone with his thoughts in an empty football stadium. The air was thin and sweet-smelling as a light snow fell and dissolved as it hit the ground. The stadium lights glistened through the cascade of soft snowflakes.

So much had happened during the fall, and now winter had brought Raymond even more questions than he had answers. Although his father's health had improved, he and his mother had discussed bringing in a full-time nurse to help take care of him. Mr. Tyler was at about 50 percent of his former self. Raymond was also debating what to do with his relationship. He and Trent had enjoyed some good times since their Chicago reunion, but there were times when Raymond would look at Trent and wonder if there were any more secrets. Could he really trust him? Finally, there was his career, or rather lack of career. Raymond's firm had offered him his partnership back, but he didn't have a burning desire to practice law or enter politics as Lisa had suggested.

So he sat on the wooden seat and watched the last of daylight drain out of the clean winter sky. Suddenly Raymond saw a man walking across the field at the fifty-yard line, heading in his direction. *Where did he come from,* Raymond thought, and was this stranger about to end his much needed solitude? The man was moving fast, almost at a magical pace, and within moments, he was standing directly in front of Raymond.

"What are you doing up here all alone? Feeling sorry for yourself?"

Raymond looked in the man's face and was shocked. It was his best friend, Kyle. The sight of Kyle was so sudden and overwhelming that Raymond felt as though his heart had stopped, but a few seconds passed and he could feel himself breathing again.

"Kyle," Raymond said as he stood up and hugged his friend. "What are you doing here? I thought you were dead."

"That's what you get for thinking," Kyle laughed, hugging his friend back.

Raymond couldn't believe what was happening. Had he finally gone crazy? He started to cry almost uncontrollably, unashamedly as he whispered in Kyle's ear, "I can't believe it's you. I've missed you so much."

Raymond felt every muscle in his body tighten as he tried to keep from trembling.

"That's okay, baby boy. You can cry," Kyle whispered.

A few minutes later Kyle pushed Raymond back softly and said, "Sit down and tell me what's wrong."

"Tell me what happened. You were dead. I saw you," Raymond said in disbelief.

"Now, chirl, you know an old gay diva like me ain't gonna never die," Kyle said. Dressed in all white he looked almost ten years younger than when Raymond had last seen him. Kyle's caramel skin was perfectly smooth and his brown eyes seemed to glow, as though an incandescent mist surrounded him.

"If you didn't die, then where have you been?" Raymond asked.

Kyle rolled his eyes skyward and said, "You know, I was going to tell you this story about how I was a human guinea pig for some of the new AIDS drugs and that a cure is on the way. Well, that's partly true. A cure is on the way, but the Kyle you knew and loved didn't survive this round."

"What are you saying?"

"Raymond, this is a dream. But I am still the Kyle you knew and I can help you. Some of this you'll remember, some you won't," Kyle said.

"So are you some kinda angel?" Raymond asked. He grinned to himself. The Kyle he knew sure wasn't an angel.

"Maybe," Kyle said coyly, just the way he used to flirt with a stranger at the Nickel Bar.

"You don't *look* like an angel. You look like my friend. You look good, at peace, restful," Raymond said.

"What did you expect? You wanted me to have some *Touched by an Angel* glow?" Kyle teased.

"But you seem so real," Raymond said.

"Of course I'm real. And, as fellow angel sister Sylvester would say, 'I'm mighty real,'" Kyle laughed.

"You look and sound like the Kyle I knew," Raymond said.

"And that's what you should think. Now close your eyes, baby boy, and let me do the talking. And this time listen. I sent you a letter I hoped you'd refer to when you needed it. But you always were hardheaded. I even called to warn you about this judge mess."

"That was you who called me?" Raymond asked. His body went from cold to warm within seconds while Kyle simply nodded his head and said, "I should have just said, 'Don't go there, chirl' . . . then you would have known it was me. But at the last minute I decided to use one of my deep man voices."

Raymond grinned, but his smile was tight with fear. This really was Kyle. Dream or not, who else would know about the letter he had received after Kyle died? Raymond closed his eyes and still didn't know if he was in a dream. With his eyes shut tightly, he saw a beautiful white house with a green swing on the porch, an evergreen wreath on the door, and snow everywhere. Then he heard Kyle's voice again. It sounded both comforting and musical.

"Raymond, life will hold many more surprises for you. And it will never be perfect. First of all, don't worry about your father. In a couple of months, he will be back to his old semi-evil self. Good as new. Now, don't expect this little close call with death will change him. But know that he loves you and Kirby the same. Don't you try and handle him either, leave that to your mother. Now let's move on to Trent. There is good and bad news there. He loves you deeply, but you've got to loosen up or he'll stray again. Remember what I always told you, most men ain't good for nothing but slangin' and taking dick. His love is genuine, but keep your faith in our heavenly Father and yourself. Don't worry, you'll never be alone. You still look good and got your pullin' power."

Even with his eyes closed, Raymond felt Kyle close to him.

"Now, I know you worry about your little brother, but he's on his way to becoming quite a man. Don't you get jealous because before you leave this earth, more people will know Kirby Tyler's name than that of Raymond Tyler, Jr. Kirby has and will continue to learn from your example. I know you're worried about Nicole and Jared and if their marriage will survive. I don't really know the answer to that, 'cause they got their own people looking after them. I do know Jared will get the child he wants, even though it might not be in the conventional way. And Nicole's going to make great strides with her career that are going to surprise even her. She's got one of Satan's assistants after her for something really stupid. But this chile, Yancey, will not succeed with her plans. Miss Thang will learn the hard way that when you sleep with the devil, sometimes you get fucked. And the next time when the devilette shows up in the form of a friend, Nicole won't be so easily fooled."

Kyle paused and Raymond, with his eyes closed tightly, felt a peace settle over his body, like all his worries were being magically lifted from his shoulders. And then he heard Kyle's voice again, serious and soft this time, speaking from his heart.

"Now, Raymond, I'm not going to tell you this again, but save some joy for yourself. Stop listening to the rain. All those voices telling you what you should and should not be doing. *Listen to the snow.* That silent voice you hear when you are totally alone, where there are no media, bosses, father, mother, brother, or lovers telling you what you should do. When you listen to the voice of snow, it will never lead you wrong. It will make a difference in your life. If you want to go back to New York and help Peaches, do. But don't do it because you think Peaches needs you. That ol' girl will be just fine and so will her kids. They will survive things I couldn't. And you know, my mama, Peaches, is like a project roach, you can't kill her," Kyle announced triumphantly.

Then there was silence. Raymond waited to hear Kyle's voice once again, but after several moments he opened his eyes and saw Kyle walking across the field. Twilight had come. The dusk that covered the stadium looked so extraordinary that Raymond knew there was a God and a heaven.

He stood up and called out Kyle's name. Kyle turned and smiled.

"Kyle, can I ask you something?" Raymond asked as his voice echoed across the field.

Kyle nodded his head in the affirmative.

"What's the best thing about heaven?"

"Everything in heaven is wonderful," Kyle said.

"But what's the best thing?" Raymond asked.

Kyle leaned his head to the left, turned, and started his journey out of the stadium. Then in a voice that sounded like it was announcing the final game score over the stadium loudspeaker, Kyle said, "In heaven . . . you can hear snow."

About the Author

E. Lynn Harris is a former computer sales executive with IBM and a graduate of the University of Arkansas, Fayetteville. He is the author of four novels, *Invisible Life, Just As I Am,* and the *New York Times* bestsellers *And This Too Shall Pass* and *If This World Were Mine.* In 1996, *Just As I Am* was awarded the Novel of the Year prize by the Blackboard African-American Bestsellers, Inc. *If This World Were Mine* was nominated for the 1997 NAACP Image Award and won the James Baldwin Award for Literary Excellence. Harris is on the board of the Hurston Wright Foundation. He is also the recipient of the 1998 Sprague-Todes Literary Award, presented by the Chicago Gerber-Hart Library. Harris's column, "For All I Know," debuted in the *Advocate* in 1998, and he is on the board of the Hurston Wright Foundation. He divides his time between Chicago and New York, where he is working on his memoirs. Mr. Harris remains an avid U of A Razorback fan of all sports!